KILL THE BOSS GOOD-E

Tom Fell, the boss, is gone, and Pander has temporarily
taken over the rackets in town. He's got some ideas of
his own how the bookies should be operating. The
business needs some fresh blood. Then Fell is back,
back from his rest at Desert Farm where Dr. Emilson
has been treating him for manic depression; back with
Cripp, his right-hand man. Fell knows he's been gone
too long, that Pander has stepped in and made some
changes. Pander thinks he's got the big bosses behind
him, but what he doesn't know is that Fell may be
manic, but he knows what he wants—power. And
nobody is going to stop him from taking it.

MISSION FOR VENGEANCE

Eight years ago they were running guns, then
something went wrong and they were all running for
their lives. Farret spent some time in a South American
prison but now he's back and out to even the score.
One of the four betrayed him, and Farret knows you
got to keep the score even on these things. John Miner
owns a ranch and is engaged to Getterman's daughter,
Jane. He's the first to find out about Farret. But Farret
isn't interested in Miner yet. First he's got to settle
with Lena; and after that, Metz. And if it isn't Metz
who set him up, Getterman is next. But sooner or later,
it all comes down to Miner. Miner brought him into
the group—and his is the biggest score to settle of
them all.

PETER RABE BIBLIOGRAPHY

From Here to Maternity (1955)
Stop This Man! (1955)
Benny Muscles In (1955)
A Shroud for Jesso (1955)
A House in Naples (1956)
Kill the Boss Good-by (1956)
Dig My Grave Deep (1956) *
The Out is Death (1957) *
Agreement to Kill (1957)
It's My Funeral (1957) *
Journey Into Terror (1957)
Mission for Vengeance (1958)
Blood on the Desert (1958)
The Cut of the Whip (1958) *
Bring Me Another
    Corpse (1959) *
Time Enough to Die (1959) *
Anatomy of a Killer (1960)
My Lovely Executioner (1960)
Murder Me for Nickels (1960)
The Box (1962)
His Neighbor's Wife (1962)
Girl in a Big Brass Bed (1965) **
The Spy Who Was
    Three Feet Tall (1966) **

Code Name Gadget (1967) **
Tobruk (1967)
War of the Dons (1972)
Black Mafia (1974)
The Silent Wall (2011)
The Return of
    Marvin Palaver (2011)

*Daniel Port series
**Manny DeWitt series
As by "Marco Malaponte"
New Man in the House (1963)
Her High-School Lover (1963)

As by "J. T. MacCargo"
Mannix #2: A Fine Day for
    Dying (1975)
Mannix #4: Round Trip to
    Nowhere (1975)

Short Stories
"Hard Case Redhead"
    (Mystery Tales, 1959)
"A Matter of Balance"
    (Story, 1961)

Kill the Boss Good-by

Mission for Vengeance

Two Complete Thrillers By
Peter Rabe

STARK
HOUSE

Stark House Press • Eureka California

KILL THE BOSS GOOD-BY / MISSION FOR VENGEANCE

Published by Stark House Press
1315 H Street
Eureka, CA 95501
griffinskye3@sbcglobal.net
www.starkhousepress.com

ISBN: 1-933586-42-7
ISBN-13: 978-1-933586-42-7

Cover design and layout by Mark Shepard, WWW.SHEPGRAPHICS.COM
Proofreading by Rick Ollerman

First Stark House Press Edition: May 2013

REPRINT EDITION

Contents

Contents

The Minds of Peter Rabe

By Rick Ollerman

Peter Rabe started his writing career with the appearance of a magazine article chronicling his wife Claire's first pregnancy. Later expanded into book form the cover credit reads, "Written, illustrated and experienced by Peter Rabe." It's a short book, with more line drawings than pages, and it has a simple pun for a title: *From Here to Maternity*.

The book is written with a wry, sardonic sense of humor and curiously, although Rabe provides dozens of drawings of various people's likenesses, including his wife's, whenever he draws himself it is either with his own head obscured or else appearing as just a scruff of hair exploding upward from his neck. The back cover contains another Rabe drawing under the heading, "About the Author." Rabe sidesteps the question by providing yet another drawing, this time with his head hidden behind a large sheet on which his wife is just finishing drawing what looks like the profile of a classic Greek sculpture. For a description he simply says he "cannot be objective about the subject" so he's asked his "wife to supply a complete picture."

Literally or figuratively, we get neither. We learn more about Peter Rabe the man than we do about his actual appearance. What we do get is a sense of his wit and charm, what seems to be a certain amount of ability as an artist, and a fairly quick and cute story of his wife's pregnancy. Notice I didn't say the *couple's* pregnancy, because Rabe keeps his role in his own story significantly in the background.

For a man who would go on to write more than thirty additional books, this attitude may be somewhat unusual. Many writers insert parts of themselves into their characters, some even saying that part of themselves is contained in all of their characters. Charles Willeford wrote that "the novel is a case history of the writer."

> It is the story of his life written as well as he can write it. It never ends; it goes on day after day, year after year. He is his own hero, his own heroine, his villain, his minor characters–the thoughts of each of these are his own thoughts twisting and churning and wrenched alive and crawling from his conscious and unconscious mind.

〖...〗

The novel is a case history of the writer. *Look Homeward, Angel,
Ulysses, The Trial, A Farewell to Arms* are great novels. They are also
case histories of the men that wrote them, and they are written with
the heart. Each is an account of what happened to the writer and also
what might have happened to him. Fact and fiction cunningly com-
bined.(Charles Willeford, *Writing & Other Blood Sports*, Dennis
McMillan Publications, 2000)

Given Rabe's near total anonymity in his small bit of autobiography, and
the variety of different protagonists in his books, it seems likely that Rabe did-
n't write himself into his books very much at all. If Willeford states the rule,
Rabe demonstrates the exception.

In his 1989 discussion with George Tuttle for *Paperback Parade*, Rabe says
that the way he conceives of a hero makes him a "stereotype" and that it is
very difficult to write about a "winner." Notwithstanding the Daniel Port
or Manny DeWitt series he wrote later in his career, most of Rabe's protagonists are what he calls "anti-heroes," people who are much more a "psychological reality" for him.

In the same interview he also states that despite his background in psychology, it has not influenced his fiction "in the least." Rabe explains that both
his fiction and his interest in psychology are independent and merely stem
from the "same kind of orientation and interest."

The fascinating part of this statement is simply that it is natural for any
reader of Rabe's work with knowledge of his background to ask precisely that
question, as did George Tuttle. This is because Rabe's work is so character
driven, and his characters are so flawed, that their psyches, their psychoses
and neuroses and thought processes, all dictate the plots of his novels.

In other words, Rabe's characters don't have mental quirks or attitudes that
are used as devices to move the plot along; rather his characters' very natures
are what dictate the plot. This exact quality distinguishes Rabe's work from
most of his contemporaries, many of whom used flaws of this type in much
more superficial ways.

For these other writers in the paperback original world, psychological elements were more a part of the general themes of their work. Raymond Chandler's Philip Marlowe must be noble above all else, or as he said in his essay
"The Simple Art of Murder," "He must be the best man of his world and
good enough for any world. I do not care much about his private life 〖...〗" Marlowe has the code Chandler has given him, and this code guides Marlowe
throughout his stories. Indeed, as Chandler has said, he doesn't care much
about Marlowe's life beyond that.

James M. Cain's or David Goodis's protagonists are in more of a psychological rut: they have no intent to cause the bad things they do, rather they fall into them with eyes wides open, powerless to stop themselves or alter events in any meaningful way. It's never clear whether they'd even want to if given the choice. For the sake of the story, they simply must march on.

Jim Thompson wrote about some clearly psychologically damaged specimens, starkly so, prototypical sociopaths and psychopaths, served up for mass consumption. When we know from the start the protagonist has certain psychological issues, we know how he will act throughout the book. The question may be in how far he will take things, or in what manner he will betray himself or be caught, but psychological elements infuse the entire narrative.

Rabe's method of using psychological attributes is far more subtle. His best protagonists are neither completely sane nor completely crazy, all good or pure evil, right or wrong, noble or ignoble. They're quite often a blend, a combination of contradictions, made up of psyches not quite working wholly together.

Like James Quinn from *The Box*, a mob lawyer intent on splitting the organization he works for in half, siphoning power away from the incumbent Ryder. Only Ryder won't take this sitting down and cares nothing for the precautions Quinn has made should something happen to him. Ryder makes it happen anyway. His men dope Quinn, seal him in a crate, and send him on a trip around the world via the hold of a cargo ship. Only Quinn is discovered early, in the African port of Okar, before he experiences the full level of despair, or even death, that Ryder intended. It's clear to the Westerner who takes charge of Quinn what has happened to him but when he seeks confirmation of Quinn's criminal past, Quinn merely tells him he has no record.

> Quinn thought that with no record he was either a very good criminal or no criminal at all, and perhaps it came to the same thing. He had not been very much interested in deciding on this because other things meant more to him. Whether he had been smart or stupid, for example, and here the decision was simple. He had been very stupid with Ryder, but that, too, was a little bit dim, since he, Quinn, was here and Ryder was not. Maybe later, more on this later, but now first things first.

So Quinn gives *some* thought to what had happened that got him shipped halfway around the world by his arch enemy, but surprisingly not much. Instead he sets about finding out who runs the local black market and immediately makes plans to take it over. A lone man, with no money, friends or resources, only a compulsion not justified or explained to the reader, only made felt by the author, is absolutely driven to take over in Okar what he couldn't back in the States. We don't know what happened to make Quinn this way. We wonder at his audacity, his self belief, and above all what could possibly make a man, any man, act this way. For Quinn it's an inevitability; for Rabe it's another subtly nuanced "non-normal" protagonist. Quinn is just *different*.

Benny Tapkow is also different. *Benny Muscles In* seems to start one way but becomes a hauntingly tragic story because the plot seems to change once Rabe more clearly defines Benny. Not just a punk trying to make a name for himself, a punk who just *knows* he's better than everybody else. The problem for Benny is, no one else can see that.

"Listen," Benny said. His voice sounded rough with impatience. "Now listen to me, Mr. Pendleton."

The white hand stopped moving back and forth.

"The more you say, Tapkow, the worse it gets." Then he almost smiled. "What do you think is the worst thing I can do to you, Tapkow? Do you remember a few years ago, a man called Murdock? Did you ever wonder what happened to Murdock? He's still alive, you know."

Pendleton paused to give things weight, but he hadn't been watching Benny. He hadn't seen the stubbornness and the angry impatience.

"The hell with Murdock," Benny said. His breath sounded tight. "The hell with Murdock and all this talk. You haven't given me a chance to say a word, Mr. Pendleton. So here it is." His voice suddenly turned quiet. "I've worked for you for seven years. I've tried to do better than the next guy because I know something they don't. I *am* better. You think so, or you wouldn't have let me stick around. I've done your crumby jobs, I've done some big ones. And then I've done some extra jobs you didn't ask for, because all I ever wanted was a chance to show I've got the stuff. And then you started putting on the brakes. 'Tapkow, take my pants to the cleaner,' while I should have been working at Imports. 'Tapkow, bring my car around,' when Turk could have done it just as well." Benny started talking faster now. "Finally I got a territory, a run-down, no-good territory, where Paddy used to rob you blind. I took that and glad for the chance. I start collecting double in my district and handed the stuff in. I needn't have. So look at it that way for a minute, Mr. Pendeleton, and then see if you're doing right. I'm not trying to tell you what to do, but you've got to remember I'm not the chauffeur around here anymore. I've done better than that."

Pendleton asks Benny if he's through and Benny tells him he is. "Then let me tell you about Murdock," Pendleton tells him, as though all that Benny had said before doesn't matter to him in the least. Benny grows quiet and tells him he is making a mistake, not recognizing that his boss is warning him by relating the example of a former colleague. The normally placid Pendleton jumps up: "Are you threatening me, Tapkow?" he asks. Gone is the "Mr." as Benny replies, "You're making a mistake, Pendleton."

> There was a white button on the side of Pendelton's desk and the white hand started to move there.

And this is where the book starts to shift in a different direction. Benny can't keep himself from putting his foot in it but he's incapable of seeing that the problem is his in any way whatsoever. His boss has the problem, his boss just *won't* see Benny's value to the organization. Narrowly escaping assassination, Benny throws in with Pendleton's rival, thinking that here's a man who can see Benny's worth, but all that happens is that Benny is used as a tool against his former boss and again, from Benny's perspective, his talents and abilities are unjustly wasted.

There is something to Benny, as we see, but it's not what Benny thinks it is, and all the time he seems to be more human than he'd want to be, he's unwittingly tragic as well. Again, it's the complex psyche of Benny Tapkow that makes the book change directions fairly early on and run out to its fascinating end.

A more obvious example is Sam Jordan, the hitman protagonist of *Anatomy of a Killer*. The book opens just as Jordan has killed his target, a Mr. Vento, whose arm unfortunately falls through the open door, keeping it from being closed. Jordan kicks the arm out of the way so he can close it as he hears someone climbing the stairs from the floor below. This seemingly inconsequential act is the start of the unraveling of Jordan as a professional killer.

After the getaway, his driver notices Jordan acting peculiarly. Later, on the roof of a house, Jordan insists that the pigeons in a coop not be disturbed. He doesn't want the animals to get out of their neat little rows and start "fluttering around."

> "Get away from those pigeons because I want them quiet."
> The driver nodded. He watched Jordan kneel down by the parapet and said nothing. They feed 'em raw meat and pepper, he thought to himself, and this is how they turn out. The raw meat is all those dames, all those dames, and the pepper's the money. All that money. And this is how they turn out. Worried about pigeons.

Jordan knows something has gone wrong inside him and desperately wants a break from another assignment. But circumstances work against him and he is forced back to work having to confront his own growing changes from within.

On the train, coming back, Jordan had sat with his shock, but then it had gone away. A thing like the arm would not happen again. If something like that should happen again it would not be like the first time, it would be without the surprise, and then there was always the trick he knew, a flip-switch type of thing, where he split himself into something efficient. Put the head over here and the guts into a box and that's how anything can be handled.

He had settled this, and then he had sat for the rest of the time, almost into New York, but the train-ride dullness had not come. He had tried to unwind, until he had found out there was nothing to unwind.

This too had happened without his having known it, like seeing his shadow which was no longer like his own shape.

There was nothing to unwind. What had wormed at him had been something else. He was dreading the nothing, between trips. The job was now simpler than the time in between.

Jordan has changed, and the catalyst was the physical contact of a dead man's arm. As he continues to unravel, his ability to perform his next assignment does as well, and where he ends up, no one can quite tell, even as Jordan himself doesn't know, until the very end.

Interestingly enough, Rabe's novelization of the film *Tobruk* contains some of his most deeply used psychological elements. The film itself is a fairly one dimensional film, with essentially one subplot and a hidden traitor that isn't all that hidden. Rabe said that he was surprised at how much work it took, that the script itself "barely provided the skeleton" for the story told in novel form.

The reader gets the feeling that Rabe is playing with us a little when he writes that a Nazi inquisitor, clearly a torture specialist who is not a character in the movie, feels his first sign of anxiety as a loss of appetite, while at the same time telling us that the first sign of anxiety for his prisoner is an overwhelming one. As the Nazi contemplates prying the secrets from his prisoner using unspecified tools at his base in Grenoble, we are treated to a description of how the prisoner, not only through beatings but through the *anticipation* of beatings, is being prepared in the meantime.

In taking us from a fairly straightforward point A to point B film, Rabe fleshes out the story to a much more fully realized three dimensional one. He does this not only through adding additional characters and modifying the plot to give more depth, but also by amplifying the personality conflicts and ethnic distrust between the mission's commander Harker and the German Jew Bergman. The identity of the traitor in their midst is fairly obvious in the movie but is handled much more subtly and deftly in Rabe's version, the traitor being fleshed out with his own distinct sense of humor and personality.

From a character standpoint, Rabe's handling of the film's token female role takes on the most depth. In what appears to be her only film role, Heidy Hunt plays Cheryl Portman in the film version and does little more than look good on the screen. Certainly nothing structural. In Rabe's novel, however, Cheryl moves from being an idealistic and naive young woman whose lover has been duped and then killed by the Nazis. Her whole world has changed and suddenly she cares no more for her father's secret mission, ignoring his attempts to shelter her from the Nazis, and proceeds to lose herself in a glut of sexual adventures that serve to unmake the character so assiduously ignored in the film.

> Whatever was feeding her sense of being seemed to have dried up. She had clearly offered her presence and he had not wanted it. He could not have known she was there! Therefore, it was possible that she did not exist–

In Rabe's hands, Cheryl searches for life within herself by allowing herself to be degraded by friend and foe alike, and toward the end, when she decides to take herself back and is held captive and cruelly used by a band of Tuareg nomads, we feel tremendous loss for the character at Rabe's choice of Hobsonian fate for her.

In another moment where one senses Rabe may be having some fun and mind games with the reader, a character tells another that a Nazi had "died well" and that he had not expected that. Not content to let that well used, even overused phrase be, Rabe has his own character challenge it.

> "He died well?" said Craig. "You mean he bled in a human fashion and then he turned properly lifeless?"
> Bergman's face became stiff. In contrast, his blue eyes seemed to glitter with life. When he talked his voice was sharp and fast.
> "I meant," he said, "that he died in the best tradition of the self-possessed human being who finally, in the face of death, handles its coming better than he has done all his life. And I mean that since I detest Von Hahn as a Nazi I am apt to overlook the possibility that he is partly human. And then, when he dies like a human being, I am surprised. I am confused. It is a dilemma with me. Did I answer you?"
> "Yes," said Craig.

And he answered the rest of us, too, I think as much as a psychologist as a writer. In the end, Rabe's *Tobruk* is a much finer story as a novel than as Leo Gordon's and Arthur Hiller's film, though the latter boasts some fine performances by George Peppard and Nigel Green. The depth Rabe adds not only to the characters but to the plot goes much deeper than the rather flat images on the screen.

A Rabe book that actually features a psychiatrist is *Kill the Boss Good-by*. After a few chapters without the main character, Tom Fell, actually putting in an appearance, we finally meet him under the care of Dr. Fredrick Emilson, M.D., Ph.D. We get Dr. Emilson's diagnosis and prognosis up front and then read on as we watch his gangster patient Fell try to function as a mob boss while dealing with his mental illness. Originally self-committed to a private hospital for an anxiety attack brought on by receiving a parking ticket, Fell leaves the facility early, under a fear of psychosis, and his lieutenant is told Fell is a potential manic:

"A maniac?"
"No! A manic. A fast-moving, cheerful guy, lots of laughs, lots of drive, and no end to what he might do or how far he might drive himself. That's what I'm talking about."

And the book itself follows that pace, where we see allegories like Fell turning off the sprinkler system for his lawn, thinking things will eventually grow when they can look after themselves, as well as a touching yet somehow not quite natural need to be near his wife. When Fell begins saying things like, "I tell him he's big, so he's big," we can't help but wonder if his curtain is finally falling. The book moves to a constantly accelerating pace and the reader is never quite sure where Fell stands or how he will make out. In typical Rabe fashion, he takes us to the final page before the resolution finally comes due.

Mission For Vengeance features another variation of mental illness, only this time it takes the form of a dangerously homicidal paranoiac named Farret. Farret believes he was betrayed by one of his former colleagues and much of the book is spent with one of them trying to stop Farret before he destroys the lives of all of them. The book has several scenes with a doctor trying to diagnose and possibly commit Farret following a murder and his less than lucid aftermath.

Interesting, too, is Rabe's use of coincidence in *Mission For Vengeance*, interesting because Rabe usually stays very far away from the Cornell Woolrich-type happenstance on which to pin a plot point. Here he winks at us, giving a rapid fire series of three quick lottery events, and then returns to his usual style of heavily character-driven storytelling. The whole book has an edge of your seat quality and shows Rabe's versatility and how he didn't write the same book over and over, although even here, he foreshadows an element of one of his best books, 1962's *The Box* (mentioned earlier). In that story we have a man in a crate shipped around the world in the cargo hold of a ship. In *Mission* we have a man wrapped in sheets and sent cross country in a furniture moving van.

At one time Rabe had roomed with Lorenzo Semple, Jr., who later became the man behind the late 60's camp version of the TV show *Batman*. When

Rabe tried to get in with the Hollywood crowd, he achieved only limited success, primarily his two *Batman* episodes, which formed a single two-part arc first airing in 1967. And guess which "Special Guest Villain" Rabe featured?

The shows aired on February 15th and 16th, 1967, and credit Rabe with the stories and Semple with the teleplays and are titled "The Joker's Last Laugh" and "The Joker's Epitaph." Whether the lines come from Rabe or Semple, the episodes are filled with signature *Batman* moments. Before the Joker is formally identified as the criminal of the day, Commissioner Gordon tells Chief O'Hara, "It's almost as if some deranged mind were trying to taunt our very sanity."

Later, after Alfred the butler, dressed in a Batman costume and quite clearly *not* the Batman, though no one seems to recognize the taller, skinnier and much older mustachioed gentleman as a fake, saves the Boy Wonder from being, ironically, stamped into a comic book page, Bruce Wayne says to Robin, "It's sometimes difficult to think clearly when you're strapped to a printing press." Sometimes it is. Indeed.

When the Joker ends up running the Gotham National Bank, Bruce Wayne is taken in by Chief O'Hara's "anti-lunatic squad." Clearly Rabe was not above poking fun at his other vocation. Always, though, as in his books, Rabe brings a certain understated uniqueness to the speech of his characters. At one point the Joker complains to Bruce Wayne about being watched closely by Batman: "Imagine my ghastly situation, Mr. Wayne, legally installed in the bank but watched like an insect by that infernal Caped Crusader."

"Yes, I can understand for someone of your dubious character that might prove annoying."

Whether the words are Rabe's or Semple's, or even both, they certainly reflect Rabe's humor, his unexpected turn of phrase, and like the rest of the works discussed here, his understanding of the psychological mind and how to use that expertise to give us unique characters and memorable situations.

Peter Rabe was an original, and one of the best not only of the Gold Medal era but of crime fiction as a genre and even as literature. While it may be interesting to muse on how his writing may have been different had he been educated in something other than psychology, that's something we can never know. What we do know is what comes through in his original novels, his novelizations, and his too few short stories and television work. And however you describe it, for lovers of fiction, it is wonderful stuff indeed.

LITTLETON, NH
DECEMBER, 2012

Kill the Boss Good-by

By Peter Rabe

Chapter One

For a town of three hundred thousand, San Pietro looked very dead, but it was noon and it was out of season. The race track was open two months of the year and the rest of the time the town just baked in the sun and spread into the prairie. San Pietro had wide streets and big lots, for there was plenty of room. The plane factories reached into the open along the rim of the town because land was even cheaper there, with more of it.

There was a traffic light at the main intersection, making useless blinks from one color to the next and then all over again. A car with a backfire came down the street and crossed against the light just when the cop came out of a beer parlor nearby. He went to the curb to look at the driver and when he recog-nized him the cop waved and watched the car pass. Then the cop lit a cigar and walked down the street, keeping under the store awnings.

The light kept changing monotonously. Once, when the color happened to turn from amber to green, four cars in a row came through driving low on their springs with the load of the men inside. The cars headed straight down the main drag, out to the edge of town, and one by one they came to a smooth stop at the big motel that was built like the Alamo. There were no other cars parked in sight and the four that pulled up made an unusual picture. It was different during the season. When the track was open they came from all over the state, cramming the town, because Tumbleweed Park was an exceptional track, and famous.

Thirteen men got out of the cars, stretched their legs, and filed through the door of the coffee shop. The place was empty except for Pearl, who said "Hi" when they came in, and Phido, who didn't say anything because he had the coffee cup to his mouth. He looked over the rim. Then he swallowed wrong, coughed, and slopped coffee where his cup missed the saucer.

The men hadn't answered Pearl. They went straight through the kitchen in back, to the corridor, because that was the shortest way to get where they wanted to go. When the door in back had swung shut after the last of them Pearl turned back to the counter and said, "What kinda business? You know them?"

"Do I know them!" said Phido, but he said it more to himself.

Being big and awkward he bumped the counter hard when he got up and Pearl made a comment about it, but Phido didn't hear any more. He went through the kitchen, opened the door to the corridor, but didn't go any fur-ther. He could see it from where he was.

He could see the room with the telephones, the blackboard where the odds were posted, and it could have been the quotation room of a broker's office except for Phido's buddies against the wall, the police captain, and the sheriff who had come along just for good measure. The sheriff backhanded one of the men by the wall and one of the others got sapped. While everybody left, the sheriff put a seal across the door lock and then he left too. They hadn't bothered Phido. They nodded at him because they knew him, but since he hadn't tried stopping them they had left him alone.

When they all got into the cars Phido ran to the coffee shop window, looking puzzled and anxious. Pearl came up too, not knowing what to think.

"A raid, Phido? How come they raided—"

"I don't get it," said Phido, saying it several times over till Pearl interrupted him.

"Better do something, Phido. Call Mr. Fell. Better tell him they got one of his places!"

Phido started cursing and turned away from the window. "Call Fell! How'm I gonna call him? If Fell was around you think this coulda happened?"

He went to the wall phone with a dime borrowed out of Pearl's uniform pocket, where she kept her tips. He called a tobacco store back in town with gold lettering on the window that said, *Cigars, Tobacco—Thomas Fell, Prop.*

This was the only place Thomas Fell owned that had his name on the door. He also owned the San Pietro Realty Company, the Tumbleweed Concessions Company, the Blue Star Taxi Cab Company, and Accounting, Incorporated, Accountants and Appraisers. He owned a big part of the race track and ran all of it. According to public knowledge he ran several other things, including City Hall.

The man who answered the phone didn't know whether Fell was back.

"I'm calling from the motel," said Phido. "I just saw...."

"Why, all of a sudden, call here? He never shows up here any time."

"I know," said Phido. "I just thought...."

"Just because you work out of this place, what makes you think he'd check in here first, after he's gone for over a month?"

"I wasn't thinking," said Phido.

"What makes you think he's back, anyway?"

"I'm just asking," said Phido, getting excited. "There's been a raid! Just now! They—"

"Raid! Are you nuts?"

"No, I ain't nuts! But somebody ought to get this to Fell. They took Mort and Jimmy and—"

"The cops?"

"Who else?"

"*They* must be nuts!"

"If Fell was here...."

The man in the tobacco store hung up, waited a second, and dialed a number. San Pietro Realty answered and a man called Hecht came to the phone.

"Raid? I haven't got enough troubles without— How should I know where he is? When Fell shows up I got enough troubles waiting for him without— All right, all right!"

Hecht hung up and called Tumbleweed Concessions. The top man there wasn't in, and besides, with Fell gone hell knows where for over a month, they had enough of a mess on their hands.

"If you don't think I'm nervous," yelled Hecht.

"Get off the phone! We got to get this thing cleared up!"

They called Blue Star Taxi to see if Pander were there, because Pander was running the show while Fell was away. But Fell's lieutenant wasn't there, nor could they find him at Accounting, Incorporated. The man there was almost as big as Pander and he checked all over town trying to find Fell's right-hand man. He couldn't find even any of Pander's cronies. The man sweated and rubbed his ear nervously. He wished Fell were around, he wished somebody knew where Fell was, but the best he could hope for was finding Pander. He finally got a lead when he reached Pander's girl friend, who thought that Pander had gone to the race track. It didn't make sense, this time of year, but nothing else made sense either.

CHAPTER TWO

The grandstand was concrete, big and white where the sun hit it and black where the curved roof made a shadow over the empty tiers. To one side of the track the prairie had been graded and oiled to make a parking lot. There was one car parked in the sun, looking very small next to the grandstand.

The dim corridors under the structure got cooler where they tunneled to the rear. The small sound of a motor hummed in the back and got stronger close to the door where the air conditioner was. It cooled the empty restaurant, the offices upstairs, the betting booths, and the rooms off the basement corridor. They had turned the thing on because Pander liked to be cool.

He was leaning against the concrete wall of the basement room and watching the three men in the chairs along the wall. They couldn't tell he was watching them because Pander was wearing sunglasses. He always wore sunglasses, big black ones with glittering brass. And his hair had a glitter where he had dented the black wave over the forehead. On Pander everything glittered. The white teeth, the shoes, and the suspenders. He was nuts for suspenders. Today's suspenders were blue with silver stitching running up and down in the shape of vines. The phone rang on the desk and Pander looked at it. Then he said, "Well?"

One of the men got off his chair and answered the phone.

"For you, Pander."

"Who is it?"

"Neddy. He's at the office."

"Tell him I'm busy."

The man made an exasperated shrug with his shoulders and told Neddy that Pander was busy. Then he listened, held the phone out and said, "Better take it, Pander."

Pander pushed away from the wall and took the phone. He said into the phone, "This better be good."

"There's been a raid, Pander. The place at the Alamo."

Pander stuck a piece of gum in his mouth and squeezed it around a few times.

"I'm sorry to hear that, Ned."

Ned made a pause and then he exploded.

"Don't you hear right? A raid! You know what that means?"

"I guess the commissioner thinks he can afford it," said Pander.

"What's the matter with you, you crazy nut! Read the signs!"

"Watch your language, Neddy."

"Don't gimme no protocol at a time like this!" But after that outburst Ned felt exhausted. He didn't like Pander to start with, and when it came to arguing with him, Ned felt useless. He took a breath and changed his tack.

"We got to find Fell. It's getting bad, Pander."

"I know. Go find him."

"Pander, don't act dumb with me! The old man takes off without a word and doesn't come back for over a month, he must have left word! You're taking his place. Where is he?"

"I'm taking his place, so don't worry," said Pander.

"Don't worry? Collections falling off, guys leaving, payoffs all screwed up, and now they get cocky at City Hall and hand us a raid! You trying to run this setup into the ground?"

"You watch what you're saying, you son of a bitch. I told you once."

"Pander, please." Ned hesitated, made another switch. "Pander, when Fell comes back, you think he's going to pat you on the back for the mess around here?"

"Fell can pat anything he likes," said Pander and chewed on his gum.

"You don't know Fell any too good, do you, Pander? You think just because he takes a shine to..."

Pander slapped down the phone without letting Ned finish and without making an answer. He knew what he felt like doing to Ned, but he wasn't quite ready yet. Perhaps later, but not yet.

He sat down on the desk, folded his arms, and stared at the wall.

"Well?" said Roy. He stretched his long legs out in front of him and threw his Stetson over one foot. Then he started to spin it.

The man next to him had a thick frame and a face like a boxer. His voice came out high and small.

"Yeah, what?" he said.

The third one didn't say anything.

"It wasn't Aaronson," said Pander, "so relax and wait."

"We been waiting," said Roy.

"I wait, you wait. I been waiting for a year. You guys can wait a few minutes."

"What did Ned want?" said Roy.

"Forget it. We're waiting for Aaronson."

"Forget it, nothing. What was it?"

Pander chewed his gum faster and acted offhand.

"There's been a raid. He's all buggered because—"

"He's all buggered? Don't you think you better make a move when that happens?" Roy had stopped spinning the Stetson.

Pander got tense. He snapped his left suspender, then the right, doing it fast, like a one-two punch. Pander always took things personally and it didn't give him much time to relax.

"I'm running this thing, and I move when I'm ready!" He made a thread of his gum, then licked it back in. "I'm ready to move," he said.

It made an effect which Pander liked, and he looked from one to the other, while they waited for more.

"See for yourself." He started to count on his fingers. "Fell's gone, and I'm running his setup. The combine in L.A. likes my work. They told me to stick close by Fell and watch for the signals. This week they're meeting, with Fell gone. I call that the signal. That's why we're here, waiting for Aaronson. He's coming down from L.A. to give me the word." Pander stopped, waiting to see how they'd take it.

"You're going to push Fell?" said Roy.

"He's getting on."

"Oh, sure," said Roy. He started spinning his Stetson again. "Getting on to his prime."

Pander sucked in air, held it a moment. When he started talking again he was sharp and loud.

"I'm getting groomed for this job, and you know it. This is it. I'm going to move and there's not going to be any deadheads in this caper."

"I'm with you," said Willy.

The silent guy nodded.

"Maybe we wait for Aaronson first," said Roy.

"That's why we're here. To wait for the word."

"What if there isn't any?" But this time it didn't faze Pander. He'd made his point and he could see it all, big and clear. Fell had been gone over a month, and there had been enough time to change things the way Pander thought best. Pander could wait just so long, and Fell didn't scare him any more. He wouldn't think of that part, but kept his eye on the part he knew best. How Fell had taught him the ropes, how Fell had always been friendly and probably not even the kind who'd ever try to push his weight around. There were other stories about Fell—that he was the kind who didn't have to push his weight around to make an impression—but Pander didn't follow that train of thought, because it didn't make sense to him. What made sense was that Fell wasn't here and that he had left things with Pander. And then Fell had never showed again, and on top of that they had called a meeting up in L.A.

"I hear somebody," said the guy who hadn't talked until then.

They listened, and at first heard nothing but the dull hum of the cooling system in the room nearby. Then there were steps coming down the corridor and up to the door.

Aaronson came in, looking sweated and tired.

"Christ, it's cold in here," he said.

"Well? Where you been all day?"

"They talked late," said Aaronson, and pulled out a cigarette. "Lots to talk about." He lit up.

"So? What's the word, damn it!"

Aaronson exhaled, shrugged. "No word, Pander. Not a thing."

They just listened to the hum from the room nearby and didn't talk. They watched Pander.

He held very still, thinking about everything, and then suddenly spat out his gum. "They didn't say nothing? They didn't say yes or no?"

"Honest, Pander, nothing. I hung around outside; I had drinks with a few of them and all I got was 'Keep your shirt on; tell Pander to keep up the good work; tell him to stay smart,' and some more crap like that."

"I'll show 'em how smart! They didn't say no, did they? They didn't check me off, did they?"

Fell was gone, and Pander was ready. Up in L.A. they were watching how smart he would be.

"I'm in," said Pander. "We're gonna move."

Roy and Willy and the silent one got off their chairs and stood around wait-ing for Pander. Aaronson opened the door and they all went out. Pander caught up with Aaronson and took him by the arm.

"Listen, you mean they didn't even say what about Fell? Didn't they say where he was?"

"Hell," said Aaronson. "They thought for sure you'd know."

CHAPTER THREE

The tall drapes kept the sun out of the room because Janice slept late. When she woke it was with a long stretch, the whole length of her, and then she sat up without transition. She got off the bed, rubbed her hands through her brown hair, and opened the drapes. She could see the race track across town. Turning back to the bedroom, she pulled the expensive nightgown over her head. She let it drop to the floor and walked naked across to the door. She opened it and called, "Rita, I'm up." Then she went to the bathroom and thought about the coffee she was going to have.

Janice took a shower and kept her hair out of the way. After the soaping she stood for a while longer and felt the sharp heat of the water massage her skin. Then she dried herself and wondered about her weight. She remembered being skinny at twenty, full-bodied at thirty, and now—five years later—exactly the same. Why think about it? She was tall and well-built, and Fell liked it.

Janice got dressed and put a lipstick on lightly, just to make her small mouth look more alive. She ran her fingers over her lids, from habit, and stroked up on her long lashes. She rarely did more during the day. She had quiet, warm eyes. She liked them the way they were, and Fell liked them.

She went downstairs because the large rooms on the ground floor looked cooler. Her coffee stood on a table by a window facing the big lawn in front. The sprinklers were on, making a mist that looked strange in the sunlight and strange over the cacti along the drive. She didn't recognize the big car parked in front.

Janice lit a cigarette, smoked, and sipped coffee. She sat like that and listened to Rita's footsteps crossing the tiled hall. Rita was answering the door.

"No," said Rita, "Mrs. Fell hasn't come down yet."

"Just tell her," said a man's voice, "the name is Sutterfield."

"But Mr. Sutterfield—"

"Just tell her, will you?"

Janice put her cup down and rose. No use putting Rita in the wrong. She would see Sutterfield and hope it was nothing bad.

"Good morning, Mr. Sutterfield." She held the door open for him.

He hurried toward her as if she might disappear. It shook the wrinkles around his jowls, and the way he stooped into his walk made it look as if he meant to peck at the woman with his beaky nose. After Janice had closed the door she took Sutterfield's hat, trying to be very calm. "Want some coffee, Herb?"

He turned, looking belligerent. "Don't you think it might be more important than coffee when I take the risk and come to this house?"

"Don't rant at me, Herb." Janice sat down, looking too disinterested.

"All right, where is he? What's going on?" Sutterfield sounded nasty.

"Herb, don't you think I'm worried too?" Her show of indifference gave way. She bit her lip quickly and tried to look angry. That would be better; better to look mean, like Sutterfield did, than to show how anxious she was about Fell.

But Sutterfield wasn't looking. He went to see whether his car was visible from the window.

"Now listen to me, Janice." Back in front of her chair, he started swinging his bent hands back and forth. "I got three secretaries, six telephones, and a whole department of flunkies to run my errands for me. But I came down here myself. Did you ever hear of a police commissioner making a call like this himself?"

"Yes."

He hadn't meant for her to interrupt with an answer, but then it nettled him enough to give her a very personal kind of pleasure. He got pompous.

"I hold more than one public office. I have my own business to run. I also—"

"I know, Herb. Believe me...."

"May I finish?"

Then Janice changed her tone of voice.

"Come to the point, Herb. You don't have to put on for me."

Sutterfield and Janice knew each other very well. He came to the point immediately. "Where's Fell?"

Janice shut her mouth. After a moment she relaxed again, slowly. "You'll have to wait, Herb."

"Wait? Do you realize what he's doing to me? I'm not in the habit of waiting for anybody, neither my kind of people or his kind! When I—"

"When you talk to me about my husband," said Janice, "you will please remember your manners as much as you do with anyone else. More so, Herb."

Sutterfield twitched his chin and stared at Janice, but didn't say anything for the moment. Then he said, "Now I'll explain something to you, Janice. He depends upon me as much as I depend on him. Where is he?"

"I can't tell you."

"You won't?"

"He'll be back, Herb."

"When? By the time this town blows up in his face? And that won't have a thing to do with what I think of him! It'll be his doing, his absence, his lack of—"

"All right, Herb. All right."

Sutterfield thought for a moment she was going to tell him where Fell was, but Janice had only wanted to stop his ranting. She tried not to show her worry and kept her face blank. She had nothing to say. If she told Sutterfield what he wanted to know, it would only make things worse. She wanted Tom Fell back more than anyone else, for better reasons, and with better feelings. Then Sutterfield started talking again.

"Do you know I haven't received my check for almost a month? Do you realize that this money must go to a number of places or else our entire arrangement in this town is apt to collapse?"

"Herb, if you need some money...."

"You seem to have no idea how much Tom pays for protection."

"No, and I don't care. Go and speak to somebody in the organization."

"They know any more than I do? They're fidgeting on their chairs as if they were wired for electricity! All they know is how to take orders, and there's nobody here who's giving them."

"I'm not interested in hearing about it."

"You don't care? You don't care about Tom?"

Janice drew herself up, and seemed suddenly very much taller than Sutterfield. He hesitated a moment, expecting her to shout, but she spoke very quietly.

"Get out. Get out, Herb."

Sutterfield went to the door, opened it, and said, "You're making things worse; you know that, don't you."

"Don't come to me about yours and Tom's business. I'm not part of it."

"Pretty soon nobody else will be, either."

Janice looked out the window and then back at Sutterfield. She wanted him to go. "Why don't you see Pander? He's in charge," she commented.

"That clown?"

Janice shrugged. "Or see Cripp. Tom and Cripp are very close."

Chapter Four

Cripp spread dust as he swung through the iron gate with the sign that said
Desert Farm. Suddenly there was no more dust. The dirt road from the highway had been yellow with old gravel and sand drifts, but once through the
gate, the road was a clean hard-top. The view coming through the desert had
had the strong colors of an Indian blanket; mesas with their sides brick-red,
sharp blue in the sky, mustard-yellow where the desert was. All the shadows
had been pure black.

Now the shadows were green. They hung dark and moist among the trees
along the drive and made the bushes look dark where they bordered the big
pea-green lawn. Desert Farm was a park, a hothouse, an artificial oasis. It reminded Cripp of Forest Lawn, except that there were no mausoleums or any
other visible tombs. The main building was a vast white thing that took
Cripp's breath away. A portico in front resembled Grant's Tomb and the rest
of the structure had a touch of a modern office building, or maybe Sing Sing,
except for the sun porches and giant verandas.

Cripp parked under a tree. He was five minutes early, so he sat for a while,
straightened his tie, ran his hands through his blond hair. He didn't seem impatient. His features were so regular it was difficult to decide whether he was
handsome or beautiful, and except for his strong neck and powerful shoulders
he might have looked like a boy.

After a while he got out of the car and with a peculiar swing of the arms
walked toward the building. It was a shock to see him walk, his whole body
making a spastic jerk each time the twisted leg took a step. That's why they
called him Cripp.

"I'm Jordan," he said at the desk. "To see Doctor Emilson."

He waited in the lobby, looking at the Indian decor. Then a young woman
wearing sandals and a hand-printed dress took him through a series of corridors; not regular hospital corridors—the first one was pink, the next one was
mauve, and the one after that was orange. From time to time the woman used
the keys that hung from her belt.

In Dr. Emilson's office, more Indian decor.

"I'm back," said Jordan. "About Mr. Fell."

Dr. Emilson came around the desk making a therapeutic smile; a slight smile,
eyes gazing deeply, and no offense meant.

"Of course, Mr. Jordan. Won't you sit down?"

Cripp sat down.

"Would you care to smoke?" said Dr. Emilson, and offered a heavy wood
cigarette box.

Cripp declined. "I'm in a hurry," he said, and watched Dr. Emilson take one of the cigarettes.

Dr. Emilson sat down again and smoked. He did it without inhaling, blowing out the smoke as if he were only practicing. He was young and smooth-skinned, with a small mustache under his nose. The mustache was meant to add age and a trustworthy look.

"What about Fell?" he said.

"You're the doctor," said Cripp. "How is he?"

"Coming along very well. Very well. You may see him, of course, but please remember the rule of the house. Keep him calm, happy, untroubled." Dr. Emilson again made his smile.

"He's got to come back," said Cripp.

Emilson thought for a moment, because he rarely said yes or no. He said, "You mean leave here?"

"It's important. His business."

This was a familiar request to Emilson, and since he already knew what to answer he waited for a moment, untroubled. He flipped the pages of a severe-looking book, full of small print and footnotes, bound in the uniform wine-red of one of the university presses. The author's name was in gold. Fredrick Emilson, M.D., Ph.D. The work dated back to the time before he had gone commercial.

"Mr. Jordan, the only important business is Mr. Fell himself. That's why he's here."

"You said he was doing fine. I'm glad. But his other business isn't."

"Does Mrs. Fell know you are here?"

"I don't think so. She's got nothing to do with the business."

"But you have."

"Sure. I'm his boy."

"Ah? I didn't know Mr. Fell had a son."

"His boy. His boy. Right hand. His aide or something."

"Ah, yes," said Emilson.

"So I got to see him about this."

Emilson wasn't sure how to handle this matter. It confused him. "Out of the question," he said, sparring for time.

Cripp went right on. "Let's ask him. You said he's better, so he ought to decide himself."

Emilson thought about how he might handle this. Cripp wasn't a relative, so the scare approach wouldn't work. He wasn't a doctor, so the clinical terms wouldn't solve anything. He said again, "Out of the question."

"Look, Fell is a paying guest. He's self-committed, and you're a private outfit. Fell can leave any time he wants."

"Let me try to explain something, Jordan. I told you the patient was well, and I meant it. I also meant it to imply that he was well here, but not necessarily anywhere else. When you brought him in he was suffering—to use your language—from a nervous breakdown, brought on typically enough by a mere matter of having been handed a parking ticket. You know the events better than I do, Mr. Jordan, because you were with him at the time."

"He was in bad shape," said Cripp, and thought about it. "Until he slowed down."

"If Mr. Fell had been under the care of a physician at the time, the physician would have told you how important psychiatric judgment is in cases like this. My judgment—"

"That was a whole month ago. And don't forget," said Cripp, "when he was home, talking to Mrs. Fell and me after we got him to bed, it was Fell himself who said he wanted to come here. For a rest."

"Yes, and it was very acute of him."

"So don't tell me he's crazy."

"I didn't. I said he was sick."

"Look, when a head-shrinker says—"

"Mr. Jordan." Emilson felt himself lose some of the smile and the patience. He found that the most trying parts of his work were the non-clinical contacts, the job of explaining to laymen. Emilson had soft little hands, and he started to stroke the book he had written.

"Let me say this. We all have flaws, and most of the time a flaw doesn't show except under stress. What really distinguishes insanity is the fact that the flaw shows sooner, that even a slight thing becomes a stress."

"That doesn't fit Fell. He's got plenty of stress in his line of work and nothing ever showed before."

"Nothing that you would recognize. But I've spent a good deal of time with Fell, and I tell you this. Now that his flaw has finally shown so much that anyone can notice the difference, it will take more than rest to mend him."

"He's been doing okay. And if he doesn't do some mending pretty soon in the way of business...."

"Look, Jordan," said Dr. Emilson. "If Fell should leave now, that might be all he needed to go over the brink."

Cripp sat up. He was finally getting straight answers.

"That's my professional guess," said Emilson, "and it's enough to warn you."

"Warn me?"

"Did you ever hear of a psychosis?"

It made Cripp think of padded cells and children's games for grown men. It made him think of Fell, whom he had known for over ten years. Fell had picked him up in New York, where Cripp was making pocket money in a cheap sideshow at Coney Island. The Brain Boy with the Mighty Memory. Tell the kid the year and date of your birthday, mister, and he'll give you the day of the week. And now the most astounding feat ever performed! Read any sentence from this paper, mister, this morning's paper, and the kid will tell you what the rest of the paragraph is. This morning's paper, mister, the kid's read it once—and Fell had picked him up after the show, kept him with him ever since. A mighty memory was quite a boon in Fell's racket. No book-keeping, no double checks on collections, no time wasted on figuring odds and percentages. Cripp did it all in his head. He and Fell weren't friends, or even buddies, but whatever they had between them was as close a thing as Cripp ever had with anyone. And Cripp made it the only attachment there was. It was easier that way.

"Did you ever hear of a psychosis?" Emilson had said, and right then all Cripp knew was that Fell was not like those men playing children's games or like somebody in a padded cell. Fell was strong, always right, generous because he was big; and he could make things sure because he was always sure him-self. Fell had two legs that gave him a straight, even walk. Fell was—

"Mr. Jordan, I asked you a question."

Cripp jerked up in his chair, the mask of calmness slipping from his face. "You trying to scare me, so he'll stick around longer? So you can suck him along and keep him wrapped up in this hot-house you run here? Let me tell you about Tommy Fell. I been with him for more years than you've had a mus-tache. He's—"

"Let me tell you," said Emilson, and the way he said it, coolly and with no effort, Cripp stopped and listened. "He is energetic, correct? There is very little that will stop our Mr. Fell, correct? There has never been such a man for being sure of success, for confidence, for making things come out the right way. And generous, correct? Even careless, perhaps, careless in his generous ways, his being so sure of things...."

Emilson saw how Cripp took it, like watching a parlor game with tricks he couldn't figure out.

"But all this is very well under control, wouldn't you say, Mr. Jordan. All this is just slow enough to keep Fell within range of the normal. And I tell you another thing, Mr. Jordan. Sometimes Thomas Fell has been depressed, just mildly, just sort of vague and withdrawn, for all you could tell."

"Just twice," said Cripp and then he listened again.

"That's all I wanted to tell you," said Emilson. "I wanted to tell you this to describe Fell's flaw. The way you've seen it, you'd hardly call it a flaw, would you? In fact, it must have helped when it came to running his en-terprises. But push it a little further, Jordan, and what do you have?"

Emilson's soft little fingers had started to fiddle with each other, and Cripp was looking back and forth from the dancing fingers to the mustache under Emilson's nose. He had been only half listening because everything had only made half sense. Then Cripp lost his temper.

"You telling me he's nuts?" he shouted.

"I'm telling you he might go nuts!" Emilson answered quietly.

"You telling me something new?" Cripp was up now. "Everybody might go nuts!"

"This type's got a name, Jordan. Fell's a potential manic!"

"A maniac?"

"No! A manic. A fast-moving, cheerful guy, lots of laughs, lots of drive, and no end to what he might do or how far he might drive himself. That's what I'm talking about."

"Fell never—"

"I didn't say that, but he might. He's got the makings to just take off into space, laughing or not laughing. And once he does that, once he cuts off his mooring, everybody better scatter because Fell isn't going to wait around and apologize."

For a while they just stared at each other, Emilson waiting to see whether he had said enough, and Cripp staring back and hoping that Emilson was finally through. Cripp had a vivid picture now. He tried not to pay any attention to it because he didn't want it to fit, but the picture was very vivid now. Not a maniac, Emilson had said, but a manic. Not somebody raving and ranting but somebody who might— No, Emilson hadn't said that. It was hard to remember what Emilson had said, and then Emilson spoke again.

"We can see him now," he said.

Cripp didn't answer, but just followed the other man out of the office.

There were more corridors painted in soothing pastels, and then the large sun porch. It could have been a hotel. Two men played cards at a small table and a group further down was arguing about cotton futures. Nothing crazy anywhere. Nothing crazy about cotton futures or about playing cards. No children's games for grown men, no white gowns and attendants. Doctor Emilson himself was wearing slacks and a Hawaiian shirt and the rest of the staff, if there were any on the porch, couldn't be distinguished from the patients, either.

Then Cripp saw Fell. He had never seen Fell wearing anything but a business suit, so Cripp hadn't spotted him right away. Three men came down the bright corridor. They all wore housecoats, and the big one had a red ascot around his neck, a diamond horseshoe pinning it down. The big one was smiling at the one with the stoop, who was talking around a straw in his mouth. That one smiled too. The one in the middle didn't smile. He had brown hair, gray at the temples. The lines on his forehead made him look as if he were thinking, except that his eyes were too casual. It was also peculiar that he should have long lashes with a hard face like his. Then the tall one roared with laughter, showing gold teeth in the back. The stooped one laughed too.

When they had come up to Dr. Emilson and Cripp, they stopped. Fell reached out and shook Cripp's hand. "Glad to see you," he said.

"The attendant will show you my room," said Fell. He pointed to the big guy, and Cripp looked at the red ascot with the diamond pin. Fell turned to Dr. Emilson. "Let me have my bill," he said. "I'm checking out."

CHAPTER FIVE

Cripp drove, and Tom Fell sat in the back. The car was a convertible, and when Cripp could see the head in the rear-view mirror he saw how the wind made Fell's hair dance at the temples. Most of the time Cripp saw only the top of the leather seat and the lines of the highway shrinking behind. Fell sat out of view, not talking. He was a presence which Cripp felt as a vague tense-ness on the back of his head and on his back where the shoulder blades came together. When it had got dark the desert had disappeared and the road started climbing gradually. But it stayed warm, a heavy night warmth that was unusual.

Cripp turned his head once to see whether Fell were asleep. Fell was look-ing back at him, and when their eyes met he smiled. Cripp turned front again and kept driving. There was a lot he had to tell. He should be briefing Fell, but after his talk with Emilson, Cripp wasn't so sure any more. Even if none of it were really true—if Emilson had been exaggerating— But Cripp had no way of knowing. And Fell was no help. He sat in the back, showing nothing. If Fell would only talk, perhaps something he'd say might give some meaning.

There were more turns in the road now, and fir trees showed black along the side. Suddenly it started to rain. It was a short rain, the kind that some-times gets caught along the sides of the Sierras and is over in a short while.

Cripp stopped the car and pressed the button which raised the top.

"Leave it open," said Fell.

Cripp drove on again.

Fell turned his head so the moist air pressed his face, a warm push that felt as if it meant to breathe for him. He hadn't seen any rain in over a month, nothing but the dry cleanliness of desert air. He liked the feel of the rain.

He was sorry when the rain suddenly stopped. He was sure something was wrong. He had seen the signs earlier, before he had left, but it hadn't been bad then. Pander, probably—only Pander wasn't alone in this. Perhaps they were just trying Pander out, the front office sending him a problem just for the hell of it. But they didn't do a thing just for the hell of it, always for a rea-son. To see if Fell was losing his grip. Ever since Janice—anyway, ever since he had married her, they hadn't been happy in the front office.

"Close the top, Cripp."

The car stopped and the top went up. Cripp snapped it down in front and drove again. Perhaps he should talk to him now. Fell ought to know.

"How's Janice?" said Fell.

How's Janice! The whole setup coming apart at the seams, and he asked about Janice.

"She's fine. She's been anxious about you, but fine otherwise. We've all been kind of anxious about—"

"She's a fine woman," said Fell. He sat in the dark under the closed roof and thought about Janice.

"She'll be surprised to see you," said Cripp.

"I'm sure Emilson has called her by now."

Cripp hadn't thought of that.

"Has it been hot back home?"

Cripp answered, "Plenty hot."

"That's good," said Fell. "Nothing like a lot of early heat for a good track when the season starts."

He was talking about the weather. And about the track season opening, as if there were nothing to do but wait for the opening, buy a ticket, and sit down to watch. It wasn't going to be easy breaking it all to Fell, all the bad news and the storm warnings. There sat Boss Fell thinking about Janice and the weather....

"Any word from the syndicate?" Fell said suddenly.

"What?"

"They're coaching Pander. Do they think he's panning out?"

Cripp had to shift right then because a road barrier led him around a rock slide that had splattered the highway.

"I'll tell you," he said, trying to catch up. "The fact is, I'd never been sure of it."

"I'm sure," said Fell. "They might want to give him a piece of this area. Perhaps all of it."

"You mean—you knew all this?"

"Sure." Then Fell laughed, a short, dry sound. "I'm not worried, if that's what you mean."

Cripp took a breath and let it go slowly, he had no idea what would come next. It had happened once that one of Fell's men got ideas and started to use muscle. Fell sent him to Mexico on a job and the man never showed up again. No mess, no stink, just a clean sweep, and whatever had happened had happened across the border. But then there had been time to plan. Maybe he had been planning, back in the desert with nothing to do.

"Ever hear of shock treatments?" Fell said.

Cripp didn't know what Fell meant. Perhaps he meant to rough Pander up, only Fell had never liked strong-arming. As a matter of policy, he used to say, you don't fix a guy by giving him a nosebleed. And what's worse, if he bleeds enough everybody wants to know why.

"They lay you out and put wires on your head," Fell said. "Then they feed you the juice."

"Juice?" said Cripp.

"Electricity. Electroshock. They gave me a series of them. Man," he said,

and Cripp could hear Fell breathe in the back, "did I used to wake up confused."

Cripp just drove.

"I had that," said Fell, "and then those talks with Emilson." Fell laughed.
"Man, did I used to come out of *those* confused."

"Did it help?"

"How can you tell? It's like living in a hothouse up there, that Desert Farm
place. They farm you in the middle of the desert. You can't tell till you leave
the farm and get out of that desert," said Fell.

"I meant the shock treatment," said Cripp. He could hear Fell moving in
the back, patting himself and grunting. "Give me a cigarette," he said.

Cripp did, and Fell lit it. Cripp could hear his deep exhaling.

"It's like with this cigarette," said Fell. "That first drag tearing down your
throat used to be really something. A real pleasure." There was the sound of
inhaling again and then the wind rushing in when Fell wheeled down the window. He threw the cigarette out. When the window was up again it shut out
the noise.

"It's like they took the edge off of things," said Fell, "and everything's
toned down."

"That's a cure?"

"You saw me throw out that cigarette. That's the cure; you don't care one
way or the other."

They didn't talk for a while and the car started winding down again. When
the terrain smoothed out Cripp went faster. The car seemed to flatten out and
the road in the headlights lost all texture. Cripp thought the faster they went
the sooner he'd be able to start giving Fell the news. As if the speed of driving—

"Go faster," said Fell.

Cripp touched the floor board and watched the needle creep up. It made
slight little trembles like a blade of grass. Outside the wind roared.

"Can you talk?" said Fell.

"Sure." Cripp held the wheel so hard his big arms felt tense with effort.

"Let's have all you know. Pander, and so forth."

Fell sounded like there hadn't been any four or five weeks in the desert and
as if he hadn't said a thing since they left there.

"About Pander, it's hard to say. He's always been snotty," said Cripp. "But
since you left...."

"That's nothing. That's his type."

"Yeah. But he's been hard on the guys. Some of them left and some of them
he sent packing."

"Any rough stuff?"

"No. Just 'or else.' You know Pander."

"Go on."

"So at first I thought we'd be losing money, the way he cut down on book-making that way; but I kept check on the weekly totals and nothing showed."

"Any replacements? Did he get any new bookies in?"

"He did, some. That's another thing. He's got a lot of new faces in town, but most of those guys just hang around."

"That figures," said Fell. "His own hoods."

"You think he's got something planned, something big? I've kept pretty close, you know, but nothing seems to be shaping up. He—"

"He's not ready. Perhaps he's waiting for the word, but he'd have his bud-dies hang around anyway. Makes him feel better."

"Yeah. Here's the next thing. We had some raids." This time Cripp could hear Fell sit up and when he talked there was more life in his voice.

"Sutterfield must be nuts. That creep must be absolutely nuts."

"That's what I figured, until I found out why. He hasn't been getting his protection money."

Fell kept still for a moment and then he said, "Son of a bitch." He said it as if he meant everybody and Cripp would have turned to look at Fell's face if the car hadn't been going so fast. Cripp slowed the car.

"What's the matter?" said Fell. "What's the matter? Come on, come on."

"Just—nothing, Tom." Cripp speeded up again. "I just never heard you swear before."

"What—son of a bitch?" The sound in back could have been Fell starting a laugh, or perhaps he was just grunting. Cripp heard the wheezing sound of the leather seat, then Fell's breathing. Fell had stretched out in back with his feet braced against the window. He was talking normally when he said, "That's nothing, Cripp. You should have heard what I was thinking." He gave a short laugh.

Cripp laughed too. "I didn't hear a thing," he said. Then he stopped laugh-ing and lit himself a cigarette.

"That's good," said Fell. "I thought you might have. It was loud enough."

Fell didn't say anything else after that, which made it sound worse. Cripp had a crazy urge to turn the car back and see Dr. Emilson, but then it occurred to him that nothing Fell had said would have sounded wrong if it hadn't been for Emilson and his talk in the first place. Cripp relaxed a little. The way the breathing sounded from the back he didn't think Fell would talk any more.

"How's Buttonhead doing?" Fell said suddenly.

It took Cripp a minute to get it straight. Fell had to say, "Where's she run-ning now?" before Cripp remembered she was one of Fell's horses.

"I think Riverdowns," Cripp said, and then added, "no. She was in Cincin-nati two weeks ago. She's at Ak-Sar-Ben this week."

"That's good," said Fell. "That's closer. She been in the money lately?"

"No. Except for show once."

"Only once this year?"

Cripp read it off the way his memory showed it to him. "Fourth twice and sixth once at Riverdowns. Fifth every time in Scarborough. She made show at Fairmount Park and fourth the rest of the time. I haven't heard yet how she's been running in Omaha."

"How's the weather been in Omaha?"

"Rain for a week," said Cripp.

"She does better on a dry track," said Fell.

"You couldn't prove it by me," said Cripp. He knew how Buttonhead had been running for two years. He didn't know what made Fell hold on to the horse, or why he had thought of the nag now. Fell kept switching topics. He made sense with what he said, but he kept switching topics. Had Emilson mentioned anything like that....

"Watch the fork, Cripp."

Cripp made the turn and drove, waiting for Fell to say something else. But Fell never did. He had turned on the domelight and was scribbling on a small pad of paper. Then he turned off the light and went to sleep.

Chapter Six

They went through San Pietro at two in the morning, when the town looked more alive than at noontime.

The plants were running twenty-four hours a day, so it made sense to run the town around the clock. And besides, it was cooler at night. They passed open supermarkets, drove down a day-bright street lined with secondhand car lots, and it didn't really turn nighttime again till the car swung into the section of town where a residence cost forty thousand and over. Fell didn't wake up till the car stopped on the drive, but then he was as if sleep hadn't interrupted a thing.

"Where's Janice?" he said.

Cripp moved up against the steering wheel because Fell was pushing the left back rest forward in order to get out that way. When he was through he slammed the door shut and looked up at the house. One light was on. Then the hall light went on, too.

"Thanks," said Fell and nodded at Cripp. "See you tomorrow."

He watched the car make the circle going out the other gate, and then he looked at the lawn. It had a dark, juicy look in the low light, and it smelled moist. Like Desert Farm, he thought, like the hothouse lawn in the desert out there. I'm going to let this one go natural. I'm going to shut off the damn sprinkling system and let this one go just the way it wants.... A shaft of light fell across the lawn and made Fell's face show sudden lines and hard creases. He turned and looked at the open door, at Janice.

She saw him stand for a moment, and then saw how his face became softer. It was without sharpness now, showing only strength.

"Turn around," he said and watched how she did it, with the light shining in back of her. She was laughing, and then she waited for him while he came up to the door.

They kissed and closed the door. The light shaft on the lawn shrank away, and then the hall light went out.

Janice dropped off the negligee and sat on the bed in her nightgown. Fell stayed as he was, except for the tie. He pulled the tie off and threw it toward a chair.

"Always the same spot," said Janice. They both laughed and looked at the tie lying next to the chair legs.

"And remember," he said, "no practice for over a month." He sat down next to her and put his arm around her waist. "A whole month! No ties at the sanatorium. Suicide risk."

Talking about it didn't seem to bother him, but it sobered Janice. She pushed his hand away and got up. She unbuttoned his shirt.

"Did they give you hot chocolate at night? Get into bed and I'll bring you hot chocolate."

"Let Rita make it. You—"

"I don't want to wake her, Tom."

"Okay. Don't be long." He watched her leave.

He looked around the large bedroom, his hands hanging between his knees, and thought how he liked the room and how Janice left things in it that reminded him of her. The whole room reminded him of her. The room of the past month had reminded him of nothing. Perhaps that had been part of the cure too, to be reminded of nothing; but what it made him remember most was this room and Janice. It was one feeling that hadn't changed, the warmth for Janice. It hadn't gone flat and indifferent like some things, like— It was hard to remember, but it didn't matter.

He took off his clothes, washed, went back to the bed. Janice had put his pajamas out, and he put on only the pants. He sat in bed and looked at his arm, a strong, short arm with good color. He twisted it, watching the muscles.

Janice came in, put the hot chocolate on the night table next to him, and pulled up a chair. For a while they didn't talk. Then he said, "It's good, Jan." She smiled at him, seeing how he was suddenly tired again.

"Doctor Emilson called you," he said.

"Yes, in the afternoon. So I would know you were coming."

"And what else?"

"He said he wished you hadn't left, Tom."

Fell nodded and looked at his arm again. He thought about moving it, like before, but then he didn't and just watched it lie still.

"He said more, Tom."

"I know."

"He said you're making a mistake."

Fell looked up. He was rubbing his arm now. When he became aware of it he stopped.

"Sometimes, Jan, I feel the same way."

She hadn't expected it, so for the moment she could think of nothing to say. But she didn't have to think, or talk. Her feeling was open, making her do the simple, direct thing. She got up and came to the bed where Fell sat and she took him around his bare shoulders, holding him close, with his head against her warm skin.

"Are you tired, Tom?" she asked.

"I don't know. It's like waiting."

"Rest, Tom."

"It's like—like before deciding, Jan."

"There's nothing to decide, Tom. We'll leave. You don't have to stay here, you don't have to keep at it. We—"

"If I only knew what I have to do—"

He put his hands on her back, held them there. Right then the warmth under his hands was the only real thing and he pressed it to make it more real.

"You always have me," said Janice. "You can always hold me."

Then he let go. He leaned back into the pillow and took a deep breath. Strength had come back to him and it felt like nothing that he had felt since the time he had left. But it was familiar, the kind of urge which was all pressure but without an object; as if Janice weren't enough, as if nobody were enough. There was only an aimless pressure.

Emilson had been interested in that. Emilson had said it was the thing he would have to learn to control; that it could carry him far, meaning too far. It was familiar: it had been behind his whole brazen history, starting with the time he had run away from home for no good reason, for the reason of running, for the joy of running, starting with the hobo jungles, and then his first winter in big, cold Chicago. And then the break. The police picked him up for breaking and entering, which he hadn't done. He took the rap. He had never been in jail before. He was regular, the cons said. He didn't take any gaff but he didn't have a chip on his shoulder, and when he got out on parole somebody was waiting for him. "—because the boss thinks you're regular. You don't talk, you got spunk, you didn't squeal on the guy what done the job." Tom Fell hadn't seen the guy who had done the job, but Tom Fell didn't talk. And because he had never been a hood before, he went along.

He stuck. For the first time he saw a clear line showing him where to go. From driving an alki truck to owning one, to running a fleet, to making the boss himself take orders. But it didn't work that way. It meant the boss had to go. Tom Fell got his way.

When Fell got older he thought everything was under control because there were no more loose ends and no more running around. Almost everything had a system. Join the combine, run your section, move west because the combine was spreading and they needed a good man with experience, stick to your racket and grow big.

Fell had run San Pietro for fifteen years before anything started to bother him again. Pander? Pushy kids never bothered him before. His age? He felt good. Was San Pietro too small? For a while it had grown faster than Fell and he had worked as he hadn't worked since Chicago. That's when it started. When he had the town in the palm of his hand he still had pressure left and nowhere to put it.

He had forgotten about that feeling, and it didn't make sense. Janice was with him by then, but it had nothing to do with Janice. They even got married because that's how he wanted it. He wanted Janice because she was the closest thing to finding an end for his aimlessness that he had ever known. But he must have been wrong—partly wrong, anyway. Why else the long hours working for no good reason, expanding his setup where there was no profit to show for it, sharpening the organization as if it had to run a whole coun-try?

He caught himself short then. It felt almost like giving up. He even took in a man like Pander, showing him all the angles, knowing why Pander was sent to him, why the syndicate always groomed the next man when the old man was getting tired. They thought he was getting tired because he checked him-self back to a slow pace for fear of going too far in the other direction. Only an old man would do that. But Fell wasn't old. It was the strain of that con-tradiction—even Emilson seemed to think so—that made Fell give.

Tom Fell knew all this. He did not like to think about it. He lay back on the pillow and ran one hand over his face. He didn't like to think about it because it didn't help.

"Jan," he said, "turn your back."

Janice turned her back. Then she dropped the nightgown down to her hips and looked at Fell over her shoulder.

"Like always. The most beautiful back ever."

She liked hearing it, and sat still while Fell looked at her back. It was nei-ther lean nor fleshy, and since he thought it was beautiful but could never de-scribe it to himself he had to look at it as often as he could.

"Are you drinking the chocolate?" she asked.

But he wasn't because then she felt his hand stroke down her spine.

"I don't think I want it any more," he said.

She got off the bed and pulled her nightgown back up because it wouldn't go over her hips. Then Fell turned the lights off and they both lay down.

Actually the first morning light was already on the plains outside of town—but when they fell asleep it could have been any time, or the first time they had been together.

Chapter Seven

He woke up as if sleep had interrupted nothing. What sleep did to him was to stop still, like a dive straight down, and when he came up again it was the exact spot he had left.

He was ready to leave at seven in the morning, Janice still asleep and Rita puttering sleepily in the kitchen. She made him some coffee and when he sat down to drink it at the kitchen table they didn't talk. Rita never talked much. She was a small-boned Mexican with a tight-skinned face and shining black hair.

He finished his coffee and phoned Cripp. He had to wake Cripp, but that happened often.

When Fell drove past his front lawn the automatic sprinklers were already on, making mist and rainbows over the grass. Fell looked at it, but didn't remember about the Desert Farm lawns. He left the sprinklers on and drove through town, out to the motel that looked like the Alamo. It was called Alamo and the big neon sign was still on with a small Vacancy underneath that went on and off.

Fell parked by the coffee shop and went in. Phido was at the counter slurping coffee and Pearl stood opposite leaning her hip against the push-button box which worked the jukebox. They both looked sleepy. Fell stopped before walking around the counter.

"What in hell are you doing here?"

Phido snapped around as if the voice had waked him up. He sloshed coffee, dropped the cup, and started shaking his burnt hand.

"It's Mr. Fell, honey," said Pearl.

"You work out of the place on Yucca Avenue, don't you, Phido? What are you doing here?"

"Morning—good morning," said Phido. He kept shaking his hand. "Gee, Tom, I didn't know you was back. Nobody told me you—"

"That figures. Since when are you working out of this office?"

"I wasn't. I just—"

"He just got up," said Pearl. "He sleeps here."

"How come you can afford fifteen bucks a night, Phido?"

"My land," said Pearl and looked down herself, "Phido and me is friends."

"I meant the price of the room," said Fell. "How come you can afford the price of the room, Phido? Business that good?"

Phido got up and hit his thigh on the edge of the counter. Everything shook.

"I'll pay for the room," he said. "Honest, Tom, there was no guests anyway on account of the season...."

"How long you been staying here, Phido?"

"Two nights, Tom. Just two nights."

"Without paying."

"Honest, Tom, I can pay it. Just give me a few days—"

"Business bad, Phido?"

"Bad? We had raids!"

"I hear that was days ago," said Fell.

"So?"

"So how's business now?" said Fell.

Phido sighed and let his arms drop against his legs with a loud slap.

"I been forgetting, Tom, you musta just come in. All the bookie joints that got raided are closed."

Fell took his upper lip between his teeth. It made his jaw come out sharply and gave him a strange look because of the way his eyes stayed soft, with the long lashes halfway down.

"They never opened again? Pander never opened them up again?"

"That's right, Tom. Pander never opened them up again."

Fell turned and went to the kitchen. Before he got through the swinging doors Phido called after him, "Honest, Tom, just gimme a day or so and I'll pay you the—"

"On the house, Phido." Fell let the doors swing shut. He walked down the corridor and stopped at the door where the first raid had been. There was a seal hanging across the door jamb. Fell flipped it with his finger and walked on.

He had an office in the back, a little room with expensive wallpaper, an air conditioner built into one window and another window with plants and a view of the motel's swimming pool. The prairie showed, further back. The nicked desk by the window was almost bare—just a phone and some pencils. Fell took the phone and called his office in town.

"San Pietro Realty Company," said the voice.

"Give me Pander."

"Pander ain't in, and besides—"

"Where in hell is he? It's after eight."

"Look here," said the voice, but Fell interrupted.

"Where can I reach him?"

"Who are you, buster, the police?"

"Worse, you son of a bitch. This is Thomas Fell. Now let's have it. Where's Pander?"

The voice gagged a little and Fell waited. "Home—I guess. He doesn't show here very often, uh, Mr. Fell."

"What's he doing, taking a holiday?"

"He does business from home, mostly. I didn't know you were in, Mr. Fell. Let me call Pander and—"

"Never mind. Besides, I'm calling from Washington."

"Washington?"

"Yeah. I just bought the Capitol Building." Fell banged the phone down, but he wasn't really angry. He just felt active, very active, and he wondered for a moment why he had made that crack about the Capitol Building. He didn't often waste time on jokes but he thought it was pretty funny. A capital joke, and he laughed to himself. Fell got up and looked out the window at the empty pool. He would have liked to see some activity there. The door opened in back of him and Cripp came in.

Cripp looked sober, concentrating on walking because it was such an effort. Cripp sat down and said good morning.

"You look sleepy," said Fell. He kept looking at Cripp because it did something to his mood. He liked Cripp, and now that he was here it meant work for Fell, step by step work without crazy distractions and the kind of sober thing that had gotten away from him, just a month ago, when he had gone to Desert Farm.

"I am, kind of," said Cripp. "I didn't think you'd be up early today."

Fell sat down and asked Cripp for a cigarette. He smoked slowly, then put it down in an ashtray.

"You told me about the raids," he said. "Did you know the places were never opened again?"

"Yes. That's why I came to see you at the sanatorium."

"You sure broke it to me gently. In fact you never said a word."

"Well, you know how things were. And then you decided to come back anyway."

"Good thing I did." Fell picked up the cigarette, took a puff, put it down again. "We got to see Sutterfield, and then Pander. Before seeing Pander I want a picture of how the money's been coming in. How much have we lost?"

Cripp squirmed his leg around and looked at Fell.

"That's what I don't get. We lost nothing."

Fell frowned.

"Pander never gave me any trouble checking the daily tallies. We lost nothing."

"What did he show you—daily totals or the lists of bets collected that day?"

"Totals."

"Perhaps that's where the bug is, Cripp. Pander hasn't been paying protection for a whole month or more."

"That's not it, Tom. The month's total is just about the same as always, *plus* the protection Pander didn't pay."

"I'll be damned!" said Fell.

"Now there's this," said Cripp. "I tried checking around because the bets must come in somewhere, but I had kind of a hard time. Pander's got lots of new help, you know, the old guys didn't know from nothing or just would-

n't talk to me. And I didn't get anywhere trying to talk to some of the customers. They pretty well know me around town and I guess most everyone
smells there's something going on and wants no trouble. But here's what it
looks like, Tom, and—"

"Never mind. Let Pander tell it. You got your car?"

"Sure. How else do you think—"

"Hell, I forgot, Cripp," and Fell leaned forward to give Cripp a pat on the
shoulder. Then he got up. "Let's take your car. You drive better," and they
went out.

They walked through the coffee shop. Nobody was there except Pearl, and
when she saw Fell she smiled at him and walked up.

"I just wanted to tell you, Mr. Fell, I think you're swell. And thanks for
the thirty dollars you give me."

"I gave you—"

"Fifteen a night, you know. Two nights."

Fell had stopped and looked at the girl without having heard one sensible
word. He was just going to say you're welcome and let it go at that, when
Pearl saw that she hadn't explained herself.

"The thirty dollars you told Phido was on the house, you remember? He's
going to get the thirty dollars anyway, and seeing how you said you didn't
want it Phido says he's going to give it to me. And I want to thank you," she
added, looking down.

Fell grinned and gave Pearl a pat.

"You're welcome," he said. "And let me know if Phido doesn't come
through."

Cripp and Fell were at the door when Pearl called after them, "And any
time you want a cup of coffee for free, Mr. Fell—and your friend too—you
just come here."

Driving in Cripp's car, Fell commented, "There's your chance, Cripp. Free
coffee."

Cripp looked back at Fell.

"Doesn't she know you own the place?"

Fell grinned. He said he didn't think it made any difference.

Chapter Eight

In one way San Pietro was wide open, but in others they liked a certain formality. So Fell didn't walk into the Town Hall and ask for Commissioner Sutterfield. He didn't even park in the closed lot where the officials had their cars, and when Fell and Cripp happened to see the mayor pass on the street they nodded, said hello, sir, and walked on. Then Cripp and Fell walked to one side of the Town Hall and went into the basement. They stopped in the record room and looked at one of the volumes with lot numbers and subdivisions.

"Would you like to come this way?" said a woman attendant wearing pink-tinted glasses.

They did, and then through a door in the back, up an iron staircase and through Sutterfield's office, to the commissioner's front room. That's where the file cabinets were, the group photos of cops for the past fifty years, and another woman attendant. She also wore glasses, rimless, and her lenses also were pink.

"He's very busy," she said to Fell. The rose-colored glass made her eyes look ugly.

"Sure," said Fell. "Tell him we're here."

"They called from downstairs," she said. "You may go in now."

That's when Sutterfield opened the door, held it for them.

"How are you, Mr. Fell?"

"Thank you, fine, Mr. Sutterfield."

Sutterfield closed the door and watched Cripp sit down. Then Fell sat down. Sutterfield remained standing.

"All right, Fell. What is the meaning of this?"

It came out so cold that both Fell and Cripp looked up. "Take it easy, Mr. Sutterfield," said Cripp. He looked over to Fell.

"I'll take it easy when I've been given an adequate explanation for—"

"That's why we're here, Mr. Sutterfield," Cripp said quickly, because he was watching Fell get up and walk to the window where he stood and looked out.

"Don't get excited, Herbie," Fell said to the window. "Just hold still till we get something straight."

"Now you listen to me, Fell. You seem to have the idea—"

Fell cut him short but talked very quietly. He turned back to the room, sat down, looked at his shoes. Fell's long lashes made him look almost sleepy. "I have no idea, Herbie. One reason we're here is to get an idea, to find out what goes on."

"Very well," said Sutterfield. He was rubbing his hands together. "It's very simple from where I'm standing. You disappear—for your health according to Janice—and leave matters in the hands of some incompetent, self-seeking assistant who seems to have the idea—"

"Mice will play while the cat's away," said Fell. Both Sutterfield and Cripp looked startled. "Go on, Herbie."

Sutterfield finally sat down.

"Now listen to me, Fell. Perhaps you have the notion that I have time to waste, or money to throw away, or perhaps that all of this is just some friendly misunderstanding." Sutterfield stopped to gather breath. Then he almost shouted, "I'm a businessman with obligations and a strong sense of what's proper. For allowing you to operate in this town—"

"Allowing me, Herbie?"

"Yes, allowing you! And for that I expect to receive consideration as arranged."

"Say it, Herbie. You mean ice."

"Your language doesn't—"

"Payoff money."

Sutterfield's sour face got livid. "I'll order raids that will ruin you! I'll get the state police and the district attorney! I'll—"

"You'll have a fit, Herbie. Any minute." Fell used the pause to say more. "I just want to straighten this out, Herbie. And then everything will be as it was before. Okay?"

"What did you say?"

"How much ice do I owe you?"

Sutterfield was quick to answer.

"Four weeks. Eight thousand."

"Cripp?" Fell looked at him.

"That's right." Cripp nodded.

"Write a check, Cripp."

"Now, just a minute," said Sutterfield. He had got over his surprise. He leaned back in his chair and felt very much on top. "Because of your inefficiency I had to handle unpleasant, unexpected incidentals which are not part of our arrangement. For example, I paid a number of functionaries, who also did not receive their due, out of my own pocket."

"That comes out of the two thousand per week," said Cripp. "Five hundred to—"

"I know our arrangement!" said Sutterfield. "I know it better, I might add—"

"Dry up, Herbie, will you, please? Cripp, who else didn't get paid, besides the guys who get theirs through Sutterfield?"

"Except for the beats, nobody got paid. The beats are paid by our bookies direct. So that makes another six thousand per week all around. Nobody got paid from Sutterfield, by the way," Cripp added.

Fell smiled. "Are you trying to cheat me, Herbie?"

"Fell, your two thousand per week is not all mine. I distribute that. Naturally I was holding—"

"So what are these expenses you keep talking about?"

"Do you think raids cost nothing? Do you think it's not going to cost something to reverse my orders, to calm down feelings which have been aroused by this entire mismanagement which forced me to expend efforts in our behalf?"

"How much, Herbie? You got any idea?"

Sutterfield certainly did. "An additional eight thousand."

"Cripp," said Fell as if he hadn't heard, "what's our average take for this time of year?"

"That's hard to say, Tom. We never worked out an average figure for the weeks just before the season."

"What was our actual take for the four weeks just before I left?"

"From bookmaking?"

Fell nodded and before he was through nodding Cripp said, "Month's average per week twenty thousand, eight seventy-two."

"And how many offices did Herbie close?"

"Ten," said Sutterfield, and Cripp nodded.

"What proportion of the weekly take did we get from those?"

Cripp thought a moment, said "About thirty per cent."

"What's thirty per cent of that weekly figure you just gave me?"

Cripp said, "Six thousand, two sixty-one."

"So we lost six thousand a week, for which you want a two thousand bonus, Herbie. That doesn't make sense."

Sutterfield pinched his lips together and looked mean.

"Or looking at it another way, Herbie, I'm going to pay you eight thousand for losing me more than twenty-four thousand. So Cripp will give you a check for the last four weeks, for the time you didn't get paid. And for that price I want you to keep things as is, Herbie—normal, friendly, and smooth."

Sutterfield seemed to shrink behind his desk, holding himself that way as if he were getting ready for something, but when Cripp gave him the check Sutterfield took it and said nothing.

"All fixed, Herbie?" Fell got up.

"Just a minute."

They both looked at the old man behind the desk.

"I'm taking this money as a gesture of good will. That's all. It pays for nothing, Fell, remember that. The only way we can run this thing is by doing it with no flaws and no hitches. I'm going along with you because—" Sutterfield never batted an eye, "—because we're old friends. If you cause a stink in this town, if you start losing control—and that's what it looks like—no amount of protection can hold this business together. And remember this, Fell. I'm watching the scene, just as I think your friend Pander is doing. And I don't do business with losers. Is that clear?"

Cripp watched how Fell lowered his lashes again and how he pursed his lips. That's all Fell did. Then he looked at Sutterfield and nodded.

"Sure. Good-by, Herb."

In the car Fell didn't say any more about it. He asked Cripp for a cigarette and smoked part of it. "Anything new about Buttonhead?"

"No, Tom. There hasn't been time since we got here."

"Oh, that's right. When we get back from Pander, remind me to call Omaha." Then Fell didn't say any more till they got to Pander's apartment.

CHAPTER NINE

Pander was out. He had left a man in the apartment to hold down the phone and answer the door. Fell didn't know him and the hood didn't know Fell so he wasn't going to say where Pander had gone. Fell asked again, politely, and the next thing, Cripp thought, Fell might start to get rough. Cripp had seen him before when he lost his temper, and there was never much of a buildup.

Nothing happened. Fell nodded good-by and left. "Let's try the Waterhole," he said, and they drove out to the edge of town where the nightclub was.

The place was built low and sprawling. The prairie started in back of it, but in front and at the sides the grounds had been landscaped like a desert. They had even carted in the sand to make a good job of it.

The front door was locked, of course, but Fell didn't want to walk around to the side. He rattled the door and finally a guy came up. He shook his head behind the plate glass, because it was before business hours and he didn't know Fell. When he started to walk away one of the cleaning ladies came by. She knew Fell and told the guy, so the door opened and they walked in. The guy was so confused he forgot to lock the door again.

"Listen, I'm sorry, Mr. Fell," he said. "But—you want me to call Pander? Did you want to—"

"He's in back?" said Fell.

"I can get him for you—"

"Never mind." They walked to the back. The room was dim and all the up-turned chair legs gave the place the air of a storage loft—except for the frescos along the wall, the grande piano inlaid with little square mirrors, and the dance floor which was shiny black plastic. Why they had called the place Waterhole wasn't clear, because there was no Western decor anywhere. Just chrome, plastic, glass, and a lot of striking angles. Pander had thought that up. Even the rooms in back were very expensive.

"You want a drink first?" said Fell.

Cripp shook his head and they walked the length of the dark bar. Past the dressing rooms in the back they came to a door padded with leather. Because of the soundproofing the laughter came at them like a gust when Fell opened the door. There were three of Pander's new crowd, there was Pander and a blonde with a wasp waist and breasts like towers. The way she was dressed, her body showed up like a slap in the face. This time Pander's shirt was grape-colored, and the suspenders white with black stitching.

And because of the soundproofing Fell standing there, suddenly, made an impression.

They all stopped laughing.

It was hard to tell how Pander felt behind the black glasses, but nobody was watching him anyway. They waited for Fell.

"What's funny?" said Fell.

Pander coughed and said, "Nice to see you."

"That's good," said Fell and walked to the back of the desk. Roy was lying on a couch by the wall. He took the Stetson off his foot, jumped up, and held the desk chair for Fell. Cripp stayed by the door and looked out the window where the air conditioner hummed. Fell sat behind the desk, turned to Pander.

"Who's the lady?" He tried to see Pander's eyes.

"Just a friend. Millie. Millie Borden."

"Borden?" Fell looked as if he might want to say something else. He said, "How are you, Miss Borden? I'm Thomas Fell." He leaned his arms on the desk and turned back to Pander. "Are you free?"

"Sure. Sure, I'm free."

"Then send out the lady."

"Who? Millie?"

"Send her out."

"She's all right. She's with me."

Fell didn't move and he didn't answer. Then Cripp opened the door, holding it. The girl moved first. The silence was getting her, and nobody stopped her as she walked out of the room. Then Cripp closed the door.

"Leave it open, Cripp. I want Pander alone."

Pander leaned against the wall and folded his arms.

"Send out the boy friends," said Fell. "You and me will have a conference."

"That's fine. Go right ahead, Tom. Is it business?"

"Yes, business."

"Good. Let's talk business. I think you've met Roy. He was here before you left. That one over there is Willie, and the other one you can call Meyer. His full name is Meyerhofer or something." Pander took some gum out of his mouth and glued it into an ashtray. "So let's talk business."

Cripp still held the door open, but it didn't make any sense any more. Fell hadn't moved, except to look down at his hands on the desk. "Okay," he said. "I just wanted to tell you a few things."

Cripp closed the door.

"Since I've been back I've heard about the raids, of course. I just saw Sutterfield and straightened things out. We're opening up again, so get the word around that everything's fixed."

"I don't know about that," said Pander. "You lost some of your guys while you were gone."

"I hear you got new ones for us."

"I can't spare 'em. They're all busy."

Cripp had been wondering how long it would take, how long Fell would hold still. It had started with Sutterfield, and now this. Fell sitting there and Pander on top of him. And Fell didn't make a move.

"How do you mean that, Pander?"

"Just the way it sounds, Tom."

"You trying to lose us money, Pander?"

"Me? Hell no. Am I trying to do anything like that, fellas?" He turned to the three hoods on the couch.

"I want those bookie joints run as before," said Fell. "Starting today."

"Go ahead," said Pander.

Fell took a deep breath and let it out as if something hurt him. The lashes over his eyes made a shadow.

"Why don't you open up, Pander. We're still running the same outfit, aren't we?"

"Sure," said Pander. He unwrapped a new stick of gum and chewed it into place. "Same outfit, Tom."

"Except?"

"Well, you been away quite a while. You can't expect everything to stand still, can you?"

"Get to it, Pander." For a moment Cripp thought that Fell was changing. But that's all he said. Then he waited.

"You left me in charge, didn't you?"

"I did."

"And you don't like the way I ran things?"

"I don't know yet. I just got back, Pander."

"So what's your beef?"

Fell made a small gesture with his hand, dropped it back on the desk. "Pander, if you're too chicken to come right out with it—"

Pander jerked up and away from the wall.

"Me, chicken? You trying to start something, maybe? You think maybe sitting behind that fat desk makes you a big shot or something?" Since his three hoods were sitting right there, Pander balled up all his nerve and cut loose. "Let me give you a tip, old man. There's been changes around here that's going to stay changed because I say so, you hear me? I took over your mess because you left me in charge, and I'm running what I'm running with no kicks from nobody. No kicks from the boys, no kicks from you, and no kicks from guys that's bigger than you, Fell. And if you think I'm just talking big...."

"I know what you mean," said Fell. "The combine. You think they gave you the go-ahead."

"I don't think—I know."

Pander hadn't thought it would drift this way, would come out clear like this quite so soon. When he didn't come up with an answer immediately, Fell talked again, without looking up.

"They didn't, Pander. I haven't talked to them, but I know. You know why? I was in on the policy making, way back, and the policy is: let the best man show himself. You haven't shown a thing, Pander, except how to take advantage while the old bastard himself is away." Fell raised his eyes and said, "And I haven't shown a thing."

Roy had started spinning his stetson, and when nobody said anything for a second or two he leaned forward. "Let's put it this way. Pander here—"

"You shut up!" yelled Pander, but Fell cut in.

"Yes. I wasn't through yet. The combine didn't tell you a thing. All they could have said was that you should learn the ropes and make yourself use- ful. And then they watch. Get it, Pander? They watch to see who shows up best. Then they decide."

"If you're so hot, Fell, how come they're watching?" Pander was smooth again, his eyes hidden behind the black glasses. But he looked mean, even though he had a smile on.

Fell made it simple when he answered. "Because that's how it goes. It al- ways goes that way, after a while."

It threw Pander off, and there was silence.

Nothing was going right, and Cripp saw it. Fell had an advantage and had lost it. Fell got it back, let it go—everything the opposite of what Emilson said. All screwed up, maybe worse than ever. Fell with the stuffing all gone—or holding back, afraid of the things Emilson talked about.

"There's this," said Cripp, and only the new guys on the couch looked sur- prised, not knowing who Cripp was. "How come you stopped paying ice as soon as Tom left?"

"If you think I'm trying to rob the kitty for that lousy few bucks—"

"We know the money's there."

"Then don't stand there and—"

"You didn't answer. How come you stopped?" Pander couldn't get out of it, so he made it a grandstand play. He laid it on thick.

"When I took over this racket," he said and he looked at Cripp instead of Fell, "I wasn't just holding down a seat. I got improvements in mind which is the only way to keep moving." He stopped, liking the sound of those words, but then he saw that Fell was hardly listening.

Pander coughed, covered up with a quick change in stance. He turned to Cripp as if Fell weren't there. "So I improve. Fell's methods are as old as him- self. They don't make sense, they're way off, and I got better ideas."

"Stop jawing, Pander," said Fell.

"Jawing? Your sidekick here asked me a question. He—"

"What's your answer?"

"That your setup stinks, is my answer!"

"Wonder boy—" Fell started, but now Pander was rolling.

"Stinks from age! What's your biggest overhead around here, bar none? Protection! Protection for what? For keeping dozens of lousy stalls open so the customer can walk in and lay down his two bits. No stalls, no protection to pay." Pander waited for somebody to make a remark, but nobody spoke. He looked back and forth. "Nobody gonna ask how I keep taking bets with no stalls open?"

"How, Pander?" Fell sounded calm.

"Mobile units!" said Pander, and liked the words so much he said it again. "Mobile units!"

"By car," said Cripp. "I had an idea that's—"

"I had the idea, sidekick. The bookie roams all over, calls in at houses, bars, or arranges for a stop at a corner. He does business, he goes home, he calls in his take to the office, and business as usual—except no ice!"

Pander looked around, but only the guys on the couch looked impressed. Fell was chewing his lip.

"Does it work?" he asked.

"Does it work! Take a look at the weekly take while I was running this show! And the way I got it planned—"

"Cripp told me the take was okay."

"Well? So what's your beef?"

"No beef, Pander. Just open the joints up again. Like before."

"I can't spare the men," said Pander and leaned against the wall.

"You can't? Listen, Pander—"

"No, you listen, Tom. I can't spare the men and you haven't got enough left to do it yourself. And I'll be damned—"

"Cripp," said Fell, "is he right?"

"He's right."

There was no talk while they all looked at Fell behind the desk, sitting there quietly, looking mild.

"Pander, look. This needs planning, not bulldozing. A switch like this can cause trouble all over. We got to live with Sutterfield and his kind."

"I don't," said Pander.

Fell looked up, but held still.

"I want those bookie places to open."

"Go ahead," said Pander.

"And we pay ice, like before."

"Not from my take."

Fell got up then, and came around the desk. He crossed his arms as Pander had done and said, "Is this the break, Pander?"

"I don't know what you're talking about."

"You think you're ready to take this thing over?"

"Call it anything you like, Fell."

They all waited, but Fell didn't take it up. And he didn't even seem to care how it looked.

"You'll choke on this, Pander," he said, but nobody thought there was any-thing behind it.

Pander just shrugged and went to the door. "Millie," he yelled, "you ready to go?"

She came in and picked up the wrap she had left on a chair, and the way she draped it over her shoulders should have made her the focus in any situ-ation, only it didn't. There was too much unfinished business in the room and the only one to finish it, Fell, didn't make a move.

"May I ask you something, Miss—uh—Borden?" said Fell.

She looked at him and said, "Sure."

"What size are you?" said Fell.

He said it so plain, just wanting to know, that everyone gaped. It gave Pan-der another chance for a grandstand play, and he didn't care who Fell was—or used to be.

"Take that back, Fell, and apologize!"

Fell just raised his eyebrows.

"Or I'll forget you're too old to put up a fight, Fell."

"Forget it," said Fell and reached for his hat on the desk.

"Fell, did you hear what I said?"

Fell turned around again. He was talking to Cripp. "Ever notice that nose on Pander? Ever notice how nice and straight that nose is?" It was another switch nobody could follow, and Fell walked to the door. He stopped there and said, "Pander used to box, some years back. Even if we hadn't set up a fight for him now and then Pander could still have looked good. A good wel-ter," said Fell and started to smile. "And then he suddenly quit. Just getting good, and he quits. No heart, you can call it."

Pander had started to hunch himself up and got ready to take his sunglasses off. Fell continued smiling.

"You see a boxer with a beautiful nose," said Fell, "and you got a fighter without heart. Look at him."

Millie Borden looked from one man to the other. Then she moved back. She hadn't understood a thing that had gone on, but she understood what was shaping up. She moved because there was going to be a fight. Pander leaned up on the balls of his feet, arms swinging free, face mean, but nothing fol-lowed. He stared at Fell and all he saw were his eyes, mild lashes and the lids without movement, and what happened to them. He suddenly saw the hard-est, craziest eyes he had ever seen.

Pander lost the moment and then Fell smiled. He said so long and walked out of the door.

Cripp followed, and drove the car. The conversation with Pander had him rattled enough so he didn't even try for an explanation. He drove toward

Fell's house, but Fell said, "That memory of yours, Cripp. No good at all for important things."

"What?"

"Drive back to the Alamo. I got to make that call about Buttonhead."

CHAPTER TEN

Cripp didn't hear what the call was all about because Fell sent him home and saw no one till late at night. Then he called for a taxi and went home. At his house he got out of the cab on the street and walked up the drive. The sprinklers were still on, hissing in the dark and drifting fine spray at Fell. He stepped back and tried to see how the grass looked, but there wasn't enough light so he went into the house.

Janice was taking a bath. The tub was a round marble thing with steps leading down and big enough for two to float around in the water all stretched out. She heard Fell come upstairs and started to get out of the water. Then she changed her mind and waited for him.

"Do that again," he said from the door.

She made a splash sitting up and said, "Hi, Tom. Do what?"

"Roll over like that."

She sat holding her knees and smiled.

"And jump through a hoop? Or grab a fish from midair?"

"For that you're not trained well enough. Just do simple things. You know, like—"

"I know."

He came closer and sat down on a stool upholstered with terry cloth.

"Now if I had me a fish," and he held out his arm, "I might just be able to train you right."

"I don't jump for fish," she said. "Gimme a kiss." She stood up.

He leaned forward and they kissed.

When she drew back again she saw his eyes, close by and open. She felt uncomfortable. She sat down in the water again, not feeling right, but when she looked up again he didn't seem different any more, just a little tireder, perhaps.

"Bad day, Tom?" She reached for her sponge and let it dribble over her head.

"Why?"

"You look tired."

"What else?" She wasn't a very good liar.

"Cripp called," she said. "He never calls here—"

"What was it?"

"He said to call him back. You know he doesn't talk business to me."

"Then what did he talk about?" Fell sounded casual.

But Janice knew that he wasn't so she said, "About how he worried about you. How everything went sort of wrong today."

She dropped the sponge and turned on her stomach. She floated that way, acting as if she didn't care whether he answered. And Fell played the game with her, not looking at her and keeping his tone casual.

He said, "Cripp worries. My first day back—you know how it is." But then he looked at her. She sat up again, and they both knew there was no reason for them to hide things from each other.

"It did go sort of wrong today," he said.

"Are you losing out, Tom?"

"What did Cripp say?"

"That you buckled under. With Herb, and with Pander too."

"Cripp said that?"

"What he really said was that it looked as if you did, but that he wasn't sure any more how you're handling things." She had to wait for Fell to answer because he was staring at the ceiling, worrying his lip.

"I wasn't sure either," he said.

It surprised her.

"But that's gone now," he went on. "That's all gone now, because I found out how wrong Emilson was."

"Wrong? About what?"

"About me. About losing my grip on myself if I don't watch out." She didn't say anything. "He used to say that I have more drive than I can control—or at least that's what might happen." Fell started to grin slowly, thinking about the day. "Christ," he said. "Christ, did I control myself."

"Was it hard?"

"Not really." He got up and unbuttoned his collar. "And you know why?"

She saw the animation in his eyes and the old strength in the way he got up.

"Tell me why, Tom."

"Because I can't lose!"

She didn't have to think of an answer then because he walked out of the bathroom and laughed. She saw him stand by the bed, pull his tie off, and toss it at the chair. It missed, as usual.

"Same place," he called to her. Then he came back. "How's the bath, Jan?"

"Nice. Want to come in?"

"It just reminded me. You know those sprinklers out front? I'm going to shut that thing off."

"It should be off now, Tom. It turns itself off at ten-thirty."

"I mean off for good. Let that lawn fend for itself. Let's just see what happens."

She thought that was all right, if Tom wanted to try it, because she didn't much care one way or the other what happened to the lawn. She got out of the bathtub and put on a terry-cloth robe.

"Let's go down now," said Fell. "We'll turn it off."

"Now?" She was drying her hair. "Let it wait."

He watched her rub her hair.

"Let's go to bed," she said.

"At eleven?"

"You should have lots of sleep. You still have to go easy. And tomorrow—don't work all day tomorrow."

"The track opens in less than a week, Jan. That means extra work."

She fluffed her hair up and turned so he could rub her back through the robe.

"I haven't seen much of you, Tom."

"That'll change. After the opening, a week or so later, we'll go to the Sierras. We'll use Sutterfield's place by the lake, just the two of us."

"Herb goes there week ends," she said. "I'd rather not see him."

"He won't go. I'll tell him to stay away."

Janice walked into the bedroom and Fell couldn't see her face.

"The less friction with Herb, the better," she said, and it was an old topic with them. It made her sound edgy.

"He'll do as I say." Fell tried to make light of the way she felt. "He knows where his bread is buttered."

"That's what I mean," said Janice, and when she changed into her nightgown she turned so Fell couldn't see her.

"Let's drop it," said Fell. "Every time that bastard comes up—"

"I know. I can't help it."

"You've had plenty of time to get over it." Now Fell sounded annoyed. "But every time that bastard—"

"Let's not talk any more."

Fell talked low. "Maybe Emilson or one of his kind should have a crack at you about this. It's not any fault of mine that Sutterfield is your brother."

She turned around so the nightgown made a swirl.

"You know that's not it."

"I know that's not it. It's worse. But just remember, when I picked you up I didn't know you had him for a brother. You know that."

"And you didn't pick me up!" she said, grabbing for something unimportant because she was edgy and troubled.

"Don't get like him, now; don't get mean for no reason at all. And besides, what would you call the way we met. Love at first sight?"

"No," she said. "But you didn't pick me up!"

That was true. She hadn't wanted any part of him when they met in L.A. She had come to the point where she only latched on to men who could do her some good, and Fell was nothing to her. He had nothing to do with the movies, he didn't even have an interest in a nightclub, nor did he promise to help her along if she just took a turn in bed with him. And Janice didn't think she could afford it any more, to horse around and do things just for the hell of it.

She had left home young, and she had stayed away. She spent her time do-

ing just as she pleased, and everything just the opposite of what brother Herbie had wanted. She hadn't compromised Herb Sutterfield, though that
would have been easy. It gave her life an extra kick never to use his name, to
keep it a secret, and to let him worry through all the years she was gone
whether she'd smudge the good family name, whether she'd be a danger to
Herbie's career and his tight-muscled sense of what is proper. He had played
the game with her, for his reasons, and hardly anyone seemed to remember
that there had been a sister, sixteen years old, who left for the East, for school,
and who never came back. His story was that she had married somewhere
abroad.

Nor had Fell known a thing about it. He had wanted Janice, and after a
while he got her. She had no luck in L.A., and then she caught onto how much
Fell felt about her, and no reservations. It made her feel very old-fashioned
at first, and then she discovered she liked the thought of marriage. They spent
a week in Yosemite Park and after that he asked her again. If he hadn't asked
she felt that she might have asked him. They married, and he was happy. And
now, for the first time, she was happy. The shock came when he took her to
San Pietro. Tom Fell was no different from most of the others, because it
looked as if he had swung a deal that gave him the whip hand. She hadn't
known Fell was building the rackets in town, that her brother was in the deal
up to his ears, and that all this made excellent business sense. And the fact
was, Fell hadn't known it either. It gave him a big laugh, and a big advantage,
only he never made use of it. Not intentionally, and Janice believed, after a
while, that Fell had married her with no devious motives. It was the truth
and it kept them together, and only sometimes did she suffer with a small,
sharp suspicion. It made her more sensitive than Fell could understand, and
Sutterfield was the only disturbing thing in their lives. It came up now and
then. When it did Fell would change the subject.

"Go to bed," he said, "I'll be right back."

She watched him leave the room and wondered whether he had gone for
his chocolate. She asked him when he came back. He said, "No, I forgot. And
I don't want it tonight." He said it, smiling, and gave her a pat on the hip
where it curved up under the cover.

"You called Cripp?" she asked.

"No. Just to show you everything is under control."

"Where were you?"

"Down in the basement, I turned off that sprinkle thing."

Chapter Eleven

He should have called Cripp, because Cripp sat up most of the night waiting for the call, worrying about the thing he wanted to talk about. When Fell called him early in the morning Cripp was asleep. So when Fell heard the voice answer in a mumble he said get some rest, I'll pick you up in two hours. Then Fell left the house and didn't hear Cripp calling back.

That meant two more hours for the thing to develop.

Fell drove himself straight to the motel to do two hours' work for the track opening, which meant he didn't see a thing. He didn't see Pander, who was busy in the room out at the racetrack; he didn't see the out-of-town cars gathering up at points in the city; and he missed Cripp's call to the office because Fell was busy with long distance, talking to Omaha.

A while later Cripp came in, worried and out of breath.

"You look like hell," said Fell, and turned back to the desk.

"Listen, Tom. Something's up."

Fell turned around, but seeing Cripp's face he didn't interrupt.

"I got it from Phido, Tom. Just a word he'd picked up about getting ready for tomorrow—yesterday, that was, and about Pander pulling some books out of the joints you reopened."

"Well? Go on."

"It's just vague, Tom, except that I checked late last night and when I talked to one of Pander's men about what might be going on, he gave me the brushoff and started getting nervous. That was at one of the clubs in town. Right then a bunch of guys I never saw before came in, and that's when he got nervous and turned away. So I left and just by chance I see those three cars outside, out-of-town plates, but when I try checking the numbers this police cruiser rolls up and the two cops inside ask me if I'd seen you around. No rough stuff, just friendly, except that I miss checking those plates because the guys come back and drive out of the lot. Then the cops take off too."

"What's it mean, Cripp?"

"I don't know. Could be just coincidence and they just wanted to know if it was true you were back in town, or it might mean they wanted to keep me busy while those cars took off."

"You sound too suspicious, Cripp."

"Maybe. But then I try calling Pander and he won't come to the phone."

"Did Phido say he heard talk about a raid?"

"Not outright, but that's what I thought it was."

"We'll see," said Fell, and reached for the phone. He got the commissioner's office and asked for Sutterfield. He even heard Sutterfield talk in the background, telling the old girl at the phone that he was busy and Fell could go hang himself, so Fell just hung up and looked puzzled.

"We'll take my car," he said. "Sutterfield's getting a visit."

"How about Pander?" said Cripp. "Maybe he knows something and that's why he got ready and pulled out those books."

"Sutterfield first," said Fell, and Cripp had to run to keep up with him.

This time Fell didn't waste time with etiquette. He didn't come in through the office john, and he didn't even look at the pink-lensed secretary who came fluttering up from behind her desk. Fell walked right into the inner sanctum, where Sutterfield stood by a book shelf putting a volume on torts back in front of a bottle. Sutterfield turned around, crushing a paper cup in his hand.

"Fell," he said, but he didn't have time to work himself up the way he wanted to.

"Why in hell didn't you answer the phone?" said Fell.

"May I—"

"No. Just listen." Fell stopped by the desk. The way he looked and the way he acted was a big change from the day before, and both Cripp and Sutterfield paid attention. "You got your dough yesterday?"

"Did I get my dough?" Sutterfield said it as if he didn't know what the word meant.

"By check, so you don't mess with the receipts. You got paid, so you should hold still like any other crooked official. I want to know if you're holding still?"

"Fell," said Sutterfield, "have you lost your mind?"

Cripp knew he hadn't. Tom Fell acted more like himself than he had done for months.

"Did you set up my places for another raid?"

"I most certainly didn't!"

"Did you bring in men from the county seat to do the job for you?"

"You can't be serious," said Sutterfield, and there was no doubt that all this was news to him. Fell went right on.

"Did you pay off your next in line, like you're supposed to? Talk louder."

"No," said Sutterfield. "There hasn't been time. Chief Dilling was out of town, and—"

"Did you tell Dilling he was getting his ice?"

"How could I? He wasn't even—"

"Is he back today?"

"I have to check, Fell. After all—"

"Shut up, Sutterfield. Call him and find out if he's got any plans to act legal all of a sudden." Fell turned and went to the door. "If he has, stop him," said Fell, and he and Cripp left. "Back to my office," he said to Cripp.

"About those out-of-town cars," said Cripp, "I didn't see if they came from the county seat. Like I explained, I didn't get a chance to see those license plates close enough."

"Never mind," said Fell. "Just so Sutterfield knows where he stands. Right now what's important—" but he got no further.

Five cars shot out of the lot where the Alamo stood, and Cripp had to squeeze close to the ditch to let them by.

Just in case, Cripp made sure to spot the numbers.

"Got 'em?" Fell asked.

"Right. But—"

"Tell me later. It looks like they hit." When the car swung toward the motel the guess looked good.

Three bookies were outside the coffee shop and two were holding the third. The one in the middle was holding his nose, blood coming through his fingers. The other two didn't look good either.

It was worse inside. They had ripped out the phones, hacked up the switchboard, torn ledgers and address books to pieces, and there was even a big, broken hole where somebody had smashed a chair into the blackboard.

"I never seen this kind of raid." Cripp looked confused.

Fell wasn't talking. He looked at the broken phones and the ruined books, then he sat down on a chair that was still whole.

"Did they have a seal on the door?"

Cripp looked and said, "Hell, no."

"And they made no arrests?"

"Just roughed them up," said Cripp.

"And property destruction?"

"This place won't operate for weeks."

"That's the point," said Fell.

"You know what this looks like?" said Cripp.

"I know. This was no police raid."

"And those license plates—they weren't county seat."

"You sure, Cripp?"

"They were L.A. Let me think..." and Cripp closed his eyes. "They were all—let me think."

"Take your time," said Fell. "Just take your time."

"I am. I've seen them before."

"L.A.?"

Cripp opened his eyes and recited. "L.A. plates, all with the same letters. The cars belong to a rental service. Comet Cars, Inc. Syndicate owned. Who owns it now, Tom?"

"It makes sense," said Fell. "Jack Martinez owns it. Buddy of wonder-boy Pander."

"Son of a bitch," said Cripp.

"It makes sense. With the joints knocked over, that leaves only Pander's setup to operate. He'll look good after the season. He makes the money and he runs the show that's making the money."

"He'll look so good you won't be needed."

"That's right," said Fell.

Cripp kept still for a second. Then, "You going to let him, Tom?"

"What?"

"Look good."

"No. Not Pander." Then Fell wouldn't talk any more about it.

It was almost the same as the day before, as if Fell weren't entirely present or as if he were holding back—but this time Fell did take some action. He had Cripp check the other joints, and it turned out to be true—they had all been hit. He made ready to fix up the damage and then he sent wires to fill out his staff. He did all these things, busy all morning, except he never did the one thing which would have made real sense: Fell didn't do a thing about Pander.

Chapter Twelve

Pander's apartment looked a lot like the club he ran and with a crowd in the big front room he acted pretty much the way he did in the club. Except there was a hectic quality to his hosting, and he kept repeating they should all have a good time. They did; they were his own hoods, and besides the liquor was free. Millie Borden was the only woman there, but she was Pander's and didn't count. They watched her, and some of them wondered how come the dress didn't bust any minute.

Roy leaned against the wall, looking uncomfortable. He would have liked to sit down but there wouldn't have been enough room to stretch his legs anyway. When Pander came by Roy reached out and caught him by one suspender, red this time and no stitching.

"Roy, boy, you having a good time?"

"Sure. Listen, Pander, maybe it's time—"

"Let 'em have fun. I'll call the meeting to order any minute now."

"Any minute now it looks like some of them might drop dead. I don't like liquor first and then business."

"Celebrate, Roy. We got things to celebrate." Pander laughed with all his teeth showing.

"Sure," said Roy.

Pander spied Millie and waved. When she came over he gave her his glass and told her to bring it back full. Roy and Pander watched her walk away, just as everybody else was doing.

"Some dish, huh, Roy?"

"A dish. Call it a dish," said Roy.

"Except a dish is flat, huh, Roy?" More laughter.

"She won't help the situation. Look at those guys all liquored up and giving her horny looks. She don't help getting their minds on business."

"She doesn't mind," said Pander. He watched Millie come back. "Good for a woman to know she's wanted."

"Christ," said Roy.

Pander just laughed, took the glass from her, and gave her a slap on the rear. Everything jiggled.

"Go have fun, huh, Millie?" He gave her another whack so that those who had missed it got a chance to study just how well fixed up Pander was.

She walked back to the table with all the liquor and put ice cubes into glasses.

Willie came to the wall and said, "Pander, it's ten already. How about—"

"I was just going to," said Pander and turned to the room. "All right, you guys!"

It was loud and they all turned around. In the silence that followed they heard the sounds Millie made, drinking ice water.

"All right!" yelled Pander. "Let go your drinks and get organized!"

Pander stood by the wall, watching the room. He felt like a benign conqueror and all the men were moving around, pushing tables and chairs together, and nobody held a drink any more except Pander. Millie was sipping her ice water.

"Get in the bedroom," said Pander across the room.

"What?" she asked, and they all saw how she looked confused.

"Just stay there!" he yelled at her and when she closed the door nobody said a word because Pander didn't have much humor.

They all sat along the tables and Pander sat down at the head of them.

"Just to remind you," he said, "now comes business. You too, Kaufman," and Kaufman looked away from the bedroom door.

One man handed Pander a stack of sheets, typewritten lists of horses and races.

"There's plenty of horsemeat this season, not even counting the possibles. And for each horse there's double that many suckers and more. So I want you bookies to keep hopping," he said. "I want you to push those bets like never before."

"I'm afraid of them odds," said one of them. "I never seen an operation go higher than twenty to one at the most."

"In this town we move, boy. Go up to twenty-five to one if the bets call for it, and keep checking in to me. The way we got this thing set up—"

"Yeah, how?" He was one of the new ones. The Fell-Pander setup had him confused.

Pander turned around as if the guy were a heckler. "What's the matter, Jack? You never make book before?"

"Not with two kingpins in the game."

They all started to buzz, but before Pander got ready to yell the bedroom door opened and Millie came out. The buzzing turned off and they let Millie walk to the liquor table so that only her dress made a sound. She was walking on tiptoe, to avoid distracting the men from their work. She got her cigarettes from the table, walked back to the door, and closed it. Then they all turned their heads back to Pander.

"What were you saying?" said Roy.

"If you guys paid attention around here—"

"What about his setup? Tell them the way it works."

"It works for us," said Pander. "Look at it this way. I run the bookmaking, Fell backs the bets. I do the work, Fell's got the money. You got any questions or anything like that, come to me. You pay in to me, you collect from me, and nobody deals with Fell except me. Clear enough?"

"I hear tell he's got a crew of his own or something. He's running the joints and you've got the floating crew or something."

Pander laughed. "Forget it. Fell isn't running a thing around here except through me."

"Fell's out?"

"Don't mix in politics, bud." Pander started shuffling his papers. Right then the bedroom door opened again and Millie came out.

"Now, listen!" said Pander. He talked loud because nobody was looking at him. Only Millie was looking at him so he yelled at her. "What in hell is it now!"

"I want my ice water," she said.

"So go grab it and then stay in that room!"

She left and there was silence except for one who said, "Ice water she needs."

"Who said that?" But Pander didn't get his answer.

Roy leaned over the table and got things back to business. Even Pander was listening. "The third race on the fourth," Roy said. "That's the one needs special attention and anybody with information on those nags speak up now."

"That's right," said Pander. "That's the money maker. Take a look at your lists."

They all looked at lists with the names of horses.

"There's four horses to watch. Rainy Day, Claret, Moon-day, and Sis. They'll all have run before by the fourth but not in the same field. Watch the performance, stack it up with their past record and go easy on those odds. Each one of those nags is a cinch horse. The suckers know this as well as you guys, so watch it close."

"How about pushing the long shots in that race, the other five horses?"

"Any one here know those five?"

"Rosebud. I been following Rosebud. Till last year she's been a half-miler part of the time. They're bringing her up slow."

"She been in the money?"

"Some."

"There's another deadbeat in this, Buttonhead. Good-looking horse, but—"

"Good-looking! You think maybe—"

"I said good-looking!"

"Only horse that's good-looking is the one in front. If you ask me—"

"No, he's right. The—"

"Shut up, somebody!" They all turned to Pander.

"That's better." He sat back and put gum in his mouth. "I don't want you guys worrying about half-milers running this nine-furlong track. That's allowed. Fact is, we like it. And what's more, the favorite in this race, that is, the favorite we want to see win is this nag— Roy, what's her name?"

"Mindy."

"Millie?" said a half dozen of them.

"Who said that?" said Pander.

"Anyway, her name's Mindy," said Roy, "and she's done well on the half-mile. She's run the mile only off the record and she's even better. She's in this race by arrangement."

"Clear enough," said one. "Do we handle it so she pays twenty to one?"

"That's the idea," said Pander. "That's why this meeting."

"And the other four long shots?"

"Go higher. Make it look good, as if no other horse mattered except those first four. Let the long shots go sky-high."

"What? Twenty-two to one?"

"Higher. Up to twenty-five. At the track we'll go more, but you guys working on the road go up to twenty-five."

"Hell, Pander, that's pushing it."

"I said—"

"All right, I'm just asking."

"But aside from this," said Roy, "keep in touch with the office. We'll be watching all bets coming in and we'll tell you how to adjust if the betting runs too heavy on any of those."

"Will you know for sure? How about the bets taken in through Fell's bookies?"

"Don't worry," said Pander. "I'll have that information. After all—" he moved the gum so he could smile— "we're all one big happy family."

"What about Buttonhead?" somebody asked. "It's her first race on this track."

"Maybe her last. I saw her in Omaha making show once out of three tries."

"At Ak-Sar-Ben? That's a half-mile track."

"A guy by the name of Dudley owns her. Nice guy. He says he's only putting her in a five-thousand-dollar race because of the training. She runs three thousand stake, usually."

"You mean he runs her out of her class just to—"

"All right! Forget about Buttonhead! I want some attention around here. Get this thing done!"

They got down to business and went through details of some other races. Millie never showed up again and they all looked sour attending to business till one in the morning.

CHAPTER THIRTEEN

It was around the time that Pander's meeting broke up when Cripp got a call. The phone woke him and he jumped up. He had Fell on his mind, first thing, and it worried him.

"Say, Cripp? This is Tom."

"Tom— Who—"

"This is Fell, you jerk. Wake up."

"I'm up. I'm awake, Tom. You need me?" Cripp leaned with the phone at his ear as if it would help him to hear.

"Wanna see a horse?"

"You say horse?"

"Sure. Put your clothes on, Cripp, and I'll pick you up in twenty minutes."

"Tom, it's two in the morning."

"I know. See you in twenty minutes. About a horse," and before Fell hung up Cripp heard him laugh at his own joke.

While Cripp got dressed he thought that he should have asked Fell from where he was calling. He should have made sure Fell was going to show up. When a man fresh out of a sanatorium calls at two in the morning and laughs about buying a horse... Cripp gave his head a sharp snap. He wasn't sure what Fell had said and went to the bathroom for some cold water. Then he'd better call Janice.

Perhaps Fell was right there, with Janice, and nothing was wrong. After the cold water Cripp heated some coffee. He stood in the empty kitchen and watched the coffee heat. Perhaps a bite—but the kitchen was empty. Cripp never bought food. He ate out and except for coffee he never spent time in the kitchen. Or in the living room. The few pieces of furniture were against two walls because all Cripp ever used the room for was to walk to the bedroom. When at home he would sit in bed where his magazines and his albums of pictures were stacked up. He clipped pictures from magazines—ships, mountain scenes, trees. He didn't know the names of any of them but he was partial to trees.

It couldn't have been more than ten minutes when the horn blew downstairs. Fell was there. Cripp gulped what was left in his cup and hurried downstairs. He slid in next to Fell and tried to see how he looked, but the car shot off and Cripp had to hold on. After the next turn he straightened up. Fell was heading out of town.

"Got a cigarette, Cripp?"

"Sure." He gave Fell one.

The match showed Fell's face, alive, wide awake. He looked at his watch, then drove faster.

"Tom, what's that you said on the phone?"

Fell laughed but kept his eyes on the road. Cripp was grateful for that.

"Do you want to see a horse, I said."

Cripp smoked, and after a long exhale he said, "That's what I thought you said."

"It's a long drive, so I thought—just for company—"

"Where's Janice?" said Cripp.

"You know Janice and horses. They don't mean a thing to each other. Janice is asleep."

"When it comes to that, Tom, I myself don't have much of a feeling for horses. Tom, could you go a little slower?"

"She starts working at four-thirty. It'll take close to two hours getting to her."

"I see," said Cripp, and watched the highway get eaten up.

"You've seen nothing till you see this little money maker of ours. That horse–"

"What horse, Buttonhead?" Cripp said it like a joke.

"That's right. Buttonhead."

Fell was crazy. He may just be a harmless dud any other time, which was enough of a worrisome change in itself, but now this thing about Buttonhead—Cripp watched Fell drive and they talked about other things. It wasn't hard talking to Fell. He seemed active and pleased. He was far out of San Pietro, he was going to see his horse, and perhaps this was all just the normal thing for somebody nuts enough to own a horse.

When the sky started to turn light blue they were close to the foot of the Sierras. Some peaks in the distance showed sun, but the rest of the land still held the dark of early morning. Where the pines started, Fell turned off the road, drove through a small town where a milk wagon was making the rounds, and then out into the open again. They passed two ranches, then Fell turned in at the third.

There were no stables in back, just a barn. There was an empty corral and an open stretch behind that. Cripp saw the fresh wood they had used to build a new railing. Like a nine-furlong track.

"They'll be up at the bunkhouse," said Fell. "Want breakfast?"

Cripp did and they walked to the bunkhouse.

The long table had two plates and two cups on it. By the stove a man was slicing onions into a pot.

"They're out," said the man. "Left ten minutes ago. Want breakfast?"

Fell said yes. The man brought plates of eggs and the coffee and then went back to his onions.

Fell ate fast. He slurped the hot coffee as if he couldn't wait and kept looking out to the barn.

"More eggs?" said the man.

"Sure. All around."

"They went to pony her," said the man.

"Whom with? Sally?"

"She won't pony with nobody but Sally."

"I know," said Fell because he had only asked to make conversation.

Then they heard the horses, Sally and Buttonhead, come around the barn.

"Look at her!" Fell got up. "Look at her, Cripp. Isn't she neat?"

Cripp looked. "But why say she? It's a gelding."

"I call 'em all she," said Fell, and then he went outside to Buttonhead.

The rider got off the pony and the two horses kept their noses together as
if they had a secret.

"Cripp, tell the truth, is she a beauty?"

"He is," said Cripp because he had to admit it.

The small head kept nodding and poking and the tall legs made little dancing steps. The gelding had a big heart, very high withers, and the long sway-
back of thoroughbreds.

"And smart," said Fell. "You catch how she's listening to me?"

"I guess so," said Cripp.

"And look at that nose. Ever see such an articulate nose, Cripp?"

"No," he said, very politely, but he thought this was going too far. So he
said, "Can she run?"

"Can she run!"

"Yes, you know—"

"Can she run, Cripp! She's born for running; she can run better than she
can walk. Now look at that pony. See that steam all over the pony?"

Cripp saw how the pony was steaming in the cool air. "Now, Buttonhead.
See any steam?"

"No steam," said Cripp. "Perhaps that's because he took it easy—like at all
those tracks where he's been following the field around the course."

Fell gave Cripp a look of pity and then he laughed. He turned to the boy
who was holding the pony and asked him if the track came next, if Buttonhead were going to be clocked now. The boy said that was next and walked
the horses into the barn.

"I see Buttonhead taking ten steps for every one the pony takes," said Cripp.

Fell laughed again and said that was prancing and it limbered the legs.

"Perhaps in a prance race—" Cripp started, but then Fell cut in. He was-
n't kidding any more.

"Those other races you mentioned. They were half-mile tracks. Buttonhead
is a one-miler."

Cripp got it. "This is news. This news is worth some money."

"Better than that," said Fell. "It's worth everything I let slide in San Pietro."
Fell wouldn't explain any more because the two horses came back from the
barn. The same boy was on the pony and a lean little guy was riding Buttonhead. He said, "Hi, Mister Fell," and Fell said, "How are you, Dominic,"
and if Fell had also mentioned the last name even Cripp might have known
that this jockey was big time. The two men rode by and Buttonhead was clink-
ing his bit. But he had stopped prancing. He walked almost like a cat.

Then the trainer came out of the barn, a wrinkled man with skin the color
of his leggings and a look on his face as if he were half asleep.

"How's it look?" said Fell, without the time to say hello first.

"We'll see, Fell," and the trainer held up the stop watch in his hand. Then
he walked by and followed the horses.

They followed him and Fell kept mumbling, "That guy's going to drive me
crazy. I swear, one of these days that guy's going to drive me crazy—"

Cripp caught Fell's fever by the time they got to the track, but then came
some more torture.

"Pony around once, Dominic. At the three-quarter mark start dancing."

"Okay, Mr. Dudley." The horses walked off.

A three-quarter-mile walk on a track takes longer than on foot to China.
Cripp started to know that and he wondered how Fell kept so still. Dudley
kept still too, except that with him it was more like sleep.

Fell said, "Mr. Dudley, why the quarter-mile before clocking her?"

Mr. Dudley. That was the second time he'd been called Mr. Dudley. First
the jockey, then the owner.

"She likes it, I guess," said the trainer.

"Look, that'll change the timing between here and the real track. I need a
sure figure."

"All owners need a sure figure," said Dudley.

Cripp was surprised to see Fell give up.

"Three-quarter," said Dudley as if he didn't care.

Buttonhead was starting to sidle, with the jockey straddling high and
stiff-legged over the horse. Then the canter got smooth: a dipping canter with
a short reach, almost as if the horse weren't leaving the spot. Then the pony
wasn't next to the thoroughbred any more. After a while the pony veered
off.

Mr. Dudley got up to stretch, the way it looked, but then kept walking into
the track. The big horse further down was thumping closer, so they could hear
it, but Dudley kept walking till he seemed almost up to the railing. He raised
a slow arm and held it. Buttonhead wasn't sidling any more and the jockey
was coming down to the saddle. He came down, smooth and slow, and the
horse's rock never reached his body.

They were going to run right over Dudley.

The trainer's arm shot up straight and the jockey was glued down flat in a monkey crouch; the trainer snapped down his arm, which must have fanned the nose of the horse, they were so close then, and they were off.

The pace was so smooth Cripp had to get impressions from the clods of earth that had started flying. They suddenly flew like shrapnel and then the horse started leaning because there was the turn.

Dudley came back and he walked watching his shoes.

"Man!" said Cripp.

"What did you say?" said Dudley.

"Just—you know, what a runner."

"He's below the half-mile," said Dudley. "That's the race he's been losing."

"This is nothing? You mean this is nothing special?"

"Nothing," said Dudley.

He climbed up to stand on the bench.

"Half-mile?" said Fell.

"Coming up."

Fell got on the bench like he was performing on a tightrope.

"Start watching now," said Dudley. "Time was one fifty-four."

"Man!" said Cripp.

"It stinks," said Dudley.

Then they watched the faraway weave of the horse, flat over the railing, and it seemed to get slower. Cripp was watching as if he owned the horse.

"Look. Did you notice, Mister Dudley, it almost seems he is, she is slowing down—"

"Looks that way."

"Getting tired at that point, must be."

"No. He's just flattening out."

But the illusion got worse. Once around the near turn all that showed was a muddled pumping of those reedy legs and the horse and rider a foreshortened lump next to the railing stretching this way.

Dudley was walking again and didn't stop till he might have leaned over to touch the rail. He just stood there watching the horse and then he looked straight ahead. It happened almost with a snap because then there was the horse. A big, long, windy stretching of neck and legs when the horse shot by with a sound like a train.

Dudley came back and the horse kept going.

"Well? Come on, give out! Dudley, what's—" Fell leaped off the bench and caught Dudley by the arm.

Further down the horse was dancing again.

"Steady climb few yards after the halfway mark," Dudley was saying.

Further down the jockey was stiff-legged over the saddle and the pony was waiting there, nodding his head.

"Too fast at the three-quarter. Dominic's got to learn how anxious she gets."

They had their noses together, nodding.

"The mile, for heaven's sake, what was the mile," Fell was saying.

"The mile was one thirty-nine and a fifth."

Fell seemed to breathe with relief.

"This is it! That Mindy they've set up for the race was clocked one forty."

"She was clocked at one thirty-nine, too," said Dudley. He kept walking back to the barn, with Fell next to him, and Cripp trying to keep up.

"Are you serious? How come my lookout never told me that figure?"

"Wasn't important. Buttonhead's done one thirty-eight. At times."

"At times, at times! Listen, Dudley—" Fell had forgotten the Mister— "I got to know what goes on. Why won't that horse—"

"He hates the railing," said Dudley. "He did one thirty-seven and three-fifths in the middle."

"So listen, Mr. Dudley. Just let her have her way and make that time in the middle, and none of this horsing around."

"The rail is faster. That horse can hit one thirty-six once he understands about railings."

"Mr. Dudley, look. See if I don't make sense. I'm satisfied—"

"That horse gets to thinking the way you do, Mr. Fell, and he'll stop paying attention to business. I can't have him thinking 'Let's play it safe,' if you know what I mean. That's lack of confidence, and I never seen a winner with lack of confidence."

"I'm going crazy," said Fell, "any minute now I'm going crazy from this talk."

"We'll hear what Dominic says." Dudley stopped by the barn.

Buttonhead and the pony were taking a walk near the bunkhouse, putting their feet down with care and wafting the blankets that hung over their backs. The boy was leading both of them and they kept squeezing him out of the way so they could get their noses together.

Dominic was wiping his neck when he came out of the barn. His face was clean where the goggles had been, but the rest was dirty, making him look like an owl.

"I slowed him at the turn," he said. "He wanted to leave the rail."

"Did you have to all along?"

"Just the last turn. He's hugging the inside on his own now, especially in the straightaway."

"He's catching on," said Dudley. "When he gets anxious he forgets. Remember, Mr. Fell, I told you he gets anxious near the last turn."

"I want to say only one thing. If he is the anxious type, very well, I can understand that there may be horses who are the anxious type. In a case like that..."

"Not really anxious. Mr. Fell. It's more like eager, too eager."

"Believe me, Mr. Dudley, that horse cannot be too eager."

"He is eager in such a way he doesn't know his own strength. What I'm teaching him is how to know his own strength."

"Yes. What I want to know is, in the few days that are left, can you con-vince— I mean can you train that horse to do—"

"He's learning," said Dudley and looked at his watch. "Tell that boy to walk a left-hand circle, will you, Dominic? Ten more minutes."

"Sure, Mr. Dudley."

"Now, what was this, Mr. Fell?"

Fell stuck his hands in his pockets and dipped on his feet.

"What's on my mind is very simple. Is this horse going to take that race? Is she going to?"

"All owners want to know that," said Mr. Dudley and then he excused him-self because he had to get a solution ready for bathing Buttonhead's ankles....

Fell drove and Cripp sat next to him. He lit a cigarette from a stub.

"I'm going crazy," said Cripp. "I think that guy's going to drive me ab-solutely crazy.

Chapter Fourteen

When they got back to San Pietro, Fell dropped Cripp off and told him he wouldn't need him till later. Cripp watched Fell drive off and went upstairs to his rooms.

The fever had left him. He remembered the way he had felt when he had watched the horse running, feeling exactly as Fell did. Fell, perhaps, felt like that often; it made Cripp apprehensive. When the phone rang he was glad for the interruption. He sat down on his bed, took the phone, and said, "Hello."

"Cripp, this is Janice."

"Yes, Mrs. Fell."

There was a pause, but both of them knew they were thinking of the same thing.

"Have you seen Tom?" said Janice. "I'm calling only because he left while I was still asleep, very early...."

"He's all right, Mrs. Fell. I've been with him."

Janice said "Oh" and then she laughed, but Cripp knew that she was still anxious.

"We went out early to clock a horse," said Cripp. "They clock them early, that's the only reason Tom had to go when he did."

"I'm glad," said Janice. "I'm glad that it was only a horse."

Cripp nodded, forgetting that Janice couldn't see him. He thought how good it would be if it were only a horse, if there were no other doubts.

"You know I don't like to do this," said Janice, "calling you about him like this. But you understand, don't you, Cripp?"

"I do, Mrs. Fell. I know what you mean."

"I don't— I really haven't anyone to talk to about this, so perhaps that makes it worse for me than it is. You know, Cripp?"

Cripp nodded again without saying anything. It shocked him to find that someone else thought about Fell the way he did; like a confirmation, as if his doubts about Fell had suddenly gained real basis.

"Of course I'm exaggerating," Janice said, and laughed again. "But I can't help being concerned."

Cripp could tell how she felt. He wanted to smile, so she would be reassured, but she couldn't see him. He said, "There's really nothing to worry about," and after a pause, "believe me, Mrs. Fell, I'm watching him."

"I'm glad, Cripp."

"Sure, Mrs. Fell. It's just that you and me don't know about these things and the way Doctor Emilson talks, it's hard to know what to think."

"That's true, Cripp. Especially when Tom seems to be all right. He acts perfectly all right when I see him."

"When I see him, too."

They paused again, and then Janice laughed, more relaxed now, and said, "I'll let you go now, Cripp. You must be busy."

"That's all right, Mrs. Fell. I'm glad we had this talk."

"This was just between us. All right, Cripp?"

"Sure. And if you like, I can call you back some time, just so you don't have to worry."

"Thank you, Cripp."

Cripp nodded again and hung up.

He would call Janice back, now and then, to tell her that there was nothing to worry about. He looked for a cigarette, found the pack empty, dropped it on the floor. He would call her back, now and then, to find out how Fell was at home, what Janice thought about Fell. That was the real reason.

Cripp got up, feeling angry, and when he took the first step he stumbled. He caught himself and started to swear, low and fast. He started to swear at Emilson, at himself, at Fell, and then again Emilson. After a while he was rid of it and went to heat the coffee. The thing to do was to forget about doubts, speculations, and about Emilson's ifs and maybes. He would go by what he saw, by the way Fell acted, and if Fell didn't keep on an even keel, Cripp would know it.

But Fell didn't show a thing. He was active and very sure, doing all the routine things required of him when the season started. Cripp noticed only one thing: Fell did nothing but routine things.

He hadn't done a thing about Pander.

For the moment Cripp let it alone and didn't remind Fell; it might not be good pushing him. On the day of the race Fell seemed at ease and very sure with himself. At seven in the morning he was waiting for Cripp in the hall of his house, and when Cripp walked in Fell was just through using the telephone. Fell said hi and Cripp just nodded because he was still tired. When they walked out Cripp looked at the lawn, wondering about the color. It was light green, almost yellow, and then there were dark green patches next to some dry ones.

"Got a disease there?" he asked.

"Naw," said Fell. "Just not enough water."

"So water it."

"It'll get water," said Fell. "Wait till the roots grow deep."

Cripp drove and Fell told him where to go. They headed out of town to the sheep ranch that a man by the name of Coon used to own; he had sold the house and corrals when the factories got big and paid easier money. A young guy called Fritters had moved in because he liked space for his kids and the place was cheap. Fritters was engineer at the San Pietro radio station, but being a short-wave bug he never had quite enough money. He had lots of expensive equipment and could listen to any place in the world but the hobby cost money. That's how he got to know Fell.

They swung off the road toward the ranch house and Cripp wondered why. He'd done a lot of things for the past week that didn't make sense to him, but since Fell had wanted them done Cripp did them.

Cripp wanted things to go smoothly for Fell. Cripp had paid money to total strangers, from fifty bucks up to several thousand. It had been Fell's own account so that was all right. And Fell knew the guys, he said, so that was all right too. Then Cripp had arranged it so Pander's men couldn't get to the new books they were keeping. Pander had no chance to check how the bets to Fell's bookies were coming in, but that didn't mean a hell of a lot because there were so few of them left. Then there was the letter to a man named Gross, a department head in the telephone company. Cripp had delivered the envelope to the man's house, late one night.

And about Buttonhead: Fell hadn't placed a single bet on his horse, even though nobody knew he was owner, but Dudley was listed. Then Fritters. "Call up this guy Fritters and tell him I want to see him," Fell had said. It made even less sense to see the guy, at his house, at the crack of dawn, before Fritters went off to work.

Cripp parked by the house and they walked to a shed by the corrals.

"Did you know Pander's bookies got radios in their cars?" said Fell.

"Good for them," said Cripp.

"Two-way radios," Fell said. "To phone in their bets. To check odds."

"Clever," said Cripp, and then Fritters stood in the doorway of the shack and said "Good morning."

The inside of the shed was all control boards, dials, and knobs. The tubes of the short-wave sets were hidden by panels.

"How's it working?" said Fell.

"Fine. I've got their wave length pegged for three days now."

"Tell Cripp about it." Fell laughed. "Cripp thinks he's still dreaming."

"Pander's cars have an assigned wave length. It's registered and licensed, and that's how I found out," said Fritters. "So I've got this thing here set up." He pointed to a wired box that looked the same as all the others. "This causes a racket on their wave length. They can barely make out voices."

"They can't radio in the bets and they can't get the odds," said Fell.

It sounded smart, but crazy.

"How about phones?" said Cripp. "They can't phone in?"

"Sure. But Pander wasn't set up for that. His dumb raids ruined the equipment we had and what he's using now can't handle the calls from a fleet of bookies."

"Man," said Cripp. "He shouldn't have gummed your setup. He could use it now."

"And he can't get new equipment in time. There's a queer log jam in orders at the telephone company."

It might ruin Fell's fun, but Cripp said it anyway. "All they have to do is figure odds at the end of the day and be ready for the next twenty-four hours."

"That's what he has to do," said Fell, "only it's risky when the bets come in fast. And one thing is sure. He can't do it for the third race today. It's at four-thirty this afternoon, and today's bets have to go by yesterday's odds. With the way bets pour in for that race Pander's running himself ragged trying to get a picture of what goes on."

Cripp said, "You've got him coming and going, but neat."

"How do you know?" said Fell, but Cripp didn't want to answer in front of Fritters and he waited till they got back to the car.

"Drive to the motel," said Fell.

"You've got him neat," said Cripp, "because he's bound to take bets on that race without being sure of the odds."

"You know what Buttonhead is paying?"

"Buttonhead?"

"We're paying the limit, twenty-to one."

"I don't mean to slam your horse, Tom, but—"

"You know what Pander is paying?"

"I can check," said Cripp. "I didn't know you wanted to know."

"I know already. Twenty-six to one."

"He must be nuts," said Cripp. "No bookie pays more than—"

"He doesn't think so. There's two half-milers in that race who don't stand a chance with the favorites. Buttonhead is one, only Pander doesn't know about her. The other one's Mindy. He knows about Mindy. He wants high odds on that horse because he thinks she'll run in the money, and giving crazy odds on Mindy he keeps away outside bettors who would collect plenty when she comes in. And it won't look like a set-up job so much because there are two long shots in the bunch."

"If that makes sense...."

"It makes sense."

"If that makes sense why do you need all that hocus pocus with the radios and the phones?"

"Because there's going to be some awful heavy betting between now and the race. On Buttonhead."

It made sense again, especially after having seen the horse train and remembering the money Cripp had paid out to those strangers. It was Fell's own money, and he stood to make a pile with the bets those guys were going to place.

"You think that will rattle Pander any?" said Cripp. "You think he gives a damn when he has to pay off those bets?"

They had stopped at the motel and Fell got out.

"I'll see that it does," said Fell and told Cripp to pick him up again at 2:30.

"How are you going to—"

"I can't lose," said Fell.

Chapter Fifteen

On top of everything else the air conditioner had broken down so Pander blamed it all on that.

"Pander," said Roy, "just keep thinking that it might rain. Just think of—"

"So then the heat gets sticky."

"I mean if it rains the track calls off the races."

"Stop dreaming and call that repair place again. This heat—"

"We got only three phones; we don't want to waste a phone on a call about air conditioning, Pander."

"Shut your face and—what? You waving at me?" Pander stalked around desks and chairs to get to the sweaty man by the far phone.

"He wants to know if we can carry a one-thousand bet on her," the man was saying.

"On whom, dammit?"

"This Buttonhead horse."

"How in hell do I know, if you guys keep tying the instruments up with conversation. Hey Mac, isn't that short-wave fixed yet?"

"How in hell do I know?" said Mac and stuck his head back behind the panel.

"I'll tell you how in hell! You're the mechanic around here, and—"

"That's right. Mechanic. I don't know from short-waves and I'm telling you again, get a guy over here who knows this crate."

The man on the phone kept tapping on Pander's arm. "—wants to know if—"

"What! What!"

"Buttonnose—the Buttonhead bet, Pander. He wants to know."

"All right, just hold it a minute. Pinky! What's the figure on Buttonnose, third race today. Come on, Pinky!"

Pinky looked across the room from the cluttered desk where he sat. "There's no Buttonnose in that race. Not on this sheet. Maybe—"

"I said Buttonhead!"

Pinky stuck his head down again, then said, "Twenty to win, twenty-two to—"

"All right, stop jabbering." Pander turned back to the man at the phone.

"Take it, tell him to take it. It's twenty to one, and I don't want no long-winded—"

"That's from the day before yesterday, Pander. He wants to know—"

"Don't argue with me. There's no change."

"But it's the third high one he's taken, Pander. He wants to know—"

"Tell him he's nuts. Tell him to get off that phone and to keep those horses straight. Those bets musta been on Mindy, the other half-miler, and besides it's not his place to worry who's covering."

"He says—"

"Hang up!" yelled Pander and turned away.

It made him bump into Roy and that brought on more yelling. Roy waited till it was over and then he said, "What was that you said about covering?"

"Huh?" Pander was winded and sweating.

"Something about who's worried about covering bets."

"I said for him not to butt in. It's not his place to worry about stuff he's got no notion about. Those damn foot-soldiers are getting so swell-headed around here you can't—"

"What bet was he worried about?"

"Julius! What was that bet? On the phone just now."

"A thousand. And he said he's already had three high ones on the long shot."

"What long shot?" Roy wanted to know.

"Button in the—I mean Buttonhead in the third."

Roy pushed his tongue around inside one cheek; then he said, "And you're not worried about that, Pander?"

"I got time to worry about every little damn brainstorm that comes jamming up the phones?"

"He had a point, Pander."

"Lay off me, for God's sake. We already went down on the odds to twenty."

"Can you cover that kind of betting?"

"Can I cover? The whole setup is built to cover, you jerk."

"Can you, Pander, if it turns out a run on one horse?"

"There's no run on one horse, just one bookie running off his mouth. Now get out of the way. I've got things to do before post time."

"Nobody else reported this kind of thing?"

"Of course not!"

"Perhaps better tell the boss."

"The who?"

"I mean Fell. He'll have to lay off those bets. Better let Fell—"

"The hell with Fell!" Pander left the office.

It was only the second time that Cripp had seen it happen, but he caught it and remembered the way Fell had looked watching Buttonhead. If Fell was excited it was in a strange way; as if the excitement had all turned into strength, packed tight and waiting.

Down below the grandstand they were letting the horses out, letting them trot their legs or look at the starting gate.

"I'll be glad when it's over," said Cripp.

"Anxious?"

"Anxious to get back on the job. You haven't done a thing to...."

"I will," said Fell. "See Buttonhead? Here, take my glasses."

Cripp took the glasses and saw that Fell was smiling. He sat in his box with arms spread back over two chairs and one leg over the other. He didn't seem to be smiling at any one thing. He was just smiling. Then Cripp put up the field glasses to look at the horse.

"Hey," said Fell. "Look who's coming."

Cripp looked and saw Pander. His head was bent and the dark glasses covered much of the expression he wore, but Pander looked worried. He ran up the steps, stopped once, and turned to look at the tote board across the track. One of the favorites was dropping from three to two and there was a series of flashes when Mindy changed from twenty-three to sixteen.

"Hey, Pander," Fell called.

Pander spun around as if somebody had insulted him, and his face didn't relax when he saw who it was. "Come up here a minute, boy."

Pander came up.

"Never mind that boy stuff. What do you want."

"Nothing, Pander. I thought maybe you were looking for me."

"Why would I—"

"Shut up a minute, boy. They're lining up."

The loudspeaker blared, some of the hands were running back to the fence, and horses looked nervous around the gates. "Ten minutes," said the loudspeaker.

Pander stayed by the box.

"You look like you want to be invited in," said Fell. "Want this seat?"

Pander turned, but when he saw Fell he didn't say anything. Fell was just being friendly.

"How's the sucker money running, Pander?"

"Huh? Coming in."

"Hope you kept tab on those odds, Pander. Big job, you know."

"Don't you worry."

"Shut up a minute, Pander, there's one trying the gate." But it wasn't. The horse had backed out again, wheeling around now with the jockey trying to straighten the horse.

"I'm just asking," said Fell, "because I haven't been in touch. You haven't shown me a thing or asked about anything."

Pander moved the glasses up and down his nose, looking busy.

"You know how it is. I was coming around tomorrow. I was going to—hell, you're here now and it isn't much anyways, but I was just thinking. How about laying off bets? Big race, this one, and—"

"Kind of late, isn't it?"

"Well, I just thought, maybe playing it safe wouldn't do any harm, seeing how the money came big on this race anyway."

"You don't need me to lay off your bets, Pander, not the way you're running this, boy."

"I don't mean that. You didn't get it what I was saying."

"You want me to take layoff money on this race. Isn't that what you said?"

"I was just checking. There are some real long shots in this one, and I figured—"

"Which one? Mindy?"

"Oh no. Hell no."

"Five minutes, Pander."

"Yeah. Uh, look, Fell—"

"You know, like I was saying, you don't want me to lay off any bet. First of all, you can always make good with your own pool, and second—" Fell leaned over with a confidential look— "that wouldn't look good, Pander, you coming around and asking *me*—you know what I mean, Pander, *you* asking *me*."

"I'm not asking a thing, Fell. I'm just discussing—"

"Quiet now, Pander. They're lining up." Fell turned front.

"I said—" But nobody was listening to Pander. He walked off, stiff-backed but looking right and left, waving a few times at people as if he had nothing else on his mind.

They had all the mounts behind the gates now, coaxing them in and shutting the doors behind them, one by one. The loudspeaker kept still and voices got lower.

"What if he'd asked you, Tom? What if he'd asked you straight out to take layoff money."

Fell looked at Cripp without turning his head. "I would have told him to go to hell."

"Can he pay up on those bets he took?"

Fell was watching the gates. The horses inside stood still. A few were tossing their heads.

"He's going to look like a horse stepped on him," said Fell, and then there was no more talk, but a second or so of everything holding still when the bell clanked out, the gates jumped open with metallic snaps and they were off. The first scramble divided into two packs. No stragglers, just two packs and clods flying.

One favorite had dropped to no odds, the others were two to one. Something must have leaked about Mindy, who had dropped to eight. Buttonhead was 20-1, next to the highest who had stayed at 24. That one was last in line, in the slow pack with Buttonhead. Mindy already showed her promise, out front with the favorites.

First turn, the two groups had pulled apart.

"She's at the rail," said Fell.

"I see."

"Behind those three. They're blocking."

Cripp just nodded.

At the middle of first turn the field stretched out—Mindy, already showing herself, with only four others ahead. The favorite pulling out front.

The last group split. Buttonhead hugged the rail and couldn't pass.

"He's cramping her style, Cripp. Look how—"

"It's only a horse, Tom." Cripp knew he had said the wrong thing but Fell wasn't listening. He smoked and watched.

At the end of the first turn Dominic must have let her have it her way. Buttonhead left the rail. The far straightaway showed a long line, some moving up, some dropping for good.

"Look at that Mindy!"

"She'll wear herself out."

"Look! Threw a wheel," said Fell, and they watched the horse buckle, then roll. Mindy was ahead of the accident so she kept right at it. Buttonhead had to swing back to the rail—Buttonhead all alone behind the bunch holding the front.

Five ahead of her.

Half mile. Four ahead of her.

"Like always," said Fell. "Jeesus! Come on."

The field flat by the rail now with Buttonhead taking the dirt from the next in line.

They started their turn and from the distance they looked tired.

Buttonhead was fourth now, holding the rail as she should.

At the top of the turn the favorite swung wide and got ready.

"I'm dying," said Fell.

Mindy had heart. The favorite couldn't get back to the rail, where Mindy pulled up and stuck.

"I'm going nuts. I'm—"

The crowd made a swell of sound.

Buttonhead was a flat form at the rail, with only a forward movement. Then she slowed. Mindy was there. Mindy in the last turn showed her wind was going. The favorite got back to the rail and in front.

"I'll kill Dudley," said Fell. "I'll kill Dudley for this," and he stopped abruptly because it caught in his throat.

Mindy was a rail runner but Buttonhead wasn't. Buttonhead swung toward the track.

When Fell started laughing it got lost. The crowd was up.

The favorite stuck to his place and looked like a mechanical pacemaker. Buttonhead's ears were back tight. She had the middle of the track and she stayed there.

"Baby!" Fell was yelling. "Baby!"

Foreshortened in the last straightaway it looked like a treadmill.

"Baby! You've got to, *got* to—"

Mindy was tired and there was space between her and the pacemaker.

Buttonhead, running the center, gave a jerk with her head when Dominic turned the crop in his hand, put both reins in one hand, and reached back. Buttonhead seemed to be nodding.

The roar got worse when the perspective got normal again.

Dominic looked to the side once to watch the favorite, and he might have thought about taking the rail. Cripp thought he might and saw how Fell bit his lip. Cripp hoped it would be over soon.

Buttonhead stayed where she was, and so did the favorite. He stayed and was pacemaker.

When the man leaned out of the tower Mindy pulled up. Where she got it nobody knew but she came up, and it wasn't too late. Buttonhead was where she liked it best, in the middle of the track. The man in the tower had his arm in the air, waiting, and it was almost done. Mindy was pouring ahead, the favorite stayed by the rail, showing power. Buttonhead was flat in the middle.

Mindy the last. The favorite. Buttonhead won it.

CHAPTER SIXTEEN

The season wasn't over, so outwardly nothing changed. Fell spent time in his office and at noon he came into the coffee shop. He stood there till Pearl saw him. She left her customer and brought him a cup of coffee. "On the house," she said, and he winked at her. Then he went back to his desk, put the coffee down, and looked for a cigarette. He didn't have any. He left the coffee there, went to his car, and drove off.

Downtown he had to crawl with the heavy traffic. He decided to walk the rest of the way and left the car in a parking lot.

Fell walked as if he didn't feel the heat, but next to the window of a department store he took off his jacket. He looked at the dummies, the clothes draped over an artificial tree, and went inside. He bought a light jacket and put it right on, and though the clerk protested Fell gave him the jacket from his suit and left without it.

The tallest building in town had four stories and Fell had space on the top. Three girls were typing and a man was working an adding machine.

"Cripp here?" said Fell.

"No, Mr. Fell, but he left a message."

Fell took the paper and didn't look at it right away.

"Did the telephones get in?"

"Yes sir, this morning."

"And there was one place needed a switchboard."

"Yes sir, that was installed too."

"Are the new bookkeepers—"

"Arrived and went to work this morning."

"Cripp showed them around?"

"Yes sir. And he said to tell you the radio was fixed and working. I don't know what radio."

"That's okay. I know."

Fell opened Cripp's note and read, "They are at Pander's apartment, starting at noon."

"About time," said Fell and walked to the door. He stopped before going out and turned back to the girl.

"New jacket. You like it?"

"Very much, Mr. Fell."

Cripp was waiting downstairs at the Pander address. He saw Fell coming and thought he looked good. He should. He had made a mint on that race.

"Hi," said Fell. "How come you aren't upstairs?"

"Wouldn't let me in," said Cripp.

"Come on," and they went upstairs.

It was a lot like before the race, bookies milling around and noisy talk, except this time nobody paid attention to Millie, nobody laughed, and there were no drinks. When Fell knocked on the door it was suddenly quiet. Millie opened the door.

"Miss Borden?" said Fell. "Of course. How could I forget that name." He walked in. He was feeling fine.

"What do you want?" said Pander. "This is a private meeting."

"Can it," said Fell. He smiled and sat down on a couch. "Is there a seat for Cripp?" he said. "Somebody get a seat for him."

Somebody did and Pander didn't make a move.

"Now," said Fell. "Go ahead, Pander. I just came to listen."

Roy got off the edge of a table casually.

"Like Pander said, Tom, this is private. We got business and don't want any kibitzing, not from nobody. So you better leave. I'm trying to say it nice, but—"

"Shut up," said Fell.

Nobody made a move.

"And don't forget it again. You're working for me." Fell looked around the room, then at Roy, then at Pander. "And I don't just mean the two top bananas. I mean everybody."

It was Pander's turn, but he wasn't ready. He was sucking in breath, keeping his teeth together and before he got ready Fell said, "Go on, Pander. You were saying?"

"Get out." Nobody had ever heard Pander talk quite that low.

Fell sat still. "You think you can swing this alone?"

"I can swing you from here to—"

"You don't get it, Pander. I'm talking about your business, this good-will meeting of yours."

"Get one thing straight, Fell. Anything I start I can finish. And anything you want to start...."

"So finish it," said one of the bookies.

"All I want to know is who's paying the damage."

"And the bus fare," said a bookie. "I don't even have bus fare to skip out from under."

"Go on, Pander." Fell was rubbing it in. "Tell him how, Pander."

"I'll tell them! I'll tell them straight who's causing this stink. I mean you!"

The bookies didn't get it, and Fell just laughed.

The laugh was the last straw to Pander. "Who's supposed to take layoff bets around here to keep things going? Who's supposed to see to it that—" he demanded.

"He means me," said Fell, and grinned at the bookies.

"You're damn right I mean you. So what happens when I ask you?"

"You didn't ask me," said Fell.

"I didn't ask you? Roy. Was I going to see Fell before the race?"

"I don't know," said Roy. "Did you?"

"Listen, you son of a bitch. You yourself were bending my ear about this. You yourself said—"

"But you didn't want to go," said Roy. "Then you did anyway?"

"You're damn right I did, seeing how those jerks over there kept taking in bets at screwy odds. Now don't lie, Fell. Did I see you at the track?"

"Sure."

"Did you take layoff bets to cover losses?"

"The way you put it you were too big to need me for covering."

"Now talk straight, Fell." Pander was enraged because Fell just sat there, smiling quietly. "Don't horse around, Fell, just talk straight."

"Putting it straight," said Cripp, and they all turned to him. "You didn't ask. You may have had cold feet, but you didn't ask."

Pander turned like a fighting dog. "You calling me a liar?"

"Yes."

Pander got livid. Some sweat rolled over his glasses. He wiped at them, took them off. Some had never seen him without his glasses.

In the middle of the silence Fell's voice dropped like a stone. "Don't tangle with Cripp, Pander," he said.

It brought the fight out in the open and Pander jumped.

From the waist up, Cripp was by far the strongest in the room. He ducked when Pander rushed him and, taking a fist in the face as if it didn't matter, coiled his big arms around Pander's middle. He squeezed so hard it made a sound.

"Leave him," said Fell. He was standing now. There was nothing mean in the way he looked, only dangerous. He looked active even standing still, and the force in him struck out like a charge. "Hold him, Cripp," he said.

Cripp twisted an arm and Pander snapped around, not daring to move because his arm might come off.

"And you guys, listen. He put you in the hole and didn't have the brains to see it coming. Then he didn't have the guts to cover. But he made a pile on it. Mindy paid fifteen to one on the nose. She came in third. How much, Cripp?"

"Eight."

"He got eight for every buck he put on that horse, and he put plenty. He used his pool to stake on Mindy, so the pool is eight times as big now, by rights. That's where your money's going to come from, to cover those bets you guys sold."

"That won't cover," said Cripp.

"Right, that won't cover. That's the part you guys have to worry about. You'll have to put that up yourselves. Here's my deal: I'll put it up and you guys work it off, working for me. Most of the season is ahead of us and you can work it off easy, with cash to spare. After that you can stick or you can blow. But nobody blows before you pay up. Is that clear?"

They said okay. Fell had himself a crew.

"Is that clear, Pander?"

Pander couldn't move and he didn't talk.

"Let him loose," said Fell.

Cripp did. Fell shouldn't have stood that close; he should have known, like everyone else did, that there was no other way for it.

Pander swung hard and connected, and with a rage from all the way back swung again. That one hit too, a sharp thud on the side of Fell's head, but when the follow-through came Pander suddenly pulled his punch.

Fell stood head up and started to roar with laughter. He had swung with each punch as if he couldn't feel pain and was roaring a loud, crazy laugh straight at Pander's face.

Then he hit.

It cracked Pander's mouth, and Fell was still laughing. When Pander recovered and flew out with a left, Fell saw it but again didn't try stepping away. He took it and laughed.

"Cripp," it was like a grunt, "what did I say about noses, Cripp?" A blow to the chest stopped him from talking but he didn't look punished. "About boxers with perfect noses." Right then Fell connected but he didn't care. "A fighter without heart! Hear, Pander? No heart!"

That's when he broke Pander's nose.

Pander tried stepping back but somebody pushed him from behind. His blood made a mess down his shirt front. When he heard Fell laughing again he reached for his gun, but even if he had found it, there wouldn't have been enough time. Pander had lost long ago.

Then Fell stepped back. He was panting and his face was cut but that's not what showed. What showed was a man who seemed all muscle.

"Pick him up," said Fell. "The bedroom's in back." Then he smiled, nodded at Cripp, and the two of them left.

The men stood around without talking about the fight, even though they had never seen one quite like it. There was a weird part to it, because through it all, Fell had never been angry.

CHAPTER SEVENTEEN

There was a smoggy sun over Los Angeles, and to keep the glare out of the room all the blinds were drawn. There were six large windows in the conference room. The drawn blinds made the beige walls even more colorless. Three men sat at the table. One smoked a cigar, one drank soda water, and one made small doodles on a pad in front of him. They all wore business suits.

"Well? What about San Pietro?" Brown didn't look up. He took the cigar out of his mouth and looked at the ashes.

"It's a problem," said Shawn.

Erwin stopped doodling. "Pander's out. No good."

"And Fell?"

"That's the problem."

They sat without talking for a moment.

"He's kept Pander. Some kind of job or other."

"It doesn't make sense."

"What does make sense? He's pushing to open a second track; he buys real estate all over. New clubs he wants; he's squeezing that Sutterfield, who can take just so much; he's throwing out money like it was his—"

"It is."

"Like hell. He made it on our losses. The combine lost and he made it. And that real estate...."

"He knows San Pietro. Perhaps it makes sense."

"It makes sense to buy up the whole prairie?"

Shawn took a drink of soda and they all waited till he was through.

"The thing is he hasn't consulted us. He's moving, and I don't know where."

"He's moving awful fast."

"Like that track deal. Two tracks make sense. It means a season twice as long. But it doesn't make sense the way he's moving. He's got the land already and he's using the same plans as on the first track."

"The point is, he didn't consult us. Can San Pietro carry a season twice as long? Are there enough customers? Is it going to make too big a splash and draw attention to our setup? The point is, we don't know. Fell can't know, because he didn't consult anyone. We got high-priced talent to check all those things, but Fell—"

"He's moving too fast."

"Don't forget, though," Brown commented, "Sutterfield's the wheel out there and Fell's got him where it hurts."

"That's another thing. Him marrying that Janice can be a problem."

"I never liked that deal."

"A problem, let me tell you. What if it gets around that the kingpin in San Pietro is the brother-in-law of the political wheel there? Even the suckers won't hold still for that."

"They've kept it quiet. I don't know if Fell ever used his advantage there."

"So why did he marry her?"

"Makes no sense."

Shawn tore a leaf off his pad and balled it up. Then he doodled on the next sheet.

"So. To get back to Pander."

"He's nothing. He's through."

"Sure. But he's still there."

"He hasn't got it. He just hasn't got it."

"He's got one thing."

"What?"

"He's got it in for Fell. Like all crumbs, when they carry a grudge—"

"He's no good to take Fell's place."

"I didn't mean that."

"He's no good, and for that matter, maybe Fell's okay."

"Maybe. We don't know."

"We got to find out."

They sat for a while without talking.

"The sanatorium. We'll look there first," Brown said. "That might do it."

"We can send Jouvet. You know, he can put it over."

"Sounds good."

"We'll send him and see."

"And Pander?"

"Right now forget about Pander."

"And Fell?"

"We'll see."

CHAPTER EIGHTEEN

Fell took a shower, dressed, and went downstairs. Since it was only four in the morning Rita was not in the kitchen. He went to call her. Once awake she looked at him from the bed but Fell just stood there and waited.

"I have to get dressed," she said.

"Do it later. Come on and get me some coffee." He stood there.

Her Indian face didn't show it but she was puzzled because he just stood there.

"Come on, come on," he said. He was looking at her, but she wasn't sure what he was seeing.

Rita got up and reached for her housecoat.

"You must be only in your twenties," he said. "Never mind the hair," he said, "leave it down. Just make the coffee."

She left her black hair in one shiny long braid and went to the kitchen.

Fell didn't follow her. He went outside and breathed the air. It smelled good, but it was already warm. Then he went to look at the lawn, kicking at the yellow dust that had started to show in patches. Some grass had died but it was still a lawn, a dry, brittle lawn with uneven color. Once he stooped to look closer. Something new was growing, something spiky and wild where the grass had given up. He went back inside.

Rita was at the sink beginning to tie up her hair. "Leave it down," said Fell.

She let the braid fall again and lowered her arms. Fell stood close now, but his eyes told her nothing. But she put her hands up to the housecoat and closed it in front.

"Open it up," said Fell.

She stood still for a moment; then she let go and started undoing her belt.

"The braid, Rita. Open up the braid."

If she felt humiliated Fell didn't notice. He watched her pull the braid around and undo it. Then she shook back the hair.

There was a lot of it, thick black hair with lights in it. Rita's housecoat stayed open but neither he nor she paid attention to it.

"God, that's good." Fell put his hands into her hair. He held it, watching her.

"Turn off the coffee," he said, finally, and let go of her hair.

"I never could tell about you," he said, "but you must be only in your twenties."

She watched him take the pot and pour coffee at the table. She came to the table and stood there.

Fell drank coffee, and when he looked up she was still standing there. The housecoat was open and the nightgown came to sharp points over her high breasts.

"Go back to bed," he said. His cup was almost empty.

Her lower lip was between her teeth. She looked at him and then turned, the lights moving in her hair. She went into her room and took off the housecoat and then the nightgown. She rubbed her hands over her thighs once, then lay down. Her hands played with the cover.

Fell finished the coffee, got up, and stretched. In the hall he grabbed the new jacket off the hook and put it on.

Rita heard the front door slam.

Fell was whistling as he drove down the street, and at five o'clock he pulled the car to one side, out on the highway. The grandstand and race track were on the left, the open prairie on the right. That's where the contractor's shack stood, the dump trucks, the steam shovels and half a dozen caterpillar tractors. Fell turned off the road and made the car dip when he stopped by the contractor's shack. It was a few minutes after five then, and the Diesels started to roar and the cats clambered off into position.

Fell got out. The super and the foremen saw him from the shack, but Fell didn't come in. He climbed over the dirt and watched the buckets take bites out of the ground. Then they reared up, swung sideways, and the trucks sagged on their springs when the earth dropped down. The cats were further away. They dug their blades into the ground, made a gouge, and when the earth had piled up they backed off and did it again. The noise was deafening.

Fell stood and watched. Once he moved because the shovel was biting close. When the sun had cleared out of the haze along the horizon the prairie turned hot and bright.

Fell finally turned and went to the shack. Under the window that faced the machines he had a desk and a phone. Every time one of the dump trucks went by, the window rattled and Fell, at the desk, looked out. Then he'd work again. He didn't interfere with the supervisor who was checking blueprints and talking to the surveyors, and he didn't bother the foreman who was studying time sheets and work plans. Then he looked up and called the supervisors.

"It's six-thirty, Jerry. Where's the equipment?"

"Half-hour late," Jerry said. "That happens."

"I want that stuff here and going."

Jerry leaned his hands on the desk and sighed. "Look Mr. Fell. You want the equipment, fine. But if you ask me, it's money thrown out the window. You got till next summer to get this track finished, and the grandstand too."

"More equipment makes it faster," said Fell.

"So you get it done three months earlier. So the track sits around for three

months extra doing nothing." Then they heard the engines from the highway.
"Like I said, Mr. Fell—"

Fell leaned to look out the window. "That's what I like to hear," he commented.

The convoy slowed at the work area and then flatbeds with shovels riding
high and earth movers and a dozen more cats came swaying across the ruts and
stopped one by one. Jerry went outside to take care of things and Fell got up
to stand in the door of the shack and watch them unload the equipment. Each
time a piece was unloaded it went right to work. That's what he wanted to
see.

He watched till seven o'clock, when Cripp arrived.

"You look lousy, Cripp." Fell laughed.

"These hours," said Cripp. He climbed into the shack and then he and Fell
sat down by the desk.

"You pick up the deeds?"

"Here." Cripp tossed a bundle on the desk. "You realize they had to open
the place special for me to get these at this hour. What I don't get, Tom—"

"Fine. We got them. How about the clubs? Did that architect guy show up
yet?"

"Last night."

"Where'd he put up, at the Alamo?"

"Yes. Last night."

"We'll go there, around noon. He ought to be all set up by noon."

"Sure. Now listen, Tom, we got to start figuring finances. All this buying
and building—"

"Keep an eye on it, Cripp. You're good at it. Now another thing—"

"Tom, listen. I am keeping an eye on it and that's why I'm talking to you.
We've got to start—"

"I got it all figured out. I'll pinch Sutterfield and make things jump a little.
You don't think he's trustee of a bank for nothing? And racing commissioner
and dummy on the real-estate board. I'll go see Sutterfield again."

"Tom, Sutterfield can do just so much, and he's bad medicine when you go
too far."

"I know. He's old and ill-tempered. But he's okay; he'll come through," and
Fell laughed.

They settled a few more things, and at nine o'clock Fell wanted some coffee, so a short time after nine he and Cripp drove back to town and to the motel.

Pearl gave them coffee and Cripp had eggs and toast with his. The coffee
was free but he had to pay for the rest.

"How's Phido?" said Fell.

Pearl leaned her hip against the jukebox gadget on the counter and shrugged.

"Fine, Mr. Fell. I don't see him much."

"You still with him?"

"He's so busy all the time. He says it's your fault."

"Excuses."

"Well, he's making book like he used to and then he's bartending all night at that new one."

"The Kitty."

"Yes, the Kitty—and all these other crazy things he's telling me about, like you sending him to pick up radio cars in L.A. and getting office furniture down here and who knows what."

"Kinda hard on you, Pearl?"

"It certainly is, Mr. Fell."

He laughed and asked for more coffee.

"He's planning for the future," said Fell. "He's making dough."

"I don't see any of that either," she said.

"So? You don't strike me as the wallflower."

She tried to look offended but then got serious. "I want Phido to marry me."

"Ah!" Fell lowered his voice. "You pregnant, Pearl?"

She answered right away. "I wish I was," and then she went to serve somebody else, down the counter.

Cripp and Fell went to the back, where Fell's other office was. The room looked bigger because the desk had been moved out to the shack at the construction site. Fell unlocked a file cabinet and flipped through some folders. Then he tossed papers on a chair and slammed the cabinet shut.

"Take this to McCann's office," said Fell.

"What is it?"

"Deed and stuff for the Kitty. Tell McCann to transfer it over to Phido. Except the mortgage," said Fell. "I'll handle the mortgage."

Cripp took the papers and said nothing. He didn't know what to think, whether to call it plain crazy or to let it go for what Fell meant it to be: a friendly gift—an overgenerous one but a straight, simple gift. Crazy?

"Beat it," said Fell. "Just let me know where I can find you."

Cripp said he'd be out in the coffee shop, and if he left he'd leave a number with Pearl.

He got his free coffee but after a sip or two felt too nervous to sit and finish the rest of it. He took a dime out of his pocket and went to the wall phone. When he got his number he tried to keep it short and anonymous.

"This is Cripp, ma'am. I was wondering how things were going. At your end."

"How are you, Cripp," said Janice. "I'm glad to hear from you." She hesitated. "I don't know what to tell you, Cripp; I haven't seen him very much. He seems very busy."

"I'll say."

"Cripp, is there something you want to tell me?"

Cripp didn't know what to say. There was nothing to tell. Nothing concrete. Except that Fell had made it back to the top, like a miracle, back on top bigger than ever—and then he hadn't stopped. It seemed as if he couldn't.

"I'll tell you what, Cripp. Perhaps you could come out to the house for a talk. You think it could be arranged so that Tom...."

"Tonight, if you're free. I don't think he'll be in before late."

"I'll be home," said Janice. "Please try to come."

CHAPTER NINETEEN

Dr. Emilson had forgotten about the letter, but when the front desk called him up and said Dr. Jouvet had arrived he remembered the name and was glad for the diversion and the chance for a professional follow-up. Dr. Emilson had thought about Thomas Fell a few times, wondering what might have happened.

"Dr. Jouvet?" he said into the phone. "Mr. Fell's physician? Send him in."

Dr. Jouvet looked correct, a little severe, and with the self-assured manner of the medical specialist. Dr. Jouvet made Dr. Emilson feel a little self-conscious.

"I got your letter, of course. Please have a seat. I'm sorry there hasn't been time to—"

"I quite understand," said Dr. Jouvet. "However, your secretary answered. She gave me this date. I did not inconvenience you?"

"Oh no, not at all. Cigarette?"

"Thank you. I don't smoke."

Dr. Emilson smiled but Dr. Jouvet didn't smile back. Dr. Emilson got through the lighting of his cigarette, feeling self-conscious.

"So you are Mr. Fell's physician. To tell you the truth, Doctor, I should have liked to consult—"

"I am his attending physician, yes, but only for the past month."

"Oh. When he was here, you know, he had been attended by a physician in San Pietro."

"I am not from San Pietro."

"Yes, of course. Los Angeles."

"New York, Doctor Emilson."

Emilson blew out smoke and gave a short laugh. This time Dr. Jouvet smiled back but it was just barely benign.

"Well, then—you came to see me," Emilson said.

This was better because now Jouvet had to talk. Emilson sat back in his chair and waited.

"As I said, Doctor Emilson, I work in New York. One month ago—it must have been shortly after Mr. Fell left here—I received his call that he was arriving in New York for immediate consultation."

Emilson nodded through his smoke. "From one psychiatrist—"

"I am not a psychiatrist, Doctor Emilson."

"Ah. I'm terribly sorry—I—"

"Quite all right, Doctor Emilson. Our own specialties tend to make us presume—"

"No, really. As a matter of fact, your letter—"

"Internal medicine, you may recall. As I was saying, Mr. Fell came to me at rather short notice. However, under the circumstances I examined him immediately, the usual symptoms, lethargy, some skin darkening, stomach upset rather severe. But you know all this, I'm sure."

"No, I don't," said Emilson.

"Hepatitis."

"He had no symptoms while he was here."

This time Dr. Jouvet smiled voluntarily. "We specialists—" and he laughed— "are all cursed with the same single vision." Jouvet turned serious, folded his hands. "However, that's the very reason I am here."

"Mr. Fell's hepatitis?"

Jouvet ignored it.

"My examinations are always quite complete, perhaps even excessively so. On that basis you will understand that I—though being an internalist—took notice of Mr. Fell's psychological problems. I am here because you are the logical one to clarify matters to me."

"Well," said Emilson, "of course. You came all the way from New York—"

"Of course not. Let me make this clear. Mr. Fell has engaged me, for the time being, as his attending physician. I have accompanied him back to San Pietro. There was some justification for his move—a man of his age has often a number of things which require attention. Under the circumstances anything you can contribute to my understanding...."

"Oh, of course." Emilson put out his second cigarette. He didn't light another one. "By my lights, Doctor Jouvet, your patient should not be out of a sanatorium."

"You don't say."

"Yes. Let me explain. Or first, rather, let me qualify. Because of Mr. Fell's discharge, against my advice, my observations were not complete. But a manic syndrome was obvious."

"A manic depressive?"

"I'm not sure it's cyclic. In fact, to classify it as manic is descriptive only, and from a psychiatric point of view not too meaningful. Clinical research seems to indicate, in most cases, that a manic depressive psychosis is actually—"

"Doctor Emilson, for my purpose the descriptive classification will do. I doubt whether I could follow you beyond that."

"Oh, it's not really—"

"Really, Doctor, this is not false modesty."

Emilson was disappointed. He had hoped for a chance to be thorough, to sit down with a colleague. But then internal medicine was really no fit background for a technical airing of Fell's case.

"Let's say we discuss the prognosis," he said.

"Again, you flatter me, Doctor. I would need a description of symptoms first."

They both laughed politely. Then Emilson said, "Has he been very active?"

"No. The lethargy induced by the liver condition—"

"Yes, that would counteract any inclination toward—"

"Except for this. I have never seen a patient respond to treatment quite as quickly as Mr. Fell did. That is, as far as the lethargy goes. And even when it was at its height it was sporadic."

"As if he were pushing it out of the way?"

"Exactly," said Jouvet.

"Descriptively, that would be one of Mr. Fell's chief attributes, to push aside all obstacles to his—to the progress of his psychosis."

"It sounds ruthless."

"No, not ruthless; inconsiderate. No moral scruples and therefore no concept of right and wrong."

"But no—ah—vicious intent."

"Certainly not. In fact, the manic's optimism and self-assurance make any sort of viciousness unnecessary. You may even find that Fell can be very generous. He will feel that he can afford to be."

"Rather an incautious trait."

"The picture is: careless, outgoing, optimistic. Quite likable, for that reason, but by no means reliably so. The patient can switch allegiance at the drop of a hat."

"Tell me this, Doctor Emilson. Would Mr. Fell tend to be dangerous?"

Emilson thought for a moment, then shrugged. "To others, no. Not by intent, anyway. To himself, yes."

"Meaning?"

"The increase of tempo in the manic is a record of his disintegration. The more he displays all I have described, the closer he comes to the collapse which ends with a full-blown psychotic delusion. At that point—" Emilson shrugged again— "the patient is very hard to reach."

"It sounds tragic," said Jouvet.

"Yes, it is. Whether this will be so in the case of Fell—"

They both shrugged this time and Jouvet said, "Then what keeps him sane?"

"That is hard to say. You say he hasn't cut down on his responsibilities, removed himself from the pressures of his business?"

"I didn't say, but you are right."

"They all have a core of health," said Emilson.

"Which sustains it in one case and not in another?"

"In the case of Mr. Fell, I believe it is his wife."

"She sustains him?"

"So it seems."

"How is this?"

"Without being clinical, he feels safe with her. And so she becomes his sane spot."

"I must remember this," said Doctor Jouvet.

"I wish you would," said Emilson, "because if he should leave her, that could be the signal."

"For what?"

"That he has broken with sanity."

When Dr. Jouvet left, Emilson was still disappointed. He felt dissatisfied with the surface descriptions to which Dr. Jouvet had held him. It did in-justice to the case and would be slight service to Jouvet.

But since Jouvet was no doctor he felt satisfied with what he had learned. It was a shame about Fell. He meant no harm. But Jouvet was sure that the men in Los Angeles, in the beige office, would think of it differently.

Chapter Twenty

Cripp didn't get to see Janice that evening because Fell kept him busy. They had a meeting with some of Fell's lawyers; they had a conference with two men from the zoning board; and then there was a long session with the accountants. Fell went home at three in the morning and Cripp went to his place. He thought he had just gone to bed when Fell called him up again, seven A.M., but when Fell heard Cripp's voice over the phone he merely told him to go back to sleep and to meet him at the motel around noon.

When Fell hung up Cripp was wide awake. He knew where Fell would be—out at the building site, watching the shovels and the bulldozers. Fell wasn't likely to leave there before noon.

Cripp knew Janice's sleeping habits, but he thought it might be important enough and called her immediately. Once he got past Rita, Janice told him to come along at any time.

She saw his car pull into the drive and a while later heard his irregular step on the tiles in the hall. Uneasily, she remembered sitting here and listening to Sutterfield come into the hall.

When the door opened she got up, came across the room, and said, "Good morning, Cripp. Have some coffee?" He said yes and they both sat down at the small table by the window. They didn't talk while she poured.

"It's a little odd," said Janice, and smiled. "I've never done this before—talk about Tom to somebody else."

"Perhaps we shouldn't," said Cripp. He watched the steam from his coffee cup and then looked up at Janice. She seemed taller than he.

She said, "We may not know what to talk about, but I think we should. It—something doesn't feel right, about Tom."

"I know, but perhaps it's just the way Emilson talked, making you feel this way."

"That would be nice. That would be the best. Except—"

"I know. It feels the same way to me."

"Cigarette?"

Cripp nodded and took one, then lit hers. He forgot his own.

"I haven't seen Tom very much," said Janice, "but perhaps that in itself is what worries me."

"I've seen a lot of him. He never stops. He does as Emilson says, keeps going all the time."

"Is he doing anything foolish?"

Cripp shrugged, then took the time to light his cigarette. "I don't know, Mrs. Fell. I honestly don't. Perhaps I'm more confused than he is."

"If he would only do less," said Janice. "If I could see him more."

"Can't you tell him?"

Janice looked at Cripp without talking. Then she leaned forward.

"That's it. That's the thing, Cripp. I can't talk to him any more. It's as if I weren't there."

It embarrassed Cripp and he looked out the window, at the lawn with the dry patches.

He said suddenly, "Perhaps you should leave. Go away for a few days and make him take notice."

"He needs me."

"But he doesn't know it."

"I'm afraid to leave, Cripp."

Cripp understood that. He looked down at his feet. "I just thought, you know, a little shock—"

Janice nodded. She took a new cigarette, then put it down again.

"Why fool ourselves, Cripp. The fact that we're sitting here shows something is wrong. Why fool ourselves?"

When Cripp spoke again he said it fast, to be done with it. "I'm going to call Emilson." Then his courage ran out. "If it gets any worse," he added.

"Yes. We may need him. I'll talk to Tom. I'll try and make him see...." She frowned, shook her head, didn't go on. It had never been like this between her and Fell. There had never been such a wall. As if he were trying to hide from her, pull away. But that wasn't it. There was nothing cagey about him. It was more as if he were losing touch and did not try to reach her.

She turned abruptly when the car came through the gate and stopped next to Cripp's. Fell jumped out and walked into the house immediately. If he had recognized Cripp's car he gave no sign of it.

"Stay," said Janice. "If he asks, we'll think of something to say."

The door to the room wasn't all the way open when Fell said, "Jan, I had to...." He hesitated when he saw Cripp but walked straight toward them. He nodded at Cripp, smiling, then bent down to give Janice a kiss.

"Pour me some." He nodded at the coffee.

He watched her fill a cup, pulled up a chair, and leaned toward Janice.

"You know where I was? Out there with those machines. And suddenly, Jan, I had to see you." He stopped abruptly, leaving a solid silence. Then he smiled at Janice. "I haven't seen you much, lately."

He patted Janice's hand and then picked up his coffee. He didn't see the smile of relief on Janice's face.

"Tom," she said, "you promised, after the season, we'd go to the mountains."

"I did, and we will." Then he looked at Cripp. "How come you're up this early? I thought when I called you...."

"I came over to talk to Janice," said Cripp. "I thought, and she thought, that...." But Fell wasn't listening. He tapped one hand on his knee and said, "You know, it's a good thing you're here. I've got to see Sutterfield—"

"Tom," Janice interrupted.

"And I want you to come along," he finished.

"Tom," Janice said again, "Cripp and I talked about you."

"You did?" Fell got up.

"Tom, are you paying attention?"

If the words made no impression, the tone of voice should have, but Fell only frowned. Then he put his hand on Janice's shoulder and gave a small squeeze.

"I'll be home early tonight, Jan. We'll talk about our trip."

Then he was at the door, and Cripp followed him out.

CHAPTER TWENTY-ONE

Sutterfield wasn't in his office and the old girl with the pink glasses couldn't say where he was.

"Call his home," said Fell. "See if he's there."

"I'm sorry, but I never call Commissioner Sutterfield at his home. We have a rule."

"Oh, come on," said Fell and pushed the phone her way.

"I am very sorry. However—"

"Come on, now." This time Fell slapped her on the back, like a comrade, and for a moment she seemed to choke. She found her voice high up someplace, sounding mean.

"I must insist. And please get off my desk or I'll call—"

"Go ahead, call him."

"—call the police!"

"But, honey," said Fell and he leaned down on one elbow, "you *are* the police." For one second he smiled, then it was gone. "Take the phone, Cripp. You call Sutterfield."

The way Fell sat on the desk she couldn't get up without touching him and that thought was enough to keep her stiff in her chair. Cripp phoned Sutterfield's home, but he wasn't there either. He called the bank without luck, the racing commissioner's office, and then the real estate board.

"Where is he?" said Fell. He was smiling at the woman, but she thought he was going to bite.

"This outrage—"

"I'll call Commissioner Sutterfield and have you arrested," said Fell. "Where is he?"

It couldn't be much worse, she thought. He was leaning so close, and leering, and he had both hands on the arms of her chair and with one brief twist could have sat in her lap.

"I refuse!" Her voice quavered.

Fell changed so abruptly she didn't know whether to be grateful or scared.

"Come on, let's have it. You're holding me up." Cripp noticed how Fell hadn't just changed for effect but was tense and meant it.

"Where is he?" said Fell again.

"In his—he is at the club this morning. The Athletic Club."

Fell got off the desk and left without saying anything more. In the car he said, "The Athletic Club. I'll give him a workout!"

Fell wasn't a member, so they wouldn't let him in, and when he said who he was they got huffy about it. It worried Cripp. He saw how Fell held one lip in his mouth, without talking, and then took his hands out of his pockets.

"Send Sutterfield out here," was all he said.

The deskman thought he hadn't heard right.

Fell took the bell off the desk and started to tap the button.

"Sir—" started the deskman, but then an attendant came running in answer to the bell.

"Never mind, Jordan." The deskman sounded hurried. "The bell—"

Then another attendant came running because the bell was still going. They both stood there watching Fell dingle the bell button up and down.

Then the deskman had an idea. The reading room opposite was empty and the two attendants were there. "Grab him!" he said. It sounded dramatic. "Throw him out!" But the attendants didn't get it.

Fell showed them. He reached out for the closest, spun him around and kicked his rear. The man sailed across the foyer. Cripp saw how Fell liked it, how he pushed away from the desk to grab for the other man.

"We don't want any trouble," said Cripp, and he stepped between the two. "We don't want a commotion, so just get Mr. Sutterfield. Please," said Cripp.

The man across the foyer had picked himself up and Fell had a smile on his face. "Hey," he said, "hey, you," and started toward the man.

"Tom, listen." Cripp held his arm and Fell must have noticed the grip because he stopped and the smile disappeared. "Tom, listen to me," said Cripp. "The clerk says he'll get Sutterfield. He'll get him right now."

Fell relaxed.

"Let's go," said Fell, "you're holding me up."

He had stepped back to the desk. The clerk looked at him, scared now because he couldn't make Fell out, but seeing the way Fell was looking at him he didn't feel like fooling around any more.

"He has the— Mr. Sutterfield is in the conditioning room. He is—"

"The what?" said Fell.

"Steam bath. He will be out—"

"Show me the steam bath."

The clerk sent one of the attendants along to direct Fell and Cripp to the steam bath.

There was a heavy man on a table and the masseur was working on him. There didn't seem to be anyone else but then they saw the row of steam cabinets along the far wall, and Sutterfield's head was lying on top of one.

Sutterfield was looking weak. When he saw Fell he made a sudden rattle inside his box, then looked weak again.

"If you're well done on all sides, Herbie, come on out so we can have a talk."

"Milton!" said Sutterfield. He was craning his neck to see the masseur and called "Milton!" again.

There was one last slap from the back of the room, then the fat man grunted as he got off the table and Milton called back, "Coming right up, sir."

Sutterfield might have had something else in mind when he called "Milton" but the masseur had his routine. He talked a blue streak while he turned off Sutterfield's steam and slammed open the cabinet.

"Up and lively now," he said and helped Sutterfield out of the box. Then he held a big sheet up and Sutterfield had to walk over to it in order to get wrapped up.

"Christ!" said Fell. "You look awful."

Sutterfield couldn't even talk. His bony legs stuck out below.

"Don't you think so, Cripp? I think he looks awful." Fell grinned after Sutterfield, who was being led away by the masseur.

They waited in a room called the Antler Den with wagon wheels hanging from the ceiling for chandeliers and a lot of ranch-type equipment all over. There were so many antlers it looked dangerous. Then Sutterfield came in, fully dressed, and sank into a chair. He still looked weak.

"How are we doing?" said Fell. It didn't sound like small talk but neither Cripp nor Sutterfield knew what he meant. Fell seemed to think they would all know what was on his mind so he just said it again, "How's the progress, Herb?"

"Progress? What progress do you mean? Do you realize, Fell, you have seriously compromised me? I not only demand an explanation, but I'm warning you—"

"You're wasting my time," said Fell. He leaned forward in his chair, eyes wide and hard. Only his face looked animated. "I'm getting sick of you, Sutterfield, make no mistake. Don't yammer, don't make excuses, just follow through when I ask a question. Cripp, you got a cigarette?"

Cripp fumbled for his pack, nervous now. There was something electric in Fell's behavior and it seemed to infect those around him. Cripp handed a cigarette over as if he could hardly wait to get rid of it.

"So talk sense, Herb. I want to hear what you did."

Sutterfield knew no more than before, only this time it didn't make him querulous. Instead he felt anxious and rushed. "What I did?" he said. "About what, Fell, I can't seem to remember."

"You heard me talk about those tracts of land. Does that ring a bell?"

"Ah, of course. You bought that land. Ah, yes."

"I've got to dump it. I need the dough. Did you set up the sale as we decided?"

"Fell, really—uh—I don't remember that we decided just then—"

"What do you think I was doing, damn it, just dreaming about it? I said the land was good for that plant expansion they're planning. My land's better than what they had in mind. So make them buy it!"

"Fell, you don't understand. As the banker, as the lending agency for the factory expansion, I can—"

"You can tell them what land you're going to take a mortgage on and for what terms."

"But—"

"And being on the real estate board you got the weight to push expansion one way in this town and not the other. So don't hold me up, Herb, I want that profit and I want it now."

Sutterfield felt he didn't have the strength to argue. All he wanted was to get away, not to feel pushed as he was, and to get rid of the tension that seemed to come from Fell. He could do the thing with the real estate. He didn't like it, but it could be done.

"Very well, Fell, I understand. And now, if you'll excuse me—"

"When?" said Fell. "When does this thing come off?"

"Really, I'm in no position...."

"You are now. When?"

"Uh—my guess, I'd say possibly three months."

"Don't be an ass. Push it down to a month and a half."

Sutterfield didn't answer. He stood up suddenly. "Now listen to me, Fell. You don't tell me my business, any more than I tell—"

"Like hell I don't, Sutterfield."

Fell hadn't moved, but his eyes had followed Sutterfield when he stood and now they went down again.

Sutterfield sat. It brought the eyes back in line.

"He said he'd do it," said Cripp. "He's going to try to put this deal through in as close to a month and a half as he can."

"Sure he will," said Fell. He threw his cigarette across the room and it landed near the screen in front of the fireplace. "Pay attention, Herb." Sutterfield snapped around. He forgot about the cigarette he'd been watching, because Fell was again making him feel on edge. "About the breakage fee," Fell said. Then he waited.

Cripp got tense when he heard it. He saw how Sutterfield took it, slumping back in his chair, but Cripp felt tense. He had been almost sure that Fell had forgotten about it. He had hoped that Fell would. The breakage fee was the state's cut from the track bets, and that tax hadn't changed in years. It was the same all over the state. Then Fell had decided the cut was too high.

When Sutterfield didn't say anything Cripp tried again. "Tom, just remember one thing. San Pietro is only one track out of a couple hundred in this state. It's—"

"Two tracks. We'll have two next year."

"All right, two. But still only one small setup out of—"

"We're getting awful big, Cripp. The way I got this thing stacked I'm getting awful big."

"For God's sake, Tom, make sense. What can Sutterfield do? You're asking a change on the state level and all you got to work with is local!"

Fell started to laugh but it didn't relax the air.

"Herb, tell him! Tell him how big you are, Herbie! Aren't you getting bigger all the time with me boosting...." Fell stopped laughing and frowned at
Cripp. "Don't rattle the guy. I tell him he's big, so he's big. Sutterfield! Say
something."

Sutterfield seemed to have shrunk into his suit and when he talked he still
didn't come out.

"Don't try to flatter me. I want you to listen to Cripp when he tells you
about this."

"To hell with Cripp!"

Fell had been looking at Sutterfield when he spoke, but Cripp made a start
in his chair. Fell's tone had gotten sharper. And Fell had never said anything
like that before.

"I set the thing up for you, Sutterfield. I told you to go to the county seat
and start pushing. You know your way around there because I showed you.
I showed you years ago and you got a solid line into the county seat. From
there—"

"Tom, listen, please." Cripp leaned forward in his chair. "The county seat
isn't the state capital."

"It's all one! Sutterfield, listen. The tax guys at the county seat make their
recommendations to the state. You know Pasquale there and the two Richies.
They got their jobs through pull from state, and that proves the connection!"

Sutterfield gaped. Cripp was wishing this were all a joke.

"And if that doesn't cut any ice I told you what else to do," said Fell. He
was suddenly very quiet.

"Fell, you've gone clearly out of your mind," said Sutterfield.

"And you, Herbie—you might find you're out of a job, sudden like."

"What—what do you mean?"

"Never mind that. Let's talk about Throkton, on the state board."

"Fell, you can't be—"

"Throkton wouldn't want you to foreclose on his properties, huh, banker?
Throkton wouldn't want you to spread it around how you two screwed the
state on that highway deal, huh?"

Sutterfield gathered himself for one more try in the old manner.

"I refuse to listen! I refuse to consider your megalomaniac schemes which
might cause the most destructive—which are tantamount to outright blackmail, the most dangerous kind of—"

"No danger," said Fell. He was still very quiet. "Push Throkton. There's
no danger. A recommendation from county, and the same time just a push
where Throkton is sitting—"

"I refuse!" Sutterfield sounded hoarse.

Fell got up then as if he hadn't heard, or didn't care. That's how the next
thing got its bite.

"Do it today—brother-in-law."

CHAPTER TWENTY-TWO

If Fell didn't come in by eight, Janice would eat alone. He came in at ten and the table was set, Rita was still in the kitchen, and Janice was waiting.

"All lit up," he said from the hall. He looked at the lights. "Hey, Jan!"

Janice came into the hall, walking fast. She smiled too quickly, but Fell didn't see it. He gave her a kiss and held her.

"Didn't see you all day, Jan. What a day—you hungry, maybe? Want to go out and have a bite before turning in?"

She steered him into the dining room and showed him the table.

"We waited with dinner. Let's sit down and eat together."

"Sure," he said. "Let me wash my hands."

He went to wash his hands and never wondered about dinner waiting this late at night.

He came back and held the chair for Janice. When she sat he gave her shoulders a squeeze, went to pull his chair closer to hers, and sat down.

"Let me tell you about this new thing at the new track. Ten shovels, four earth movers—you know what an earth mover is, Jan?"

"Tom, have your soup."

"Fine. Let me tell you, Jan, you're looking good." He smiled at her and kept looking until she answered it. Then he ate some soup.

"Janice, listen. Four earth movers can do the work of—I forget. I forgot how many cats. These cats, you know. Eat your soup, Janice."

She laughed and said, "I was wondering when you would notice. I've been looking at you all this time."

"How do I look?"

"Fine, but nervous, I think. How do you feel, Tom?" She leaned on one elbow and stretched her hand over to his.

He started to pat her hand but then he slowed down. He stroked it slowly, then held it.

"I feel good with you, Janice."

"I want you to," she said. Rita was taking plates away and Janice waited. "I would like to see more of you."

"I'm so rushed," he said. "I want to be less rushed and with you more."

She smiled. "And your earth movers?"

"Forget them," he said.

They ate quietly, and then they had a cigarette together while Rita cleared the table.

"Did you ever see Rita's hair?" said Fell. "I mean down. Did you ever see it all loose?"

Rita had stopped in the middle of brushing the tablecloth. She gave Fell a look. Then she went on because Fell was talking about something else. She left the room, and Fell and Janice opened the balcony doors upstairs and sat there, with the bedroom light behind them and the darkness in front.

"I'm relaxed now," said Fell. "I feel big and relaxed."

"You need that, Tom." She sat closer on the small bench and took his hand. "Tom, will you listen to me?"

He looked at her and nodded. His hand felt warm.

"Herb called me," she said.

"Oh?"

"Because you saw him today."

Fell gave a snort.

"Tom. I was very upset. Please tell me what happened."

"Just business, Janice. What did he want?"

"He said you threatened him."

His hand had started to move, working her fingers.

"He better learn something," said Fell. "That guy better learn something, and fast."

"You know what I'm talking about, Tom. I'm trying to be calm about it, I'm trying to think it was all—the excitement, perhaps, because he acted up the way he does, Tom. Are you listening, Tom?"

Fell was looking straight ahead. Only his hand seemed to be with her. He was bending her hand back and forth and then he started to tap it with hard fingers.

"Herb means you no harm. You know that, don't you? He can't harm you, Tom."

"Keep out of this, Janice. He tried to get in my way."

Janice pulled her hand away and sat up. "I can't keep out of this, and you know it. I'm in this, I'm the part that matters."

"Don't get that way, Janice."

"You threatened him and you used me—you used us—to threaten with. You used our life for—for—"

"Stop that. It's got nothing to do with us. There comes a point when every-thing stops moving because this puny jerk gets the idea I'll stop because he's out of breath or something and I give him a kick. That's all. I give him a kick, that's all."

Fell had jumped up and his hands made sharp little movements. He tapped the rail and looked down to the lawn.

"Tom, look at me."

"You look at me! Look at the size of it and don't mix, don't mix up—" he faltered. "Look at the size!" he yelled, and threw out his arms. "I'm showing you he can't get in the way."

"Tom. What are you talking about?" Janice was standing now too but she hadn't moved closer.

"Come here," said Fell.

She stared at him, and took a long breath. She tried again.

"Hear me out, Tom. We can't have this thing between us, this constant, ugly thing with my brother. We love each other and that's for us, for you and me. It's for nothing else."

"Nothing else," said Fell.

"We want it that way. I know that about you and me." She held her wrist and twisted it in her hand. "That must not change. I won't let that change, Tom!"

"He wants to get in my way. He's in my way."

"Tom, leave him alone. Leave it all alone. You don't need him, you don't need any of this, the chasing and straining for I don't know what. Give it up, Tom, please. You don't need—"

"Give it up?" His voice was too loud. "Give up what I haven't got? I'm moving, Janice, and I don't stop till I've got what I haven't got. That's what I'm saying!"

"You have me."

"And more! Everything!"

She felt confused and it made her want to cry. "Tom, please. You can't hurt us like this. Tom, we must go away. You need help."

"Help?" He laughed. "I don't need help any more because I can have everything—"

"You need help, Tom, and rest. I'll help you all I can. I'll hold—"

"Hold? Anybody that tries holding me back—nobody holds me back any more."

She stopped him with a sharp slap on the cheek, hard so he wouldn't go on, so the weird, uncontrolled thing in Fell would stop long enough for him to remember her, but then she was afraid to come close. He stared at her, as if waiting, but she was afraid. She said, "We agreed to it once. I said if you ever used my name, or the fact that Herb is my brother, I said I would leave."

He held his lip in his teeth and watched her.

"I said that I would leave," and she tried hard to make her voice even.

"Just don't get in my way."

"Did you hear me, Tom?"

When he didn't answer she ran into the room.

He heard a door slam. He started to say something but instead ran into the bedroom. Janice wasn't there. "Come here," he kept saying. "Come here."

Then he sat on the bed. He got up and pulled back the covers, knocked his fist into a pillow, sat down again. He sat there for a while and then he started to curse, low and fast, over and over. Once he said "Janice?" and then he started to curse again.

Nothing else happened and then he got up. Fell walked fast, with a spring that showed how awake he was. He got downstairs, went through the hall and outside. The shaft of light from behind him showed the dying grass, the bare patches and the spiky weeds. Then Fell stepped back and slammed the door. He went to the kitchen, through that to a hall and into the room where Rita was. When he tore the door open he saw her asleep with the rich hair spread out wide. Fell laughed. When he yanked back her blanket and then the gown she had on, Rita was still barely awake.

Chapter Twenty-three

He got up at the same time and he didn't change tempo. He left the house before five. There was an envelope on the hall table, just one word on it— Tom. But Fell didn't notice and the letter was left there for days.

He drove out to the construction site where the truck was waiting and two men were loading his desk on the back. All the equipment was standing around without noise, and nobody was out there except three men further away, surveying and waving at each other. There had been a mistake, because of the rush to get started, and now the machines stood idle, waiting for the mistake to get ironed out.

Fell gave it just a glance and then went to the truck.

"It goes to the Alamo. Know where that is?" Without waiting for the men to answer he said, "Follow my car. Come on."

He got back in and drove off. The truck lost him on the way but they knew where the motel was so they met him there later.

Fell was on the phone in his deskless office and he kept phoning while they moved in his stuff. He paid the men and each got a ten-dollar tip. It embarrassed them and they wanted to say something to him but Fell waved them out and banged the door shut behind them. Then he opened his file and pulled out papers. He left some of them on the floor but the deeds he spread out on the desk, side by side. They spread all over the desk. He stood back. Then he took a pencil and tagged some of them off. He made two piles and wrote on a sheet of paper. Now and then he looked out of the window but since it was barely past six there were no people around the swimming pool.

Then Cripp came in. He didn't say hello and his tie wasn't on right.

"Tom, it's worse today. You got to try doing something. Listen to me."

"I'm busy, Cripp. Here, take these deeds and—"

"To hell with those deeds!"

"What?"

"Tom, drop everything for a minute and listen."

"I got a better idea. That track project is so screwed up I think we'll start fresh at the other end, east side of town. Here." He tapped one pile of deeds.

"Where'd you get those? They're the ones I took to McCann's. We got a purchase agreement for those. The factory deal."

"I'm going to cancel. Fresh start."

Cripp groaned. Then he set his legs wide, swiped out, and the deeds flew all over.

"Now shut up and listen, Tom! You got trouble—"

"Nothing like it. I got lawyers coming to buy those factories. I got an idea—"

"You got nothing! You're losing your grip!"

Fell gave Cripp a steady look. "Will you listen? Sutterfield's skipping out!"

"Like hell."

"He couldn't hold out any longer, you know he was losing his shirt brib-ing that real estate through the board and forcing the—"

"Stupid bastard. I just told you I canceled out on that." Fell jumped up and said, "Come on. Let's tell Sutterfield the good news."

Fell went down the corridor and every second step he tapped his hand on the wall.

"Tom, you don't get it!" But Fell wasn't listening to Cripp.

In the coffee shop Fell waved at Pearl but kept going. "Mr. Fell!" she called. "Wait, Mr. Fell!"

He stopped and she came rushing up. She threw her arms around his neck and gave him a kiss.

"I'm getting married, Mr. Fell, I'm getting married to Phido!" She stood back, out of breath. "And I want to thank you, honest."

He grinned and gave her a tap on the chin.

"You're a winner, honey."

"Wait, Mr. Fell."

He stopped at the door.

"It's in two weeks. And we want you for best man. Will you be, Mr. Fell?"

He laughed again and said, "Sure, I am. I am the best man." He went out to the car.

In the car Cripp tried again. He said to himself that he'd make that call for sure today, if he didn't get through to Fell now. One more try and he'd have to call Dr. Emilson.

"Tom. You won't do any good with Sutterfield. He isn't running from you. It's the authorities."

"I know them," said Fell. He was driving too fast. "When it comes to au-thority—" They swung a curve and had to hold on. Then Fell said, "I got a job for you, Cripp. After Sutterfield."

"What now?"

Fell was quiet and even his driving looked controlled. "You know where Jan-ice is?"

"Janice! She gone?"

"I want Janice," said Fell.

Hearing it Cripp lost the anger he'd been trying to hold back. The way Fell sounded Cripp couldn't be angry, impatient.

They swung into Sutterfield's drive and a car was parked there. Sutter-field's houseman was throwing a suitcase into the back. Fell ignored it and since the front door was open Fell walked right in.

Sutterfield saw them from his den. At first he tried to duck but saw Cripp waving at him, so he gave up and waited. He might as well. It didn't really faze him any more.

"Hi, Herb," said Fell. "I got good news. Sit, Herb," but before anything else could happen Cripp took over.

"Mr. Sutterfield, this is important. You must explain what has happened. Tom won't listen to me but he's got to understand. Tell him. Tell him now, before you leave."

Sutterfield shrugged. He talked with a flat indifference.

"It's over, Fell. I might still be able to—"

"You crazy, Herb? We're just starting to roll."

The lack of comprehension was like a sting to the old man and once more, suddenly, he started to shout.

"Throkton is coming down! You know what that means?"

"Sure, Herb. I called him. I took the load off your brain and called him myself."

"You called him yourself! I couldn't go through with it so you, like an idiot, called him yourself. Well, the fat's in the fire! He's not coming down to play ball or anything like that, Fell. He's got other ideas!"

"I'll show that son of a bitch—"

"You'll show nothing. He doesn't care about me any more. I'm through. Ruined. I'm off to the capital for one more try to save myself, or to save what's left. I got a chance, Fell, because Throkton doesn't want me, he wants you! He won't touch me because he's in as deep as I am, but you're deeper! You made that call and you sent that letter. Blackmail! In writing! And I'm counting on you not to talk any more, Fell, because Throkton is covered, by me, and anything you say against me cuts off your own nose. You—"

"Mr. Sutterfield, hold it a minute." Cripp talked fast. "Fell isn't responsible. I want you to stay and we make a deposition or something. We'll call Emilson—"

"What did you say?" Fell was roaring. "You trying to cramp my style?"

"You don't get it either," and Sutterfield lowered his voice so it sounded like the start of a cough. "Throkton's coming down with a tax investigator, with a team to look into gambling, and here's more." Sutterfield suddenly shouted again. "Not just state-level. They've got the F.B.I.!"

"Jesus," said Cripp. He looked at Fell and saw he was biting his lip.

"You did that, Herb?" Sutterfield wasn't listening to Fell. He had left the room, not caring about Fell any more.

"Cripp, you listening to me? I've got to do a few things."

"What is it, Tom? I'll do them."

"I'll do them. I've got to find Janice—"

Chapter Twenty-four

The blinds were drawn in the beige conference room, even though there was no sun at that time.

Brown held a cigar but it wasn't lit, Shawn played with a cigarette pack which was crumpled and empty, Erwin was tapping a pencil against his chin.

They all wore business suits. So did Jouvet.

"You shouldn't wait any longer. What this Emilson said—"

"Never mind now what he said. We got eyes to see."

"But remember he said it wouldn't get any better."

"We waited too long. For a while there—you know how it looked, real clever—"

"What about Sutterfield now?"

"He's arrested."

"So what now? Do we stop him?"

"Can't be done. The stink...."

"And besides, all he knows is about San Pietro. That's boiled over anyway."

"Fell then."

"I don't know. In a pinch, I've seen him do it before, he might even help by taking the heat."

"He'll take nothing. You heard what Jouvet said."

"So it's a hit?"

"No other way out. I see no other way out."

They sat a while watching Brown light his cigar. Jouvet said, "Perhaps look at it this way. He's not responsible. He could even be helped if...."

"No more risks."

"But a man like Fell, think of him."

"We can't do that. That tack is no good."

"So it's a hit."

"Do we use Pander?"

Brown shook his head. He pressed a button by the side of the table and a girl stuck her head into the door.

"Send him in," said Brown.

The man that came in was slight. He had a head like a thinker, except that his jaw ruined the impression. It was blue and curved up. Like some kind of fish.

"It's Mound," said one of the men.

"Because we got to be sure," said Brown.

Mound kept his hands in his pockets. It made him look cold.

"All right," said Brown, and nodded at Mound. "Like we discussed."

Mound nodded too and went to the door. Nobody talked while he was leaving.

But before Mound closed the door he stepped back, unaccountably, and held the door open. He nodded at the man who came in and then went out and closed the door. Still nobody talked while they watched Fell come all the way to the table.

"I'm glad you were in," he said, and pulled up a chair.

He looked from one to the other. "Did I interrupt?"

Brown put his cigar into an ash tray, doing it slowly. "Why are you here, Tom?"

Fell looked bad. His face looked more lined, making his long-lashed eyes seem strangely out of place. He smiled and looked from one to the other.

"I had to see you sooner or later, that's why I dropped in. I'm in town looking for Janice."

When nobody answered, Fell looked at his hands and mumbled, "I guess you wouldn't know."

"You going back to San Pietro?" asked Shawn.

Fell seemed to wake up. He kneaded his hands for a moment and then he talked clearly, very sane.

"I want you to send a man to San Pietro, someone who knows his way around. I've got to leave."

"Leave?"

"I've got to. I'm going to take some time off, Janice and me. I've just got to."

"Where you going, Tom?"

"I'll be back in a month. Meanwhile we need someone to handle my job. I'm leaving Cripp there, who can help better than any. Whom can you send?"

They looked at each other, puzzled, and they thought about Mound who was now on his way to San Pietro. "I don't know if you can do that, Tom. I understand...."

"I know," said Fell. "I made a mess, a bad one."

"So we hear."

"I'm not sure how it happened, but the thing got away from me."

They were puzzled, but not impressed. They hadn't thought Fell would admit, or know, this much. That's why they really sat up when he went on.

"We're losing money on the second track I started building, and I almost did worse with a real estate thing I was setting up. But the worst is the team. They're sending a team down, from the capital, to look into things."

"I'll be damned!" said Brown.

"But I can make good. I'm going to make up the track loss out of my own pocket, the real estate deal is back to normal, and I've figured a way to head off that team." Fell paused. "After that, you got to give me a replacement. Janice and I...."

"You can fix it?" said Shawn.

"Yes. There's a man by the name of Throkton...."

"We know all about that," said Brown.

"Then you know I can tie him up. I couldn't before Sutterfield got arrested, but now his testimony...."

"I'll be damned!" said Brown.

They all looked at each other. They knew what Fell said was true.

"The way Fell here works, the way he's worked in the past," said Jouvet, "I think he can do it."

They all tried to catch Brown's eye and when he saw it he frowned, then nodded.

"I got to be sure first," he said.

"What do you mean?" said Fell, who didn't know what had gone before.

"He has to make a phone call," said Shawn. "After that...."

"Not yet." Brown picked up his cigar and pointed it at Fell. "Can you show what you said in black and white? The track expense, how much you can raise, the real estate shuffle, the Throkton frame you got in mind?" Brown coughed. "What I mean is, so that the man we send to hold down your place will know what goes on."

"Sure," said Fell. "When do you want it?"

"Soon. The sooner the better."

"I can run down and be back tonight."

"We'll be here," said Brown, and they all watched Fell leave the room. Then they looked at each other.

"Perhaps we should have asked him to come in before," said Jouvet. "I don't think Emilson knew what he was talking about."

"How about Mound? You better call right away."

"No," said Brown. "I can't reach him before evening anyway."

"Are you sure? I'd hate to see something go wrong."

"We'll wait for Fell."

"It's up to him."

Fell was driving through L.A., checking all the old places. Once he drove within a few blocks of the place where Janice was, but he didn't know it.

Chapter Twenty-five

Cripp couldn't find Janice and he couldn't find Fell, and when he was at the end of his rope he went home. He sat down on his bed and dialed the Desert Farm, asking for Doctor Emilson. He was running with sweat by the time he got his connection.

"... of course, I remember you, Mister Jordan."

"Now listen close, Doctor Emilson. What you said turned out—like you said it might. Tom Fell needs help, Doctor Emilson. He needs real help!"

"Yes," said Emilson. He seemed to be thinking. "I'm sorry that I was right."

"What next, Doctor Emilson, what do I—"

"Have you spoken to Doctor Jouvet?"

"Who?"

"Doctor Jouvet, his physician. He saw me recently to discuss the case."

"What was that name?"

"J-o-u-v-e-t."

"No!"

"Is anything wrong, Mister Jordan?"

Cripp didn't answer. He went over it again and again, trying to see the angle, but then he gave it up, knowing the angle all along. They wouldn't send Jouvet just for a stunt. They would send him to get the expert's verdict on what had been going on, and if Emilson told Jouvet....

"What did you tell him? Fell was sick? Getting worse?"

"Substantially what I told you, Mister Jordan."

"You told him that?"

"Mister Jordan, I fail to see...."

"Emilson, listen! We got to find Fell, and quick."

"You mean you don't know where he is?"

"No, he went after Janice, his wife, he said. She—"

"She's gone?"

"Yes, both of them."

Then Cripp heard Emilson curse. He had to wait a while and then he broke in.

"You've got to understand, Doctor Emilson, that Jouvet was a phony, sent down by the—by Fell's competitors, and all it can mean—"

"I think I understand. Now listen to me. You must make every effort to find Mister Fell. And once you find him, don't let him out of your sight. Do you know where his wife is?"

"No. She left because—I don't know why but she left."

"If she comes back, if you see her, impress upon her to stay at home, where Fell can find her."

"Stay here? But I just told you I think they're after Fell here."

"Jordan, it is very important that Fell find his wife, and if he comes back without having reached her it would help tremendously, Jordan, to find her at home, to find her as soon as he can. You understand that? And I'll be in San Pietro early tomorrow morning."

"As soon as you can, Doctor Emilson."

"I will. And don't worry too much. If he can find his wife, and as soon as I get there, we'll have things under control. Meanwhile, if you find him, do not let him out of your sight!"

Cripp hung up with an empty feeling. He would have liked to close his eyes, open them, and find it was morning. He got off the bed and went across the room, dragging his leg worse than ever. Under the shirts in the drawer he found his revolver. He checked it and stuck it into his pocket.

It never rained that time of year. The clouds blew in from the Sierras but they all steamed away before they got to San Pietro. It should be another month before rain came. But the heat felt sodden, there was a haze, and beyond the town clouds had piled up.

It confused Fell. He hadn't felt so confused in a long time, though it wasn't confused in the head, because he knew where he was. The dry lawn in the sun, all but dead, with small things starting to grow that had blown in from the prairie. Fell nodded to himself and then he smiled. The lawn was growing. If it wasn't one thing it was another, but something was growing. It would spread and get bigger, like the prairie, and then the thought took hold. Fell turned away from the house and decided to walk out to the prairie. There was nothing bigger than— He jumped back, thinking the car was going to run him over, when Cripp came to a fast stop.

"Tom," he yelled. "Wait!"

Fell had no intention of leaving and smiled when he saw Cripp come up.

"Where in hell have you been, Tom! I've been looking for you ever since...."

"L.A. I just got back." Fell frowned. "There was something...."

"Did you find Janice? Did you look for her, Tom?"

The thought gave Fell a painful sensation, almost making him cry. Instead he laughed. When it was over he felt suddenly beat.

"I didn't find her," he said. "Listen, Cripp, I got to find Janice."

Cripp took Fell by one arm and steered him to the house. He told him they would find Janice, would wait for her here. In the hall of the house Fell stood by the table while Cripp talked to Rita. No, she said, Mrs. Fell hadn't been in and hadn't called. That's how Cripp didn't see it when Fell picked the envelope off the table and stuck it into his pocket, because Rita was looking at him, distracting him.

"Let's go sit down," said Cripp, and held the door open to the room where he had drunk coffee with Janice. Fell nodded, came in, and sat down by the window.

They would wait, thought Cripp. They might talk about this and that but they would wait, the way Emilson said. But Fell didn't talk. He sat back, hands folded behind his head, and watched the thoughts that came by. They were of all sizes and colors, but in the middle was Janice. Fell stayed that way until Janice disappeared, and instead he saw the window opposite, and beyond that the yellow lawn. Fell took a breath and looked at Cripp.

"Anything new here?"

Cripp wasn't sure yet. He looked away and shrugged, not wanting to see Fell's eyes.

"Janice and I are leaving. I talked about it to Brown."

"You what?"

"Brown. I just came back from L.A. I told you."

Cripp chewed his lip, leaned forward.

"What did he say?"

"We talked about how to arrange it." One side of Fell's face started to smile. "I think they had other plans. Before I walked in."

"Tom, do you know what in hell you're talking about?"

"You know how it is in this racket. You're on good behavior, or out. And you and I know—together with everyone else—that I haven't been panning out so good lately."

Cripp stared, then looked away. Sane as sane. How else could he talk like that?

Fell walked to the window and looked out.

"It'll take some recouping, but it can be done."

Cripp got up, smiling, and stepped up behind Fell. He put his hand on Fell's shoulder and gave him a pat, a warm gesture which, had he thought about it ahead of time, would have embarrassed him. Fell gave him a quick look, then turned back to the window.

"Take a look at that lawn, will you?"

Cripp still had his hand on Fell's shoulder, but now he felt awkward about it.

"Remember my telling you about that lawn getting on by itself? Look at it."

Cripp dropped his hand and looked out.

"Yeah. Some sight."

"You think so, huh? Come on, Cripp, let's take a walk."

"Wait a minute. Where?"

"Out to—" Fell had started for the door, then came back. "Why? You don't sound right."

Cripp didn't know what to say, whether to say anything.

"First thing I asked you, Cripp, I asked you is anything new here. You didn't answer."

"Because I don't know," said Cripp.

He watched Fell come closer and when Fell reached over to pat Cripp's pocket neither of them talked for the moment. Then Fell gave a short laugh.

"You really aren't sure, are you?"

"That's right."

"Last time I saw you carry that gun was—when was it, seven years ago?"

"All right, Tom, listen. I found out Jouvet—"

"I just saw him today. In L.A."

"You didn't see him a few days ago. He went to see Emilson."

"I haven't seen that one in over a month."

Cripp didn't take the joke up.

"He went to see Emilson to check up on what's what with you. You know what that means?"

"I know. They're worried. Like I thought when I saw them."

"You think you changed their minds, Tom?"

Cripp really wanted to know and he watched Fell very closely, but the face looked like always. Lines through the tanned skin, the lidded eyes, the temples grey.

"It's hard to tell, Cripp."

Sane as the sanest. He could have said, sure, and that would have been crazy.

"Let's take a walk, Cripp."

"Why? The best thing to do...."

"If Janice should come in the meantime, we'll leave a message with Rita. Janice should wait here."

Sane.

"We'll just make a quick check. Come on."

Emilson had said don't let him out of your sight! The way Fell acted there was no reason to hold him back, and he had made no attempt to go alone. Fell told Rita he'd be back in an hour and if Mrs. Fell should return she should wait in the house. Then Fell and Cripp left.

Cripp drove downtown without knowing where Fell wanted to go. No need to ask until they got to the center.

"Pull over," said Fell. "I just saw something."

Crip stopped and looked around quickly. There was some traffic, a few pedestrians, a department store. Cripp didn't see anything.

"Where are you going?" said Cripp.

"Windbreakers growing on trees," said Fell. "Ever see anything so crazy?"

Cripp followed Fell out of the car quickly, but Fell was waiting for him, and behind Fell, in the store window, were windbreakers growing on a tree.

"That's crazy all right," said Cripp, and even laughed. "Come on back in the car. You didn't say yet where you wanted to go."

"Wait a minute," said Fell.

He walked into the store and found the counter with the windbreakers, as if he had been there before. Fell shook his head. Crazy thought. He bought a windbreaker and gave the clerk the jacket he had been wearing.

"Tom," said Cripp.

"Wait a minute."

Fell walked out of the store.

"Tom, where are you going?"

"Come on, this is it."

"Listen to me...."

"His place is around the corner."

Cripp grabbed Fell's arm because he couldn't keep up.

"Come on," said Fell, "this is it. A visit to Pander."

To check, Fell had said. What better place to check but with Pander. Cripp tried to keep up, breathing hard, not noticing that Fell was breathing hard too, as if in a rage. But Cripp's bad leg didn't give him a chance. He didn't catch up with Fell until he came to Pander's door, and there was Fell, standing by the door, waiting for Cripp.

"This is it," said Fell and drove his foot into the door. It crashed open.

When Fell saw only Pander and the slight man it confused him.

And the day before he had been confused, forgetting to go back to the office, where Brown and the other three had been waiting till late.

And now, he didn't even recognize Mound.

Chapter Twenty-six

The way some can smell a cop Cripp could spot a professional. He slammed the door shut and had out his gun. Then he blocked Fell.

"Move and you're dead," said Cripp.

Pander stopped, halfway up from his chair, and Mound held still.

"Move," said Fell. "This is it, move!" and with a sudden slam of his arm knocked the gun out of Cripp's hand. The physical act was like a tonic to Fell and he jumped free of Cripp to stand crouched in the center of the room.

The gun had scuttled under a chest.

That's how they stood. Pander afraid to make a dash for it because Fell was too close. Cripp not daring to move because it would take him too far away from Mound. Mound sat still and Fell stood waiting. Cripp caught it, watching, and relaxed a little.

Cripp had no gun. Pander had no gun. And Mound, sitting, he had no gun.

"You guys stay put," said Cripp. "I got something to say."

Fell watched. The situation had gotten away from him and he had to gather himself.

Mound got up from his chair and straightened his suit with small movements.

Pander was grinning.

"Talk all you want, Cripp. Talk and watch this."

"The first guy that moves gets his back broken. You remember how, Pander?"

Then Pander stopped grinning. He tore his mouth open and yelled.

"Now, Mound! Your setup! Those bastards, both of them, now, Mound!"

Mound coughed.

"I'm leaving," he said.

"Are you out of your mind? You crazy hopped-up bastard, are you out of your mind? The hit! Come on, Mound, the *hit!*"

Cripp saw he had been right. No gun. He even saw that Mound might not have done it if there had been a gun. This was not his way of doing business.

A hit was a secret and personal craft, done alone, with no one around.

"This is not my way," said Mound.

He ignored Fell, because Fell was crazy. He ignored Pander, because Pander was nothing. And Cripp, he saw, was a cripple.

Mound walked to the door.

But Cripp was faster than expected, lunging for the door, missing Mound by no fault of his own. Fell was there, wrestling with Cripp, and hissing in his face.

"The wrong one, Cripp. I want Pander. Let this turd be and then Pander—"

So Mound, as if he hadn't been there, got away.

Fell was no longer confused. Pander was his focus and there was nothing to interfere. Cripp couldn't leave. Stick with Fell, stick close and keep him safe.

When Pander saw Fell come across the room he got up and moved back.

"Your nose," said Fell. "It's broken. A fighter with heart. Cripp, look at the fighter."

"Tom. Hear me," said Cripp and reached for his arm. "He's nothing, Tom. Leave the bum."

Pander had stopped, flat by a wall. He looked worn. "Listen to him, Fell. You hear what he says? Not me, Fell, I'm a bum, just a bum."

Fell had stopped moving.

"Fell, listen to Cripp. He says I'm nothing, he's right, dead right."

"Stop yammering," said Fell.

"Tom, did you hear—"

"Stop yammering, Pander, or I'll throw up."

Then Cripp let go of Fell's arm because it looked safe. He took a deep breath only it didn't help. Fell was again radiating an edgy tension, a strong nervous force without aim. So far, everything held.

"Cripp," Pander was still by the wall. "Is he safe?"

"Just don't move."

"He isn't looking at me, Cripp. Just the chair. Let me get to the chair."

"Stay there."

"Let him sit," said Fell. "I don't step on worms."

Cripp, between two poles, had to hold both of them. With Pander it would be easy.

"You stay put, Pander, or you'll never—"

"All right!" Pander held still. He watched Cripp stop without coming nearer, saw the deep line down one side of the mouth disappear. Pander breathed again but didn't move.

For the moment Fell seemed controlled. How to keep him that way, how to make him turn his attention for good. Steer him outside, perhaps.

"Tom," said Cripp. "We're through here."

"That bastard just moved," said Fell and came closer.

Cripp spun around but Pander stood still.

"I tell you, Cripp, that bastard just—"

"Tom, don't bother. We've got to go now," but Fell was holding the lip in his teeth, hardly listening. "Tom, I've been looking for Janice."

"Janice," said Fell.

"We'll find her, Tom."

"I know."

There was nothing laughable about it, because at that moment Fell was sane again. His face was quiet and he ran one hand over his eyes the way anyone would, anyone with his heavy troubles. Anyone anxious to find his wife.

"I tell you, Cripp—"

Cripp was listening.

"The bastard!"

Fell's shout was mad. He grabbed Cripp as if to get him out of the way and spinning Cripp saw where Pander dived for the gun under the chest. Fell tried to go after him, with Cripp reaching out, when Pander was up, quick like a jack-in-the-box but this one a killer. The gun came around and there was just time for Cripp to toss himself forward making Fell bounce to the wall when the shot crashed out, then another one, and Cripp took them both.

He rolled on the floor waiting for the pain, even seeing the blood on his leg, the good one, and then he saw what was happening to Pander.

Fell was an animal and the gun didn't matter a damn, scudding across the floor out of reach.

When Fell got up he breathed hard and seemed tired. He paid no attention to what was left on the floor. What was left wasn't worth living for.

"Cripp," he said, "are you all right?"

"Run, Tom—"

"Cripp, are you all right?"

Fell reached down to pick up the wounded man and it hurt Cripp so badly he clawed his hand into Fell's side. It tore the pocket, making the envelope fall to the floor.

First Fell lowered Cripp gently, then he wiped the sweat from his face, then he waited for Cripp to relax and open his eyes.

"Lie still," said Fell.

Cripp turned more, staring to see.

"Lie still and relax. I'll get you—"

"Tom, what is it?"

Fell looked down, where Cripp was trying to reach the envelope, then reached for it, tore it open.

The message was very brief. *Please come for me, Tom,* and an L.A. address and a phone number.

"What is it?"

"Janice," said Fell, and gave the sheet to Cripp.

"When did you call her? Tom, answer me! When did you call her?"

"I didn't."

"The phone over there, Tom, hurry up!"

Fell brought the phone over to Cripp but the cord didn't reach. He put it down on the floor and said, "I'll call her." He read from the sheet and told the operator the number. Then he sat on the floor, holding the phone, and stared out of the window. Cripp saw no movement, no expression, and he began to tremble without control.

"Hello, yes?" said Fell. He was silent and then he said, "I want Janice. Jan-ice." He looked over to Cripp who was straining to get nearer the phone.

"Oh?" said Fell. Then he hung up.

There were red and grey swirls in front of Cripp's eyes and his jaw hurt from clamping his teeth, fighting to stay conscious.

"What—" he said. "You hung up...."

Fell walked to the door.

"She was gone. She wasn't there any more," and walked out.

The rain was coming for sure now. The night was cool. Small gusts of wind pushed it closer, moving the clouds together so they piled over the town. It was too dark to see the clouds but they were there, almost ready.

He held the letter in his hand and every time there was a wind he walked faster. He stopped when he saw his house. Because of the wall he couldn't see much but he saw the upstairs. The window was lit.

"I'm back," he said.

He crossed the street and went up the drive. He would look up again. Step under the window and look up. He walked to the middle of the lawn, watch-ing his step. There was some light where the front door window let it through from the hall. Fell saw dust under his feet where the lawn had dis-appeared. He kicked at the spiky things that had started to spread there.

"Must be a disease," he said. "It needs rain."

He looked up and called, "Janice?"

He waited a while and then he turned. He couldn't see it, by the drive, but he knew it had moved.

"Janice?"

If Fell would move just a little he would be more in the light.

"Over here," said Mound.

He saw Fell step into the light and he saw his face brighten.

"Are you there?" said Fell.

Mound didn't answer. He had wanted to say, yes, it's me, or something like that. He didn't say it.

"I can see you!" said Fell. He waved, a big wave with both arms and any moment he was going to laugh.

Mound hadn't wanted to say anything, but when he was closer he said, "No. She's not there."

"Oh?"

"I'm Mound."

His gun was up.

"Oh," said Fell.

He lowered his arms and the shot killed him.

There had been some thunder and then the rain burst down. Janice stepped to the window. She looked down at the dead lawn, soaking up rain, but it was too dark to see anything there. She turned to the room, sat down, and held her head in her hands. She sat like that, as if she were waiting to cry.

THE END

Mission for
Vengeance
By Peter Rabe

Chapter One

When the train comes through the pass it lets out a hoot which I can hear from my place. After that the train winds through the valley and doesn't get to Great Rock until half an hour later. By jeep, from my ranch, it's ten minutes.

The waiting wasn't easy. I thought of saddling a pony and taking a quick turn down the north fence where the two hands and the foreman were working, but that would have meant changing clothes or it would have meant getting my clean ones splattered. I could have sat on the porch with a bottle of beer, watching the morning fog over the pastures and the blue Rockies in back. But I would have smelled from beer afterwards which was no good either. Or sit in the kitchen, maybe, except Pauline was there. Her Indian name was Slow Water, an image which fit the old woman well, if you can imagine a big pond with no ripple but smiling most of the time. And if there was anything I couldn't stand then it was being smiled at.

"Mister Miner?" she called from the kitchen.

I went to the kitchen and said, "What do you want?"

Pauline stood there with her big arms white to the elbow; and a sweet odor of cake-making all over her and, of course, she was smiling.

"You coming straight back from town or you going to linger a while?" she asked me.

"Linger? I'm coming straight back from the station. I don't see, Pauline, why you...."

"I'm asking because of the kitchen." She kept smiling at me all the time. "If you linger I got a chance to clean up before you come back. Why don't you and the young lady linger somewheres on the way...."

"You can stop using that word," I said. Pauline now started to giggle. "And stop acting like a catastrophe. You yourself got married four times, by your own count."

"Only once, for the first time," and she slapped the dough on the table and laughed like a donkey braying.

I left the kitchen.

"And never," she yelled after me, "as late as you're doing it." More braying.

I slammed the door shut and went out on the porch. If it had been up to Pauline she would have arranged for some damn fertility rite, something tribal and terrible.

I felt cold about ceremonies. I felt very warm about Jane—warm is an inadequate word—and all she and I wanted was to be together, live here together, and no more trips from here to Frisco for a short, hectic visit and then months of waiting again.

I had never been married before. There had been a lot of things I had never done before, but then they had turned out all right. I had never raised cattle before, I had never owned land, I had never before committed myself as much as now.

Eight years is a long time or a short time. It depends on whether anything changes. In my case, things had changed a hell of a lot.

Far down the valley the train was just coming out of the woods. The locomotive tossed white cloud puffs into the air and moved out from under them. On the next puff nothing came, which always happened just before the train hooted. Then the whistle shot out a long jet of steam, then another moment or so because of the distance, and then I could hear it. That was the second signal. The train was up to the cattle pass which meant twenty more minutes to the station.

I couldn't wait any longer. If I drove fast I might even catch the train where it ran along the south highway for a while and if Jane sat at the right side of the train we could wave at each other going fast in the same direction. Then I would wait for her at the station and having seen her just a short while ago, perhaps the meeting wouldn't be such a strain for me.

The whole thing was ridiculous, chasing along next to the train. I crossed the yard to the barn, walking stiff and hard. If this was a big step it was the best big step I'd ever taken. Bar none. Not even eight years ago— I went into the barn to get out the jeep and no matter what time it was I would drive straight down to Big Rock and wait at the station. I would be nervous as hell and happy because seeing Jane had never failed to do that to me and she'd know it for what it meant, that I loved her and wanted her for all time.

Luke had cleaned up the jeep for the trip because I wanted it to look good and not so much like a mud crawler. I did not own a car then but just the jeep and a carryall. I walked all around the jeep. Luke had cleaned it good and I knew Jane would like it. But then I saw that the tires were clean on one side only. On one side Luke had washed down to the black rubber but on the other side he had left clods of the yellow mud paste hanging all over the tires. I thought, Damn that Luke bastard. He's good for nothing but digging fence posts and singing to the cattle. He can't count higher than two. But then I knew Jane would just laugh about it and she'd probably like Luke best of all because he was gentle and had a peculiar way with the cattle, like a good mother with a small baby. But nevertheless to hell with that Luke bastard, and I started to clean up the tires myself.

When I got to the depot the train was just pulling in with the bell in front going slower and slower. There were crates of chickens on the platform and when the train rattled by, all the crates came alive with squawking and feather fluttering, all of which could have been funny some other time but not a good background for me taking Jane in my arms. I was now too anxious about see-

ing Jane to worry about chickens or anything and just watched the train doors
when the brakes made their final squeal and the row of cars stopped.

Jane came out first. Or I saw her first. She had to come down the steep steps
from the car, stretching her legs. It was a pleasure to see. And then she saw
me and just jumped down to the platform not caring how it looked. It looked
very good. She came running with her hair flying and her face all open; it was
such a pleasure I didn't know what was happening to me because I could have
been crying or laughing or both; it was all the same.

We had a long hug and a long kiss as if we didn't mean to let go ever again,
which was true in a way. A great deal had changed for me over the years and
having Jane now was part of that and nothing was going to change it back.

"John," she said, and "John, let go a minute," so I gave her some room.

She smiled up at me but it didn't have the same spirit, as when she came
running to me. It was a small smile, almost mannered. "I was going to come
alone, John, you know that. But I couldn't help—" she stopped when she saw
me look up and I looked back to the train door where she had been. "John,"
she said, "be nice to him. He won't bother us—"

Getterman came out of the train, stooped as ever, small as ever, but there
he was. Getterman was Jane's father.

If I had not known Getterman I would never have known his daughter. I
had known Getterman for many years, but that had been business and all that
had changed. He and I didn't dislike each other but that's the most I could
say about it. Even when I used to come to see his daughter he and I had little to do with each other. What we had in common we didn't discuss, and if
it pleased him that I liked his daughter, he kept that to himself too. Nor had
he ever tried to interfere between me and Jane—unless this was the switch,
because here he was, walking up the platform.

"Miner," he said, "how are you—" His smile was more an apology than a
gesture of friendship.

"Fine, Getterman. Fine." I let go of Jane and looked at him. "You come along
for the ride?" I wasn't especially friendly about it. I mostly wanted an answer.
When he shrugged and didn't answer right away I said, "You come along for
the wedding?"

"Don't mind me," he said. He smiled at Jane, looked at me, glanced at the
chickens, looked back at me. "I don't want— I just wanted to see you, some-
time..." and there was something so pathetic about him now, I hated to look
at him. He turned aside for the suitcases.

"Be nice to him," she whispered to me. "He isn't..." but then she had to stop
because Getterman was back carrying suitcases.

"I don't know how you're set up, Miner, but I can get a room here in town
someplace. I just wanted to see—"

"Don't be an idiot," I said. I felt curt and awkward. "Lemme have those suitcases."

Then I jerked my head at both of them and went ahead to the jeep. I was-
n't being nice to him, the way Jane had asked it, but I did let him come along
to the ranch.

He sat in back with the baggage and Jane and I sat in front. There was no
talk on the way back. Jane tried to talk to me and took my arm with both her
hands around it, but I couldn't pay any attention. I fought the wheel back
and forth a lot as if there were plenty of hidden ruts but that was just for dis-
traction. The dirt road to the ranch was nice and smooth and the swell of the
grazing land with the big pines in the back was some of the prettiest landscape
I had ever seen. It had been my thought to tell Jane about this, to show her
how far my land went and what else I was hoping to buy in time, if the beef
prices held, but none of that came to me now. I didn't even see anything except the road in front. All I felt was a place in the back of my head, something
spreading like a fluid itch down over my neck, the place where I felt Getterman was keeping his eyes, sitting in back there and watching me. I had to turn
around then, doing it fast, but Getterman wasn't even looking at me. He sat
in back holding on with both hands, his head drawn in and eyes closed. He
looked pitiful.

"Don't go so fast," said Jane close to my ear.

I felt like a bastard. I slowed down right away and the next time she
squeezed my arm I looked at her and was able to smile. She smiled back and
sat close, almost as if we were alone.

When we pulled into the ranch I made a wide swing through the yard, past
the barn, the bunk house, the stalls and the silo, and up to the main house
which looked big and flat with the long porch in front. We had painted it
white just a week before and Pauline had put a geranium pot on each side of
the steps. The big yard had been raked, and the hitching rail had a saddle on
it. That was no place for a saddle, of course, however Luke had wanted it
there, because he had seen that type of thing in the Saturday movies.

"It looks beautiful, John," said Jane.

I enjoyed hearing that. She had seen the place once, but that had been right
after I'd bought it, a mess everywhere.

"Yes. Very beautiful," said Getterman.

That spoiled it for me. I didn't answer and got out of the jeep. Then Pauline
came out of the door and stood on the porch and I introduced her around.
That should have been a fine occasion too, because Pauline loved Jane sight
unseen, but it was all wrong now. There was one of those idiotic struggles
for the luggage between me and Getterman, ending with Pauline carrying
most of it into the house, and to top off my mood Pauline had to sidle up in
the hallway and casting her eyes down—a thing she never did normally: "Had
no chance to linger, did you—but don't worry. The kitchen's all clean."

I went through the showing of rooms, offering cake and coffee in Pauline's
kitchen, then a short walk through the barn and a look at the corral, but it

was all just a prelude. Jane knew it, going through all the motions quickly, and Getterman must have known it, trailing along and saying nothing. When I saw Luke riding in that was my chance and I called him over to have him meet Jane. They were friendly with each other right from the start and Luke took her back to the corral to show Jane how he sang to the cattle. I said, "Come on, Getterman," and he and I went back to the house.

I sat down on the porch and he sat down next to me. I put my feet up on the railing, but he didn't, sitting drawn up the way he must sit at a desk.

"Beer?" I said.

"I would like a shot."

I called this out to Pauline and we sat in silence while we waited for the shot and the beer. I could see Luke and Jane by the corral, Jane leaning there with one foot up on a rail in spite of her skirt and Luke calling. There was just a cow in the corral and her calf and they both watched Luke, or listened to him. In a while, so help me, if that calf didn't leave her mother and come trotting over to Luke and suck on his fingers. The cow stayed back, staring.

Pauline gave me the beer and she gave Getterman a waterglass partly filled with whisky. He spun the ice cube around while Pauline went back in the house and I took a long pull from the bottle. It had a cold bite going down which is what I wanted. I waited for Getterman to take his drink but when he had done so he still didn't talk. He looked at the blue mountains.

"What is it?" I said. "What worries you, Getterman?"

He said, "Farret is back."

I put the beer down and very slowly worked one hand into the other. It made the knuckles crack....

CHAPTER TWO

Eight years ago and maybe five thousand miles away we had this set up. I was in it, Getterman was in it and that Farret. Farret also had a girl working with us, his girl, and the fifth one was Metz. If anyone was the leader I sup-pose Metz was the one, because he had the money to start with and he was the oldest. Metz worked the end on the mainland, Getterman was on the is-land, and Farret, his girl, and I, we worked the run in between. We ran guns.

Cervales was the man in the mountains who bought our guns and the one to watch out for was Duz, General Duz, because he was in power and mean-ing to stay that way. In his eyes we were revolutionaries, just like Cervales, though this was not true. I, for one, never knew just what they fought about and not until later did I find out that Cervales was really no better than Duz.

Metz had the money and contacts to procure arms and ammunition. He set it up on the mainland.

Getterman was on the island, running a tourist bureau at the time, and that's how he was the business contact for the deal with Cervales who used to send his instructions, and sometimes the money, to one of Getterman's offices.

I made the run across the Gulf. I had a twenty-year-old Chris Craft, a beat looking 28-foot scow with a rusty pulpit over the bow and a big cockpit with the chairs taken out, because I had the boat fitted for bottom fishing. The cabin slept four, there was a small galley, and I had a head which was all chipped enamel. Nothing looked new. Not even the engine. But the engine was a 1000 H.P. Marine Buddah and the bronze prop would have looked good on a 50-foot dragger. The hull was fitted with white oak ribs, built in extra to take the strain, but that didn't show. The whole hull was double and so was the deck. The fantail, the poop, everything double. This gave me cargo space.

Farret was a bum. I found Farret. We needed a man to take the stuff into the mountains or at least partway up to a rendezvous. I did this for a while but it wasted time and most of all it kept the boat inshore too long.

That day I was in the capital because sometimes I picked up the money there to take back to the States by boat. I had four hours to kill so I went to the *Donna Mobile* which was a good eating place. It was large and cool, with white marble all over the walls, with two espresso machines, one at each end of the counter, and the counter carefully done in heavy mahogany, showing columns, leaves, naked maidens and so forth. A stainless steel machine squeezed sugarcane juice and the other thing I remember was the large bin with sweet rolls. That, and the little tables, was the restaurant.

I went through to the back, nodded at the cook, went out through the court which was all overgrown with fat plants, and into the door to the shed. It was dim and moist there and only one card table was going. There were five men at the table. The pile of chips, I saw, wasn't big. In a while one man got up and gave me his seat. He was wearing the uniform of the Duz army, a corporal, and he must have been out of money. I bought his seat and sat down, telling the rest of them that I had just three hours. There should be no misunderstanding, in three hours I had to go.

The game went back and forth, never much either way, and we mostly ganged up on one man who was a pigeon. He was small and fat, sweating heavily, and he lost all the time. He kept saying *Oi, oi, oi,* in the most comical way and keeping his humor, so we all laughed when he did it, when he lost—which he did most of the time—and we bought him the drinks and *fritos*. It was a friendly game.

Except for one man, which was Farret.

He was a young man. I saw this by his hands and his neck. But he had very old eyes. I don't mean old and wise in any poetic sense, but old eyes because of the veins that showed and because of the sick-looking skin around them. His eyes stuck out and he moved them fast. The reason I didn't like him was because his eyes moved too fast. That's the only reason.

He had clammy-looking hair which he kept tossing back, and his clothes hung badly on his thin frame. He looked hungry. He was hungry then, but later when he wasn't he still looked the same.

The little fat man's name was Julio and this time only Julio and Farret were left in the game. Julio was a hopeless bluffer, so we all dropped out one by one, except Farret, the hungry one. He sat over his cards bent like a vulture and for once he was even grinning.

"Raise me five?" he said to Julio. "As long as you're teasing, I'll play along. And raise you five more."

Julio sweated, but he always sweated. He looked at all of us but we all looked bored.

"I die," said Julio, "but I can't die ignorant."

"Cost you five," said Farret.

"I see you," said Julio and put his chips in the pot.

Farret dropped his cards so they ended up on the table in the form of a fan. Pair of five, pair of jacks, and a king.

"I die!" said Julio. "I have the same pictures!" A five, a jack, and three kings.

We all laughed and stomped and slapped Julio's back. But not Farret. He said nothing. He sat there, and as if he were just passing the time and it meant nothing, he gathered the cards around him and fingered through all of them. But the deck must have been all right because he said nothing.

Next hand, Julio took the pot with a flush. Farret was the loser. Next hand, Farret lost again and this time Julio beat him with a low pair.

"You son of a bitch!" said Farret in English and slammed down his cards.

"What did he say? What's that?" and Julio smiled back and forth from one face to the other nervously.

"I said you're a son of a hoor," in Spanish this time, "and I'll take it back if you got the guts and show me how you cheated!" said Farret.

"The outrage—" Julio got up when Farret grabbed him by the front of the shirt. It ripped.

"Nobody cheats *me*," said Farret and he practically spat this in the little man's face. "Nobody...."

"Let go of him," I said and got up too.

I was going to say it a second time when Farret let go of Julio and turned on me. "You been feeding it to him! You lousy...."

"Get out," I said. "Get out now."

"Make me!" and Farret was clear of the table now, facing me. He was crouching and a switchblade snapped in his hand.

He held it well. He stood crouched, somewhat like a tackle, one foot forward, one back. Both his hands were forward of the line of his head, the knife looking at me, weaving, like a snake testing the air. Then, without looking down, he switched hands. Right, left, right, left, so I wouldn't know which side would strike—

But Farret switched hands much too slowly, just to impress. I could see when he tossed the knife and how it sailed in an arc from one hand to the other, he did it that slowly. It looked very menacing.

I was younger then and pretty nervous, which meant I could be quite fast. Next toss and my foot came out while the knife was in mid-air. Farret, who did not want to lose his knife, had to hold still where he was in order to catch it and that's how my foot clipped his hand. The receiving hand. The knife fell to the floor, Farret ducked to retrieve it and so put the target where I wanted it best.

I kicked him hard in the temple. He slammed into the table but before he sagged I was up close and kneed his chin. Not hard—I wasn't that angry—but enough to make a good thud and to snap his head back and give him momentum to a slam lengthwise on the floor. He hit the back of his head which hurt more, I think, than what I had been doing.

By then everybody had left. That's the convention in such a place. I sat down on the table and smoked while Farret collected himself. I didn't know what next but I wanted to see Farret up. He was a rat, a vicious rat and intense. Somehow, that gave me a feeling for him. Maybe it just meant that I wanted to hit him again.

He got up slowly, he weaved a little and came just a little closer. But from that dreamy condition he suddenly windmilled at me, landing several times, before I could roll myself over the table and out of the way. I was down on the floor, watching him come, with my legs doubled and feet his way. He remembered about my feet then and stopped out of reach.

"Had enough?" he said.

My ribs hurt on one side and he had cut me over one cheekbone with the ring he was wearing. I thought it was fine for him to think I was mortally wounded.

"Yes," I said. "Now step back."

To my surprise, he did.

"I always even the score," he said, watching me.

"Must keep you busy," I said, but he didn't see the humor of it.

"Keep the balance sheet balanced," he said. "At all times." He said this like it was a creed.

I looked at him and lit a cigarette because he had knocked the other one out of my mouth. He was a rat all right. A hungry rat keeping alive on his principles.

"You broke?" I said.

"Not the first time."

If he had said it was temporary and he had a big deal on, something big that would break any minute, I would have walked out right then.

"How come you don't make a touch?" I asked him.

He spat and said, "You don't owe me nothing."

A real fine set of principles I saw there. I didn't give a damn about his principles but the fact that he was stiff that way interested me. Somebody predictable I can handle.

"Come along," I said and went to the door.

He didn't ask why or argue, he just came. That was good to know too.

We went through the leafy court and into the restaurant in the front. The cook was there and one waiter and I had meant to walk through when the waiter said, "Señor Miner? There is a meal here for you, and for the other one," he nodded at Farret.

"For free?" said Farret.

"From Julio," said the waiter.

Julio had meant to keep it a friendly game, to the end. I appreciated that and said yes, I'd have a meal. Farret sat down too, because he hadn't eaten in a day and a half.

That's how I met him. We talked a while longer and after I had softened him up with some stories about the things I'd been doing—about gambling in Florida, about rum-running for some of the fancy hotels who weren't too fancy to cheat on the liquor tax—after that he told me what I wanted to know.

I didn't explain to him how I had gotten to the point where I was, that I had been too much of a drifter to stick out the slow grind of legitimate work. I had been a shrimper. My father had left me the boat. But to say I was a drifter would have been to say I was like Farret himself.

"I'm on the lam," he said.

"You sound like you're proud of it."

"Look," he said, "I just ate. I feel heavy. Don't bother me." He sat back and started to poke his teeth with a toothpick he had in his shirt pocket.

It was fine with me that he felt this way, slower than he had been before, because with the touchiness gone he would be easier to talk to. It wasn't a question of liking him better but of learning to know him better. I needed an extra man and there were these few things I had noticed which might be just right for the job; needing money, being in hiding, that curious code of playing by the rules, the predictable way he had about principles.

"How long you been on the island?"

"Three years."

"You know any people here?"

"I'm friendly and trusting," he said.

His eyes weren't going so fast any more, as a matter of fact he kept staring at me. He did this without trying to hide it, but kept looking at me as if to make it insulting.

"You don't want to talk?" I said.

"Why should I?"

I shrugged, as much to gain time to think a moment as to show him he couldn't rile me. I was beginning to wonder just how useful that new behavior of Farret's might be.

"I'm asking," I said, "because if I knew you better I might tell you more."

He just raised his eyebrows—making sure I saw it—and sucked on his toothpick.

"Because as long as you're not eating regular," I kept at it, "you might be interested."

"And I don't know you from Adam," he said.

It started to feel as if I was the one applying for a job with his company. I lit a cigarette and said nothing. Maybe if I talked less he'd show more—

"All I know about you," he said, "is you fed that fat guy the cards."

I said, "Crap." Nothing else.

"Maybe," he said. "Maybe yes, maybe no. And if there's one thing is against my principles, it's hanging around guys that don't play by the rules."

I was getting bored. He was still stuck with that problem of having lost at the table, which was no recommendation as far as my interest was concerned. I put out my cigarette, and without expecting an answer I said, "So why in hell are you hanging around?"

"I'm trying to figure out if you fed him the cards," he said, "because if you...."

I interrupted to tell him he should go to hell and got up. He got up too. He walked to the street with me and gave a slight nod when I said, "See you," which was something I said out of habit. Then I walked towards the harbor and could see him still standing there in front of the restaurant when I turned a corner. He wasn't looking at me but was talking to a small kid who had stopped to ask for a cigarette probably.

I had two hours left and nothing to do till I picked up the money so I stopped in the next *bodega* which is a place where you get coffee, rum, groceries, lottery tickets, and food across the counter. I stood at the counter and had an idea that a cold bottle of beer would be good now when I saw the kid walk into the place. He was ten, maybe, and looking around for a tourist. But there were no tourists in the *bodega* which the kid must have seen almost immediately because these places are small.

"Yes?" said the counterman.

"*Café con leche.*"

I picked up my cup after the pouring was done and turned towards the street. The kid was still there, looking, but then he left.

I had two coffees and two cigarettes and then I walked toward the harbor. It would be cooler there, with the wind coming in over the water, and I find it easy to lose time when I look at boats weaving up and down on their moorings. Then I saw the kid again. He was sitting on a bollard and spitting into the water.

I watched him for a while but he wasn't watching me, except every now and then when he'd look straight at me.

I walked away from the water and into the first street. I stopped right past the corner and waited. There was the kid again. He walked along the quay, looked at me once, kept walking and bent down to pick up some stones now and then. He tossed the stones into the water.

I'd been shadowed twice or maybe three times before to my knowledge and those had always been times to be taken very seriously. Once it had to do with gambling in Florida and the other times, the more serious ones, it had been on the island. My shadows had been men who were pretty slick at their job and the idea had always been that neither would let the other one know he was watching or being watched.

But this? A ten-year-old kid who stares me straight in the face?

I did some more walking and once, on a double back, I almost lost him but then he spotted me at the last minute. After that, he stayed right on my heels.

He didn't want to talk to me, he didn't care if knew about him, he wouldn't let me out of his sight. I couldn't let him follow me where I was going and for a moment, because this was so unorthodox that it was ridiculous, I didn't know what to do. Then I stopped and turned around.

"*Niño.*"

"*Señor*"

"*Cigarillo?*"

"*Gracias,*" he said and held out his hand.

I gave him a cigarette and took one myself. We were standing next to a low wall which went around the big lawn of a public park and I sat down on the wall. He sat down next to me and waited for a light.

"You getting tired walking?" I asked him.

"A little, *señor*."

"Me too."

I lit his cigarette and then mine. We sat and smoke for a while. The way he handled all this, out in the open, I didn't know what to do except to handle the same way.

"Why are you following me?"

"Not to lose you," he said.

"Why so?"

"So I know where you are."

The boy kept smoking and he looked at me, waiting for the next question. That's all he did. He wasn't brazen about it, he didn't think it was funny, he just waited.

"Uh—look, *niño*. I want you to beat it."

"No," he said.

Obviously, I wasn't doing this right.

"Would you like to know where I'm going?" I asked

"No," he said.

Still not the right question.

"Who paid you?"

He flipped his cigarette into the street and said, "The thin man. You know, the one who came out of the restaurant with you."

For a second I thought this was very funny, but then I thought of Farret and it didn't seem funny any more. It was a little crazy. Or perhaps it was dangerous—

"Will you take me to him?"

"Of course," said the kid and got up, waiting.

We walked for twenty minutes. We passed the restaurant where Farret and I had eaten and turned up a street with old apartment houses.

There was a section of the city with houses built in European style, turn of the century. They look big and massive on the outside, dripping with senseless ornaments of stone and plaster. On the inside they are dark and cramped. The stairs are narrow, the ceilings are very high, and there are too many apartments crowded on each floor. Still, I didn't think that Farret lived here.

We walked up to the third floor.

"Who lives here?" I asked the kid.

"I don't know. He said come to the end of the corridor. This house, third floor." The kid waited for me to follow him.

The corridor was long and dark. I didn't know Farret at all, it occurred to me. It was an uneasy feeling—

A door opened in back and Farret came out. He looked at me and the kid and waited till we got closer. Then he gave the kid money, nodded at him to leave, waited till he was out of earshot.

"I guess you're all right," he said to me.

His thin face didn't change much when he said it but stayed cold and serious. It gave a patronizing air to his approval.

I took a deep breath because I didn't want to get angry.

"You sent the kid after me?" I asked him.

"Sure."

"I think you and I, fellow, better have something out." I took his arm and led him to the end of the corridor. We stood there by the window. "I don't care why you did it and I don't care that it didn't work, but I'm going to promise you...."

"But it did work."

What had been in my mind was to give Farret a stiff threat and then a stiff punch in the solar plexus, just so he was going to understand me for sure. I stuck my hands in my pockets and tried to feel calm. I could always lean on him later.

"What worked?"

"He brought you back," said Farret. He lit a cigarette and seemed very satisfied.

His pitch wasn't clear to me but what became clearer all the time was the cold, ominous quality of the man. I said, "Do you know who I am?"

"All I wanted to know."

"The more you find out, Farret, the closer...."

He interrupted me with a laugh. "What you going to do? Beat up a ten-year-old kid that's following you around on the street?"

He was very clever. I had respect for that trick of the using a boy, but I still didn't know what went on.

"You going to tell me why you had the kid bring me back, or do you want...."

"Of course," said Farret. "Like I said, either you did feed him the cards or you didn't."

"You can't let go, can you?"

"I can now. Like I said, you're all right."

"I didn't cheat you?"

"No."

"And if I had?"

"Why think about it? You didn't."

I did think about it, because in those days, on the island, any number of things could have messed me up and a cold bastard with a monomania like Farret's could really get dangerous before he'd let go.

"I couldn't ask you and be sure of the answer," Farret said to me, "so I asked Julio. And I wanted to tell you what he had to say. That's why I got the kid to maneuver you back here."

I said, you son of a bitch, or something like that but then it struck me what he had said about Julio.

"Where is he?" I said. "Where's Julio?"

"He's all right," said Farret. "He's fine," and he looked at one of the doors in the corridor.

Julio was on his bed. There was just the one room with the bed and the rest of the furniture, and when I came in Julio was staring at the high ceiling. Then he turned his head to look at me. He looked sick.

"You hurt?" I asked him and went to the bed.

He tried to smile but it was a pretty weak smile. One side of his face was a little bit puffed, and, he explained, his stomach hurt. Farret had hit him hard in the stomach. Farret had seen to it that everything hurt quite a bit and in that way made sure that Julio wasn't going to lie. No, Julio had insisted in spite of everything, nobody had cheated.

"I believed him," said Farret. He had come into the room. "Or else he wouldn't be lying there *talking.*"

I turned around and went to the door. Farret stepped aside for me to get by but I kicked the door shut. I didn't want Farret to leave. I looked at him and the amazement must have showed in my face because Farret got belligerent right away.

"Look," he said. "I don't want trouble from you and I don't want trouble from him there, but you rub me the wrong way and I don't forget. I keep the...."

"...balance sheet balanced," I finished for him.

For a moment he didn't say anything because it seemed to surprise him that I should know as much as he did. He started to say something else when Julio talked from the bed.

"And my money," he said. "He took the money—"

"You did?" I asked Farret.

Farret just shrugged and started towards the door.

"Give it back," I said. I felt it was time to set up the proper relationship.

"You can go frig—"

It was time. I backhanded him over the nose so the knuckles would really dig and he bumped into the door backwards. He was blind with tears and the nose must have hurt him all the way up to the roof of the skull. I then used his kind of language to get through.

"Same as you, Farret, I'm going to keep it even. He didn't cheat when he got the money, so give it back."

He gave it back.

Then Farret and I walked out together.

I thought about it for a moment and then decided that Farret was a prospect again. The same qualifications like before—no money, a stickler for rules, the predictable way he had with his principles—same as before; more so.

He would do fine for the job, and I tried to think of him that way and nothing personal. Perhaps I should have thought more about the lengths to which he would go, but I only thought about him as a short range problem.

I took him to the first *bodega* and I bought the coffee. I told him to sit, to keep his mouth shut, and to listen. He did all that and I told him about the job of taking the guns up to the mountains. I just teased him with some of it and he was interested. I got him some makeshift job with Getterman's tourist bureau and while that went on, for another week, I checked on him stateside. Metz was a great help there, since Metz knew a number of people who know a great deal. It had been through Metz in the first place that I had started to get anywhere. The gambling at first, then the rum running, then this. Metz and I had set the gun business up together.

Farret, it turned out, had knocked over a filling station some place in Louisiana and the town constable had caught him cold. But the constable had been old and friendly, which meant only one thing to Farret, an advantage. Before they even got to jail Farret had jumped the old man, beaten him, and had bolted away in the police car. Furthermore he had crossed the state line.

Farret, just as he had told me, had been on the island three years. He had to sit out several more to get past the statute of limitations.

I gave Farret the job. He took the guns up into the mountains. Even when he used a guide, it was Farret who was the head man. He was loyal or what we used to call loyal, meaning very jealous of proper authority: he was boss here, I was boss there, somebody else elsewhere. That kind of thing. It made him a good tool. A while later he sent for his girl, whose name was Lena. With his cool sense of duty, Farret assigned functions to her. She was a dull girl but with a soft, sexy body, and she was very blonde, a premium attribute in that part of the land. By shacking her up with the right kind of people Farret improved his work and saved himself a great deal of money.

That was the five of us. Metz, Getterman, Farret, Lena. And I was in it. In the end we got caught very badly, but we got away by the skin of our teeth. We all cut out in different directions and for my part, at least, that was the end of it.

CHAPTER THREE

"He's back, and looking," said Getterman. He finished what was in his glass with one toss.

"You're worried?" I said. I didn't know what else to say at the moment. I myself felt worried.

"Anything that's got to do with *that* time, John, worries me."

I would have been more specific. Anything that had to do with Farret in particular was worth watching out for—

"What did you mean, he's looking?"

Getterman got up and walked back and forth on the porch. He looked at his daughter down by the corral but I don't think he saw her.

"You know what I'm doing now," he said. "I'm an eighty-a-week office man and I don't mind. I even like it that way. I do nothing else and I look nowhere else. Except we deal with cargoes. Tea, balsa, corned beef."

"I know."

"So you know." He was excited and it made him snappish. "You also know we handle payrolls? Crew payrolls?"

"I have tried to know as little about you as possible," I said. I wanted to tell him that I, just as he, wanted no contact since that time eight, or nine years ago, when everything split.

He paid no attention to what I had meant and said, "We deal in cargoes. Only South American cargoes. That's how the crew is, South American mostly."

"Is it important?" I picked up the beer while I said this and I'm sure it looked offhanded. I was nervous as hell.

"It's important because Farret was in one of the crews mustering out in Frisco!"

"Still a bum," I said.

"Bum? Believe me, Miner, I looked into that. I know one or two people in Frisco and they looked into Farret just so I don't have to worry."

"They looked and now you're worried."

"Yes. My friend spends an evening with him, two evenings maybe, and you know what's what with him?"

I said nothing, just waited and drank some beer.

"First of all he's got money!"

"That's why he shipped out as a deck hand."

"He shipped out of Chile as a deck hand because he couldn't let on there that he had a pile. He says he has a pile. He spends like it."

"Mustering out pay."

"Don't argue with me, Miner. Please. He has all this money, he says, and he says he's going to have more. Lots more. He's using the money he's got for one thing, he says. For an investment. He's investing in an all-out search for the fifty thousand owing him from a big job in the past. Now what do you think, Miner, he means by *that?*"

"Maybe he's talking about eight years back?"

"You bet he's talking about that! There's five bastards, he says, who are going to pay up what's owing him."

I got up. I looked at Getterman, who stood there worn and pathetic, and I nodded at him. I even tried to give him a smile, just for his benefit.

"I'm worried too," I said. "Believe me."

It helped him and it helped me. It was the truth.

"I don't remember Farret being a braggart," I said. "Maybe he does have dough."

"And if he does he can move that much better!"

"You sure he thinks somebody owes him?"

"Am I *sure?*"

"Don't screech, Getterman. You know nobody owes him. Everything went to pieces, that's all that happened."

"Am I sure?" he said again. "My friend, just to dig more information out of him, made believe he didn't believe Farret. You know what happened?"

"Come on, what?"

"Farret gets rough! They start hitting each other and then Farret did something to him with a cigarette! My man's in a hospital!"

"I'm sorry to hear that," I said. I walked away a little, so that old Getterman would stop talking. I wanted some quiet for just a while, to get the picture. It sounded like Farret all right. It sounded like the same man of eight years ago, only more so. More rigid, more proud, more fanatic and so, more cruel.

"I think he's crazy," said Getterman.

Even that, maybe. I said, "I'll have to think about this."

"You mean you're going to sit here and wait for him?"

"I don't want him around here," I said. "I'm sure of that."

Then I walked to the corral, looking for Jane.

She was at the silo where Luke was trying to show her something. He was trying to make her come closer and look into the small door of the silo, but Jane was shaking her head and holding her nose all this time. I heard her laugh and then she saw me. She said something to Luke, waved at him, and ran over to me. She had taken her shoes off and her stockings, which was sensible considering the high heels she had worn.

"Did I stay long enough?" she called, coming closer.

Too long, I thought, much too long.

"It's something serious," she said, and took my arm. We started to walk back to the main house.

I said, "It has to do with eight years ago, when your father and I were running guns. You know about that."

"Yes," she said. "I know about that."

"It's over. It's meant to be over. You know that."

"I know."

"One of the men who was in it," I told her, "has shown up and perhaps it means trouble. Your father thinks so."

"He worries, John."

"I worry, Jane." I stopped and put my hands on her arms. I turned her my way and said, "I have reasons to worry now, because I care. I love you and you are valuable to me."

"Give me a kiss," she said.

We held each other a moment and then I had to finish.

"Even meeting you has no strings with the past," I said. "I met you after that business, and I met you in spite of your father."

"He almost quit his job and moved out," she said, "that time you ran into him, in Frisco."

"I feel the same about him. It's all right that way. It's artificial, but it's a price for having two lives in one lifetime and wanting to kill one of them off."

"And now it's alive again?"

"I don't know," I said. "But I have to find out."

We got back to the porch then and there was really much more to say.

"You stay here," I said, "while I'm gone."

"Gone?" she said, and her laugh was a little bit nervous. "You make it sound so ominous."

"It won't be long," I said. I waved my hand around and looked at the house. "This is going to be yours, Jane. Stay here, wait for me, and in a day or so when I'm back...."

"It's just a notion," she said, "isn't it? Like a rumor. Something my father has built up in his mind, and in a short while it's going to pass and evaporate. Isn't that right, John?"

There was a great deal of hope in her voice, and a stubborn note. If she just kept believing that way, about its all being Getterman's fears, then she would stay safely here and the whole thing might pass before she would have to start thinking differently about Farret's being back in the country. I wanted to think of it that way myself.

"Yes," I said. "It's one of those lousy things, one of those little things that comes up, nags at you and then passes."

"Then I'll go with you," she said. "I want to be with you while it passes and then we can come back here together. And we'll start together, the way it was planned." She smiled at me. "Did I fool you?" she said and then put her head down, against my chest. "I didn't fool you, same as you didn't fool me. Maybe father didn't make something up that's going to evaporate. You're worried about it, and I am."

I put my hand on the back of her head and held her. "But let me do it alone," I said. "I'll worry less, with you here."

"I'm going along."

"Jane—"

"I'm going along." She pushed herself away so she could look at my face. "John, the way I love you I *must* be with you."

"I know. I feel the same way, Jane. But I couldn't have had you ten years ago, darling, and I can't have you now. Not till I know...."

She stopped me by just shaking her head. I felt a great warmth and love for her, for feeling the way she did and for acting the way she did. And the whole Farret thing wasn't so real anyway. Mostly Getterman's fear. I would take Jane along and it would be all right.

I took her face in my hands and kissed her and we didn't say anything else about this. We felt it would make the trip back to Frisco much less important.

On the trip to Frisco Getterman could tell me no more than he had already and when we got out at the station in Frisco he and I were relieved to be able to go our own ways. "Call me at home," he said, "or at the office," and I said, "Of course, I will, and don't worry." I stood in the big hall with Jane and watched Getterman walk away. He could have been a stranger.

"What do you do first?" Jane asked me.

"I'll get a room," I said, "so there's a place where you can reach me."

She frowned but I picked up my overnight bag, took her arm, and started to walk out to the taxis.

"You can stay at my place," she said. "You don't have to get a room."

Jane didn't live in her father's apartment. I knew she still had her own place, in spite of the marriage she and I were planning, because her rent wasn't up and her things hadn't been shipped to the ranch yet. I didn't want to stay at her place for a simple reason. Just in case there was anything to this thing with Farret, just in case he was here and looking, I was not going to stay in the same place with Jane. If I tracked Farret, he might track me. I didn't want him to track me to Jane.

"How come you're still maintaining," I said, and I used the word maintaining to make it sound funny, "how come you're still maintaining separate quarters while coming to my ranch with the notion of marriage? How come you find it necessary...."

"Don't try to lead me by the nose," she said. "You don't want to come over so you can keep me out of things. All right, get your own room. It'll feel more illicit," and then she grinned at me while I tried to look stern and hailed a taxi.

I took a room in a little hotel downtown and paid for one night. With luck that was all I would need. Then I told Jane to go home, I'd call her later, because my first step wouldn't interest her very much anyway and I'd hate to bore her, I said, with something undangerous. She surprised me by making no objections.

It wasn't much of a contact. I didn't know where Farret was and for that matter I didn't know what I would say to him should I meet him. The only concrete thing I knew about Farret was the man Getterman had sent after him.

The man who had tried to help Getterman lived on Decker Street and his name was Al Marco. It was getting dark now, around seven, and Decker Street was a sight of gloom. I got out of the taxi and stood there under a light. The taxi bounced down the slanting street, the taillights looking fuzzy from the moisture in the air, and when the car turned the corner the street was quite empty.

I found the door to Al Marco's place on the top floor of his tenement building. I smelled mold in the hallway. I knocked and he yelled, "Come in."

I walked into the kitchen.

Al Marco looked short and mean. He had his feet on the kitchen table and watched me while I closed the door.

"My name's John Miner," I said. "Getterman sent me."

"Go to hell and get out," he said. When he talked he slavered. A vicious swelling distorted his lower lip, with the soreness inside and yellow salve on that.

I went to the kitchen table and sat down on a chair. Marco had turned on a gas heater to burn the wet out of the air. There was a lot of close heat in the room.

"Don't you want Farret?" I asked him.

He let me stay then. He swore and he talked a lot, but said nothing new.

"Where does Farret live?" I asked Marco.

"When I saw him, he told me the Colony Towers."

I looked around for a phone but didn't see one. It could wait. "You met him there?" I asked.

"I met him in a crummy place on a crummy street by pier five. That's where."

"Look, Marco," I said. "I hate to put you through all this twice, but I'm asking for a reason. I want to know if Farret is loaded. A guy that drinks at a crummy place and talks about living at the Colony...."

"He bought all the drinks and so on. That's all I know. And the next time I meet him—"

"It makes a difference if he's got dough," I cut in on him, "because it tells me how fast he can move, how thoroughly he can look for whatever he's looking for. You understand?"

"He wore a pea jacket and he was shaved clean."

"He's always shaved clean."

"And smelled from toilet water. Five bucks a bottle, he told me."

"He could still be just on a spree."

"He mentioned the traveling he's going to do. All over the States."

"Where? He mentioned places?"

"Everywhere, he said. But first, he said, he's going to stretch his legs here. Stretch his legs, he said."

"What did he mean? Stay here?"

"If he's here," said Marco and wiped spit from his chin, "I'll find him."

"Yes," I said. I thought about what I knew and it came to nothing. Farret is going to stay and he's going to leave. He's got dough, or he doesn't. He brags and he's cagey. I said, "What do you do, Marco, may I ask?"

"Docks. Union steward." He put his feet down on the floor and looked into his palm. "Now, as soon as I'm better," he said, "I'm going to comb...."

"Marco. That ship Farret was on, is it still here? Is the crew still here?"

"Sure. Four days for loading. And that's exactly what I'm going to do. Find me a crew man off that boat...."

"Where?"

"Where what?" He didn't like being interrupted.

"Where do you look for that crew?"

"Empire Arms. You know where that is? A bunch of them went to the Empire Arms. One of those Mexicans runs it, from Chile."

"A Chilean."

"What I said. They get rates, if they're Mexicans from Chile."

The hotel was on Mission Street. That's quite a ways from the waterfront and more like skid row than sailors' territory, but the crew got rates and the host was a countryman.

First I found a phone down the block and tried calling the Colony Towers. There was no such hotel. That took care of that.

It took me half an hour to find a taxi. I felt cold in the wet street after Marco's hot kitchen, and by the time I got to Mission I didn't feel in an interviewing mood.

Looking down Mission Street you see more seatown missions than bars, which should make the sight of so many winos a mystery. Unless they need hymn singing and confessionals as much as they need to get drunk. I found the Empire Arms between a place called the Harbor Light Haven and a boarded-up store. I had a time finding the hotel because the sign wasn't lit and the building was no wider than the size of a room. But there were four stories, and the desk, for some reason, was on the third floor. I had to wake up the clerk and was in a fine temper by then.

"No rooms," was the first thing he said.

He looked smooth and blank. The Inca face and the hooked nose reminded of a hungry bird. The next contrast was the tight, white shirt, buttoned all the way up, and starched. It destroyed the face.

"The crew of the *Veronica Mendes* lives here," I said. "I have to see one of the crew."

"Which one?"

"Juan," I said. I was sure there was a Juan.

"They have a party. You can't see."

The man wasn't the clerk, he was the owner. When he was finished talk-ing he sat down.

I pulled out a five and kept folding it while I was talking. "I've got to see him. It won't take very long. He can go back to his party...."

"You can put away money," he said. "They have a party. Two months at sea and now they have a party. Nobody talks."

I took a deep breath and just stood there for a while, wanting to give all this up and reminding myself that I couldn't, not as long as there was doubt about Farret.

It was very quiet in the hotel, dim and quiet. I saw a corridor lined with nothing but doors, narrow and distorted. The sight could have been painted on two dimensions.

"They don't talk," said the man again. "They drink wine quiet and they have women." He thought I had been listening for the party.

It was a strange image he drew. Silent wine drinking and sex quietly, in a house built in two dimensions, and a ritual with it perhaps, something from the Andes.

I said, "Look. I understand this. I'll come back—"

"Four more days," he said. "Come back then."

I ignored this. His English confused me. "But in the meantime maybe you know where Farret is. He's on the crew."

"He left," said the man. "He was here two days ago."

Just like that.

I said, "Two days ago? Where to?"

"Uptown."

"Uptown? You don't mean out of town?"

"He didn't say that. He didn't say he would leave yet."

"Not yet?" I pumped the man as much as I could but all he said was Farret had left here, Farret was thinking of staying in town, and later—who knows when—he had plans of traveling.

I left and went to the phone in the first bar on the street. I called Getter-man who was already in bed and told him to lock all his doors and windows. I told him all I knew at this time was that Farret might still be in town. No,

Getterman's name hadn't been mentioned, but nothing else had been mentioned either. I would spend a few days, I didn't like this any better than he did.

Farret had time, he had money, he had four names on his list. Maybe Getterman would be the first.

Chapter Four

I've sat out a number of things. I've waited for a good hand to come up or even a miracle hand to make good for a week's losses. I once sat out five days in the Channel of Yucatan, the propeller fouled with the net and the short wave getting weaker and weaker. And other things where you do nothing but sit in the dark. But none of that was like two days in Frisco hoping that Farret would show. Or hoping he didn't show and perhaps this whole thing was just a nervous old man's conscience, or worry. Nothing happened to Getterman; nobody saw Farret. I called the hotels, rooming houses, I called my ranch. Nothing there, either. If Farret had come to Frisco looking for Getterman he would have done so and shown himself. He did nothing like that. He didn't know Getterman was in Frisco and I didn't see how he could know about me.

I sat in Jane's place where almost everything had been packed and stood around in boxes and cartons. Her rooms looked unsettled and made both of us feel as if we weren't wanted.

"I'm ready to drop it," I said.

I sat by the window and Jane came over with two cups of coffee. She sat down on a box next to me and we held the coffee cups.

"This man left San Francisco?" she asked.

"Yes. I'm sure."

"And you're sure it's over?"

I wasn't sure it was over. The thing about Farret was, I didn't know anything. All I knew was that I remembered Farret from a long time ago and that he was a rat. And that he was back in the States, for some reason. I didn't have to explain this to Jane because she said, "This way, I think you'll never be sure."

"Not till he shows up."

"Can you wait?" she asked me. "Can you sit it out?"

I shook my head.

Ten years ago, maybe. But not now. Not that kind of life any more.

"Drink your coffee," she said.

We drank coffee and I smoked. Then I said, "I'm going to see that crew once more. In the Empire Arms."

"This time I'll go with you."

She had been very good about staying in the background and now, since I felt sure Farret was out of the city, I saw no reason why she couldn't go with me. I liked her with me. Seeing Jane showed me the one good reason why I was looking for Farret at all. I smiled at her and said, fine.

It was the third day when we went to the Empire Arms together and the fifth time I had been there. The mistake had been to go there in the evening, so this time I went at ten in the morning.

The Empire Arms is not a hotel that looks right in the daytime. The stair-case is for walking up tired or beat, at the end of a day. The high corridors are night time passages to go into an anonymous room. The desk is a night desk, where a yellow bulb burns over the switchboard and the clerk needs sleep. I woke the clerk—a man I hadn't seen before—and he got up to shove the register over the counter. He barely looked at us.

"Smith or Jones?" he said.

"Smith and Jones," I told him, but it didn't sound like a joke to him nor had I meant it funny and the clerk said nothing. "I've been here before," I told him, "to see somebody in that Chilean crew."

"Which one?"

"Who's in?"

"Five are in. Which one do you want?"

"The first one," I said. "The one closest."

"Number ten," said the clerk. "But knock first."

We walked down the corridor to number ten and I asked Jane if she felt properly illicit. She said no, it was too early in the morning.

I knocked on number ten and nobody answered. I knocked again, and still nothing.

"Let me try," said Jane. She stood close to the door and called, "Are you in there? Yoohoo, are you in?" There was an immediate answer. The voice was a little sleepy, but became alert very fast. "Huh— In— Ah, yes! Come in, come in, *chiquita!*"

Jane gave me a look as if she were an expert and opened the door.

There was a very old man in the room. His face was pink from shaving. He was wrapping a blanket robe over his stomach and came towards us from the bathroom. He was smiling but then he looked a little bit puzzled.

"You came to see *me?*" he asked, and looked back and forth between me and Jane.

"Of course," said Jane. "You sounded as if you were expecting us."

The old man sighed and sat down on a chair. He had a few white hairs stand-ing up all over his skull and he did not seem to be South American.

"Oh, well," he said. "I just thought, a sweet voice at the door, I might as well say 'come in.'"

"Are you from the *Veronica Mendes?*" I asked him.

"The oldest mate of the line," he said. "Why else would I be alone here," and he smiled. He had few teeth but a very nice smile.

I smiled back at him and then Jane and I sat down on the bed.

"The reason we're here," I told him, "I'm looking for Farret."

"Oh," he said. "I know him, but he isn't here."

"You know where he is?"

"He is a friend?"

"No. I just know him."

The old man smiled again and said, "Same with me."

It seemed we understood each other.

"I don't know where he is," said the old man, "but if Ramon is around, perhaps he knows."

"Where is Ramon?"

"He went out to eat. If you wait till I dress—"

"Thank you. That's nice of you, but I can try some of the others. Someone
who's still in his room."

The old man explained that it would be no trouble for him to get dressed,
he always got dressed in the morning, and going to some of the other rooms,
he explained might not be the right thing to do with the lady.

"Does he eat nearby?" asked Jane.

"A few houses down. Why don't you wait and let me get dressed...."

"We'll wait," said Jane and we got up and went out to the corridor.

I didn't want a wild goose chase up and down Mission Street and miss some
of the other crew men who were still in the hotel, so Jane said she would go
with the old man and I should stay here and look. We'd meet at the desk. I
felt that was all right. I asked her if she didn't think it might be too illicit, but
she told me to stop making unseemly jokes and she liked the old man. He came
out, wearing a pea jacket and an old, visored cap, and he and Jane went down
to the street. I asked the clerk what other room I could try and he sent me to
number seven.

I knocked on Number seven and after the second time somebody called,
"*Pase. Pase usted.*"

I did and stayed in the door. There were two people in bed, a man and a
woman. I couldn't see the man very well because he was turned the other
way, snoring. The woman looked at me from the bed and one of her legs was
out on the cover, as if hot. She looked tired. "Yes?" she said.

I said, "Nothing. Pardon me," and turned to go.

She said "Hey," so I stopped and turned back to her. "You got any cigarettes?" she asked.

I gave her a cigarette and an extra one and lit the match for her. She was
very young and very tired.

The clerk said the next room after number seven would be all right to try.
I knocked and I heard a grunt but this time I just stuck my head in the door,
knowing there might be no point to go any further. There were two women
in the bed, both asleep, one with blonde hair and the other one dark. The man
was in a chair, with his clothes on. He looked at me but said nothing. He

seemed very tired. I closed the door and tried the next one, without knock-ing. When I came in the man there said "*Pase.*"

He did not have a woman in his bed but lay there with a bottle of beer. He had made a heap of the blankets and another heap of the pillows and was cra-dled between the two hills very comfortably. He was quite young, I thought, though it is hard to tell with some of the Indian halfcasts. He did not look sleepy, just dreamy. "You are of the *Veronica Mendes?*" I asked him in Span-ish. He jerked up very suddenly almost dropping the bottle. He looked frightened and wild. "Ai!" he said. "What day? What hour?"

"Thursday. Ten-fifteen."

He kept staring at me for a moment so I said it again. He collapsed back into his valley and a slow smile came over his face. He sighed deeply. "I was afraid," he said. "I was afraid you were from the company and I had missed a day. I had missed the *Veronica.*" He sighed again and said something else, something full of vowels and sounding happy. Maybe it was Inca.

"I won't bother you," I said. "I just want to ask you about a man in your crew. I can't find him."

"Please," he said, "go ahead." Then he handed the bottle to me. "I am very grateful to you for the day. I thought I had lost it."

The beer bottle was empty so I put it on the floor. When he realized why I had done this he again became very upset. He apologized at great length and kept saying there was more beer, we would have a fresh bottle. But he stayed on his bed.

"In there," he said and pointed my way to the bathroom.

I could hear water rushing. In the bathroom I saw that the toilet was run-ning, a swift whirlpool of water. I looked around but saw no bottles.

"In the toilet. The toilet," he kept calling after me.

I found them after a while, in the toilet tank. There were three quarts in there and all the wire gadgets and levers were bent in the tank.

We finally talked, though I had no way of speeding it up.

"You know Farret?" I asked the sailor.

"Ah. I'm glad he's gone."

"Where to?"

"I will tell you where I would like him to go. I am from a small village, and back there....."

"Where is he now, do you know?"

"Give me the beer."

I gave him the beer and waited.

"Where is he now?" said the sailor. "We throw him out."

"From here? When?"

"When? I will not even try to answer that question. Just a few moments ago I lost and then found a day, with your help, which shows you....."

"I know. Let me have the beer."

I took several swallows. It helped interrupt him and I hoped to be able to think of a better question.

"You threw him out, you said?"

"Yes. We did, and I did."

"What did he say? Why were you mad at him?"

"We were angry with him because we don't like his way with women. He has no respect for a woman and what she can do."

"I see."

"Yes. We did not allow him to our party."

"I understand. I know that he isn't pleasant. But what did he say he would do, when you didn't allow him?"

"Nothing. We made him leave swiftly."

I felt useless. The sailor was on his bed, in his nest, smiling across at his knees. He drank from the bottle and gave it to me.

"Not that I understand it," said the sailor, "but this Farret told me at one time that he himself had a girl. Rather, I do not understand the girl."

"Girl— What girl?"

"I forget her name."

"Was he with the girl? I mean, when you came to San Francisco, did he go...."

"No. She isn't here. He isn't here."

"He's with her?"

"He was bragging about it, about going to her, but you yourself know how much one can trust...."

"Where, for Christ's sake is this girl?"

"Useless," he said. "I can't remember such names. It is her home. Was her home, said this Farret, years ago when she was a virgin." The sailor made a short sigh, like a cough almost. "The way he would talk about women. It is strange."

He invited me to come back in the, evening, when he would be rested.

I left his room and hoped that Jane and the old man would be back at the desk. They weren't back yet. I went downstairs fast and waited in front of the hotel.

Farret was three days ahead of me, gone after the girl friend he had had years ago. The one who had been a virgin. I had heard that story. He used to slap that girl on the rump, look around, give her a pinch, and say, "Would you believe it? But this one used to be a virgin!"

Her first name was Lena and I was hoping I could remember the second. She had been from Denver—

I saw Jane and the old man down the street, coming out of a restaurant. When Jane saw me she waved and then she stopped with the old man and they talked for a while. Before I reached them they had said good-by and the old man had gone back into the restaurant.

"He hasn't had breakfast yet," said Jane. "Did you find out anything?"

I didn't know what to tell her. I was sure of only one thing. Farret was in Denver, and Jane wasn't going along with me to meet him.

"I met this Ramon," she said, "but he didn't know anything."

"Nothing at all?"

"Let's walk," she said. "Let's not stand on the street. He did know a little," she said. "He knew that this Farret came back here to look for some friends of his, but that he wasn't looking in town. In fact, he said Farret left town for sure. He made that quite clear. The old man did the translating for me because Ramon...."

"How did he know that Farret had left Frisco?"

"How did he know? Oh— Farret had told him. Farret had packed his things, had a ticket, a bus ticket...."

"To where?"

"I don't know, John. He didn't know. Here's a taxi. Will you hail it? I'd like to go home."

I hailed the taxi and worried about Jane's nervousness. She did not usually talk very fast, or so much. We got into the taxi and I gave her my address. She started talking again. "Even though I love San Francisco and have lived here a long time, you know what those last few days have done? They've made me wonder whether I've really known this town until now. There's this new side to it now, like that hotel, that restaurant which was pretty awful, all that running around we have done and for no pleasant reason— I'm tired, John. Let's just go home now?"

She leaned back in the seat and said nothing else. I took her hand and we sat for a while. Then I said, "What is it, Jane?"

She looked at me and then she put her head under my chin and sat close. I usually like this but it felt this time as if she was doing it so that she didn't have to look at me and so I couldn't look at her.

"You're not clever hiding from me, Jane." It made me feel guilty saying this, because I was doing the same to her. "What's upset you?"

She stayed where she was and talked very low. "He must be a terrible person. Some of the things Ramon said about him, or what the old man allowed me to hear. A mean man, that Farret. The way he acted on board ship, vile, suspicious, looking for things to get nasty about." She took a deep breath but her hand moved uneasily in mine. "And that he should have come back. That he should try to get between us—"

"But he needn't," I said. "And he's left town."

"Yes. That's good—"

Then she wouldn't talk anymore. We were both quiet for the rest of the ride because I hadn't told her my part yet, because we weren't really sharing a thing.

The mood didn't leave us in her apartment and for while we just talked past each other. I smoked, trying to think what to say, and she walked around doing some odd packing and looking in boxes.

I would have to tell her, or the mood would get worse. It felt terrible to me, holding back from her, which was the same thing as lying.

"You want some coffee?" I asked her.

"Coffee?"

I got up to go to the kitchen when she said, "No. I don't want coffee. You don't want coffee, John." She came over and took my arm. "Let's rest for a while. Please?"

I didn't feel like resting. I felt nervous and jumpy.

"We'll talk later, all right? We'll lie down a while and you hold me."

What I wanted to do was go to the phone and call the airport for a flight to Denver. But it was the wrong time to tell her she had to stay behind.

We laid down on the bed and I held her, with her head on my shoulder.

"Jane," I said, but she didn't want to talk.

"Just hold me a while, John," and she pressed herself closer.

Then she moved around and turned her face for a kiss. Jane and I were not in tune and what I felt, she didn't feel, and the same went the other way too. She hung on to the kiss, which was terrible because I didn't want it, but she hung on and the hand on my arm tightened.

"John, please—" she said. "Please, John—" and her breathing came short.

There was something desperate in all this and it was this desperation which made me respond to her. We both moved on the bed and tried to think of nothing else. She tossed herself back and her eyes were closed. She pushed my hand off her breast and her fingers got tangled undoing the buttons. She pulled open her blouse and arched when my hand went around her back.

It was like a frantic fight, as if our clothes were enemies, and then when we touched, her skin against mine, the whole length of us, the intensity to each other was hard like a cramp. She gasped when I came to her and we both trembled. From there on the desperation shook both of us, almost like the real fire, and all I remember is our strong violence for each other, but something different from love, something desperate for love.

When I woke up she wasn't there. She wasn't next to the bed and she was not in the apartment. I felt almost panicky. I didn't find her note until later.

Chapter Five

Water pearls lay on the blue of his pea jacket. He took a lapel in each hand and shook, to throw it all off. He buttoned the jacket and felt warm inside. He had time now and he had money. It was five in the morning and it would even be safe now.

Farret stepped out of the underbrush and the wet grass and up on the high-way. It curved and dipped, the way it did all through the State of Utah, so that Farret could hear a car coming before he could be seen. Then he would hide in the underbrush because a man without luggage on a highway at five in the morning was a little conspicuous, and, of course, it was only twenty miles back to the place where the car lay in the quarry and the driver tied into a bundle under the steering wheel. This'll ruin him on hitchhikers, thought Farret and laughed. The laughing shook up his stomach, causing a cramp, and he remembered how hungry he was. This was all right though. He had money now. He walked faster, with everything giving him the sting of hunger now; the jar in his feet from the grey highway, the bite of the pine odor in his nose, the wet touch of the wind which drew up his skin. Five miles to the border of Colorado and he'd find a town there, if not sooner. He would eat, he would smoke, he would take a bus. He would make Denver today. And if she was-n't in Denver then somebody in Denver would know where the bitch went. Eight years was a long time but that girl never was much for moving. And besides, eight years older now, she probably looked like hell. Farret laughed on that thought, laughed with the sound getting lost quickly among the big trees but with a feel like fire inside him. That Lena bitch would be the first. Why? He had no idea where the others might be. Why else? She was a dame, and a dame—above all—shouldn't get away with nothing.

Where Denver petered out into clapboard construction and railroad sidings there was a diner next to the foot of a bridge. The bridge was very high—a railroad pass, which made the diner look squat. *Hubert's 24 Hours.*

Farret watched the place for fifteen minutes. He watched a bald man come out of the back, watched him disappear across the siding, and then Farret went to the diner. It was eleven p.m. At nine he had come into Denver. At nine fifteen he had taken a free shower at the Salvation Army Shelter for Men. At ten, smelling freshly from the use of his five dollar cologne, he had walked into the candy store which was owned by Lena's uncle. "Sure, Lena's back. Years now, I forget just how many. And who are you."

"Friend," said Farret.

"Hers or her husband's?"

"Both," he lied.

"You know where he's got his diner? If you hurry you'll catch him. He goes off at eleven. Hubert's is open twenty-four hours. Then she goes on. He goes to sleep."

Farret walked into the diner and kept his head down with the pea jacket collar turned up. He sat down at the counter and watched the woman serve stuffed cabbage at the other end of the row.

She had gained weight. Her breasts looked round now, much bigger, and made heavy movements. Her hips had always been big, but they lifted differently when she walked, with more fat. Her face wasn't older, being smooth, but a largeness was there which made her age hard to determine. Her hair hadn't changed. It was blonde and she hadn't changed it in any way. This seemed wrong.

"Want something?" she said from the other end. Her voice seemed slower than he remembered.

"Coffee."

She went to the urn while Farret lit a cigarette, and when she reached to the shelf, for a cup, Farret flipped it. The cigarette made a neat arc through the air, hardly spinning, and with a soft plop fell into the cup Lena was touching.

She drew back her hand and the cup fell down. She was very startled. The cup rolled on the work shelf and the cigarette came out. The man with the stuffed cabbage laughed.

"Herbie!" she said. There was a small shaking in her voice. "Did you do that?"

The man shook his head and thumbed over to Farret. The man kept chuckling for a long time because it had been the damndest trick.

Lena turned around to look at Farret who raised his face for her to see.

"Baby—" she said, with the smallest breath. And, "Mother Mary—"

"Coffee," he said. "A clean cup."

Drawing the coffee gave her time. She was not very emotional but the cigarette thing and then Farret had all come too fast. She felt confused and then injured. To play such a trick—

"I take it half and half," said Farret.

She said, "Oh, yes. I'm sorry," and went back to the urn where the cream gadget was.

"Don't spill it," said Farret and watched her bring the cup which was much too full.

She put it down in front of him, spilling some, but she ignored it. She could hold just so much confusion and after that she would go a little bit blank.

"Aren't you gonna wipe it up?" he asked her.

"Baby," she said, trying to whisper, "whatever are you doing here?"

He just grinned at her. He took out a cigarette and lit it without ever look-ing away from her face.

"You lost a tooth," she said.

He closed his mouth. The sudden anger drew his face into lines so that it looked longer and old. She saw this. She knew this about him, and for the first time since he had come her feelings became something more than just being startled. She felt fright.

She walked away. The other man had asked for his check. He paid her with the right change, then left.

There was only Farret and the woman now, just looking at each other. The coffee urn made a slight sizzle noise and it smelled of linoleum in the diner.

"When are you free?" said Farret.

She had seen that he was going to talk, but she gave a start just the same. "Free?"

"Yeah. Like I said."

"Baby," she said, "I'm married now."

Farret drank the rest of his coffee and got off his stool. "Call him up."

"What?"

"Call him up and tell him you're sick. He should take the shift. You're go-ing home."

"He's *asleep*. He works sixteen...."

"*Listen to me!*" said Farret. He said it straight at her and he seemed to go stiff when he said it.

Lena felt that she could do nothing but what Farret asked. She called up home, she let the phone ring for a long time, and when her husband came on she talked with much confusion. But he was coming down, if only to find out what was the matter.

She came back to the counter where Farret was standing and she watched him take out another cigarette. He was taking his time. She watched him light it and then smoke. He just stood there and smoked. She couldn't stand it any longer and said "Baby, please. He'll be here in five minutes. We only live five minutes from here."

"Please what, Lena?" said Farret and kept on smoking.

"Please *go*. Wait outside someplace. Baby. *Please.*"

He grinned at her and said, "Uh-uh."

"I promise, Baby, I'll meet you outside as soon...."

"I'm not worried. I want to meet him, is all."

"Mother Mary—" said Lena but Farret would not go. He sat down again and asked for another coffee.

Lena's husband came in a few minutes later. His bald head looked pale and a few little hairs way in the back were standing up in different directions. He was short and perhaps he had been strong but there was tired fat on his body.

"What?" he said to Lena. "What now, what, what—" He was very tired and walked to the back of the counter before she explained herself.

"Hubert, I got this terrible...."

"Sick," he said. "Big pink woman and sick. I don't understand. Go home, go, go—" He was putting his apron on and changing his shoes.

Lena went out very fast.

"I tell you," said Farret, "you work too hard, Hubert."

Hubert didn't bother to answer. He looked at Farret and gave a snort. He ignored the man at the counter and drew himself coffee, black, which he started to slurp standing up.

"And not even customers to show for it," Farret said.

"What time is it?" said Hubert. There was a clock on the wall behind him but he did not feel like turning around.

"Eleven twenty."

"Ten minutes the next bunch comes. Goes by shifts."

"Ah," said Farret. "And twenty-four hours of it. Must be a goldmine," and then he said "must be a gold mine" again because Hubert hadn't answered.

Hubert said, "I'm Rockefeller."

Farret laughed, so Hubert would notice it and then he said, "I wouldn't argue with you. Wouldn't be the first guy hides his dough with hard work and complainings. Huh?"

"I'm a little bit tired," said Hubert. "I can't laugh."

"Stashed safe and sound, I bet," Farret went on. "And one day, when the time comes, you and that lovely wife of yours close up this greasy spoon, pack one little bag for the clothes, one big bag with the money, and...."

"Listen," said Hubert. "I don't know you from nothing. So don't kid like that." He sounded hurt.

Four men came in, wearing railroad caps and the red bandanas tied inside their collars. They looked scrubbed and close shaven and their striped overalls made the sound of starch. They said, "Morning, Hubert," and, "the same as usual," and one of them asked, "Where's Lena?"

Farret looked at the clock again and considered that Lena had been waiting outside for over ten minutes. Let her wait a while longer? Perhaps not. Ten minutes, Farret was sure, was a long time for Lena at present. And besides, he didn't like Hubert.

"Your wife collected for the coffee," he said and went to the door.

"All right," said Hubert. "All right. All right."

Chapter Six

He found her in the dark by one of the slanting girders which went up to the roof of the bridge. She stood there holding herself as if she were cold. When she saw him coming she said, "Baby?"

He stopped close to her and looked at her face. "The way you keep saying 'Baby,' Lena. How come you keep saying it that way?"

She stepped back a little, looking down and sideways but never at him. "I don't know— Because I *used* to call you that, I suppose."

"Nice," he said. He tried to catch her eye.

"I'm cold," she said. "Please tell me. Please tell me why you came, and acting this way."

"Because I love you," he said and slapped her face.

He waited a moment while she cowered. When she didn't look up and kept her arms over her head he said, "You can come out now. I won't do it again."

She looked up and saw that his hands were in his pockets.

"Who's at home?" he asked.

"Home?"

"You got a home, don't you?"

"Nobody."

"No children?"

"I got no children," and then added, "I will though. Later."

He didn't answer to that, because her remark meant nothing to him. He took her by the arm and said, "Show me where."

They walked across the broad bed of tracks and on the other side up the street which had no lights. He kept holding her arm just where the sleeve ended and started working his fingers over the skin. He held her arm so he could feel the side of her breast with his knuckles.

She said, "Baby— I mean, please— I'm a married woman."

"That all you think about?"

"I like being married."

He laughed, nasty, and said, "I didn't mean that." He dug with his knuckles.

She said nothing else. And if he says nothing else, she thought, then perhaps nothing else will happen because then I won't have to answer. It's only when I say something to him things go wrong.

They came to a bungalow where they went up on the porch. Farret let go of her so she could get the key under the mat and unlock the door. They don't have the money at home, he thought. Inside, she did not turn on the light but went to the windows to pull down the shades. Then she turned on the light.

Farret saw nothing special; catalogue furniture and a carpet with flowers. There were more colors woven into those flowers than he had ever seen on a carpet. Maybe the carpet was very expensive.

"Sit down," he said.

"Where do you want me...."

"*Sit down.*"

She sat down on the edge of the blue couch which had a tassel at the end of each bolster. She brushed the tassel away from her knee and watched Farret lean by the opposite wall.

"Lena honey, I'm going to get it from you or I'm going to get it from Hubert. I'd much rather get it from you."

"Huh?"

"Fifty thousand, in round figures. Dollars, I mean."

"Mother Mary—"

"I understand that," he said, enjoying it. "There was fifty thousand in that last gun run, but perhaps you didn't know it. But you know, don't you, how much you got paid? How much did you get paid when we broke up?"

"Baby— I think, I feel like I'm going crazy— Baby, what is this?"

He walked all the way across the room to her without saying a word and he stopped without saying a word, standing in front of her. She saw how his face changed, and what it meant, but she could not look away now.

"*I was suckered,*" he said. "And that doesn't happen to me." He stepped back then. His voice changed again, lower now. "How much did you get at the split-up?"

"Nothing!" Her voice went out of control. "Mother Mary—I got nothing at all—will you believe me! I ran! I just ran!"

When she felt like herself again she thought she had perhaps made an impression. Farret was chewing his lip and then he started to chew on his thumb. He kept watching her all the time but said nothing. He looked at her, up and down, but his eyes were in shadow. It gave her a start when he talked again.

"Get up," he said.

She started to say, "Please, Baby—" but got up without finishing it.

"This the only room you got? What more rooms you got here?"

She grabbed at the chance in the same way she would suddenly struggle if she were about to drown and at the last moment would feel bottom under her feet. Her hands started to gesture and her eyes blinked very quickly.

"Well—this was a one bedroom place when we first got it. When we first— Oh well, you didn't ask that. So Hubert—he's good at this, with his hands and knowing tools like he does, he made the bedroom into part of the kitchen—I can show you— Well, later. Let me first finish. Made it part of the kitchen and part of the kitchen into a breakfast nook, a cute—well. And he took the back porch, doing something with it, and built this new bedroom and next to it—"

"Show me the bedroom."

"Yes. But here, let me show you first where...."

"Just the bedroom. Just that."

Her mouth stayed open a moment and when she closed it her face felt very lax to her, very tired, as if it might drop right off and she would even be too tired to care about that. He took her arm again, like before, and then she moved. She went into the bedroom and flicked on the overhead light, the light they never used since they got the little bedlamps, one by each bed and with Soft-Glo bulbs in it—

"Well," he said. He stopped her in the doorway and let go of her arm. "Twin beds."

He now put his arm around her and moved his hand very freely. I don't feel a thing, she said to herself. I don't feel a thing, I don't feel his hand, I don't feel his hand there—

"Which bed do you sleep in?"

"That one."

"Hmm."

I'm glad I lied when he asked me about the bed, which one was mine. I'm going to shut my eyes to this thing and just let it happen, let it happen fast on the wrong bed, and then I'm going to run back to the diner and tell Hubert he should go to sleep, he's so tired, and I'm not sick anymore and I'm sorry—

"Hubert works sixteen hours, I hear," said Farret.

Mother Mary— don't let me feel a thing, I don't really feel a thing—

"You grew some," said Farret. He slowly opened all the buttons on the front of her uniform and looked at her breasts. "Of course, you were just a growing girl at the time, but some tussler. Huh? Remember us tussling?"

I don't remember a thing, not a thing now or after, just quick, let it just be quick—

He stepped away from her at that moment and went to the window to close the shade. "Seeing as you're a married woman," he said.

He walked around the room once and then sat down on the cedar chest. He did everything very slowly. Any moment, Lena thought, I'm going to tremble.

"Take off your clothes."

"Baby," she started. Her voice felt like it was way up in her mouth someplace and she had to swallow. He looked thin and mean in his large jacket, sitting there on the cedar chest, but she was not going to offend him because she was taking her uniform off already. "Baby—I just want to say one thing—" She dropped the uniform and stood there in her brassiere and her smock. She thought about the uniform lying there, so she bent down and hung it over a chair.

"Take off the bra," he said. He watched how it tightened, squeezing her

when she reached back to open the hook. "When did you start wearing a bra?"
he said.

"Fourteen," she said, automatically.

It made him laugh. "I don't remember you wearing a bra much." He was-
n't looking at her. He was getting a pack of cigarettes out of his pocket. "And
you weren't fourteen then," he finished.

She stood with her bra in her hand and finally put it on top of the uniform.
She itched where the left strap had been on her shoulder but was afraid to
reach up and scratch.

"Next floor," he said. "Come on, come on." He was lighting a cigarette but
as soon as he had done this he put it on the edge of the cedar chest.

Lena pulled the smock down, stepped out of it. At the last moment she
caught the heel of her shoe in the fabric and almost fell to the floor. Instead,
she let the smock rip. She did not have the natural impulse to check on the
damage because she had to look up and see Farret, see what he was doing. She
was sure he would make something of this, say something now, she having
stumbled like this, almost naked— She dropped the smock on the chair and
looked over at Farret. He was lighting a fresh cigarette. Then he put it next
to the one which was already lying there on the edge of the cedar chest.

He looked up and said, "You're not wearing any stockings."

She just shook her head. She'd rather not speak.

"S'a shame. Would have liked to see you roll off those stockings."

If he asks me to put on some stockings and roll them off I'll say I don't have
any stockings. I'll say I have stockings but they're wet on the line— And he'll
say 'do it wet,' he's sure going to say 'do it wet'—

Farret was lighting a cigarette. Like before, he put it next to the others.
Then he looked up.

"Come on. Take the pants off. First the shoes and then the pants."

She did this and stood there naked. There was a faint line running across
her middle, where the elastic had been, and she felt like rubbing herself again.
It came to her that she always rubbed herself when she took off her underthings, just where the elastic had been or a strap. She felt terrible not being
able to do this now and for a moment that made her forget everything else.

"Hey," he said. "Lemme see you walk over there."

She would move fast now, she thought. Get there, maybe rush it a little once
she got over to him. There were certain ways she had not thought of for a very
long time.

She walked over slowly, hoping that nothing would move on her. When
he looked up, with a new cigarette in his hand she stopped walking.

"Just like he said. Pink all over."

She said nothing. She watched his thin face and thought that something dis-
pleased him, which was true. Farret felt suddenly peeved, out of nowhere,
and lit one more cigarette to be doing something. He hardly looked at the

naked woman. He remembered her mostly white.

"Baby—" she said. "Can I close the door?"

"You shut up," he said.

The door stayed open, the woman stayed where she was. She felt like rub-bing herself again, over the belly.

"Now I want you to get over to that stool," he said.

If he had said something she expected, or done anything like she expected, it would have been all right. She would have just done it, because even now she had forgotten about being naked. She felt suddenly naked again, a wide, helpless nakedness, and when she sat down on the stool in front of her van-ity her breathing felt painful and flat. She was very frightened.

Farret moved a little on the cedar chest, in order not to tip his cigarettes. They lay in very neat alignment, the glowing heads sticking out over the edge of the chest. Farret was holding so still that all the blue smoke ribbons stood still in the air.

"Did you know I been in prison since you skipped out on me?"

She tried to answer but he had said more than one thing. She had not known that he had been in prison, she did not know why he had mentioned it, she did not know in her confusion what to answer about skipping out on him but she had to say something to him because he was wrong—

"Well?"

"I— didn't."

"Didn't what?"

"Didn't know. About prison—"

"Three years," said Farret. He seemed to be thinking about it. "I get suck-ered out of my share on the island, I have to run like hell to keep from dying but I made it to Chile." He cocked his head, looking at Lena's thighs. "You know what I got three years for, in Chile? Trying to beat unemployment."

She hardly listened to him, just watched what he was doing.

"Three years with nothing to do," he said. At that point with care, he picked up one of the cigarettes. "There's a smudge on your nose," he said.

Lena touched her nose without thinking, then looked at her hand.

"You don't see it?" said Farret. "Show me your hand." She held out her hand and the cigarette smacked into her palm.

The shock was so great that she sucked in her breath and held it for a long time. It wasn't the pain. There was none, that time, just the impact and a small spray of sparks. But Farret's intent and the terror which he meant for her overwhelmed her.

"I've got a whole row yet," he said. "I can hit anything."

Her nakedness was like pain on her skin—

"Where's the money?"

She couldn't talk yet. She moved her head stupidly, back and forth.

"Left shoulder," he said and hit her there.

This time it burned. She started to scream but it stuck in her and she heard him again, "Where's the money?"

"Money? What money? I don't...."

"Sit down," and then, "Right shoulder."

He hit her there and a warm trickle of ash rolled over her right breast.

Then she started to scream. She opened her mouth and closed her eyes, only opened them again when she stopped for breath. Then she saw that Farret was leaning forward, way forward, a cigarette aimed at her face with his hand held out. She shut her mouth with panicky suddenness when he said, "The money. All of you split after the break-up. Where's yours?"

"I don't have—" she stopped, ready to duck, but Farret just put the cigarette in his mouth and took a drag. While he did this he nodded at her.

"I don't have any!" She started fast. She rushed it out. "I never got any, honestly! All I got when I found out about everything was the two hundred you had in your pants at home. I took that to get back to the States when I found out that there had been the raid and nobody left to help...."

"Left knee," said Farret and hit it.

But she only stopped long enough to gasp. She had to tell him what happened, he seemed to be listening when she was talking— "Please, Baby, please! I'll give you the two hundred dollars. Hubert and I have a little, we have four hundred, all the money we have—"

He only dragged on the cigarette, but she hadn't known why he had moved.

"How come you found out so quick that I got jumped on, the way up to the mountains?"

"Four hundred dollars," she kept on saying, "is all there is and you can...."

"Stop yammering."

He knew he was going to have four hundred dollars. Perhaps there was no more, perhaps she had not gotten her split because she was stupid that way and had no real title to anything, now that he thought of it. She was much too dumb and scared to lie. Then what? He had to know more about the time everything tore down the middle. It had nagged him and bothered him. It was, and he knew this, the real reason for his coming back to the States. Those things don't happen by chance, getting beat out of a setup. Somebody had done the fingering!

When he, Farret, lost out, it became a certainty, a law to him that somebody had deliberately cheated him; just as much as it was the law that you go kill the squealer. It's laws like that which keep a man going.

He aimed the cigarette at her and liked how she snapped her arms over her front.

"You knew," he said. "You knew I was taking the long way to the hide-out. Just that afternoon I told you."

"I don't—I didn't know...."

"I told you I'd be back in three days. That's how you knew I had changed plans to the long way!"

"Please— Baby— I never stopped to think it meant that. I never told any-body!"

"I even know whom you told," said Farret and let fly another cigarette. He felt the hate make the back of his mouth go sticky and hot. *This* bitch! "Where did you go that night I'm talking about. You remember?"

She remembered. She wished he'd sit down and not stand like that with his face black over her, with the light behind him—

"Salvato!" she said. "You sent me to Captain Salvato!"

"I know that." He sounded too calm. "Every Wednesday night you got laid by Salvato."

"And don't you remember," she said fast, "you were still home when Salvato's orderly picked me up with the car?"

"Sure. No slip-up there. The good captain does me a favor, and I see to it you're delivered. No slip-up there. The good captain always stayed off my back."

"So that night when they ambushed you...."

"You know who jumped me? Fifty men in the woods and machine guns? Captain Salvato!"

"But I never told him! I never told him which way you were going that night—I never *saw* him that night!"

"What? Where were you?"

"The orderly. He drove me the other way, not to Salvato's station. Down to Del Ray, the beach there."

"What for?"

"What for?" she said. "In the car. He was afraid of the mosquitoes. It was Del Rey," she went on, "because I could see the light on the point. Once a ship came into the bay and lay there. A battleship, the orderly said. I saw all the lights."

Farret sat down again. He had no more cigarettes so he put his thumb to his mouth and chewed on the nail. There had been a battleship in Del Ray Bay that night because he had seen it. He could see it from the cove where he picked up the arms from Miner's boat. That was another bastard, that Miner. Lena could not have known about the battleship if she had been at the patrol station inland, where Salvato was, where Salvato should have been. Of course he hadn't been there. The raid had been planned in advance. They had just picked up the girl, so it looked like the usual. Every Wednesday night and then Salvato the bastard does this! It hadn't been Lena who told him. Some-body else fingered this—

"When did you get back?"

"He kept me all night."

"I said when did you get back?"

"In the morning. I don't know what time...."

"Who told you the whole business was shot?"

"Nobody. Nobody told me. I waited around for a few days and never saw anybody. You didn't come back, I never saw John. I'd sometimes see John because he used to drink beer in the...."

"Don't talk to me about that sonofabitch."

"And then I went looking for Getterman. All his tourist places were closed and that's when I got worried. I even called Mister Metz...."

"Where was he?"

"I called him at his place in Florida, in Tampa that was, but he wasn't home so they told me to try...."

"You finally talked to him?"

"Sure I talked to him. He was the one told me to come on home. He was very nice."

"*That* sonofabitch knew! All the way in Tampa!"

"He was very nice," she said again. It was one of the few nice things she could remember and liked to think about. She hung on to the thought of Mister Metz and could have been talking to herself. "He told me to come see him right away and when I did he told me to buy some clothes and gave me some money for that. And told me I should go back home, back to Denver, I should have a nice life and go home. He gave me the money for that too and I went home."

"Where's the money?"

At first she didn't understand what money Farret was talking about because she was thinking of other things. She sat looking down at her hands and could see the butts on the floor. One of them was still smoking. She was back in the bedroom, hers and Hubert's, with the overhead light on, the one they never used anymore, cold and naked on the small stool and Farret there in the pea jacket. "He told me to write to him sometimes," she said with her voice low and hopeless. "And I did. He wrote back too. And when he moved to Miami he wrote me again, asking about me—"

"I'm going," said Farret. "Where's the money?"

"Going?"

"In the bank? Come on, wake up?"

"Bank? No!" She jumped up, not believing any of this but trying to believe what Farret had said. "Here, in the house," she ran to the kitchen, talking all the time. "In a box. Hubert doesn't trust banks. Here, no, I don't need a light."

Farret watched her crouch by the sink where she opened a cabinet door, pulled out a plasterboard panel, and then a box. A cigar box with papers in it and a few bills. They came to four hundred dollars. He took them out of her hand and let her go by. She went to the bedroom and stood there for a moment rubbing her belly, then one shoulder where a strap would go. She looked at the chair with her clothes and picked up the brassiere, not too fast though. She looked at Farret who stood watching her but Farret said nothing. He watched her put on the bra, the panties, and a slip which she got from a drawer. When she reached for the waitress uniform he just shook his head, which was enough to give her a start and pull back her hand. It looked as if she meant to take off the slip again when Farret said, "Put some clothes on. I mean real clothes, dress and so on. An overcoat."

CHAPTER SEVEN

When she got off the plane in Denver it was late. She could see as far as the airport lights let her and on the other side of the lights she felt the night was something solid and black. For a moment she thought of nothing else. She felt the difference in the air immediately, the dry thin coldness, a contrast to the wet atmosphere of San Francisco.

In the airport building she looked at the restaurant counter behind the glass doors and wondered if she should take the time for a hot cup of coffee. She felt exhausted but the thought of delay made her tense again. She had been afraid and on edge ever since the morning on Mission Street, when she had decided.

Ramon had told her plenty. He had told her that Farret was after three men, three 'friends' who had cheated him out of a fortune. And he, Farret, had come back for just that. Whether for the three men or for fortune or both, Ramon hadn't known. But Ramon had known Farret's first stop. That was Denver. He would start looking from Denver, said Ramon, because he knew only one address for a starter, the name and address of this girl. She had been on the island with him. Nobody important, this girl, not as important as the three men, but a starter. Lena Crowly. Perhaps she had married? Didn't matter. Her aunt would know, Bess Crowly in Denver, some street by the railroad tracks.

That's all Ramon knew, but Ramon also knew that nobody else on the *Veronica Mendes* had been in Farret's confidence. So John didn't know about Denver.

I did right, she said to herself. She went to the telephone booths and started to look for Bess Crowly in one of the books. I did right, even to the lying and that desperate act on the bed. Even that. If John went and met Farret, they would be into each other like animals, each for his reasons.

She had done right. She would not look for Farret and even if she did meet the man, he would not know her. She would find the girl and persuade her to lie to Farret so he would go off in some wrong, harmless direction. It was possible for two women to agree on such things, to do things without violence. And if Lena still loved this Farret, a thing which was entirely possible, that would make everything that much more certain. There was no Bess Crowly in the telephone book. Still, nothing to worry about. The aunt had no phone and finding her would just take a little bit longer.

Jane walked past the restaurant and did not think about wanting coffee. There was no time. There was less time now than when she had still been in San Francisco because delay now meant a whole night wasted, if she could not find Bess Crowly before the old woman went to bed.

Jane took a taxi and asked for the police station. They had a directory at the station and the desk sergeant found Bess Crowly in a few minutes. No, there was no Lena Crowly, but Elizabeth Crowly lived on Plusher Road.

"Kinda late, don't you think, Miss?" said the sergeant.

"She's expecting me," said Jane. "Thank you."

"Welcome, Miss. Hope you find her. This directory is eight years old, you know. The last census was taken—"

Jane didn't hear the man out and wished he hadn't told her about the age of the list. It seemed to make the night even later and the time more pressing.

Plusher Road went up hill from the railroad tracks and the taxi had to go very slow to spot numbers on the old frame houses. The street was without lights and seemed almost rural.

"Here's twenty-seven," said the driver. "But it's dark."

"No, I don't want twenty-seven. I want *thirty*-seven."

The cabby thought that the girl in back was close to tears.

Thirty-seven looked the same as all the other houses, and there was a light in one window.

"You want me to wait, Miss? This neighborhood...."

"No. Please. I'll be all right."

"I'll be at the diner," said the cabby. "See that diner across the tracks? If you want me within the next half hour."

She didn't hear him out. She ran up the porch steps and knocked on the door. There was no sound inside. When the door opened a little ways and jerked to a stop on the short chain, the sound was like a blow.

"Who is it?" said an old voice.

"Oh—Mrs. Crowly? Are you Mrs. Crowly?"

"Miss Crowly," it said from the dark crack. "What is it, girl?"

"I'm terribly sorry to knock on your door this late at night but I wanted to be sure—I was very anxious...."

"You don't sound right, girl. Wait a minute."

The door shut. The chain made a noise and then the door opened. Jane couldn't see the old woman but she sounded nice.

"Now you come right in here, girl, and let me look at you. You been running up the hill, you're so out of breath?"

Jane went into the dark hall and the woman in there took her arm and led her to the door where the light showed a little.

It was the kitchen. The old woman was small and pink, and except for her shapelessness and the white hair she could have been less than fifty.

"I don't know you, do I?" she said and looked at Jane with a short-sighted stare.

"No, Miss Crowly. I've just come to town. I came straight to you because

I'm so anxious to see Lena. You know Lena?"

The woman laughed and said, yes, of course she knew Lena. Then she asked Jane to sit down by the kitchen table.

"I don't want to keep you, Miss Crowly. I just wondered if you'd tell me where I could find Lena. Tonight maybe. She and I used to know...."

"Sort of late," said the woman. "Don't you think? How about some coffee, uh—"

"Jane. My name is Jane."

"Oh." The woman went to the stove and put a pot on the flame. "I don't remember Lena mentioning any Jane."

"Well, the fact is I haven't seen her in a long time, but I was kind of anxious...."

"Wait a minute. I think she's working tonight. Let me think—"

There was cold coffee in the pot and with the heat started to smell strong and good.

"Maybe not," said the woman. "Maybe Hubert is working tonight. But in that case, I doubt you'd find Lena up. She's always been a long sleeper, you know, and going to work at six in the morning—"

"Then she lives here in Denver?"

"She lives right across the way," said the woman. "Come here, I show you."

They looked out of the window at the black street and a grey shape of a house across the way where all the windows were dark.

"No, wait a minute. Don't I see a light?"

There was a crack of light coming through a shade.

"She's up!" said Jane. "Let me just run across...."

"That wouldn't be Lena, honey. Maybe that's Hubert. You'll like Hubert, you know. When you see him and get to know him good—"

But Jane wasn't listening. She didn't care what the old woman might think and started to edge to the door, apologizing.

"But wait. The coffee...."

"I'll be back. I'll be right back. Just let me check if she's there," and even though the old woman was talking again Jane walked out of the house.

There was just that one crack of light by one window and the rest of the house was all dark.

She hesitated when she came to the porch, because she did not know what she would say. It seemed there had been no time to think or to do anything but to get here as fast as she could.

The door opened and a man came out. They looked at each other and both of them seemed to go stiff.

"Hustling?" said the man. It sounded hard and mean.

You'll like Hubert, the woman had said, when you get to know him.

He looked back into the house, then came out and closed the door behind him. He seemed very thin in the big pea jacket.

"Well? You must be selling something."

"Oh no—"

"Come here."

She didn't move. She couldn't have gone one way or the other. He came down the porch steps and then stood very close.

"What do you want?"

"My—my name is Jane. I'm Jane. I'm a friend of Lena's."

"She's got friends?" He laughed, a nasty sound. "How come you're hanging around?"

"I came to see her. I was wondering...."

"She's got cute friends," said Farret and looked her up and down. "Real cute, busting in here at the crack of dawn."

There must be an easy way of handling this, she thought. It can't really be this hard, talking to Lena's husband. There was no reason, except her exhaustion and anxiousness, to make her feel the terror nipping at her—

"Where you going?" he said.

"I thought I'd come back—I better come—"

He was suddenly patting himself with small gestures that seemed oddly violent.

"You got a cigarette?" he said. "I ran out in there," and nodded back at the house.

She took out her pack and gave it to him. He took it, pulled out a cigarette, then offered her one. That would do it. She would smoke a cigarette and the commonness of the act would clear up her feelings.

He sat down on the porch steps after having lit both cigarettes and looked up at her.

"Cute as cute," he said.

Jane took a deep drag and blew out the smoke like a man. It looked tough but made her feel awkward.

"If you don't stop this," she said, "I'll tell Lena."

He laughed and then he shut it off very suddenly.

"Tell her what."

There was a threat in his voice but she would ignore it. She would *have* to ignore it or not get anywhere. And besides—it suddenly struck her—Lena's husband would be on her side! Lena's husband could not possibly like Farret!

"Listen," said Jane. "You've got to listen to me."

He was listening. He had heard the change in her voice and he waited.

"You've got to let me talk to Lena, and to you too."

"Why?"

"I've come to warn you," she said. "You understand? There's somebody coming, somebody your wife used to know many years ago."

He said nothing and she could not see his face. He was now turned so that the distant light from the track no longer showed his face.

"And he's perhaps going to cause trouble, all kinds of trouble, because he's that kind of person."

"He is? What's he got in mind?"

"I don't know exactly but let me explain. Many years ago your wife knew him. Not here, somewhere else. There was never anything to it, really."

"There wasn't?"

"I'm sure not. Besides, he's not coming here because of love interest, or anything like that. He's not that kind of person."

"Ah. You don't like him, huh?"

Jane frowned, because she could not see his face and the change in his tone had no clear meaning for her.

"Tell me," said Farret, "what's he ever done to you? And how come you know him?"

"I *don't* know him. What I'm saying...."

"You talk like you hate his guts. How come you hate his guts?"

Jane tried to step back, because Farret had gotten up and come closer. She could see his face now because he was very close. Then he reached out and held her wrist.

"How come you know this?" and he kept holding her wrist.

There was too much to consider now. Whether to run, to scream, to tell what he wanted to know, to explain everything at great length.

"Lena told me," she said very suddenly. She did not even know what had given her the idea. "Lena told me he'd come some time and I heard about this man who was asking around...."

"Cute," said Farret. He was working his fingers up her arm and grinning. For a moment the suspicions had been cutting into him like sharp knives, but not now. What she had said made sense and he could relax. He could relax enough now to think of just how to take care of this one. Scare her good and proper so she'd keep her mouth shut afterwards.

He suddenly sucked in his breath and yanked the girl's arm painfully. She'd been lying! How could he have overlooked the obvious lie. Careful. Much more careful now, from now on and in the future. If this one was such a good friend of Lena's, how come she didn't know what Lena's husband looked like?

"You bitch," he said. "Where'd you hear all this guff? Answer me!"

Answer, answer something fast. Don't scream with fright or he'll get worse. And don't talk about Farret to him, because Farret seemed to upset him a lot, like a weak husband's impotent rage about the men his wife used to know before they were married.

"Here in town," she said. "I just came to town, just tonight, and I was looking for Lena. I haven't seen Lena in years, many years, so when I asked around that's when I heard about the man who was looking for her."

"Oh," said Farret. Perhaps she had not lied. She had only scared him. There was nothing to get even for except that she had scared him for no reason at all. The bitch was going to learn something, and he moved his hand high up on her arm.

"Let go!" Her voice was furious and she pulled away. It surprised Farret, but not for long. He had one standard attitude toward women and that was dislike.

"And now that I let go, now what?" he said.

He wasn't through with her and Jane couldn't leave. It was worse now than when he had held her, because now she could try and run but would not know what he would do.

"Gonna tell me some more about that bad man who's coming after Lena?"

"I'll not bother you any more," she said, trying reason. "So if you'll just let...."

"I'm not through with you yet," he said.

Jane did not dare to move. It had to do with the stare he had, like something waiting, and with the large hand he dangled over one knee. He had his leg up on the steps, leaning his arm on it, and his hand hung down limp except for the small, snappish movements it made.

"You move, lady, and you won't move for long."

It was all cheap-sounding talk, third-rate tough talk, except that she was sure that he meant it.

"If you don't leave me alone...."

"...you'll scream," Farret finished for her, and before he was even finished his hand had reached out and pulled her close, twisting her arm. "You and me are going inside," he said close to her face. "You been wanting to see Lena, isn't that right? You and me are going inside and you'll see her. Me and Lena got a unique relationship." She could feel his wet breath on her face when he talked. "She won't mind. She'll watch and won't mind."

He started to move her by twisting her arm. He's insane, she thought. If I scream he'll hit my face, break my teeth or my arm. If his breath weren't so close—

"Jay—neee!"

They both froze. Farret did not let go of her arm but he straightened up and stared across the street. "You coming back, girl? Your coffee—"

"One word out of you, and I'll make it hurt," he said. His voice rushed and hissed.

"That you over there, Jane? Who's that with you there, Jane?"

"Don't answer. Just hold still and don't answer."

But she could hear that the man was confused. Perhaps he was afraid. It took the fright out of her and she was suddenly angry.

"Yes!" she called, very loud. "It's me, Miss Crowly, I'm coming over!"

Her opposition had startled him and he let go of her arm. There was a hell of a lot at stake here. Why gamble now, just for the kick of scaring this bitch. He moved back up the steps.

Jane started to run. She ran down the hill, towards the tracks. The running alone didn't take care of her excitement and she ran crying, loud and hard. She didn't think about her sudden strength and the courage she'd shown, she just ran, crying, because she knew that the man must be Farret and how close she had come to knowing about him, more even than John knew. That perhaps Farret was not through with her yet.

CHAPTER EIGHT

I couldn't get a reservation to Denver till the next day. I wired for money, I carried my overnight bag around all that day looking for the old man and Ramon, because that's where she must have gotten the information which had sent her ahead of me. I read her note over and over, and I cringed each time I read the few sentences. *Don't worry, darling, please.* That's how it started. I cursed Jane, myself, Farret, taxi drivers, odd strangers who bumped into me on the street, because '*Don't worry, darling, please,*' was almost too much to take. The rest read: *I'm going to talk to Lena. It'll be easier for me and please wait for me in the apartment. I'll be careful. I'll call you.*

Every time I felt the brief dullness come over me which happens with too much tension I read the pathetic note again which made me scream on the inside with frustration.

The old man, the clerk told me, had gone to a museum. He went to museums every day. Ramon wasn't in either, and no hint where he might have gone. I raced around and I raced back to the apartment because Jane might call. I did this all day and part of the night. Next day I took the plane. The trip was hell.

By the time I got to Denver there was no excitement left. I had even slept on the plane. I got to Denver in a fake state of calm and that's how I went through most of it. I would look for Lena and I wouldn't mention Jane to anyone until I knew what went on. I had a feeling that this would protect her. I had a weird superstition that it would keep Farret away.

At the Denver airport I went to the telephone booths and stood there with a directory for fifteen minutes. Her name was Crowly or Crowder or something like that. Or the same spelled with a K. It was going to take me a while. There was no last name that rang a bell which also had the first name Lena. Not that I had counted on it. Not that Lena had a phone, had the same name, or was still in town. But somebody with a name like hers would be related, which was the most I could hope for. I copied out six likely names with the addresses so I could make my rounds. I wasn't going to phone. It would be too hard to explain.

I didn't know Denver so the first two names on the list turned up in an unlikely neighborhood. My taxi drove down some quiet streets with large houses. There were no railroad tracks. It was dark now, maybe ten, but I knew there were no railroad tracks. I remembered that Lena had mentioned the yards. *I used to feel the shaking in the bed at night and see the light flit across the ceiling when the trains came by.*

The Crowly which was a candy store turned out to be it. There was the candy store, then a Salvation Army place, barber shops advertising showers for fifty cents, and the bars. The railroad tracks were two blocks away.

The very old man who I figured must be Mister Crowly was sitting behind the counter, looking at nothing. All the colors of the hard candy, all the jars and the old trays with licorice ribbons and penny candy, he must have been looking at them for half a century. There were magazines across from him, all kinds and tastes, but I'm sure he couldn't see that far. I said, "You got Gum Babies?"

It was a very old kind of candy, nothing to do with chewing gum, and I just happened to know that there was such a thing.

"One?" he said.

"Five."

He hadn't looked at me and when he got up and reached into a counter he didn't look at that either. He took out five Gum Babies and dropped them in a bag. Then he took out another one and put it in his mouth.

"Ten cents," he said. "Used to be two for a penny—"

I paid him and rattled my bag around, to look at my candy.

"Nice and pink," I said. "No candy was ever that pink."

"Turns white, chewing it. And your tongue gets redder."

He sat down again and said nothing else. I hadn't done well trying to start a conversation.

"Crowly," I said. "Crowly. Do you know a Lena by that name?"

He looked at me for the first time.

"That would be a chance," I said. "A coincidence."

"Looks like one," said the old man. He had stopped chewing. "She's married now. Know her husband?"

"No. I met her years ago."

"Hubert's Diner," he said. "If you hurry you're likely to catch him. He goes off at eleven."

It said *Hubert's 24 Hours*. And painted near the door Kowalski Proprietor. The sign wasn't lit but a lot of light came from the row of windows with some of them steamed. That kind of sight, in the middle of a cool night almost anywhere is something I like to see.

It was nice and warm inside. All the seats were taken. They were railroad men, maybe taking a break, because I could smell the grease on some of them and they had gloves hanging out of their pockets. The thing was, none of the men were talking. The coffee urn made a sound and a man drinking coffee made a small sound here and there, but nobody talked. They sat all in a row and the man on the other side of the counter, he looked very quiet too. He was bald and chunky. His arms were folded and he kept his face blank. Must be Kowalski. I would wait till he got off.

It must have been eleven right then because a woman came in from the back, wearing a clean, white uniform. When she walked by Kowalski, behind the counter, she said, "Okay. Go get some sleep."

Kowalski moved very slowly. He took off his apron and changed his shoes. All that time, with the blankness on his face, he kept looking at the woman who had come to relieve him. And then the weirdest thing happened. Kowalski's bald head seemed to get redder, he moved his mouth, squinted a little, and I swear the man looked like he was going to cry.

It meant nothing to me then because the woman he had been looking at didn't give any clue. She was nothing in particular. She was plump, had curled hair, and wore rimless glasses.

Kowalski left then.

I caught up with him half way across the tracks and he made a movement which showed he knew somebody was coming but then seemed to give it up. I was walking next to him and he still didn't look. I said, "Mister Kowalski?"

"Yes?" He looked up once but kept walking.

"Mister Kowalski, my name is Miner. I don't think you know...."

"It's late. It's very late," he said. "Come tomorrow."

I thought I should start again.

"Mister Kowalski, you don't seem to know who I am, but it's very important."

"Can't wait?"

"No."

"But no news," he said, which meant nothing to me.

We went up the incline of an unlit street. I could hear how his breathing got heavier.

"You live nearby?" I asked him.

"That house. There."

I thought I would wait till we got there, especially since he didn't seem to mind, and getting there might make it all easier. I would talk to Lena, which was the important thing, and avoid battling with him and his tiredness.

The door wasn't locked and he went in ahead of me. One light was on, in the kitchen, and Kowalski didn't turn on any others. He sat down on a couch with tassels, just sat and waited for me. The light from the kitchen gave a depressing effect.

Lena was asleep or she wasn't home.

"I'm sorry about the late hour," I said, "but you'll see this is important."

"I know."

"About your wife, Lena."

"Talk, talk. Don't wait to talk. All you police fellers start out like the same. So what do you want to know now: Have I seen Lena? No. I ask you: Have you seen Lena? I ask you that question. Everytime you ask me your question I ask you my question about Lena. So talk. Talk."

Farret had made it! Farret was back and there was now no speculation. Lena was his first.

I tried playing a role and was glad that Kowalski wasn't paying attention. It was bad enough I had told him my name and it would be worse if I told him everything. The police were in it. The last thing I wanted was the police and me in the same thing.

"Just to make it official," I said, "my name is Lieutenant Meyerberg, Joel Meyerberg."

"All right. You told me already. All right."

It went fine, so I kept it up.

"We have a new line of inquiry, Mister Kowalski. You will have to remember some names. Incidentally, has the name of the suspect been mentioned to you?"

"You got one?" He sat up. It was his first sign of life.

"No. Just the usual. I asked because it has to do with the names."

"Ask me." It was automatic again. "Ask me."

"Getterman?"

"Who is this?"

"Has your wife ever mentioned this name to you?"

"No such name."

"You realize, Mister Kowalski, that your wife, in the past, knew a number of people. I don't mean this in any...."

"I know my wife. I know from before I know my wife, everything. And then we marry. So talk. Talk."

"Thank you. Now this name: Metz."

"Mister Metz? He was very nice. Very nice. He used to help Lena."

Pay dirt. If he knew the next answer.

"Does your wife know where he lives?"

"The last card he wrote he said he was living in Miami." Kowalski looked up. "Mister Metz is in this thing?"

"No, no. Certainly not. Please forget any such thing. I asked you the name just for a general roster. Any other names she has mentioned—from before?"

"I know from before, but no names. We never talked names. What does it matter?"

I felt safer. Nobody knew any names from the time when the five of us had been together. Not Kowalski, therefore not the police. My name hadn't meant anything to him. He had even forgotten it ten minutes later, and the same for Getterman. And the same for Farret.

Metz was something else. He had written to Lena, she knew his address, he was, in fact, the only one whose address Lena knew! Aside from that none of us knew each other's whereabouts. Which included Farret; or else he would not have gone to Denver. In San Francisco he had been ten minutes away from Getterman's office and half a day's train trip from where I lived.

And now, after getting it out of Lena, Farret knew his next stop. Old man Metz.

"Your wife disappeared—uh—that was—"

"Yesterday. Only yesterday."

One day's head start.

I knew all I needed to know and got up. What I didn't know was why Lena was gone? Maybe hiding, ashamed, frightened. Maybe Farret was really insane. It worried me, having known the girl.

"In the past, did your wife ever disappear?"

He stared at me with dislike. "No," he said. "You insult her." I tried to tell him that I had meant no such insult.

He seemed to believe me, when the phone rang.

Kowalski went to the phone while I waited.

He said very little. He said, "Oh" a few times and "Yes, yes" and then a long time he said nothing while he nodded his head, with his eyes shut. He hung up, came towards me with pain and bewilderment on his face. He blinked and some tears rolled down. I felt very bad.

I saw nothing else, felt nothing at first. His thick fist drove deep into my middle with no sound, it seemed, with no motion, just pure force.

I remember I doubled over and then wished I could curl around deeper and more completely, to be nothing but something small shrinking away. The pain was terrible.

In a while I could hear Kowalski crying, or wailing perhaps. He stood over me but I felt he was not really concerned with me there on the floor.

"Why?" He sobbed. "Why? Why this? One comes, he takes her. The next comes, he sits in my room and asks questions. Has she done anything? Have I done anything to them? One comes and asks about her, then takes her. The next comes in the same way, goes to the same place. You," he was suddenly close to my ear, "you don't move!"

I could see his shoes now. I had rolled towards his shoes without knowing which way I was moving. I had moved mostly from pain.

"Why?" he said. "What do you want, you and the other one?"

I couldn't talk yet.

"You go to the candy store and ask about Lena. Like the other one did."

I couldn't concentrate on what he said, but the irony struck me, that I should have tried finding Lena the same way Farret had done it. The old man in the candy store, it seemed, had seen me well enough to call up and describe me.

"Please," I said. "Please hear me out. You don't understand this—"

"I don't understand this," he said after me. "Yes. I don't. So I call the police!"

His shoes moved away, towards the telephone.

I tried to get up, but it was very hard. It must have looked foolish or useless because Kowalski stayed by the phone and didn't bother to stop me.

"Police," he said into the phone. "Operator, give me the real police now."

I buckled back down to the floor. There wasn't enough strength.

Chapter Nine

This house, unlike the others nearby, had three stories and seven chimneys. All the other houses were low, plastered white, long split-level houses with flat, graveled roofs. Some had Spanish tile on the roofs, some had nonsensical balconies, and all of them, each in its tropical park, looked low and flat under the royal palms.

The three-story house was dark brick, reminiscent of the north. The seven chimneys never showed smoke, because if the weather should ever get coolish there were little gas panels in every room to take out the chill. Where feasible, these gas panels stood in the fire places.

The house was a conspicuous monster which first of all made the owner out to be rich and next either a wilful man, or a man of no taste. Or a man with humor.

This was Metz. He was in a large, sunny room on the first floor, lying in bed. He was dying of cancer.

His bed linen was blue, because he liked it that way, because he had snow-white hair which made a fine contrast. His midnight to eight nurse was combing his hair, a job she enjoyed, always leaving this job to the last after bathing him, changing him, and doing the other things that needed doing when a bed patient woke up and wanted his morning toilette. When the eight to four nurse came in she would see a very neat old man in an immaculate bed—a very thin man and his skin color too far towards gray, but it all gave an impression of orderliness, which was the thing between these two nurses who had their rivalries.

The day nurse, her color and plumpness almost a flaunt next to the old man, would wait till the other one left, and then would start tucking and slapping the bed on her own, saying "Well, well, well. And what kind of a night did we have?"

"We?" said Metz. His eyes, maybe by contrast, looked very alive. "We had no night of any sort, girl. You know that."

Metz's voice sounded offhanded and hoarse. Some of the growth was in his throat.

The sun had been shifting and a patch of it started to crawl up on Metz's cheek. He lay still under it, his eyes closed, but when he heard the shade make a soft chatter and the sunlight disappeared from his face he opened his eyes and looked at the nurse by the window. "Open it," he said.

"But, Mister Metz."

"Open it, girl."

She was not a girl. She was in her late thirties and took Metz's way of address as a personal compliment. This made her more lenient with him than was her habit and she opened the shade again. "If you say so, Mister Metz. But soon it's going to be in your eyes."

"Very soon I won't know it," he said.

The day nurse laughed so heartily that it startled Metz. She laughed all the way back to the bed and started patting and tucking again. "Now, now," she said. "We don't want to be gloomy now, do we?"

"We?" said Metz. "I don't know about you, girl, but I got gloom all through my insides. Or don't *we* really believe that?"

"Now, Mister Metz. I have my instructions, and not the least of them is to keep you cheered."

"You can't keep me cheered," he said. "I'm too weak for that business."

He looked her up and down and then stopped with his eyes on her belly. So she knows I've got life-like interests, he thought to himself. So she leaves me alone with her dutiful cheer.

"*Mister* Metz," said the nurse. "Now we shouldn't talk like that."

"If you say *we* once more—" he took a pause, because he felt tired, "I'll die on *our* shift, girl."

She said nothing. She stopped tucking and slapping his bed, as if to punish him, and went to the door. "I will get your tea, Mister Metz." The mention of death by a patient was like a demerit to her.

Metz watched her leave the room. When she was gone he craned himself to see the bedstand which stood too close to his head. It was always too close to his head and he would die before they would change that habit. He got up with his elbows behind him and managed to see the clock. He reached out with one arm, managed to move the clock over, and looked at its face. Then he sank back on his pillow.

He had now learned several things: that it had cost him more effort today than yesterday to manage this daily maneuver; that his pain was starting earlier. He closed his eyes and breathed slowly. With all their technology, tricks, routines, time honored mannerisms, with all these things he could buy for money, he was still left completely alone in the thing that mattered most. He felt quite alone with the task of facing his own disintegration.

He moved his head around to find the spot of sun on the pillow. Then he moved his face into it.

"Now, have we been restless again?" said the nurse from the door.

She's griping about "our" bed being mussed, he said to himself. She can't stand it when the bed looks like somebody's living in it. *Living* in it, he repeated to himself. He looked up at the nurse and said, "No. All is serene. Daily more so—"

"That's fine," she said. "That's lovely."

She cranked up his bed and swung the bed table over in front of him. The smell of the hot tea seemed too penetrating to him, and too sudden.

"Aren't we—aren't you going to drink it, Mister Metz?"

"Give me my shot," he said.

"But Mister Metz," and she looked at the clock, "not for thirty minutes yet."

"Times change, girl. I need it, believe me."

"Now, we don't want to...."

"I'll wrinkle your bed, girl. I'll foul it."

The nurse made an embarrassed sound, quickly tucked something at the foot of the bed.

"You can kid me all you want," he said to her. "You think that's the bed-side manner. But don't kid yourself, girl. You know I need it. Don't kid your-self, girl."

She wished he did not keep his face in the sun. It looked wrong and horri-ble, it upset her.

"Very well, Mister Metz." She said it very low and did not look at him, but prepared his injection and gave it to him. Then she sat by the window and looked out on the lawn where the traveler palms stood all in a row. They looked pressed and starched to her, not like live trees. She did not turn around again till she heard Metz drinking his tea.

"All right?" she said.

"Fine. All is serene."

When he looked more relaxed and his eyes slower she walked up to the bed, folded her hands, and smiled at him. "And now I have a surprise for you, Mis-ter Metz."

"Please. Don't."

"While I was heating your tea there was a phone call and...."

"Was it Bernstein?"

"No, Mister Bernstein hasn't called."

"Good, good. Days of grace," said Metz. "Bernstein and his money worries will soon be over."

"How nice," said the nurse. "I'm glad he's straightening out your money worries, and then that will be over."

"Not he, I'm straightening it out. Soon as I'm dead."

The nurse took this very valiantly, keeping a stiff smile on her face. "Your surprise," she said. "Don't you want to hear it?"

"Go ahead, girl. Tell it to me."

"Well, this young lady called up, an old friend of yours. She said she's an old friend of yours and your man Howard downstairs, I asked him, and he said yes, she's an old friend of yours."

"Who?"

"A Mrs. Kowalski."

"No. Here?"

"She would love to see you, Mister Metz, and if you promise not to get ex-cited...."

"Call her. Tell her to come," said Metz, smiling.

"If you promise not to get too excited."

"I know. What I'm trying to tell you, girl, if you call her now and she gets here in half an hour, then she'll hit me right at the fifty-five minute peak of that shot you just gave me. I'll be fine, she'll be fine, and you won't have to worry. Call her, girl. Lena and me with my shot, it'll be like a nice old dream."

Metz lay in bed feeling the drug go into all of him. He felt soft and without any hard boundaries, and out of this indistinct cloud he reached around him with just a few senses; with his eyes to see the bright light on the window panes, with his ears to hear sounds from outside. That's all he needed, just those two feelers to reach around, just those two senses to carry his interest. It gave him a good feeling of concentration, so that he could have sworn he had heard the taxi outside long before anyone else did. But when he turned his head to say something about this he already saw the nurse at the door, opening the door, and the voice he heard said, "Mrs. Kowalski sent me. May I come in?"

"No excitement," said the nurse, and left the room.

Farret walked up to the bed.

The two men looked at each other and both were smiling. Metz was smiling because he thought he would now see Lena, Farret was smiling because he was pleased with the sight. There was Big Metz. There was a thin heap of bones which was Metz.

"Well, well, well," said Farret. "We've changed, haven't we?"

Metz dragged it out of the depth of his cloud. The habit helped very little now. "We," he said. "I don't know about *we*. I think *you* have, Farret."

Farret pulled up a chair and sat down. He took out a cigarette, put it in his mouth, then took it out again. He didn't think he should smoke. It had nothing to do with his feelings for Metz, so he told himself, but was a general law about sick rooms. Metz was looking at him now. There had been a change in the man, thought Farret.

"How come you got away?" said Metz.

They had never liked each other and Metz, with the rights of the older one, had never been polite about it. Even now, half dead there on the bed—

Farret took out a cigarette, put it in his mouth, and lit it.

"It could be the drug," said Metz. Thinking was less of an effort now, because his dislike gave him a feeling of life. "It could be just that, or is it taking you a very long time to get to the point?"

"I've come to the point," said Farret. "I'm looking right at it."

"You must want something," said Metz. "You brainy rats usually want something for nothing."

"Maybe you even know what," said Farret. "I got this feeling I got my man."

Metz, considering his state, was very alert. The friction was a tonic to him, something he craved and would enjoy, no matter what came after. Actually, he was not that much aware, or he would have wondered about Farret's tone.

"I'll take a guess, if it kills me," said Metz. The drug was coming apart in his head like mist blowing. "You want money."

This time Metz noticed the quality, because Farret looked very intent and his voice was the same. "No," said Farret. "You don't buy me off."

"You *have* changed."

"No. I just got sharper."

"You sound, pardon the phrase, as though you're on a mission," said Metz.

Farret sat back in his chair and seemed to expand. He liked that phrase. He relaxed, put out the cigarette on the heel of his shoe. On a mission was a very good phrase. It pulled together, he thought, all the strong feelings and all the nagging feelings that had kept him going for the last eight years, that had kept him from going down and under, because all that time he had had a mission.

"I got a raw deal on the island," he said. "Then I got eight years of time to think. When I lost out...."

"Of course you never lost out in your life except that one time," said Metz.

"Be quiet." Farret had wanted to say, "shut up," but the old man there and that face had changed the words for him.

"Don't mind me," said Metz. "Just talk. Say something, even."

Farret leaned forward and Metz, drug or no drug, couldn't miss the expression. That rat did have a mission.

"I've had a rough life," said Farret. "The kind of life that can break a man. But not me, Metz. Not me. What keeps me going, what always keeps me going, is principles! And one of them is, I hate doublecrossers!"

Metz almost laughed, but nothing weakened him like laughing so he turned it into something else. "You are an avenging angel," said Metz. "I can see that clearly."

"You laughing at me, you son of a bitch?"

"Oh no, I'm too weak."

"You watch yourself, Metz. You watch yourself with me."

If Metz had been less certain of dying he would have worried more about Farret. But even so he saw that the man was dead serious. A rat with nothing has at least principles, and preferably principles which blame somebody else. It had been there all the time, with Farret, but then he was doing well enough to leave principles be. He had been just a rat running guns, making money, making one or two people jump when he yelled. Lena for instance. But then eight years of bad luck or eight years of nothing but kicks in the pants, that had brought out the mission in Farret. It had brought out the full flower of the rat. He wasn't even interested in money!

The nurse opened the door to check if there was any excitement. "Everything all right, Mister Metz?"

"Just talk," he said. "Nothing serious."

The nurse left and the two men stayed together. Metz closed his eyes because he wanted to save his strength. He felt he had nothing to lose but that and he wanted all of it to have his game with Farret. All his life he had wanted to care as little as now and had wanted to show it. Farret would see this, how little anything mattered.

"You must have a plan, Farret. Some grand plan to set everything right."

"I'm gonna take you apart," said Farret without raising his voice. "I've got it clear in my head now how you tipped off the police, back on the island, and made me lose out."

"I'm a mastermind," said Metz. "I ruin a ten thousand a month setup, just to get a rise out of you, right, Farret?"

"You were headman," said Farret. "Nobody but you...."

"I thought you were headman," said Metz, and his face with the dope behind his deep eyes looked all wrong grinning like that.

"If you weren't so sick," said Farret and got up to stand by the bed, "if you weren't so sick in the head, Metz, I'd take the trouble and show you how right you are."

Farret stared down at the old man, thinking what to do about Metz, how to hurt the old man in the worst way.

"Going to eat me alive?" said Metz.

Farret felt suddenly sick. "You son of a bitch," he said. "I'm gonna make you wish you were dead."

This made Metz laugh.

"I'm gonna make you tell how you did it, how you crossed me up."

"Just ask me," said Metz, enjoying the way Farret looked, how he stood there by the bed, almost like a crazy man but very sharp in the head and very eager.

"I don't see you denying a thing," said Farret.

"Of course not. I'm not afraid of you yet," said Metz.

The day nurse stuck her head in the door, but all she saw was the two men talking quietly and Mister Metz smiling. The visit, she thought, was doing a world of good for Mister Metz. Such a nice man, the other one, to come and spend time with a dying man. But she said, "Five minutes, Mister Metz. We mustn't overdo it."

"We're reaching the climax," said Metz to the nurse. "It can't possibly last five more minutes."

Such a brave old man, after all, thought the nurse. And cheerful. She closed the door and decided that even ten more minutes would be all right.

Farret sat down again and folded his arms. He had decided to come back day after day for a while, till he knew better how to hurt the old man, but right now he would spell out what he knew. It would make the old bastard less snippish.

"You," he said, "sent the guns from the States. Nobody but you was ever sure when a shipment was coming, sure enough and long enough in advance to arrange a doublecross good enough."

"I'm a master...."

"Shut up. So you arranged...."

"Why?"

For a short moment Farret was caught by the question, because he had never thought about this. Then he laughed. He didn't have to think about this question, did not have to raise it in the first place, because the answer was built in.

"Because I was getting too big for you!"

Metz had his eyes closed, his insides weaving with dope. To Farret it looked like shock.

"I was the key man for deliveries and without deliveries there was nothing. No arms, no deals, no dough. I was the key man! I kept the local junta in the palm of my hand...."

"Lena's, you mean."

"I needed the local help for the convoy...."

"Like beating the bones out of your guide, that little fellow, Enrico or something?"

That was a fine memory for Farret: Enrico the sugar cane farmer who lived at the foot of the mountains and who could smell his way up to the hideout or rendezvous almost the way a dog would do it. It was a fine memory first, because Enrico was getting rich through Farret's employing him and second, because it gave Farret the chance in the end to break Enrico back down to size. A lousy peon telling him, Farret, not to cache arms on the sugar cane farm; telling him, Farret, to keep away from Enrico's daughter, a thing no better than Lena except darker in color—

"You lost a good guide there," said Metz. "Maybe you got ambushed because you lost your way without him taking you by the hand up the mountains."

"He wasn't no good with both legs broken," said Farret without any humor or intentional viciousness.

"Anyway," said Metz, "I pulled off the doublecross. A day before you went up the mountains I gave Captain Salvato the word you'd be coming through, did I?"

Farret stared at the old man, wondering how Metz lay there without being afraid.

"You know a hell of a lot," he said. "Like I thought."

"I couldn't have told the good Captain before then, because he wasn't available," said Metz.

"Ten-day leave. How did you know that?"

"Through you," said Metz. "You didn't want to move any arms till Captain Salvato was back, remember?"

"What a memory," said Farret, truly impressed, and mostly impressed with his own rightness: Metz *had* been the one! It was a shame he admitted it all with so much ease. A sick man. No accounting a sick man.

"You look ten years younger," said Metz. "It must be wonderful to feel so right."

It's going to feel even better, thought Farret. It's going to feel best of all when Metz won't take any of this so easily anymore. Why is he taking it all this easily?

"But you're still not sure, are you, Farret? And you got to be sure you have the right man, don't you?"

The bastard was playing with him! He was now starting to—

"But don't worry," said Metz. Then he changed his tone. "You got Lena along with you?"

"Why? What's she got to do with this?"

"I'd like to see her," said Metz.

Maybe this would be the thing to give Metz a twist. Something with Lena—

"But mostly," Metz went on, "I want her here so I can prove to you, about myself."

"Lena?"

There was a phone in the room, out of Metz's reach, and it started to ring. It had a soft, purring bell, but both men turned as if at an intruder.

"Would you bring me..." Metz started but Farret was already up and lifting the receiver off the cradle.

"Mister Metz?" said a voice.

"Yes, what is it?" Farret made no move to give the phone to the old man in bed.

"Will you give the phone to Mister Metz, please? This is Howard. I'm calling from downstairs."

Farret gave the phone to Metz. He watched the old man very closely but Metz looked mostly tired. He listened with eyes closed and opened them only once, to look at Farret; it made Farret turn away from him.

"No," said Metz to the phone. "But we'll arrange something a little bit later. I'll tell you when, later." Then Metz asked, "Bernstein didn't call back, did he?"

Bernstein, Metz's accountant, hadn't called back. Just as well, thought Metz, and then he asked Farret to put the phone back in its place. He watched Farret do this and said, "You go bring Lena. I'm tired now."

Farret thought about it, wondering what the trick might be, except that Lena was dumb and Metz was sick and what tricks were there between the two that could stop him.

"You want to know who crossed you, Farret?"

"I know already!"

"But a moral bastard like you, Farret, you need proof. Come back tomorrow. With Lena."

Farret stood there and frowned.

"Scared? Scared of tricks?" said Metz.

Metz would suffer for this, for the things he was saying and for the way they came out, he would suffer for this whether he was dying or not, guilty or not.

"Time," said the nurse from the door. She came into the room and smiled at Farret. "But you must come back," she said to him. "Old friends of Mister Metz's cheer him so and there haven't been any visitors here in a long time, isn't that true, Mister Metz? Don't we like...."

"We do," said Metz. He turned in his bed so nobody could see his face. "Tomorrow, Farret. Same time."

Chapter Ten

It would have been good to be able to say to Kowalski, "Look, you and I are after the same man. A terrible thing has happened to you and I'm afraid the same might happen to me. Help me find him and it will be the same as if you found him yourself. And I'll see that your Lena comes back to you."

It was too late for that. He wouldn't listen. I was on the floor in his cheap front room with only the light from the bulb in the kitchen. The carpet looked like night and day, dark and dull-colored where there was no light and the very bright patterns close to my face where the light from the kitchen made a streak into the room. The carpet there had vivid colors, too many colors it seemed to me, with shiny reflections on the pile, all painful.

I said, "Kowalski, please." And I think I tried saying I'm sorry, but he was on the phone asking for the police and then he hung up. From where I was lying he looked very large and bullish. The wetness on his face didn't distract from that.

"Lie still," he said, "or I hurt you bad."

I could hear him open a drawer and when he came back into view he stood there holding a hammer.

I understood very clearly, as clear as my pain, that there was no point talking to him. There was no point to anything now but to get away, because once the police came, once they found me and started unraveling, it would be the worst.

But Kowalski was not a man like Farret and that was the way out, if any.

"Lie still," he said again and came closer. He said this with a lot of meaning but it was mostly pain, mostly pain and confusion over what had been happening to him.

"Kowalski," I said. "Help me. I can't move."

"They will move you."

"Help me, Kowalski. The blood inside—"

"What?" He came closer, to hear me.

"I can't move. I got to move, Kowalski. Sit up. Or the blood inside, where you hit me, might kill me. You'll kill me, if you leave me on the floor."

I needn't have gone that far because he was already holding me under the arms. He still had the hammer. It was in his right hand, sticking out next to my chest.

"The couch," I said. "Please."

It hurt like hell when he moved me and I wasn't groaning to make an impression. He put me down quite gently and then he stepped back. I was on the couch and he was in front of me. He was holding the hammer but no longer thinking about it.

"Five minutes maybe," he said. "And you'll be all right. They come from the station."

I wanted to try once more.

"Kowalski. You and I are after the same man."

He held the hammer again, knowingly, making it jerk in his hand with a quick tightening of the muscles.

I said, "All right," and then I mumbled something which he couldn't understand, which was nothing but mumbling, but it made him step closer. He almost stepped between my stretched legs.

"What you saying? What? You have to move again?" and he reached out his hands to help me.

I hit him hard on the knee with my foot. The sudden impact almost made me throw up but Kowalski fell. He jackknifed. I was afraid I had broken his knee, which is easy.

But when I was up he was almost up, using one leg mostly, with the effort making his bald head a near purple.

It would have been good to say something to him, that he and I were not enemies. I could hear the siren howl up from the tracks. I hit Kowalski hard, on the side of his head.

Then I ran. The sirens were growing louder, whipping some kind of life into me. I knew by the motion that I was going down hill, away from Kowalski's house. Get away. And after that get to Miami. I must get to Miami. For what? To catch Farret and lose Jane? I couldn't leave Denver without having found Jane!

I stopped on the street and right then I didn't hear sirens or anything. I only felt the sinking inside me, a sensation like a helpless fall, because I did not know how to solve the dilemma. If I stayed they would catch me and I wouldn't find Farret. If I left, if I could make it, I would leave Jane somewhere behind.

I think they caught me because I could not solve the dilemma.

Once in the cell I slept.

There was a window in the hall which ran past my cell and the light woke me. The light hurt my eyes and for a moment I lay there and thought that closing my eyes would stop everything and I might go back to sleep. I did not want to wake up.

A piece of routine got me on my feet, for the time being. The turnkey came down the corridor saying, "Six clock. Stand up if you want breakfast," and so on the whole length of the hall. On the ranch I would eat breakfast at six o'clock and that's why I got off the plank and stood by the bars waiting for breakfast. Not that I thought I was back home. I felt stiff from the night on the plank and I wasn't hungry. But I would do this routine thing so that there would be no problems.

They brought a plate of oatmeal and a mug of black coffee. When I sat down with the stuff another trustee came by and asked if I wanted milk and sugar. I shook my head and didn't look up.

"Drunk again, eh?" he said and then walked on to the next cell. He said the same thing each time he stopped but he got very few answers.

It would have been nice to have landed here, drunk and disorderly. The way I felt, nothing could have been nicer than to be in this place for that reason. All of a sudden the oatmeal was finished. Figuring five minutes for eating it, maybe ten, I had managed to spend that much time without knowing it.

I found cigarettes in my pocket and had one with the coffee. But the trick with passing the time didn't happen again. I was awake now and nothing else. I was awake and could do nothing with it.

I couldn't see anything out of the cell except the wall of the corridor and the window. The window showed me some sky and it brought in the sound of a clock. Every half hour I could hear the clock. I spent the time picking up problems and dropping them. I didn't solve my problems but I learned, sitting there, to leave an unsettled problem alone. That's not an easy thing but it is valuable. It's like learning to live with an impossibility.

That's how I saved my strength. I felt I would need a great deal.

The turnkey let me out at ten in the morning and took me through two other locked doors, up a staircase, and into a room. There was a desk, a bench, and some chairs. The turnkey explained nothing and I didn't ask him a thing. The last thing I wanted was to get a no-answer. The turnkey left when a lieutenant came in.

"John Miner?"

"Yes," I said.

They would have gotten that information from the papers I had in my pocket.

"Known Kowalski long?" he asked. He didn't look up but was doing things with some papers. We seemed to be sitting here, just killing time.

"No," I said. "A very short time."

"You make friends fast."

It was a snide crack and I sat up, getting ready for the business end of the conversation. What I had decided to do was to tell the truth more or less, depending upon how severe the charge. Some felonious assault charge, I figured, would be the worst. In that case, I thought, I would tell them about Lena and Farret. It would be a dangerous thing, what with my own past being tied in with them, but the worst had already happened. I was caught, up to my neck, and the best I could do now was not to antagonize them.

The door opened and Kowalski came in. He had a big gauze patch on his skull and he nodded to me. In one hand he carried my bag. He set it down on the bench and said, "This is yours. I brought this for you."

I had two answers for that. Either he had been asked to bring it along because they were moving me to a more permanent jail, or he had brought it
along to get the taint out of his house.

"Sorry about our fight," he said. "I'm sorry it happened."

I said nothing, because I understood nothing.

"Sign this," said the lieutenant to Kowalski, and Kowalski signed something
on the desk. Then the lieutenant said, "Beat it, Miner."

I coughed, because if I had said something now it would have come out a
squeak.

"But don't leave town. And we want you to report here tomorrow at
eight."

"Just a minute," I said. "I'm out?"

"You're out. Kowalski dropped charges."

"I'm out." I got up and walked to the bench where my bag was. "If I'm out
I don't have to report."

"You take that attitude, Miner, and we keep you here. There's more to this
thing than Kowalski's charge. We still got a kidnapping problem."

I shut my mouth. I didn't know, and I didn't want to know, how much
they were interested in me. I just wanted out so I could look for Jane.

Kowalski had left the door open and when I picked up my bag I could see
out into the hall. Jane sat there.

I don't know when I had started but when I had her in my arms there were
tears in my eyes. She and I didn't talk, and Kowalski didn't, and we walked
out to the street without saying a word. Kowalski opened the door of an old
car and Jane and I sat in the back. Kowalski drove to his diner and didn't look
back at us.

Jane and I just sat close together.

"You had breakfast?" Kowalski asked.

"Yes. I ate." We got out and went into his diner.

There were three yardmen at the counter and we walked to a booth. We
sat down with Kowalski. I said, "I'm sorry too, about last night. Really."

"I understand it," he said. And then, "She came to me, your lady, and explained about you when she found out."

I didn't know what to say, but something had to come out so I squeezed
Jane's hand.

"At least something good came of it," she said, "of my running away to do
this alone."

"You're safe."

"It was terrible," she said and explained about meeting Farret. And how
she had come back the next day to find Kowalski after Lena had left, and how
she had stayed one extra day because there had been no flight back to Frisco.
"I called you and called you," she said, "and then I thought I might catch you
here. I was sure you were coming."

"And there I was," I said, "snug in jail."

"I read it in the paper this morning. I read about the arrest and went back to Mister Kowalski."

"You go after Farret now?" Kowalski asked.

"Yes."

"It is better than the police." Then he got up and nodded at me. "If you find her, tell her she should come back. Tell her," and he went to the part of the diner where he had the kitchen.

I took Jane to the airport, and it was good that there was very little to say. She had been terribly close to the worst about Farret, his willful anger with anything that aroused his suspicion. She would leave him to me.

She understood that it was better. She left to wait for me at the ranch and she knew I would come soon. She believed that completely. However, I don't think she would have gone easily, if she had not been able to help me before.

Chapter Eleven

I left Denver by plane, going to Miami. The Denver police were expecting me at eight the next morning but I took great care to find out if they were watching me and when everything looked normal to me I took the chance. The lieutenant might have been talking big, or he might have hoped I would come because he had no good legal way to detain me. Or they had been careless about me, or had even lost interest. The question didn't bother me at first and I mostly thought about Farret while I was on the plane. I tried to sleep a few times but that didn't work. When we landed at Miami's International Airport I got suddenly jumpy. Perhaps it was the knowledge of getting closer to Farret, or it was because of too little sleep, but everyone at the ramp, waiting and stretching their necks, was waiting and stretching for me. I forced myself not to pay too much attention, but then again, I had left a trail like an elephant. If Denver wanted me, they would have no trouble. Nothing happened though, and the jitters went.

I took a room in the Cuban section and I called a few people to help me with Metz. On the third call I got his address. Then I called Metz. He didn't answer the phone himself but the man said Metz would call back. I had to give him my number which made me nervous again, though by this time it was getting ridiculous.

The hall phone rang five times in three hours and I got there first each time. Once Mac wanted Joe, then Rita wanted Desi, then somebody wanted Desi again, and next Rita again, wanting Joe this time. The last one was for me.

"I'm Miner," I said. "Who are you?"

"Metz, boy. Fancy...."

"Metz?" I didn't recognize the voice. "I'm not sure about this," I said, very nervous again. "You sure you got the right party?"

"It better be you," he said, "because we're having a reunion."

"Look, fellow. I don't belong to any...."

"Lena and the weasel-diesel are here," then a laugh which didn't sound right to me. Even the expression he had used when referring to Farret could have been picked up by somebody else. Only Metz had ever used it, between him and myself, but somebody else could have picked it up.

I said, "If you're in this for the money, how come you don't quit?"

That's how we had met. He owned more and had more money than he could hope to spend while in his sane mind, but he had been at the poker table in a private room in his own club, playing against his own house, losing to himself or to me. I had thought that was very funny or maybe eccentric but then he had answered me and from that time on we had exchanged the remarks between each other on a few occasions.

"I'm in this so I learn not to give a damn," said the voice on the phone, and that had been the remark Metz had made at the poker table when he dropped fifteen hundred to me.

When he had spent fifty thousand to set up the gun running deal with me, I had said to him, "If you're in this for the money—" and he had answered, "So I learn not to give a damn."

The exchange had been a great joke at that point, because that same day the papers were carrying news about the island revolution being just about over. As it turned out there was a new one a week later and the split in the island affairs lasted and lasted. Metz never did lose his money.

Then we had used the remarks once again, when Metz had blacked out one day and was in the hospital for observation. They took him off cigars, off liquor, off good food and off his feet. Two weeks later he was out and doing the opposite. "If you want to stay alive," I had said and he, looking like death from the ordeal, said, "So I learn not to give a damn."

"You still there, John?" said the voice on the phone.

"Yes. I didn't recognize your voice, Metz."

"It's me though," he said. "What throws you is my death rattle. I'm learning not to give a damn," and he laughed again the way he had done a short while ago.

His humor had never been orthodox or very easy on the nerves. He sounded bad, and something else worried me now. With Metz half-gone and so free to be irresponsible, how much help would he be with Farret?

"Metz," I said. "I don't know what you know about this, but Farret worries me. I called to warn you."

"Have you seen him?"

"No."

"I have. He's looking for blood."

That settled one thing for sure. I wasn't on any wild-goose chase and the Lena-Metz circuit wouldn't stop there.

"Is Farret in town?"

"He's coming back to see me, Miner. He'll be here at least till tomorrow."

"Where is he? If I can get to him...."

"Oh no. Don't do that. I want you to know what my doctor said when he saw me after Farret's visit. He said, 'Mister Metz, you have a remarkable pulse today.'" Then Metz laughed again.

The joke went over my head.

"Metz, listen to me seriously for a moment. I don't know how much any of this means to you but Farret...."

"I know. Better come today, Miner. Two this afternoon."

I felt reassured when he said this and his tone hadn't been flip or sarcastic.

"Is Farret going to be there?"

"He comes tomorrow, I told you. We better meet first. We can figure something."

"Right."

"I'll discuss it with you, Miner. Maybe there's one or two ways to change his tack for him."

Metz was all right. His macabre jokes just meant that he hadn't changed. By the time I hung up the phone even his voice seemed familiar again.

I had three hours before seeing Metz which I used to take a bath in the community shower at the end of the hall and to eat my first meal of the day, both welcome tasks. My suitcase was back in Denver. Then I flagged a jitney which took me across the Venetian Way into Miami Beach. I took a taxi all the way to the gate of the Metz place which looked properly deserted the way all the big houses did.

I counted change out of my palm and at that moment looked up and saw the man on the sidewalk. It seemed obvious to me the man was trying not to look at the Metz house and my taxi in front of it.

"Drive."

"Huh?"

"Drive," I said. "Just beat it out of here."

We passed a parked car that I checked automatically. Chevrolet, one year old, Florida license, district of Miami, pink and cream. And empty. Just parked there, on a visit. Fine. Why not. But better be cautious.

When the taxi swung into Alton and started running down the wide, four lane boulevard I noticed a Chevrolet, one year old, Florida license, district of Miami. Two tone, pink and cream—

Chapter Twelve

Alton gets cheaper going south, a street now instead of a boulevard. At the first light I dropped a five on the front seat and got out of the cab without having to explain any more. I got to the curb when the light changed but crossed too fast. I crossed all alone. Maybe that was when he spotted me. I was well down the cross street and into the bend where the residences started again when I saw the pink and cream car back at the intersection. It was parked there and the man got out on the side of the curb. He didn't look my way but came walking my way as if he had nothing to do.

There was a truck entrance in the building ahead and a lot of big boxes. They said *This Side Up*, and *TV*. They stood there, all empty, and there couldn't have been a finer setup for building a fort or a kid's club house on a back lot. I walked slowly now and looked at the boxes, appreciating the sight.

My man was closer now. I could hear his steps. Right then he was nothing but heel thuds in a rhythm but they suddenly had a lot of personality to me and a lot of meaning.

At the truck entrance I slowed, then stopped. I hoped I was giving him time for his maneuver and then turned around. I hoped he saw this because I didn't see him. I had given him enough time. Then I walked through the gate and stopped by the boxes.

It wasn't as good as it could have been because none of them were high enough to reach over my head, even the stacks of several boxes on top of each other. And in the back of the entrance, inside the building, there was a truck ramp, a window showing an office, and there was a man on the ramp checking sheets on a clip board. He turned to look at me while I stood there and looked over the boxes. I waved at him and kept checking the boxes.

"Don't take any of the big ones," he said from the ramp.

I said, "Okay, I won't. Okay, thank you."

Then he left.

This happened just in time because I heard the footsteps, fast now and then suddenly slow. I crouched down to be out of the way. I saw my man before he saw me. He came into the entrance, slow and easy, looking at all the emptiness and at the boxes. He did all this slowly and with ease because I think that's how he felt. He had just this one job, to do tailing, and it was no strain on him.

He moved, coming along the boxes, when I jumped. I hadn't let myself go since this had all started. I did now. It felt right and sharp. My hand cut him hard at the base of the skull and to keep him from going forward too much I jammed the heel of my other hand flat over his nose.

Those two punches must have met on the inside of his skull like two trains hitting head on because his eyes rolled up white instantly and his legs melted down.

He wasn't heavy. He was rather small, with fine bones, and dark like some South Americans are. He smelled of soap, the kind they call beauty soap, and was dressed well. Money in one pocket, car keys in the other. Handkerchief in the left back, nothing in the right. In the jacket cigarettes, in the other side pocket a broken cheroot. I must have broken that, dragging him. A Florida driver's license, name Luis Gambello. Something else. An English-Spanish phrase book and the same in reverse.

No holster, no gun, no badge. But he carried a knife.

"Hey. Hey, you there—"

The man with the clip board was back on the ramp and I didn't know how long he'd been watching. He stood there, more upset by his own fear at the sight of us than by anything else. It helped me get over my own sudden fright.

"Stay where you are!" he said now. "You make one more move...."

I straightened up just the same. The clip board he pointed wasn't going to hurt me and besides, I wasn't going to stop now.

I said, "Listen. Be glad I'm shticking wif my fren here. You wanna manipu—manipperlate him yerself?" I was walking up to the ramp now, an aggressive walk and drunk. "You gotten idee the trouble a drunk is when he's drunk like my fren here? You wanna maybe finout what...."

"Don't you come any closer! You get out of here this instant or I'll call the manager!"

The manager. I could tell who scared my clip board man.

"The manjer unless he's a drunk too ishn't gonna know howter mannipurless he's a drunk too gonna—the hell wid you," I said and went back to the boxes.

The manager did come while I was still there, standing at the edge of the ramp with his belly out and his arms akimbo. I didn't pay much attention to him because I was moving my drunken friend and when the manager started to shout it wasn't at me but at the clip board man. About what kind of way is this to run shipping and receiving and how long have those bums been living in those empty boxes and no wonder sales have been dropping off—

I never got the connection to the last comment because I was out on the street by then, dragging Luis Gambello like a bona fide drunk. He helped a little, trying to move his legs, but he was still badly shaken up. I got him back towards Alton where his car was parked and dropped him into the seat next to the driver's.

He and I were not finished. Gambello wasn't a cop but he had been following me. He watched me when I got behind the wheel which was all right. I looked at his nose which was tight-skinned from the swelling and then I hauled out for a backhand.

There is nothing like a sensitive nose to make a man forget anything else. He saw my face getting ready for the hard swing and my arm hauling back and he cringed down into a small knot of fright. He stayed that way, waiting for the hit.

"So we understand each other," I said.

I never had to hit him because we understood each other. He stayed far away from me, his hands up like a little rabbit so that he could get them over his face very fast, should the need arise.

"Sit on your hands," I said.

"For heaven's sake," he said. He had a soft voice, with an intonation of the Spanish language.

"I'm not going to hit you," I said. "I want to reach into your pockets."

He sat very still, very worried, because he wanted to give me no cause to come near his nose.

I took out the spring knife. The fact that I had found it didn't seem to disturb him at all. Then I took out his driver's license, looked at the address, gave the license back to him. I started the car and we drove.

He said nothing during the trip. Once he lowered one hand to put it inside his jacket pocket so I said, "The cheroot is broken." He accepted that information and did not put his hand in that pocket. "The cigarettes are all right," I said. He looked at me with a very faint smile, as if my knowledge amused him, took out the pack and offered a cigarette to me. We both smoked but he never talked. He was poised now, calm, the sort of calm which meant no strain or worry, at least none of the generalized kind. He was still very cautious about his nose.

The address on the driver's license was in the southern part of Miami, almost in Coral Gables. It was a large, bland apartment building in a row of others. Except for the regimental row of thin palm trees in front, the place could have been any well-to-do city.

When we got out of the car he said, "Apartment E-5."

"Thank you."

His poise was infectious. I did not know who he was, I did not know where he was leading me, but I felt polite and in need of displaying good manners. I could have questioned him in the car and he would not have told me a thing. I could have beaten his nose back in his face and perhaps gotten something that way, but not much. Not with this Luis Gambello. Since that small bit with the cheroot and the cigarettes he and I had established a relationship and it had absolutely nothing to do with brutalities. In a way it felt weird, he and I on the elevator, he and I walking down the long corridor, gesturing to allow the other to take the lead, nodding in thanks, that sort of thing. Until we got to the door of E-5 I had even forgotten the immediate pressure: it was close to four and Metz had been waiting for me since three.

But Farret wasn't due until the next morning. There was time, there had to be time, because so far Luis Gambello had not been explained.

"There is no one at home," he said when he put the key in the door. "Just my lady friend." He smiled, swung open the door, walked into the apartment.

It seemed he was right. The large front room was empty, the kitchen seemed empty, and when Gambello went to the bedroom he knocked on the door.

"Magdalena?" he said.

A girl answered in quick Spanish, something I did not catch, but it sounded happy and eager. Just before the door opened Gambello had time to say, "We have a guest, Magdalena," very quickly, so that the door never quite opened. I never quite saw the girl in her white negligee, but she made a surprised sound and drew back. Then Gambello came back to sit down on a very modern, very expensive easy chair, nodding at me to sit opposite. We both sat and looked at each other for a moment and then he smiled briefly.

"Apparently you wish something from me. It would seem you have to talk first."

He was right. Politely and correctly so.

"Who are you?" It sounded coarse to me, in the face of his manners.

"Luis Gambello," he said, politely and correctly.

At that moment the bedroom door opened and Luis Gambello stood up. I felt it necessary to do the same.

"Miss Gonzales," he said, which was equivalent to saying Miss Smith, which may or may not have been so but established Gambello the gentleman. "The lady friend I mentioned to you."

She was no lady in the sense of having been trained as such. She wore an expensive dress, selected by Gambello most likely, wearing it as if it were in her way. And in a way, it was. She might have been an innate lady, or a potential lady, but any signs of this were overpowered by the quality of strong sex.

She was very young, very developed, and probably from one of the islands. She said, "Howyado," and sat down on the couch. It made her uncomfortable in her dress and she pulled on the top of it, to free her breasts. I felt that nothing would free those breasts except taking off everything.

"My friend," said Gambello to the girl and nodded at me, "has been in a fight with me." She gasped when he said it and looked at his nose. I myself became very uncomfortable. "But without my friend's help," he went on, "it would have gone very badly."

The girl started talking to him in rapid Spanish. I couldn't place the accent exactly, but thought she was Puerto Rican. She talked about her compassion for him, should he not go to bed, he must be more careful, and also that she had a strong brother whom she could call on the phone and if he, Luis, would reveal his assailant's name then her brother would be available to beat the man's face in. This girl was completely in love with Gambello.

"None of that will be necessary," said Gambello to the girl. "My friend took care of everything and your devotion alone, Magdalena, heals me."

What interested me was Gambello's attitude. He did not want the girl to know about his business. She probably knew nothing of his business.

"And now," he said to the girl, "I think I will sit with my friend for a while." He got up and the girl got up. I did too. Gambello took money out of his pocket, gave it to her and told her to spend a few hours at a remarkable double feature he had seen, mentioning a house which was way in the north of Miami. The girl gave him a strong look of devotion, kissed the side of his face, and left.

Gambello went to a cabinet, then came back with a bottle of brandy and two pony glasses. We sat down again.

"You have a phrase book in your pocket," I said. "But you speak beautiful English."

"Thank you, Mister Miner. I had bought it for Magdelena."

I didn't remember having told Gambello my name. "She was born here in Miami," he was saying, "but you know the kind of cultural isolation in which some of the poor are living."

"And you?"

"I have travelled a great deal." He was pouring the brandy.

"Starting from where?"

"Ciudad de Gambello."

There was one city by that name, small and ancient, and it was on the island!

"After one of my ancestors," said Gambello. He waited for me to drink from my glass and then he drank too. "But do you know which city I have liked best? Lisbon. Lisbon to me is the best and the worst of Paris, Rome, London, and Prague—prewar Prague—all rolled into one. It is fabulous."

If I allowed it this would go on until tea time and then he would offer me tea. We would have tea until dinner time and then he would offer me dinner. I had to remind myself of Jane waiting for me back in the Rockies, of Metz waiting for me in his bed, of Farret.

"How did you know my name, Gambello?"

He smiled and got up. I followed him into the bedroom where he opened a drawer while I watched over his shoulder. He handed a picture to me which had my full name on the back.

"You were thinner then," he said.

The picture, I guessed, was at least eight years old. Then he showed me four more, of Lena, Farret, Metz, and Getterman.

"Where did you get these?"

"From my government. Shall we go back to the living room?"

"General Duz," I said and followed him back.

"Oh no," he said. "Presidente Cervales. You hadn't known he won in the end?"

I hadn't known. All I had done was help ship guns.

"And you?" I said. I sat down again and picked up my glass. It seemed the best way to keep Gambello talking fluently.

"My family has always been in governmental affairs," he said. "I was abroad during the revolution but joined the Ministry of the Exterior upon my return." He picked up his pony and sniffed. "Cervales happened to be in office by then. Would you tell me, Mister Miner, where you live?" He asked this without any change in pace.

"Where I live? Why?"

He smiled and shrugged. "I didn't think you would tell me. It would have made things easier."

"What?"

"Finding you. But no matter. It was foolish to ask."

"Finding me? Who's looking? Cervales?"

"Our government," said Gambello. "I'm sure you remember supplying arms to us?"

"Us? You weren't even there!"

"But I am here now, governmentally."

"Cervales is looking. He is looking for whom?" I said.

"For all five of you. I showed you the pictures."

"Why?"

"Because your interruption of arms supplies were extremely hard on the Cervales faction. And most welcome to Duz."

I said, "Christ. Christ almighty."

"The possibility exists that you were traitors to the government."

"Traitors to the government?"

"Duz became a traitor, you understand. By virtue of Cervales taking over the government."

"I've never seen Duz except on posters," I said. "And all this was over eight years ago!"

"Yes. Duz is dead now." Gambello sipped. "Meanwhile justice continues to search out its victims."

I could have sworn he was smiling into his drink. That, together with my confusion, made me finally blow up.

"You mean to tell me your lousy operetta government is so damn bored they got time to chase all over this country and who knows where else...."

"Uruguay, Chile, Paraguay, Brazil."

But I didn't let him interrupt me. "...to drum up some unlikely treason case for your local consumption?"

"You are quite right," said Gambello. "It amounts to just about that. The Cervales government is quite without internal problems. We have bread, but no circus."

I got up and went towards him.

"But, Mister Miner," he said getting anxious, "you are asking for this information!"

He was right, of course, and I had nowhere to go with my anger.

"What's this crap about Uruguay, Paraguay, and so forth?"

"Your Mister Farret," said Gambello. "He was there, and in Brazil and Chile. Illegally in some of them, but that is to be expected."

"Don't side track. What about Farret?"

"He was the only one whose whereabouts we could trace. We are close to the countries I mentioned." He saw me getting impatient and came back to the point. "We found he intended to come back to the States and find every one of you. A falling out of the thieves, you might say. We followed him to San Francisco, we followed him to Denver."

"What happened at Denver?" I said.

"We almost lost him. Our man on that leg of the journey gave Farret a lift, Farret was hitchhiking, and in the process got himself robbed and tied up to the steering wheel."

"And now here we are in Miami. Now you got Farret, Metz, and me."

"And the young woman."

"Now what?"

"I don't know. The matter then goes to another department. And besides," said Gambello, "we don't know Mister Getterman's whereabouts, nor yours. You haven't told me yet." He smiled, trying to encourage me to see the humor in this.

"Typhoid Mary," I said. "The sonofabitch is like Typhoid Mary."

Gambello, not understanding the reference, kept politely silent.

I went to the door and locked it. I came back across the room and put my hands into my pockets to feel for the knife.

"You alone in Miami?"

Gambello shrugged, looked at his fingernails. Then he said, "Yes. I might as well tell you."

"How about the girl?"

"She is just a local lady friend, Mister Miner." He got up and looked at me. "You would like me to say I never found any of you?"

"That's so," I said.

"And my promise to give no report wouldn't do?"

"Would you give it?"

He had a very frank smile. "No," he said.

"The Gambello honor, or something."

"I have not tried to insult you, Mister Miner," he said.

I bit my lip, wishing I were in the mood to apologize.

"In any event," he went on, "I wish you would not think it necessary to kill me."

"Turn around," I said.

"You haven't answered me."

"No," I said. "I won't kill you."

He turned around and I hit him fast on the temple. It worked most of the time, with the right force, and Gambello was frail. He was out before he hit the ground.

CHAPTER THIRTEEN

Farret walked into the mahogany lobby to the Fort of Biscayne and stopped there for a moment. The high ceiling, the gilt on the columns, the four large chandeliers, all this pleased him. This was splendor. Farret was still wearing his pea jacket, but that didn't bother him. There was even design behind wearing the pea jacket. A bum? A bum sailor out of work? Farret had been hoping and waiting that somebody would try and treat him like that and then he, Farret, would straighten the sonofabitch out. He, Farret, was neither a bum nor a sailor. He was a consistent planner over several years now and everything was coming ripe. Two leaps and he had found his man. Foolish to have thought it had been Lena, but not so foolish to go to her first. And to keep her around now. Punish her.

But she was muck. Punish Metz for having deserted him, for having dropped him, Farret, back into the gutter. Punish the old man for having had the power. Last of all, but the shiniest reason, for breaking the code! Tracking a doublecrosser was like having religion!

Farret walked up to the desk, watching the room clerk. If the creep didn't look up any minute and smile as he should there'd be some rough talk coming his way. But at that moment the room clerk looked up, said "Good afternoon, Mister Farret," and held out the key.

"And get me somebody to carry these packages," Farret said.

The son of a bitch should have offered, thought Farret.

The creep shouldn't have to be told. He dropped the long carton and the two small ones on top of the desk, covering the record book which the clerk had been working on. The packages were candy-striped and a fancy name was printed at an angle. The stuff had cost a fortune. Farret had less than one hundred dollars left. However, there would be more. There was a plan, and in Farret's case that meant everything was as good as reality.

He unbuttoned his pea jacket and followed the bellhop into the elevator and then to his room. He sent the man away at the door. The tip was five dollars.

"Open up, Lena," he said from the corridor.

She opened the door and watched him come in. He was carrying the packages and the doorkey.

"I run myself ragged for these things," he said, "and you can't show enough appreciation to open the door when I ask you?" He dropped the packages on one of the single beds and turned on Lena as if he expected her to defend herself.

She did nothing like it. She closed the door quietly and was afraid to look up.

"Come here," he said.

She came over.

"I'm sick of looking at you in those Sunday bests from the Denver bargain basement. Throw 'em away."

"But, Baby, this dress...."

"You arguing with me?"

She shook her head. She even knew what would come next, because under one pretext or another he had made her do this maybe a dozen times.

"Come on, come on! I go to the expense I want to see some results."

He needn't rant, she thought. He needn't screw up his voice to that pitch like a vicious bite. She undid the belt on her dress and then the zipper.

"Easy! I told you a hundred times to stop rushing and doing it nervous. I don't want that because it gets on my nerves, this rushing and jittering." Farret took a deep breath, as if to show his exhaustion, and sank down in the chair by the window.

And why does he have to pretend, she thought. He wants me to undress, I undress. He never used excuses for anything, a long time ago, and that was all right. But now, cheap excuses as if she, Lena, was stupid and needed them. He was bad now. He was very bad.

"Now roll down the stockings," he said.

She put the dress on the nearest bed and bent down to roll off the stockings. Once she looked up to see him by the window but she couldn't see anything clearly. The light came from his way. The face black in shadow, and then the bulk of the pea jacket bunched up from the way he was sitting. Why did he never take off that jacket? And at night, why did he never undress?

"Turn around," he said. "Stop trying to look up and staring."

Another excuse. He always asked her to turn around at this point so he could look at her in this way.

She heard him say, "Fine, fine," and this was part of it too, his voice no longer irritated but a mumble, almost as if he were asleep.

When she was done with the stockings she turned around and started unhooking the bra.

"Come over here. Right here." He tapped with his foot.

She stood there and took off the bra.

"Stop scratching," he said.

She stopped immediately. She would rub herself later where the strap came over her shoulder. She just stood now and looked out of the window.

"The lipstick is coming off," he said. "Put more on."

She went to the dressing table to pick up the Fire Red lipstick, keeping her head down so she would not have to look in the mirror. Her nipples were unusually red.

"Turn around while you do this."

She did. She had meant to. She put the lipstick on the tips of her breasts and it felt to her as if it weren't herself she were painting.

"Now take off the rest and start powdering all over. If there's anything I can't stand it's that thick, shiny skin on a woman."

She did this and never looked in the mirror. She would not recognize herself and that would be worse than everything else—

"In the small boxes you find underwear," Farret was saying. "Black stuff, to give class. And in the long box is a dress. I'd like to see you appreciate what you're getting from me and the fact I'm making a lady outta nothing."

His voice was sharp again because the main part was over. She was getting dressed. She put on the black things he had bought her and the flower print dress which was much too small. Even that was part of it and not a mistake.

"All right. The shoes now. We're going out."

"Oh," she said and then swallowed the rest of it. "How nice," she had wanted to say, but how could it be?

"Don't you want to know where we're going?" He got up from the chair and went to the door.

"Yes. Where, Baby?"

"First we're going downstairs." This, he thought, was a joke or at least a teaser to raise her suspense.

"Could we eat in the hotel restaurant this time?"

She was a cow. She was no more anxious than she had been before and the most thrilling thing she could think of was food.

"We're seeing Metz," he said.

He didn't see that it gave her a start, that she wished above all not to have to see Metz now, like this, with Farret, but none of this showed. She said, "I thought you wanted to see him tomorrow."

"I changed my mind."

He walked out of the room and when he stood in the corridor, waiting for her to close the door, he was still thinking about his change of plan.

"No good reason to give Metz more time. More time means more tricks," and he smiled with appreciation. "Right?" he suddenly snapped at her.

"Yes. Right, Baby. You're very smart."

"I don't need you to tell me," he said because once she had said it he had no further use for her.

At two in the afternoon the taxi pulled up in front of the Metz house and at two-five the nurse up in the sick room interrupted her cleaning to answer the phone.

"Certainly not," she said into the phone. "Doctor Temple just left and you know how exhausted Mister Metz is."

"Listen, girl," said Metz from the bed. He was very weak. "Who is it?"

"Now you shush now, Mister Metz."

"Who is it, damn you!"

"*Mister* Metz!"

"Come here," said Metz from the bed. He said it with such a weak voice the nurse put the phone down and came to the bed immediately.

"Listen closely," he said. The pain was gnawing at him and he talked through his teeth. "No drug for an hour, Temple said. You know what that means? This time of day is the worst."

"You can't have it."

"I don't want it. I want whoever it is downstairs."

"Now you know, Mister Metz, if this were a hospital there would be regular hours...."

"It isn't. I'm dying at home so I can do it on my time."

"I don't think you should talk that way, Mister Metz."

"I'll roll out of bed and break a hip, damn you!"

"If you're going to be unruly I'm just simply going to give you an injection, Mister Metz."

"You want me to die an addict?" She was shocked enough to give Metz time to say more. "Get him up here, girl. It keeps me alive."

She gave the message over the phone and went to the door to wait.

"Cheer him up," she whispered to Farret. "He likes you. And you too, Miss," when Lena passed her.

It was just a politeness on the part of the nurse because she did not really approve of female visitors, particularly the kind who wore dresses like that and flaunting themselves in two sizes too small.

When Metz saw Farret come in the disappointment was like a physical blow. It should have been Miner, he thought over and over. He had closed his eyes and kept saying this to himself.

"Hey." Farret's voice wasn't far away. "Don't play possum with me, Metz."

It was hard to tell if it was meant as a joke or a threat, because everything felt like a threat now, with the pain.

"Hello, Mister Metz. You remember me?"

"Damn it," he said. "Damn if I don't!" and for a brief moment, seeing Lena, he paid no attention to the pain at all. He even smiled, and his fingers made nervous movements.

"If you want us to go, Mister Metz...."

"No, no! Please, Lena. I'm really glad to see you." He smiled.

"Sit down," said Farret to the girl. "Over there." He waited till she had gone around the bed to the chair Metz wasn't facing and then he walked up to the bed himself to look down at Metz and start working his plan.

"You look like an archangel," said Metz.

Farret ignored it. "What makes this hard for me," said Farret, "is you're a sick man in bed. It would have been simpler, otherwise."

"To pass judgment?"

"Shut up." Farret said this for the insult alone, not because he was concerned about being distracted. Nothing distracted him now. "You did a very evil thing, Metz," he said, "pulling the rug out from under me. But you're flat on your back now, so giving you yours is more complicated."

"You are not an archangel," said Metz, "you are a saint."

"I brought Lena here along so you can see for yourself she's alive and kicking and happy to be with her man again."

Metz turned his head to see Lena.

"Right?" Farret called to the girl.

"Oh yes," she said. "Yes. I'm with him now, Mister Metz."

Metz said nothing.

Farret leaned over the bed and looked closely at the sick man. The position pleased him, with the other's head deep in the pillow.

"Like your nurse always puts it, we wouldn't want to have anything happen to Lena, now would we?"

Metz tried to turn his head to see if Lena had heard, but Farret's face was so close and his eyes so steady, it was difficult to do anything but stare up.

"You're sicker than me," said Metz, while the pain made him flick his eyes. Farret just smiled.

"And complicated. You could do something simple, for instance. You could pull the pillow out from under my head and put it over my head, for instance." Metz heard himself say this and thought that he himself was going insane.

"No. You," said Farret, "don't care enough about that."

It was clever of Farret. Or rather, it had been stupid of Metz to play up that point in the past. But then, it was really what kept him alive.

"So to save all that grief, and seeing you owe me something," said Farret, "we'll start out with money."

Bernstein should hear this, thought Metz. He'd die sooner than I.

"A big check every week," said Farret, "or every week a little report about Lena, and how badly she's doing. Until I think of something else," said Farret and straightened up again.

He had found his man, he had passed his judgment.

He felt good and really alive for the first time in a long time.

Metz moved a little because it seemed the pain was much duller now. It went that way. Or perhaps his thought made him feel better.

"Lena," he said. "Come over here, honey."

The girl looked at Farret but Farret wasn't doing a thing. He stood by the bed looking very calm and tall.

"You're such a just bastard," said Metz to Farret, "you'll want to do this by the rules."

Lena came to the bed and waited.

"All this extortion," said Metz to Farret, "because I doublecrossed you."

"The rules."

"I was head man and did this from Tampa. How long in advance?"

"How in hell do I know?"

"Two weeks in advance?"

"How in hell do I know?" Farret was getting irritated.

"I couldn't have done it two weeks in advance, or three weeks in advance, because of the way we ran the operation, could I now?"

"No," said Farret. "So what?"

"Because we fixed shipment dates all within a week, all the time, right? To keep leaks and doublecrosses to a minimum."

"I was the one worked that out," said Farret.

"I think Miner did," said Metz. "But no matter. So I pulled this thing on you all in one week in advance."

"Right. Only the head man...."

"Lena," said Metz. "Leave the room a minute, honey."

While she went out of the room Metz closed his eyes. It should be close to his time now, the time for the drug. He could distract himself just so long.

"Well?" said Farret. "What?"

"The whole week before we got caught," said Metz, "I was in an oxygen tent."

Farret blinked. Going by the rules, this was terrible news.

"Call in Lena," said Metz.

She came back and stood by the bed, looking from one man to the other with an anxious face. It was strange, she thought, how poor Mister Metz, with a face like a skull, looked so much warmer than Farret.

"Honey, you came to Tampa to see me, remember?"

"I remember, Mister Metz. You were so nice to me."

"Yes. Where was I, in Tampa?"

"In the hospital. You were so nice to me in spite of being in the hospital all that time and just out of the tent, too."

"Did you hear, Farret?" Metz looked up and his eyes held on to Farret.

By the rules this was terrible. Farret hunched himself, working his shoulders as if the pea jacket was too tight.

"So I'm not your man," said Metz. "You were wrong." And he laughed.

Farret remembered having made a mistake once before, blaming Lena. But that didn't really count. That was just sort of for exercise, sort of for scaring the bitch for all the other things she had done wrong in her life, and besides, it had worked out all right anyway. She found Metz for him.

Farret suddenly shouted. "Tent?" He was glaring at Lena. "What tent?"

"Why, Baby! Mister Metz is a sick man."

"Answer me!"

"Oxygen tent!"

"The day you came to see him in Tampa, right?"

"No. He was out. The week before, two weeks, I think."

Farret started to curse. He wasn't yelling any more but cursed with a low, intense voice to drain off the disappointment. Still, the Metz bastard must have been in on it, being top man. So he left the details to somebody else. There were two others to pick from.

"Who?" he said suddenly, turning on Metz. "Who'd you tell to do it? Who did it?"

Metz didn't answer right away. He felt weak. He felt sick with a sudden pain that ran up and down all his bones.

"Who crossed me?" Farret's face was very close again. "Miner? Was it Miner?"

It had to stop now. The shouting hurt him and the close face did, too.

"Miner," said Metz with a weak voice, "almost drowned trying to get away when everything busted."

"Getterman! He was in touch with the island end, right there in the capital, right there with Duz and his palace two blocks away! Where is Getterman?"

"Please," said Metz. "Call the nurse."

Farret grabbed Lena's wrist and kept her from turning to the door.

"Where is Getterman?"

"Please—"

"Where is Getterman?"

I'll vomit my stomach, thought Metz. I can't stand it any longer. And then he said, "San Francisco."

Farret straightened, feeling tall and right.

By the rules! He wasn't breaking the rules, so help him. So it was Getterman!

He stood by the bed and took out a cigarette. He looked down at the sick man and wondered how he had ever been able to think that this sick man could have been the one. A figurehead, was all.

"Mister Metz," said Lena. "If you want me to I'll just stand here and scream for the nurse to come in." Metz opened his eyes and smiled. The wave was passing and for a moment Lena looked like an angel to him.

An angel to say what she had said. He smiled at her and carefully shook his head.

"Not worth it," he said. "Farret would be mad."

Farret blew smoke and then he grinned.

"Yes. We don't want that to happen."

He kept grinning, more to himself than for effect, because now he knew it was Getterman.

"You forgot about the money," he said. "I'll take a check now."

"We better go now," said Lena.

"Stay out of this."

Metz looked up, at Farret and then at Lena.

"Why not. Why not." Then, because of his strength starting to leave him again, he talked with a lassitude which made it sound as if he didn't care. "The bureau, Farret. You see the brown bureau back there?"

Farret turned and looked at it.

"The left drawer, there's a checkbook."

"Check?"

"I don't have ten thousand cash in the house, Farret. You said ten thousand, didn't you?"

Farret hadn't, but he thought it was a fine figure. He went to the bureau and brought back a checkbook and pen.

They all stayed very quiet while Metz wrote the check. He seemed to take forever and even Farret saw how hard it was for the old man. Then Metz tore the check out of the book and held it up.

It said ten thousand, signed by Metz, and made out to Mrs. Lena Kowalski.

But there was nothing for Farret to do then, because suddenly Metz started coughing with a strange croak in his throat and his face turned a slow blue. Farret and Lena ran out of the room, both of them calling the nurse, and they passed the nurse in the hallway when she came running, but Farret kept Lena's wrist in his hand and kept going to get out of the house.

CHAPTER FOURTEEN

Luis Gambello out cold on the floor didn't solve anything, of course. I should have been with Metz and I wasn't quite clear right then about what to do next with Gambello. Knocking out an official of a foreign government with the clear purpose of fouling up his mission isn't a very soothing subject to think about for a long time.

I checked Gambello to see he was out good and cold and then went to the bedroom. I came back with two leather belts and used those to tie up his hands and his ankles. Then I picked up the phone and called Metz. It was close to four now and he had been waiting almost two hours.

Nobody answered for a while and the beep on the phone started to drive me nuts. When the phone came alive finally it was a woman talking.

"Hello," she said, "please call back later."

"Just a minute. Don't hang up, Miss. Is this the Metz place?"

"You can't talk to Mister Metz now," she said, sounding rushed, "please call back later."

Then somebody in the background called the woman and she answered, "Yes, Doctor," away from the phone, but I could hear it.

"Listen, is something wrong there?" I said but she hung up without having heard me.

Maybe Metz hadn't been joking when he had made that remark about death rattle.

I looked down at Gambello and his charm and good manners didn't mean a damn to me any more. He was a man who would come to in a while and start all over. Getting trailed by some circus government was not a ridiculous matter. Having sport with "traitors" was a serious necessity to Cervales, just as it had been with Duz, and citizenship or international complications had no meaning in the way they handled that kind of thing.

I called up a night club which wasn't open at this hour but a place where I used to have some connections. That way I got the name and the number of somebody else, a man I used to know as a buddy, and unless he had changed in the last ten years, he would be my man now.

"Ernie's Garage," said the voice.

"Is this Ernie?"

"Depends on who you are," said the voice. Ernie hadn't changed.

"This is John. You remember the...."

"Miner? John Miner?"

"Your only friend," I said because that's the way he and I used to talk when we knew each other.

"I thought you was dead, John," and he laughed. "How come you made it?"

"Maybe I won't," I said. "Are you free?"

Ernie and I didn't owe each other a thing and never had. He was one of the few men I've met whom I've liked for no special reason, just getting along well with him, and vice versa. That's all there was between Ernie and me. Ernie used to be bouncer at a place where I used to gamble. At five in the morning when business was over, he and I used to drink coffee together or give each other a lift back to town or go fishing sometimes. That's all we had between us but it seemed enough.

"Where are you?" is all he said.

I told him and then asked if he could come in a truck, a closed truck.

"How big?"

"I don't care, just so it's closed."

"Wait a minute," he said and then I could hear him ask somebody called Dick if the furniture thing was ready to go. It seemed to be ready because Ernie came back on the line and said he'd be there in twenty minutes, but what-ever I wanted would have to look good, like a legitimate pickup, because oth-erwise he would be breaking the law driving the truck in that neighborhood.

"It's a pickup," I said.

Twenty minutes was a long time under the circumstances and I tried keep-ing time out of my mind by doing a hundred things that hadn't occurred to me before. I put a gag on Gambello, I went over his whole apartment trying to find something in writing, such as a report of his work, for instance, and as a matter of fact found such a thing. It was a typed itinerary which Gam-bello had kept in the folder together with the pencil notes from which he had copied. He hadn't put down yet that he had run into me but I burned the whole business anyway, in a coffeepot on the stove. I called the Metz house again but this time the line was busy. I had found no luggage in the apartment so I took Gambello's keys and went to the basement. I found the locker there with the same number as his apartment and there were several fine trunks. I brought up one of them in the service elevator.

That's how I saw Magdalena before she saw me, though it didn't help. I wasted time cursing so before I got back into the elevator she had turned and seen me.

"Ah! Hello!" she called, waving at me. "I am back early."

That was true.

"Are you bringing a trunk?"

I got out of the elevator and brought the trunk to the door where Magdalena was waiting. She had a small package in her hand and showed it to me.

"I came back early and brought this," she said, "because I was worried about his nose."

It was a salve, something her mother put up. She was worried, she said, that Luis would not like the smell and would therefore refuse to use it.

"We'll see," I said. "Please open the door."

My tone of voice mustn't have been right because she gave me a look while she opened the door. I couldn't worry about that. I was worried about a million things now. Most of all, I wanted to get away to see Metz.

Of course she saw Luis Gambello on the floor as soon as she got through the door. She pushed across the room to him with loud cries of pain and love and started to fondle him. That's how she noticed that he was bound.

I was in the room then, the door closed and the trunk out of my way, ready for her. She got off her knees and turned around, her face like a fury. But I was pretty close to the end of my patience by then and it must have showed. She had meant to yell and maybe leap at me, scratching, but she did none of that. She lowered her eyes and took a slow breath.

"You will let him go," she said. "I will help you forget him," and she walked towards me quite slowly.

She was a sorceress: the slow roll of her hips, the round push of her thighs under the dress while she walked, and the hands which suddenly seemed very delicate, opening the buttons on the front of her dress. Her breasts were pushing the dress apart by the time she was up to me.

I caught myself wishing that Farret was a dream or that the girl was a dream with nobody in it but she and I. It made the reality that much more repulsive. I could see the bound man behind her and his eyelids were fluttering in a sickening way.

And Metz was sick and Farret was sick and if this didn't end soon the same would happen to me. "No," I said. "Don't." It was very short and extremely hard.

"I am not teasing," she said. "We go in the other room," and she took my arm, pressing it against her. I pulled away, hoping it would offend her. It only confused her.

"I show you," she said. "I mean it. I love Luis and I mean it," and she reached for my hands to put them on herself. "I will give you my all," she said.

I was very glad she had said that. She had heard that expression somewhere, or had read it, and it fitted her as badly as clothes do an animal. It jarred me right out of her spell and she was a girl now instead of a sex dream.

"No," I said. "Believe me, Magdalena, I'm much too distracted at the moment." I looked at my watch to make it all very flip.

She surprised me again because of all the expressions she could have worn now, the last one I would have expected was a look of deep sympathy. She had her dress off and stood there in her white underthings which seemed very small, but she wasn't using any of that now. She went to the couch and sat down there, folding her hands and looking at me.

"That is something," she said, without taking her eyes off me. She shook her head. "It must be terrible."

"What's this?"

"The men who can't. I have never met one before."

I understood her then and noticed that her look was one of frank curiosity. If a man doesn't want to sleep with her, was her reasoning, it can only be because he is incapable.

"I never thought I would meet one," she said.

"Magdalena," I said. "You are not likely to ever have that experience. *Now get your damn clothes on!*"

I don't know how she took that because at that moment there was a knock on the door.

"Let me in first," I heard Ernie's voice, "or I break down the door."

I gave another look at Magdalena and saw she hadn't moved.

"The guy that's coming in," I said, "doesn't have any affliction. So beat it," and I nodded at the bedroom door.

"Arriba!" said Ernie when I opened the door, but he wasn't looking at me when he said it but at Magdalena who was just walking across to the bedroom.

I slammed the door shut and took Ernie by the arm.

"Listen to me," I said. I kept holding his arm because he had walked right past me and towards the girl. But he had meant it more as a joke and stopped now, looking at me.

"Good to see you," he said. He was short and squat, with a pushed-in face, and when he smiled you couldn't be sure what he was doing unless you knew him well. "You mean it's like a movie, with one girl and two lovers?" He jerked his head at Gambello on the floor.

Gambello was awake now, looking at us.

"You want me to tell you what it is or you want to do this blind?"

"If you say so, John, I'll do it blind."

"It's better."

"Who gets the trunk?" he said, looking at it.

"It's for him, Gambello. Just to carry him out of the building. After that comes the hard part, Ernie."

He looked at me and shook his head once.

"Some things I don't do, John."

"He, Gambello, he's got to be out of circulation for about six, seven days."

"Oh," said Ernie. "Ah. That's all right."

Magdalena came back out of the bedroom, but she still hadn't dressed. She walked across to Gambello and sat down on the floor next to him. She held his head and murmured to him. I caught just a few words. She was comforting him.

"You remember Long Pine Key?" I said to Ernie. "There was that shack we used by the mangrove swamp?"

"Also," said Ernie, "there is a prison farm on Long Pine Key."

But that didn't concern me. What counted now was to get provisions, to get Ernie to take off a week which shouldn't be difficult, and to find out if he had brought the right kind of transportation. The Key was about a hundred miles south and the last two miles went over a pathway which would take some nimble driving.

"What kind of truck did you bring?" I asked.

"A beauty," said Ernie and nodded for me to look out of the window.

It took up six parking spaces; a long, aluminum semi-trailer, and it said *Thru Way Van Line* on the side.

"Christ," I said. "How did you get that?"

"I repair 'em. Big, huh?"

"Not yours?"

"I just love to drive them," said Ernie. "Every time I give one a grease job even, I take it out for a test run. Like this one. She's all ready to go, soon's I get it back."

"Going where, Ernie?"

"This one? Due to leave in an hour I don't know where exactly but it's in Dakota. One of the Dakotas. First stop Kansas someplace," and then he started to smile because he'd gotten it too. "This will be Mister Gambello's first trip to the Dakotas?"

"I think so, Ernie," and then we went to work.

They would probably find him on the first stop, in Kansas, but that would still be too long for tying his wrists and ankles with belts. We wrapped him in several sheets, up to the shoulders, and some belts around that. Before that we took all identifying material off his person, and also his money. I didn't want it to be too easy for him to get around once he came out of the van.

But there also was Magdalena. She was no longer worried about Luis getting killed but she loved him and did not want to leave him.

"Now listen to me," I said. "I'm not going to kill him but this is still a matter of life and death. You don't know the half of it."

"I don't care about that."

"He won't be safe till he's in Kansas or beyond that. If he comes out of that van someplace before Kansas, he will be shot. There's a car to follow that van, to make sure of that."

"I will do anything."

"I know. I want you to. You can stay in the van with him and see to it he doesn't budge."

"I can do it!"

"I don't mean that, Magdalena. I don't want those sheets off him till Kansas. You watch him, or he'll try and get out. You can feed him, you can turn him for comfort, but no noise, and no getting out. You...."

"Anything!" she said again and this time ran to put on her clothes without having been told.

I found a paper bag in the kitchen and put bread in it, some bananas, cheese, and some cold hot dogs I found there. I put water into an empty milk bottle and wrapped all of this up.

Gambello had a bad headache probably but was awake now and watching everything. With the gag over his mouth it was hard to tell how he felt about this. But he gave us no trouble when we put him inside the big trunk. The way he was wrapped I felt like a grave robber.

We put Gambello on a sofa in the van and then brought down Magdalena in the other trunk, together with the bundle of food. We helped her onto the same sofa where she and Gambello were walled in by two closets, a vertical bed, and a mirror.

"Remember what I said to you." I pointed my finger at Magdalena and made myself look mean as hell.

She just nodded. I slid Gambello's gag over and showed Magdalena how it was done. This gave Gambello a chance to say something to me.

"Closer," he said. "Put your ear next to my mouth." I did and he whispered to me.

"I appreciate everything you have done for my comfort. I am not complaining. You mean well, but must do what must be. However," he took a breath to be able to speak very quickly. "Don't send the girl along with me, for heaven's sake! She will do everything you have told her and fearing for my life she will be here with me from Miami to Kansas."

"Love's lovely reward," I said but he started hissing again and I bent my ear closer.

"Three days? Four days? How long does it take from here to this Kansas? And all this time she and I this close on the sofa and I myself wrapped in this sheet!"

"Love's lonely labor," I said and climbed away from both of them.

CHAPTER FIFTEEN

I took a taxi to the Metz place, the second time that day, and sat on the edge of the seat all the way. It was a good guess that Gambello would be out of action for a few days which was fine. Now Farret would have to be put out of the way, somehow. After that, maybe they would have another revolution on the island and Cervales wouldn't have time for any other diversions like this. I let the taxi go at the gate to the Metz garden and ran down the drive. It was four-thirty now, hours after my appointment. Maybe I wouldn't even get in. Maybe they had hospital rules for him. I rang the bell.

There was no answer. I rang again and nothing. I don't think I would have gotten in except for the fact that the door was open, had been open all the time.

I walked into a large hall and called hello a few times but nothing happened. I could smell disinfectant.

I had a notion of following the smell except that didn't work. It smelled the same at the foot of the stairway, at the end of the corridor which led into a dim back, and no difference to my nose at two of the doors which led off the hall. But when I finally stopped walking around in the hall I was able to hear the sound. It was very dim but it was conversation. The sound took me the length of the corridor, into a pantry, through a room which looked like a baker's kitchen, and from there into the kitchen proper. The last words I heard before they stopped talking were, "Can't you wait till he comes back?" and the other one, "Comes back?" which was the point when I came into the kitchen and they both turned around to look at me.

A man in a narrow business suit and a man in a pin stripe isn't a common sight in a large, empty kitchen, but I don't think it struck me at the time when I walked towards them where they were drinking coffee. The one in the business suit was slim and pale and the other one seemed stockier, though it might have been the build of his jacket.

"Yes?" he said, coming towards me. "You want something here?" He was still holding the cup but put it down on his way.

"Is this the Metz house?" I asked.

"Yes. And who are you?"

"My name is Miner. I had an appointment with Mr. Metz."

"I'm the one answered the phone," said the man in the pin stripe. "I'm the one connected you."

"Oh. Howard, was it?" and I held out my hand.

"Yeah, Howard," he said and I had rarely shaken a hand quite that disinterested.

When I let go of his hand he went back to pick up his coffee. Then he said, "You're too late."

"He's in the hospital," said the other one. "He's alive, but in the hospital."

I lighted a cigarette, out of sheer nerves.

"Coffee?" said Howard.

"Yes. Thanks."

"Whatever it was," said Howard, "will have to wait."

"Some things don't wait," said the other man to Howard and it sounded like the conversation which had gone on when I had come in.

"He's a dying man!" said Howard. "What do you want from a dying man, Bernstein!"

"I? Nothing. I'm *his* accountant, but all...." Bernstein stopped himself and poured more coffee. He said to me, "Was there something I could do for you?"

"How bad is he?" I asked. "Is he conscious?"

"If he is," said Howard, "they still wouldn't let you see him. He's had all the visitors he's gonna have for a good while. Straight from the doctor."

"When did he leave?" I said. I couldn't think of anything else. "Did he leave before my appointment?"

"I don't remember," said Howard. "I forget when it was. But he passed out right after this Mister Farret was here. Him and that woman he brought."

"Farret? Was here?"

"Just this afternoon. You a friend of his?" he asked.

I would have liked to have shown him how I felt about Farret. I would have liked Farret to be here right then to show him and anyone who cared to watch.

"I guess he's no friend of yours," said Howard.

"Where does he live? Either of you know that?"

"No," said Howard, and Bernstein shook his head. "I would like to know that myself."

"You know him too?" It was a thing to ask when there were no leads. It was a lame way of starting to question when you wanted to know everything and didn't know whom to ask.

"No," Bernstein said. "I have never met this person. But whoever this person is, and regardless of my opinion of Mister Metz's present business acumen—" He took a breath then which allowed me to interrupt him.

"I'm sorry. I don't follow this."

"He took a check!" said Bernstein. "He makes a dying man write him a check!"

I knew Farret better than Bernstein did, so the story did not surprise me.

"And do you know what the amount was? Ten thousand! And do you know that was the last of the money?"

"Metz?" I said. "The last of Metz's money?"

"The last cash and that's it. This house? They're going to foreclose! His bar? He's got this *one* bar. In the red to the hilt. His few stocks? There's a lien for debts outstanding on everything! He's broke, kaput. All right! But at least, so help him, we had this cash for the doctor, the nurse, the equipment and so forth." Bernstein started to laugh and put his coffee cup down.

I could understand his problem. He was the accountant and a loyal man, so when he said, "Maybe he'll die," that made sense too.

But I wasn't through. I had lost Farret by a few hours—except that Farret had cashed a check!

"Mister Bernstein, about that check you mentioned."

"It's been *cashed*, if that is what you were thinking!"

"Listen to me. It isn't five yet. They're still working at the bank. Call them up and get them to give you Farret's address. They must have asked him an address."

"He's from out of town," said Howard, but Bernstein was already across the kitchen, picking up the phone.

Farret had given a San Francisco address. They didn't want it. They wouldn't cash the check for him unless he could tell them where he could be reached locally. Biscayne Hotel, he had said. There was one and the bank called to find out if Mister Farret was living there. No. Nobody by that name. So Farret explained his mistake had been natural. Biscayne Fort was the name of the hotel, and the bank checked that too, even spoke to Mrs. Farret in her room. Then they had given him the ten thousand dollars.

"You going to visit him?" asked Bernstein.

"Like the plague," I said.

Chapter Sixteen

The Biscayne Fort lobby was crowded with men wearing name cards on their lapels and paper hats on their heads. There was a crush in front of the room clerk's desk and there wasn't a bellhop in sight. But the bell captain stood at his upright desk, drumming the palm of one hand with a pencil. I walked quickly over to him.

"I'm looking for Mister Farret's room," I said. "One of your guests."

"The room clerk is over there," he said, pointing at the desk with the crowd in front.

I got mad without having to put it on. "I'm Doctor Spence. I received a call from Mister Farret and I doubt whether he would take kindly to your...."

"Three-ten," said the bell captain. He must have had dealings with Farret.

It was crowded all the way across the lobby, it was crowded inside the elevator, and there was a bunch waiting when the doors opened on the third floor and I got out. A man asked me what had happened to my name card or whether I was just one of them shy sonsobitches who don't like to be neighborly. He was drunk and I got away without answering.

Around the bend in the corridor there was no one. It was very quiet and all the doors looked the same.

Three-ten had a wastebasket outside the door, with some candy-stripe cartons in it.

I knocked on the door and waited. I knocked again.

"The door is open," said a woman.

I came in slowly, to give myself time to look. Twin beds, open closet, a woman getting out of a chair by the window. When she came closer I saw it was Lena.

She was older, more like a woman now than ten years ago when she used to give the impression of hothouse growth, like something too much developed. She could have looked good now, except for her expression. A careless face, movements that gave up.

"Lena," I said. "You remember me?"

I thought it took her too long. She looked and then she started to smile. But I didn't have time.

"Lena, where is he? Farret. I'm looking for Farret."

She looked the way I had seen her at first.

"Gone," she said. "He's gone."

She stayed where she was while I went to the bathroom, looked in the closet, came back.

"*Where*, Lena? It's important." I took her arms. "Where, Lena?"

"San Francisco."

"When? When did he leave? How?"

"Getterman is next," she said.

"Did he fly? Train? How, Lena? Hurry up!"

"He took a taxi," she said. "The airport. I don't know when, exactly." She went back to the window and sat down in the chair. The way she acted now, we could have been seeing each other year after year.

I called the desk and asked them if they had made a reservation for Mister Farret.

"Yes, Mister Farret," said the girl. "Haven't you left?"

"What flight was it?"

"TWA, five-seventy," said the girl and then she wanted to ask me again if I hadn't left but I hung up to get the operator and the outside line.

TWA flight five-seventy had left an hour ago, said the airline desk.

I had missed again. I sat holding the phone, hating Farret all the more because he had slipped me again without even trying.

"Miss. When does that flight get to San Francisco?"

"Ten tomorrow morning, San Francisco time, sir. But that is scheduled arrival. The actual arrival time hasn't been announced yet. Flight five-seventy is making an unscheduled landing in Lamotte, Louisiana, on account of unexpected tornado conditions."

"Lamotte? Where's that in Louisiana? What other city near there?"

"I can only give you the closest town which has commercial air traffic, sir, because those are the only maps we have."

"Fine. What town?"

"Baton Rouge, which is perhaps eighty miles from Lamotte according to our map. You see, Lamotte isn't a regular stop."

"How long is flight five-seventy going to be there?"

"That is hard to say, sir, but at least the night."

"I've got to join that flight, Miss. How close can you get me to that town, before morning?"

There was nothing. Several flights crossing in that direction had been cancelled and the next flight to Baton Rouge, which wasn't affected by the tornado conditions up north, didn't leave until morning.

"The Delta Line, sir, has a much more active schedule in that entire area. If you wish, I'll look up their schedules."

A Delta flight left for Baton Rouge in three hours. I would get to Baton Rouge before midnight. She switched me to Delta and I made my reservation. In one way or another I was going to be in Lamotte that same night.

"Lena," I said from the phone. "Does Farret carry a gun?"

"No," she said. "Not a gun."

I hung up, feeling much better. The three hour wait didn't bother me then because Farret wasn't moving. I knew where he was and he wasn't moving, not till I had caught up with him.

I left the phone and walked over to the chair by the window. Lena looked very bad.

"He left you?" I said.

She must have felt there was no reason to answer that and kept still. She had her chin in one hand and looked out the window.

"Cigarette, Lena?"

I held it out to her for a while and then she took it. Her hand, I saw, was a workhand, rough and strong-looking, not like the rest of her.

"Is he coming back?"

She shrugged.

"Are you going home?"

I couldn't see her face because she turned to look out of the window.

"Tell me if he took all the money, Lena. Or did he leave you some?"

She kept looking out of the window and said, "He made me sign the check."

"Made you sign the check?"

"Mister Metz had made it out to me. He made me sign the check."

"How?" I felt the anger come up inside, but if she heard the change in my voice she gave no sign of it. She talked as before, very even.

"I'm weak. That's how. He did that and then left. I don't know if I'm going to leave, or what, because he didn't pay the hotel bill. And even if he paid the hotel bill," she said and stopped without any effort to finish.

We both smoked for a while before I said anything else.

"Let's start over," I said. "I'm coming into the room, we see each other, and you smile."

She looked at me, nodded her head a few times, but did not smile. Then she looked out of the window again.

"You did smile, you know. Remember?"

"I forgot myself," she said. "I was glad to see it wasn't Farret, or I forgot and thought it was ten years ago."

"You liked ten years ago better?"

"I didn't know so much."

"Lena," I said. "Farret is gone. I'm not saying forget him. That's stupid. But he's gone, Lena. He's over."

"He's over. I'm over. A lot is over," she said.

It was hard to tell how she meant all this. She smoked very slowly and watched the blue spirals move in the air.

I said, "Lena. I haven't seen you in about eight years, and even then I didn't know you too well. But we were friendly. I know nothing about what happened to you in those eight years, except that I met your husband."

She crushed the cigarette out on the window sill. I was sure she had never done that before, just putting a cigarette out anywhere. She got up.

I said, "Listen to me, Lena." She was walking away. "Don't you know he wants you back?"

She was by the bathroom door and I went there. I put my hand on her arm and said, "You're a good woman, Lena. Farret's gone and it's fine now."

"No!" It was very loud. "No!" and she pulled her arm out of my hand as if the touch hurt her. She pulled away, crying suddenly, and slammed the door to the bathroom. I could hear her inside, crying louder and louder, and then I heard her turning the shower on.

She started to worry me, the rush of the water behind the door and the girl crying with a wide-open sound as if she were breaking.

She had the door locked. I stepped back and then rammed it with my side, twice, before the door gave and I got into the bathroom.

There was a lot of steam already. There was a pile of clothes on the tiles and Lena was inside the shower stall. The plastic curtain stuck to her side and then detached itself which showed me that she was moving. The curtain was not all the way closed and I saw Lena there under the water, soaping herself hard and not stopping even when she saw me. And she was still crying.

I left the bathroom and sat down on the chair in the room. She might come out of that bathroom all done with whatever she felt she had to do there, or she might come out and feel the same way she had felt before. I wanted to wait for her because she might be worse then.

I had smoked two cigarettes when the shower went off, and after that, except for the sound of the towel, Lena gave no other signs. I was sure she had stopped crying.

Lena looked different when she came out. She was wearing a robe and when she walked by me she smelled damp and warm. It was a good smell. I didn't realize until then how much she had smelled of perfumed powder before. She went to the dresser and picked something up which she dropped into the waste basket, lipstick maybe.

"You look better," I said. "You feel better?"

"Thank you."

She held her robe together, which she shouldn't have done if she had meant to make herself demure, because it threw long, gathering lines into the cloth, winding over the shape of her body. Lena was built sexy. It was an unconscious thing though, which had nothing to do with the way she felt.

"Could you leave me a cigarette?" she asked.

I got out of the chair. She had gone to the bed and was sitting down. I said:

"I wasn't leaving yet, Lena. I thought we'd sit a while, maybe go down for a cup of coffee."

She didn't answer. She sat on the bed and was fluffing the hair away from her neck. It moved her robe but she hadn't noticed.

"Why did you think I was leaving?" I said again.

"Well, Farret's gone. You came for him."

"I know." I went over to her and gave her the cigarette.

"But don't act like everybody is going to step on you, Lena. Not everybody does that, Lena. You listening to me?" and I tried to take her chin in my hand to make her look up at me.

She did look at me and was crying again, not loud this time but just with tears, and when I reached for her face she drew out of the way and let herself fall on the bed. She turned away from me and covered her face.

"Lena. Lena honey," I said and sat down on the bed next to her and put my hand on her hair. "Don't be afraid any more, Lena. Farret's gone," I said.

"God!" she said, and turned to look at me with such suddenness that her hair flew up and settled around her head on the pillow. It gave an impression of wildness, and her face was alive. "He's gone, but he took it out of me. God, did he take it out of me!" and she rolled her head from side to side a few times.

"Lena!" I said, sharp to make her listen.

She stopped. She took a deep breath and lay on her back now, looking up at me.

"John," she said. "He took it out of me." I thought she was going to cry again.

I leaned on my elbows and put my hands to the side of her face. It made her look small and gentle. Or perhaps it was her low voice.

"John," she said again. "I've changed since then. I was ten years younger and nothing meant very much."

I could feel her hands. She moved very gently. She put her hands on the side of my arms and held them there. And she breathed under me with a small, hesitant movement, but I could feel that too because her softness came and went against me.

"Don't go, John," she said. "I want to tell you this."

"Go ahead, Lena."

I stayed the way I was because what changed happened very slowly, the woman under me was no longer Lena, Farret's cow, but a woman in her own right, with the warm smell still on her from the bath, and the very fine skin which I could see, and the round flesh barely touching me from beneath and then gone again.

"You know how?" she said. "How he did it?"

"Lena, you don't have to tell me a thing."

"I do. Please stay, John," and her hands held my arms. When she talked again her fingers kept moving and holding me. "It means nothing to me, in words, John, and I don't even have the words."

"What he did?"

"He took it out of me, John, is all I can say."

She looked confused, even unhappy, and didn't know what to say next.

"When you see your husband," I said, "he'll understand. He'll know that you were too afraid to do anything else."

"John," she said. Her eyes were very wide now and I felt her fingers curl. "Would you believe me, John, but Farret never touched me?"

She said it so violently, her whole body moved. She pushed against me and then did not go away. Her robe was open. I saw this, and felt it.

"Do you know he never slept with me once?"

"He's nuts," I said. "Christ."

Her heat came through to me and the movement against me could have been hers or mine. I wasn't holding her face anymore. She stretched her head up and my hands were not holding her any more, not for that moment. She was so close. The neck, a round neck warm to the touch then I pressed my hands down more pushing the robe out of the way to feel her bare shoulders. She moved them to shrug the robe off her body.

"John, take me! I've never said that to anyone, John, I've never said that before, will you believe me? Please don't laugh, John. I've never asked, I've never *asked!*"

She was big and hot under me, and all naked now, my doing, her doing, what was the difference? She held me around the back and I felt her under my hands and everywhere, a strong animal. She did not have to ask.

Chapter Seventeen

The plane had started to pitch and every so often sagged, very suddenly. It was black outside the portholes so that the glass was like a mirror. At first, Farret tried to see out of the window but he only saw himself. He then moved his head, his whole upper body, to catch the light in a certain way.

He felt that the lines in his face were quite strong. They showed strength. He looked at his face and saw how the pea jacket collar framed him from behind, like a mantle almost, the way generals used to be painted, and other important aristocrats.

Farret took out a cigarette, lit it, and watched himself smoke. He saw there was real dignity in the gestures, while the strength in his face was a threat.

"Will you fasten your seat belt please, Mister Farret?"

He turned and looked at the stewardess, but she stayed where she was, didn't change her gladhanding smile at all, didn't notice a thing. The bitch was simply frozen with fright, must be it. Frozen that way with the trained smile covering everything. She was a mess inside and trying to hide it.

"Mister Farret, will you please fasten your seat belt? We're running into a little weather and in a moment the captain will explain about it."

"That's all right," said Farret. "Carry on."

For a moment he thought that the girl was staring and he narrowed his eyes at her. He thinned the line of his lips, the way he had seen it in the black glass. That broke the bitch.

The young stewardess, when she saw Farret had pulled his belt snug, went to the next seat and then down the rest of the aisle, checking her passengers.

The bitch, because she was wearing a uniform, thought she was something else, something trim and efficient. Farret stripped her with his eyes. He saw the same shape on her he found on every woman and this one obviously too thin, except for the soft spots. What he called the soft spots were the rear, the belly, and breasts which seemed big with the rest skeletal. A revolting image which he enjoyed.

He took out another cigarette and held it near his face. It wasn't lit yet and he wanted the stewardess to come over to light it for him. He caught her eye but she didn't come over. She smiled at him and shook her head. She shook her head and pursed her mouth as if she were kissing him. Smoking a cigarette is what she meant. No, no, she said from a distance. The light over the cockpit door was on, fasten your seat belts and no smoking. The bitch was playing favorites! She was talking to somebody else! She was leaning over the seat and doing the belt for somebody and grinning that grin from very close up.

"This is your Captain speaking."

The young stewardess stood up and looked up into nothing. The bitch must adore that flyer.

"We're running into a bit of weather," the loudspeaker said, "and for the safety and comfort of all of you our weather people advise us to sit it out on the ground."

Of course! He's been going down for miles, for an hour at least, without telling anyone! Why? What else, besides the weather?

"The landing field which we are going to use is not one of our regular stops. As a matter of fact, you might find the town rather small. However, because of the threatening wind conditions it isn't advisable to go any further or to turn off towards Baton Rouge which is separated from us by a weather front."

He was trying to say something else, the bastard behind the door with the lights. He was making a picture of being walled in, walled off, no way out.

"Your airline will of course provide you with all available facilities for the night. We may not have to spend the night in Lamotte."

Louisiana? Baton Rouge was in Louisiana, and Lamotte?

The plane was descending very obviously now and a steep bank showed small lights down below. The porthole was now in a position of a funnel waiting and it was possible to imagine that by letting go of the seat—

"Mister Farret? Are you all right? Would you like some gum?"

He became aware of his hands clamped into the armrests of the seat and that the stewardess was staring at him from up close. She held gum and was grinning with love.

"Gum? No, thank you. You serve whisky on this plane?"

"Whisky? No, sir."

"How about some food? Aren't we supposed to get something to eat? That's part of the paid service."

The girl made an embarrassed laugh because passengers were looking at her and her problem.

"We're landing in a minute or so," said a man across the aisle. "Don't worry, sailor, we'll be safely down in a minute, right, miss?"

Farret let go of the armrests and folded his arms over his chest. He wanted to look into the black glass to see how it looked but now there were two of them, the stewardess and the tweed suit, both badgering him. Farret felt he was swelling inside his pea jacket and something of that strength, just as much as he cared to show, would appear on his face.

"Did you call me a sailor?"

"Well," said the man in the tweed suit, "I just thought...."

"I got to wear gold stripes to show you what's what? Who are you, anyway?"

"I'm navy myself," said the man in the tweed suit. He gave the young stewardess a reassuring smile and then he turned it without change towards Farret. "I don't wear my uniform either," he said leaning over a little. "Just like you."

Farret took a deep breath. This man in the tweed suit, you might say was a fellow officer. You can always tell. Fine caliber. Always recognize each other. Farret, in his turn, smiled at the man with a knowing look and the other one smiled back and turned front again. He didn't talk to his neighbor or look at anyone else but just sat. Farret watched that part closely. In fact the man sat so still he was probably scared stiff with the bumpy descent and hoping nobody would spot it. But he, Farret, he saw it. He'd keep the secret and just laugh every time he saw the man later. Just he and the man would know what it was all about and the right kind of relationship would then exist.

Farret smiled to himself, feeling wonderful suddenly. As a matter of fact, no reason not to test the relationship now.

Clearing his throat and shifting around under his belt Farret reached into his pocket and with a long sigh pulled money out. It was a fat roll of bills, mostly fifties and hundreds. Making a bored sigh now Farret peeled two one hundred notes off the roll, snapped them a few times, and leaned over the aisle.

"Sir?"

The man in the tweed suit looked over. The man looked apprehensive, which was as it should be.

"I need some change," said Farret. "Would you kindly break these for me, sir?"

"I'm sorry. I can't," and the man looked front again.

Farret went through the grunting and straining again, putting the money back in his pocket. Then he sat relaxed. Of course the bastard couldn't change that kind of money. He, Farret, had known this all along. Just so the bastard in tweed knew it!

After the plane had landed and they had filed out on the runway they felt how strong the wind really was. A school bus and two taxis took the passengers to the town proper. Because the wind had knocked down powerlines, there were no lights in the town. The passengers didn't see much of the town. They only saw a large gingerbread hotel with an old-fashioned lobby and kerosene lights on a few tables. Most of them went to their rooms and some played cards in the lobby. The card-players went to bed by twelve midnight and the lobby was almost empty.

"Go to bed, Janet," said the pilot. "You'll only have six hours sleep as it is."

"We like our stewardess pretty," said the co-pilot.

"If you think it's all right," said the girl. She got up and looked at the pilot writing out his forms by the kerosene lamp and then across the lobby where she could see the back of a fat chair, the blue sleeve of a pea jacket and the man's legs.

"Don't worry about him," said the co-pilot. "Not part of your duties to put the passengers into bed."

"You know what he said to me before?" she sat down again and fingered the co-pilot's pack of cigarettes. "He said he wanted to buy my uniform. If I'd sell it to him for two hundred dollars."

The pilot looked up, snorted, started writing again. The co-pilot smiled at the girl.

"Afraid he'll try forcing the sale?"

She got up again and laughed nervously. Then the co-pilot got up too.

"Come on," he said. "I'll lock you in."

She took his arm and they walked to the stairs.

"Will you?" she said.

"From the inside."

She held on to his arm and they walked up the stairway together.

Farret turned in his chair just enough to see them disappear up the stairs. She was going to take that uniform off and that punk pilot would be watching. They couldn't kid him. Not the way she rolled those hips going up the stairs and him so close he was liable to stumble. That would be the treat of the trip, him rolling down those stairs breaking every bone in his body.

Farret suddenly laughed and got out of the chair. He felt wide awake. Go to bed? That would be like suffocating in the small room instead of being out there in the black wind which scared everyone except him.

He stood outside the hotel and looked down the street as far as he could. He could not see very far but saw sudden swarms of leaves scuttle through the light in front of him and then the same leaves further down, black against the yellow square of light from a kerosene lamp in a restaurant window.

Maybe something to eat, he thought. He walked up the street and as soon as he was out of the light from the hotel lobby he thought, now I'm invisible. At the moment he walked up to the restaurant, the waitress inside picked up the kerosene lamp and left through a door in back. The place was dark now and Farret found that the door was locked.

It did not make him angry. He stood in the dark for a while and thought whether they had seen him coming. Would anyone know him in Lamotte?

Then he started walking again but did not realize right away that he was leaving the town. He kept walking to find a light large enough to mean something like a bar or a restaurant. He saw a yellow light in the distance and walked there. He didn't notice that there was nothing but brush and big swamp trees on both sides of the road. The light was close now but then disappeared because of a bend in the road. Just light specks showed through foliage and those specks jumped and moved because of the wind in the leaves.

It gave him a sense of speed, pushing against the wind like this. The wind rushing past his ears and pulling his hair felt like his own great speed and strength.

He came around the bend in the road and saw the light clearly now, and the building. There were kerosene lamps in several places behind the large window and two battery lamps in positions in front of the building.

Farret stopped. Now he knew he had left the town. And what town he had left! He stared at the gas station, remembered the gas station. When was it? Maybe seventeen years ago when he had knocked it over for ten lousy bucks! And the cop, the hick cop! How he had beaten that lousy hick cop. The whole Lamotte police force he had beaten into a pulp. They just had that one cop.

But the joke didn't do anything for him now. Nothing mattered at the moment but the terror, the terror of knowing that he had no plan to meet this plan: the flight schedule changed, the fake forced landing at Lamotte, all the lights doused so he wouldn't recognize anything till the last moment, the girl in the restaurant making him go on down the road. All this because seventeen years ago he'd robbed a lousy gas station.

Farret laughed. The dumb hicks don't know about the statute of limitations? That, of course, explained his own lack of caution. He had known all along that he was safe! How else to explain his falling for such obvious tricks?

He put his hands in his jacket pockets and walked up to the filling station. He did not walk too fast and he was no longer laughing. Neither that nor fear was any longer necessary. He knew their plan and he knew he was untouchable.

"You got gas trouble, feller?"

Farret stiffened when he heard the voice but then he saw the man come around the station and he had to answer.

"No. I'm walking."

"Fine night for it," said the station man. "You ain't from here, are you?"

Was it the same man? Hard to tell in the light.

"You come from the bayou? You ain't from town."

"I flew in," said Farret.

"Oh!" said the man. "You one of them off the plane."

"Of course," said Farret. "What did you think?"

"I wish I was you," said the station attendant. "Flying in for a night, staying in that big hotel, all that. Me, I'm staying open all night. Can you figure why I'm staying open all night?"

"No. Why?"

"Beats me!" said the man. "Boss says stay open all night to catch the stray ones coming through. Now you know there won't be more than one car coming through here tonight."

Farret saw that the man had a very sensible complaint. Very sane. Farret became absorbed in the problem of the station attendant having to stay up all night for nothing, and envying him, the plane passenger, for the big hotel and the warm bed.

"I'm going back now," said Farret. "Hit the sack."

"Good night. I sure envy you."

"Good night."

A five minute walk back to town and when Farret got there the wind seemed to die down. Everything seemed much calmer, more like night time. The hotel was on the left, looking the way he remembered it, with light in the lobby and one or two on the upper floors.

Farret felt very calm now. He would walk a little while longer, till he was entirely calm. He did not feel entirely calm, he said to himself.

A light went off farther down the street, then another one. Should this be? They should all be off. This is a small town, and it was after midnight. Why weren't all the lights off?

Farret walked close to the edge of the buildings and stayed there. Bunk, he said to himself, and "bunk" aloud. He had come into Lamotte in the middle of the night, very late, way past the statute of limitations, very late at night and in such a way that nobody knew he was coming. Landing here had been a fluke, plain and simple. Look at it, everybody is going to sleep. Just the red light on in front of the fire station and the white light from the window next to the big door. It's the damn wind, causing all this imagining, sounding like the far off howl of a motor, and trees waving high into the sky, same as the palm trees used to, during hurricane season. That was the best time to make the run up to the mountains. The noise, the darkness, the movement, all that and he would get through to the mountains best in that kind of weather. Used to be hell on Miner, though. He used to hate coming over with the boat in that kind of weather, but damn John Miner, let him drown. Too big for his britches and always with his nose into everything. During the hurricane sea-son nobody and nothing was out in the night. Just the way it was here, in the middle of Louisiana.

Farret jumped back to the side of the buildings, jumping before he knew he was doing it. Natural instinct, because the howl wasn't the wind but was a motor, there *was* somebody else out in the night besides himself.

The car came down the wide street fast, but slowed suddenly. Must be a stranger, not knowing which way to turn. Like the hurricane night on the is-land, far up the side of the mountain when Miner suddenly showed to warn them.

Miner! Damn Miner! There, in the car was Miner! Here, past now, gone down the street!

Farret was fighting for breath, to get the air in and to kill the racket inside his throat at the same time.

My God, the whole damn town was watching him from dark windows. And Miner in on the whole thing. God, run!

"You all right, Mister?"

Farret, just past his first shock, didn't have the strength to react again. He turned his head very slowly. He saw the old man lean out of the window, the only lit window, two buildings down in the fire station.

"You been sick on the sidewalk, Mister? Come here. Come on in here, if you want."

The old man kept talking like that all the time Farret was walking up to the fire station. First of all, Farret wanted the light. No more black wind and the street empty except for ghost cars and ghost drivers and ghost thoughts. And this was a nice old man with white hair, and all doubled over with age.

"Come on in. Here, I'll open the door."

Farret walked into the small room in the side of the fire station. It was bright and cluttered and very warm.

"Heat'll do you good," said the old man. "Can't do without it, I got the pains so bad."

Farret looked at the cannon stove, probably the only cannon stove full of fire within hundreds of miles from here. The stove looked very old-fashioned and beyond the stove, through a door to the rest of the building, Farret could see the red fire engine, a big, shiny truck with polished brass.

"If you're too hot sit there by the desk," said the old man. "It's the draftiest place. Tea?"

"Sure."

Farret watched the old man pour water and dunk a teabag into a cup. The old man was very bent. Even his face seemed twisted, as if his jaws didn't fit right. He limped on one leg and the arm on the same side hung crooked.

"Accident," said the old man. "It knit bad, here," and he nodded at his elbow which pointed out.

"Too bad," said Farret. The tea cup felt good and warm in his hand.

"You off the plane?" said the old man. "You look like you're off the plane."

"I am." Farret sipped tea. And then, "What do you mean, *look like* I'm off the plane?"

"Call me Mort," said the old man. "Everybody does."

"What do you mean, look like I'm off the plane?"

"You look like a furriner, like off the plane."

"I am off the plane."

"What I said!" and the old man laughed. He held his lower jaw in a weird way when he laughed and it squeezed his eyes. They were very wet and the color of milk with blue. One had a black dot for a pupil and the other one, Farret saw now, had none. The black hole was washed over and blind.

"How's the tea?"

"Fine."

"All I drink. Good for the bowels. Mine aren't so good."

"Comes with age," said Farret, drinking. He had both hands on the warm cup and sat hunched. The warmth was good.

"Naw," said the old man. "Accident."

"Oh."

He did not like the talk as much as he did the small place and the warm cup. He felt like sitting a long time.

But Mort, the old man, was mostly glad for having someone to listen to him.

"All alone here at night," he said.

"Oh? No fireman?"

"Volunteers, in this size town. They sleep at home."

"You take the calls."

"I take the calls." The old man waited for more, but Farret said nothing. "Not that I done this all my life, you understand. I been in public service most of my life, but not here. Not just with a telephone."

There was that hopeful grin on the old man's face again, waiting for Farret's question and for his interest. It revolted Farret to see that jaw come out wrong when the old man grinned.

"Stop doing that," said Farret.

"Huh? What I do?"

"You're going to throw out that jaw, pushing it that way."

"What are you, a doctor?"

Farret put down the cup and leaned one arm on the desk.

"Yes."

The old man said nothing. He swiveled his head back and forth to get a clear view with his good eye. If he doubts my word, I'll push that in, thought Farret. If he thinks I'm a bum just because I wear a pea jacket, I'll push that jaw in.

"Sa-ay! Sa-ay!" The old man came closer. He dragged his leg rapidly and his crooked elbow jutted out more for balance. "Doc?" he said. "Listen, Doc."

Farret didn't like the old man any more. He was a cripple and standing much too close.

"I got these pains, Doc, and I'll even tell you how they come about. This arm here, for instance. See this part? All thick here, in the bone? Feel it."

Farret's skin crawled when the old man bared his arm and held it up close.

"Feel it, Doc. That's where the thing was broke. Compound here, simple there, and just crushed inside where the thick part is. Now this pain here, the one in the arm and shoulder, it comes direct from this old accident wound I'm showing you."

"Old age," said Farret and stood up to get out of the way.

"Wait. Now the leg. Let me show you the hip and the leg."

"Leave your damn pants where they are," said Farret but he said it so low the old man didn't catch all of it.

"What you say? Eh?"

"I said just because I'm a doctor, old man, gives you no call to display yourself."

The old man let his pants leg slide down again and his jaw hung open. For the longest time his eyes didn't blink.

"You making fun of me, Doc?" He talked low, and with more force behind the voice it might have been threatening. "You ain't got the pride in your work to take an interest?"

"Dry up," said Farret. "Dry up and go to hell," Farret disliked the old man with a real, skin-tightening disgust.

"You newfangled crop of men," the old man kept on, "ain't got the pride in your work and the interest. Now you take old Doc Chambleau, or take me! Now I ain't no doctor and I ain't gonna pretend I'm a doctor."

It made Farret hold his breath and his eyes got narrow.

"But I'm a man got a pride in his work. I'm no old bum no good for nothing but sit here and answer the telephone. See this leg, this here, the arm all twisted that way, huh? And this here jaw, huh? I'm *proud* of them injuries!"

"And you wrecked the train getting them," said Farret.

"Now you listen here! I got them doing my work. Public service all my life in this town. You know who I am?" The old man came very close with his neck out like a turtle's. "I was the chief of police in this town for well nigh thutty-five years!"

Without saying a word—he was too busy thinking—Farret pushed the old man out of the way to be able to step back to the door and look carefully at the old man.

"And them wounds here what's crippling me, you know where I got them, huh?"

Farret was barely breathing.

"Yeah," he said, staring at the old man.

"Eh? What you say?"

"Been waiting here all these years, haven't you, cop? Planning this all these years, to get me in here and feed me that poison tea."

"Huh?"

"How'd you get those *wounds*, cop? Tell me." Farret was in form now, enjoying the cruelty of what was coming.

"In line of duty, Mister! I was escorting a criminal...."

"I remember," said Farret and laughed. "But go on."

"You remember?"

"Take a look, cop!" and Farret stuck out his face.

The old man, nettled and confused, looked hard at Farret.

"I fixed you good, didn't I?" said Farret. "But not good enough to keep you out of my hair."

"Jesus!" said the old man and his jaw was working hard.

"Don't put on, you bastard. Don't try to fool me!"

"You're *him!*"

Farret straightened up, his face very cold and serious.

"I know you know," he said. "I'm just here to give you a chance to stop pretending," and he struck out like a snake.

The old man flew against the hot stove and screamed. But not long.

To Farret it was a cold business and not much of a job. The old man was dead very quickly.

CHAPTER EIGHTEEN

As soon as I got to Lamotte the wind seemed to let up. I was there before I realized it because the town was without electricity. Lamotte Ice Cream Parlor, Lamotte Methodist Reformed Church or something like that went by before I slowed down.

There wasn't a soul on the streets and the red light over the fire station glowed like something forgotten. They must have their own generator, just to light up that little red bulb and to light up a little office built on to the garage. I didn't see anybody.

There was only one hotel in the town, according to the outfit where I had rented the car, and I was looking for that. It looked like a stage set when I found it, a three story clapboard structure with frilly balconies. I stopped the car and got out.

The lobby was empty. A kerosene lamp on the desk and a kerosene lamp on a table with magazines made a dull light which seemed almost brown. I woke the colored man behind the desk and asked for Mister Farret's room.

"Third down on the corridor going left," he said, "second landing. Better take a lamp, Mister Farret," and he pushed one across to me.

"Key?"

"Don't need no key, Mister Farret."

I lit the wick in the lamp and went up the stairs. The lamp was very bright close in front of me but the light dulled out all around, giving me no clear view further on, just shadows, brown shadows.

All the doors were painted yellow. There were no numbers but the colored man had told me the third on the left and I stopped there. Then I walked in.

The room was small, so my light seemed very bright now. The room was empty. A bed, a nightstand, a chest of drawers. No one had slept in the bed and there was no luggage. There was nothing that anyone had left behind. But I did not think that the room had been unoccupied. Someone had turned down the bed, lifted the sheets, moved the mattress. The various drawers had been pulled open, furniture had even been moved away from the wall. Almost like a search. It made no sense, searching an empty room and I wondered about Farret. The colored man had called me Mister Farret, so chances were that this was Farret's room and he had just not come back.

I left the lamp on the chest of drawers and stood near the door. For a while, at least, I would wait.

When I heard somebody come up the stairs I didn't know if it would be Farret and if it was Farret how he would act. I stood close to the door and waited.

The feet did not stop outside the door but the door opened immediately and the man came in fast. I hit him with a hard uppercut which came all the way up from the soles and stepped back as soon as I had my balance. Then I closed the door, before the man hit the floor. It was Farret.

He made a ball on the floor and would not open up. A small sound came out of him, something I could not describe, and making this sound he started to weave himself back and forth on the floor, back and forth, like a child in a cradle.

I bent down and looked at Farret. He was holding his face but I could see enough to notice the small changes; his eyes seemed larger, perhaps because he had lost weight or because of the dark rings underneath them, "Farret," I said. "You remember me?"

His eyes blinked rapidly, almost like a spasm, and he made the sound again. He was saying something, but I couldn't make it out.

"Get up, Farret." I stepped back to give him room.

He sat up slowly but he didn't get up. He sat up with a queer, frightened look in his eyes and without making a sound. He twisted his face but said nothing. I could hear the wind outside. Farret's jaw, I thought, was at a strange angle.

"You move wrong, Farret, and I break you in two."

He blinked at me and tried to look away a few times but apparently couldn't. For one reason or another he had to keep staring at me, even though the sight seemed to upset him.

"Please," he said, "please, Miner."

He worried me. I had a different picture of him, not like this, small on the floor, confused and very tired.

"Come on, Farret. Get up." I stepped closer to him to give him a hand.

He squeezed himself back against the bed.

"Please, Miner. You hurt me. I'm sick, I think. Don't hurt me, Miner."

I sat down on the chest of drawers and took out a cigarette. I certainly did not want to go closer to him if it upset him so much. He was confused? I was. Something bad had happened to him, and had taken the strength out of him, or else the whole picture I had formed of Farret was wrong from beginning to end.

"What happened?" I said to him.

He gave me a helpless look and then closed his eyes. I wished he would not hold his jaw the way he was doing.

"Farret. You know why I'm here?"

"I know. I didn't know it was planned so good, Miner, but I know now. I'm sorry. I'm sorry, sorry."

I smoked too fast, making the smoke hot and unpleasant.

"Farret," I said. "Stop trembling, will you for Christsakes?" He tried, I could see that, but it didn't help. His hands stayed very flighty and his damn jaw was getting on my nerves.

"Look. I didn't hit you so hard you have to keep your face all twisted around, Farret."

"It hurts," he said. "What are you, a doctor?"

I think the remark surprised both of us; me, because of Farret's change in tempo, and him, because he seemed to think I was now ready to hit him again. He started to talk very fast and a whine came into his voice.

"Miner, please. I can't any more, I'm through. I feel sick and through."

"I'm not going to hit you. I want to talk about something else."

"No, Miner. Let me be. I can't go on. I want out. Please, I want out."

It was pathetic. It wasn't the picture I had of him, and it wasn't even the same man of ten years ago. He must have gone through plenty during the years in between. He must have been getting it in the neck hard.

"I wish you would get out," I said. "I wish you had never started."

"I want to, God, I just want to be left alone."

I did not have the feeling that he was pulling an act. What had he done, really? He had made vague threats, so I had heard, and he had taken another man's wife. And then he had dumped her. And Metz's money. Metz had given it to him, dying anyway. I said:

"Farret, let me get this straight. You came here...."

"I'll leave! Don't do anything else. I've felt it before coming here, before you and they got me here."

"What?"

"But not clear enough! Not till the trap sprang! And that, Miner, was terrible, terrible." He looked down at the floor, then got up slowly.

I watched him get up. He was very awkward. He had trouble with one of his legs and something seemed wrong with his arm. The elbow was twisted out at a weird angle.

"Let me rest," he said. "Let me sit."

I let him sit down on the bed. Something had knocked the wind out of him, perhaps something recent. I had no name for it, but whatever the name, Farret was nuts.

"All right," he said. "I'll come. You got me, Miner."

I gave him a cigarette, not because he had asked for one but because I wanted the time. I had to think about how to handle him right.

"Watch this," he said suddenly.

I looked up and he was holding the cigarette in his hands ready to flip it. He flipped it without making a movement and it flew in an arch towards me, to one side of me, where the kerosene lamp was. It fell into the top of the cylinder and made a plop when it hit the bottom.

"Good?" said Farret.

I looked at him and he was grinning. He was suddenly tense and seemed to be waiting for me to answer.

"Very good."

"I know."

Then he exhaled and rubbed his jaw. It wasn't sticking out anymore.

Lamotte, I knew, was too small. I would take him to Baton Rouge. I would first ask him if he would go with me and then if he said yes, it would be easy. Either way he was coming to Baton Rouge.

I didn't like the way he looked now, with head down and his eyes fast.

"I want to go," he said. "I've got to get out of here. It's like the whole place is wired."

He got up and waited for me at the door.

"See? There's one of them," and he pointed at the surface wire that ran from the switch to the ceiling. He was the way he had been a few minutes ago.

"All right," I said. "Where's your luggage?"

"I don't have any. Listen, Miner. All I want is out of here, fast."

"We're leaving now, Farret. My car is downstairs."

Nothing happened on the way down and nothing happened when we sat in the car. Farret had some trouble getting his bad leg into position and then he moved around to favor his arm with the pointing elbow. But then he sat still, keeping close to the door as we started back to Baton Rouge.

"There," he said. "There. The trap."

We weren't out of town yet, passing the fire station, and I didn't see anything which could have made sense with his remark.

"We're leaving town now," I said. "So relax."

He didn't answer. He sat the way he was and stared out through the windshield.

"You know where we're going?"

"Just go faster," he said. "Faster."

"I'm going for help," I said. "Help for you. You understand, Farret?"

"Just go fast."

It was a two hour trip to Baton Rouge, but there were branches blown across the road and once I had to make a detour which hadn't been there on my way down. Farret said nothing during the whole trip. In a way I was relieved because I had no idea how to talk to him. He sat hunched in his corner and soon after leaving Lamotte he fell asleep. In Baton Rouge I had to wake him.

I held the car door open for him and the first thing I noticed when he came out, he wasn't limping anymore.

"How do you feel?" I asked him.

"Why?"

I didn't answer that. His jaw looked normal and his arm too. I walked up close to him and he didn't draw back.

"This way," I said.

The big building was marked very clearly and Farret read what it said. *Central Police Station.* He stuck his hands in his pockets and his face seemed to tighten. He didn't take a step.

"Farret," I said, close to him. "It's all part of the plan. Come on. Walk."

He went up the steps with me. Inside, at the window where it said *Infor-mation*, I stopped and looked at Farret again. I think I had reached him, be-cause he just stood there, waiting for me. Whatever had made him tick back in Lamotte was still active, though it wasn't so dramatic anymore.

A uniformed man came up to the window and nodded at us.

"Your problem?" he said.

"I need information. I didn't know where to go at this hour except to come here. How do I commit a man in this State?"

"Commit?"

"Psychiatric."

"Oh." He looked at both of us, first one, then the other, and bit his lip. "Any criminal act involved?"

"No," I said.

Maybe that meant the end. Maybe now I would have to wait until morn-ing, would have to get a physician's deposition, or who knows what all might be involved. I was improvising the whole thing but it was the best thing I could think of with Farret's turning out the way he had.

"Room Five. Ask for Lieutenant Harmond. End of that corridor."

Perhaps my relief showed because Farret looked at me and frowned. The why of his frown didn't matter on me, because I had no time to figure it out. But just the frown, the fact that he changed expression, put me on edge.

"We're going," I said, "down to that door back in the corridor, Farret. We go there and get help. Come on, it's arranged." I added that because all I knew about him was this bug he had about secret arrangements and plans.

He just nodded and when I started walking he walked along.

All the rooms down the corridor had numbers and then a legend, giving the name of an office, like *Traffic Control*, *Squad Room*, *Clerk*, *Night Court*, that sort of thing. There was nothing on Room Five, just the number.

We went into a room which was unfinished. Walls weren't finished, there was only one fixture on the ceiling which had broken holes for two more, and in one corner of the room were two saw horses and a pile of painter's canvas. The back of the room had a new partition but the doors hadn't been hung.

"Excuse the mess," said a big man in mufti.

He came through the doorless partition, put a coffee cup on a desk, and sat down. The name plate on the desk said Lieutenant Harmond.

He had the face of a healthy country boy and if he had been in that room painting a wall I wouldn't have thought twice about it. But he was the man to decide the Farret affair.

"Well, sir, what have we here," he said.

He switched on the desk light, which seemed to make a new room out of the place, two rooms. A cluttered place with an untidy desk and a small, yellow light, and then the rest of the room, bare, smelling of paint, fluorescent light high in the ceiling.

"Sit," he said. "One here, one there. Pardon me while I have my coffee. I'm listening."

He slurped his coffee and sat way back in his swivel chair, without looking up.

"I've come to bring my friend for commitment. Psychiatric commitment."

"You mean request for commitment."

"Yes."

"Your deposition or will he be self-committed?"

He hadn't even looked up yet. I was beginning to feel the same way about him as I did about Farret, both were strangers whom I couldn't reach.

"It's him, isn't it?" and he looked up, nodding at Farret.

It relieved me, as if he were now on my side.

"I don't know the technicalities," I said, "but I brought him in and he came voluntarily."

"Voluntary commitment?" he said to Farret. "What do you say, friend?" and he grinned at Farret.

Farret's eyes got narrow and he flicked one lid.

Harmond waited, Farret said nothing, and I thought the air was too thick to breathe.

"Farret," I said. "You want a cup of coffee while we talk?"

"Is there somebody back there?"

"Sure." Hammond leaned over the desk now. "There's Joe, fiddling with the files, and there's Mel. Mel will give you a cup. You'll see the urn right next to the files."

Farret had been getting up and was walking to the partition. He looked in and then said to Harmond, "I see the urn."

Either Mel or Joe stuck his head through the partition and looked at Harmond. Harmond winked at him and waved with his hand that Farret should stay there. The man disappeared again and I could hear him talking to Farret, about the coffee, and how about sitting down till it cooled, that kind of thing.

"All right," said Harmond, "what's your name?"

"Miner."

"Now let me explain this. You come at a bad hour, but we can hold him. We can hold him on your deposition, stating he's a danger to himself and society. Or the same thing with him signing it, except it don't hold water as good. If he is crazy, you can see it won't hold water what he's signing and somebody else has got to be responsible."

"I'll do it," I said. "Just so it gets done."

"Now wait." Harmond opened a drawer and rummaged around with concentration. He came up with a pack of cigarettes and offered me one.

"No, thanks."

"Well, I'll have one," he said, and when he was done lighting it, which took a long time, he said, "Now let me explain this. This is a court matter, you know. Not police. We just hold 'em for court on your say so. The court, meaning the court psychiatrist, *he* decides whether the man should be committed or not. That's why your coming here is just a *request* for commitment. Get it?"

"I get it. All I'm interested...."

"Now wait. I got to explain this, by law." Harmond gulped coffee. "Because you know what happens if the bug doctor says he's sane. He says that, and you're wide open for a suit, and I mean heavy!"

I hadn't known this because I hadn't thought that far. Not that it mattered to me. I had caught up with Farret, I now had him in a better way than I could have planned. I couldn't explain this to Harmond, nor was it any of his business, but I had a good answer for going ahead with this thing anyway.

"Once the court psychiatrist takes one look at him there'll be less question in his mind than in yours and mine about Mister Farret. I'll make that disposition."

"If you say so." Harmond opened his desk drawer again, looked around for a while, then came up with a triple form. I took it from him and looked for the place for the signature.

"Now wait."

I was getting jumpy from that phrase he kept using.

"Read what you're signing so you see what you're in for."

I looked through the form more for Harmond's benefit than for mine taking no more than a minute or two. It said I'm the one who did the committing and to the best of my knowledge and belief, etc. I signed and gave it back to him.

"Your address," said Harmond, pushing the paper back.

"I don't have a local address," I told Harmond.

He got ready to say, "Now wait," or something similar, when Farret came back into the room.

He walked up to me, there was no sign of his limp anymore or any other damage, and said, "What are you signing, Miner?"

"How was the coffee?" said Harmond, trying to help. "Was the coffee good?"

"Yes. Thank you. Just like Hubert's. You ever been to Denver, lieutenant?"

"No, sir. Can't say I have."

"Place there called Hubert's. Best damn coffee there, next to yours."

"Why, thank you kindly," said Harmond.

He could figure Farret as little as I could and looked confused. The talk he had just had with Farret had been nice, normal, and flattering. Nothing wrong anywhere. I was starting to boil.

"Before you sign anything here, Miner," said Farret, "read it good. So you know what you're in for. Believe me."

"I read it," I said to Farret. "It's about the help you and I came for."

"Help?"

"You remember back in the hotel, Farret? What went on there?"

"Why, yes," he said.

"And the wiring," I said. "You noticed the wiring."

"Old-fashioned," said Farret and turned to Harmond. "You remember in the old days they used to wire on the outside of the wall?"

"Yeah, I do."

"And your wiring here," said Farret. He looked up at the ceiling where two of the fixtures were missing. "I'd call that dangerous. See those leads? They're not even taped."

"Damn if that ain't so," said Harmond. "I happen to know about the code on that. Imagine," and he laughed at both of us, "broke the code right here in the police station, those bums!"

"Yes," said Farret. "All bums break the code. That's their danger."

The lieutenant laughed over that, but not Farret. The only thing that hadn't changed in him was his lack of humor. And I wasn't laughing either.

"I've signed that," I said to Harmond. "It's your baby now."

"Oh. Yes." He looked at the form, then back at us. "You were going to give me your address before leaving."

"Leaving, Miner?" Farret was frowning. His frown was like a tic.

I looked at him and we both could have been made of stone.

"You're staying here."

"But Miner, you can't go."

Either I was going out of my mind or he sounded like he was pleading with me. Farret! Pleading with me!

"We made it, Miner! Why break that up?"

"As a matter of fact," said Harmond and he got out of his chair with a lot of noise, "maybe your friend here's got something. Since you don't have a legal address, any address here...."

"He's from the Keys," said Farret. "He used to run a boat."

Harmond was watching closely now. He was squinting as if a strong sun was in his eyes.

"Before we go any further," he said, "let's get this straight. Sit down, both of you."

Farret sat down immediately, but I didn't. It seemed to be all Harmond needed.

"You hear me, Miner?" he yelled at me.

I'd had it. I was crippled between having to say more and having to keep my mouth shut. So I blew.

"If you don't honor that request I put in," I told Harmond, "I'm going to shovel a pile of dirt into your department that you and your coffee cup aren't half equipped to handle. I've made a legal request, now you're bound to act on it. I jeopardize myself coming here and then I can't get any cooperation out of you."

"Shut your damn mouth!" Harmond yelled at me. He came around the desk, livid.

"Lieutenant Harmond." Farret sounded very calm, very serious. "You have no business talking to Mister Miner that way. Remember that."

It set both of us back. Harmond, for being reprimanded, and me because Farret was now my sober friend.

It helped when the door opened. I didn't care who was coming in, as long as it was an interruption.

"You fellers having a spat?" said the voice and then it cackled.

He was in uniform, shirt sleeves rolled up, and very old. He had white hair, an old, sunken face, and a chin which came out too much because he wasn't wearing his lower plate.

"Close that door, Freddy," said Harmond. "I'll have this straightened out in no time."

"Now don't you be beating up no prisoners," said the old cop and cackled again. "Can't a body get him some coffee without walking through a street brawl in this here station?"

"Can it," said Harmond.

"Yes. Just shut up," said Farret.

It made us all look at Farret. He wasn't calm any more. Farret was bent a little and with his face gone all dead suddenly his eyes looked terribly alive.

"Son," said the old cop. "Good thing I'm hard of hearing."

"What he say, Freddy?" Harmond stepped closer.

"Nothing. Nothing at all," and the old cop tried to go to the partition.

"There's no tea there," said Farret. "Don't bother looking."

"Huh?" The old cop looked up at Farret and then said, "Tea?" He thought it was meant as a joke and started to laugh. And trying to pass he put out his hand so Farret would move out of the way.

That's when Farret swung.

He missed, he was that excited, but the fury in his face set my teeth on edge.

Maybe I should have left then. Harmond was in his element, holding down Farret, and the signed deposition was on the desk. And they had Farret now, dead to rights with no more convincing needed.

But I didn't make it. I wanted this to be a sure thing, so sure I was ready to tell them about Farret, a little thing here and a small story there, just so they would hold him for the right reason, hold him for the court examiner in the morning, and thinking about that took just enough time for Harmond to look over at me and say, "Don't you leave, Miner. You're wanted on this."

There were four cops in the room now and Farret suddenly calm again. I stayed for the rest of it.

Chapter Nineteen

Having no local address I had to make one. A squad car took me down to the Rouge Arms after I had returned my rented car, and the cop watched me register and then came up with me to the room.

"Sleep good," he said. "You have only four hours," and then he closed the door for me.

It was dawn outside. I could see the city which looked gray in the thin light and I saw planes in the distance. I couldn't see the air force field where they kept coming and going but the radio towers and high installations still had their red lights on because of the gray dawn.

I thought of calling Jane at the ranch, to tell her I'd be home soon and it would all be over, but it was three in the morning where she was. And I wasn't so sure. I felt terribly tired and not sure about anything then. The real crisis, after all, was over. They had Farret and all it needed now was the expert to judge him. All of which they could do without me, easily. And the further I was away from their questions, the deader the past.

I called the desk and got the airport. The next plane out of Baton Rouge to San Francisco left at nine in the morning. Nothing sooner. I made my reservation and hung up. I thought of leaving then and sleeping on a bench in the airport but here was the bed, I was sitting on it, and I felt like lead. I called the desk again, left a call for eight, hung up, lay back on the bed. I didn't even undress.

I woke up a minute or so before eight, thinking I hadn't slept yet. But the sun was up now, the heat in the room was oppressive, and my shirt stuck to me. The phone rang and the girl said, "Good morning, sir. It is eight o'clock." I smacked the receiver down, stripped, and took a cold shower. All the cold water did was make me long for the bed, a warm bed and dryness. I didn't remember ever having felt so rotten. I had no time to shave, I had no clean shirt, and the only thing that kept me going was the thought of that plane waiting, and the thought that once in the air the nightmare must be over.

I took my canvas suitcase with the few things I had bought in Miami and went down to the lobby.

I had paid in advance the night before, a few hours before, and so I didn't take time to check out. I threw the key on the desk and waved away a bell boy. Nobody stopped me and I went straight to the revolving doors.

"Man, you're early," said the man behind me, and there was the cop who had brought me down. "Had breakfast yet?"

I stopped and took a deep breath. It was the safest thing I could think of. Then I said, "You mean you poor son of a bitch sat in the lobby all this time?"

It hadn't sounded friendly enough to him, not that I had been trying.

"What's the matter, you had a bad night?" he asked me.

I said, "I'm sorry you had to wait around. But there was no point to it."

"Huh?"

"I know the way," and then I tried leaving.

But the bluff didn't work.

"I got orders to drive you to court and I'm driving you to court." And then he added, "So you don't blow outa here on that plane you been thinking of."

I had forty minutes to catch the plane, I had one half-asleep cop in an empty lobby, a revolving door, taxis outside, and enough of a desperation to try something quick.

I also had a trail from San Francisco, over Denver, to Miami, and then here. I had Denver cops looking and Gambello's crowd looking. To have Baton Rouge on top of that while Farret was just about out of the picture was foolish. I gave up.

"No," I said. "I haven't had breakfast yet."

I had mostly coffee and I didn't watch how the cop ate. I was hoping the coffee would sharpen me. All that kept me awake now was irritation.

The court house was nice and cool. The cool air almost made me feel clean. The cop took me to a waiting room which was very large, dark, and paneled. The intricate patterns in wood made the room look very expensive. The cop left me there and I waited alone for maybe ten minutes. I didn't try to leave or to move because the only thing I had to do now was hold up my end and it would be all right. As long as they had Farret. Maybe I should have felt that way when I had first walked into Harmond's office, and so saved myself a lot of wear, but the habit of having a secret can make you over anxious in feeling, in thinking, in everything. Everything up to ten years ago was supposed to be dead, but it wasn't. I didn't want it to wake up anymore.

A man opened an inner door and looked at me through his glasses. He had a tired face, oldish, and he acted shy. "Mister Miner?"

"Yes," I said.

"I'm Doctor Barnett. Would you come this way, please?"

I followed him into a room which was small and looked makeshift. There was paneling again, but only on one wall. It ended where a new partition had been built across. The partition was cheap and cut a large window in half. The room that was left hardly held desk, chairs, files, and a glass cabinet. The cabinet was full of boxes and I saw blocks in some of them and just paper in others.

"I'm the court psychiatrist," said Doctor Barnett. "And you are Mister Miner?"

"Yes. I'm Mister Miner."

"Will you sit here, Mister Miner? We'll talk about this quickly and then we are done. Fine?"

"Yes. Fine."

He sat down behind the desk and I sat next to the desk and said nothing. I was hoping he would say enough quickly, so I knew what went on.

"You look tired, Mister Miner."

"I am."

"Me too." He shifted folders and didn't look up. "I've been tired as long as I can remember. Cigarette?"

"Thank you." I took one, but he didn't.

"You brought in Mister Farret."

It wasn't a question and he didn't sound so tired anymore. He took off his glasses to clean them. "You've known him how long?"

I finished lighting my cigarette and sat up straighter.

"Have you seen Mister Farret?"

"No," said Barnett.

"But you're going to."

"Of course." He looked up this time and put his glasses back on. He kept looking at me as if there was something for me to explain.

"I just wanted to know what goes," I said. "Why I'm here. That's why I asked you."

He smiled at me and looked tired again.

"You seem relieved."

"I am."

"You can be," he said. "Mister Farret spent a good night in the police jail and he'll be here in fifteen or twenty minutes. You don't have to worry."

I was glad he understood so much without my having to explain anything and fifteen or twenty minutes weren't going to bother me. I said, "I don't know how long I've known him. Off and on over a long time."

"Uh-huh," and he wrote something down. I was glad I had said enough for his needs.

"Why did you commit him?"

I stopped breathing and was aware of the fact that I had my lip in my teeth. But Barnett didn't look up, which was good. I was grateful that he was tired and all this was routine to him, so that my shock went right past him.

"I just want to say," he still kept looking down, "that the answer is taking you an unusually long time."

Then he looked up but he was smiling, which helped.

"I haven't the knowledge," I said, "to explain this the way you might be able to explain this, Doctor Barnett. To me Mister Farret simply acts crazy. He talks in a way that I can't understand, he refers to things that don't mean anything to me, and he tried to hit a cop last night." That, I thought, was a good clincher.

Barnett smiled again, even tried a brief laugh. Then he said, "I just want to point this out to you, Mister Miner. You're doing it again, taking an unusually long time to say nothing. Did you notice?"

I sucked on my cigarette so I wouldn't have to answer.

"You noticed." Then he leaned on the desk. "Look. I'm not here to diagnose you, and I haven't tried. But you are trying not to help me, and I think you are doing that because you feel it would mean you are not helping yourself. You sit there and you're trying to help yourself by saying as little as possible. Huh?"

I stomped out my cigarette and said, "You're right." Why not. He was right and he knew it and I knew it.

"I'm not the police, Mister Miner. All right?"

"You're not?"

"I'm not. What you say here about yourself doesn't concern me, officially, and so won't go any further. All right?"

"All right."

"So whatever the nature of your past association with Mister Farret, don't worry about it. Not on my account, at any rate. All right?"

I nodded.

"The reason you're here," he said, and now he looked down again, "is to substantiate your claim that Mister Farret should be committed. That interests you, doesn't it?"

That interested me greatly. I suddenly wanted to say a lot because nothing like Farret had ever happened to me and all of it was bad, so bad that the anger came up inside me, feeling like a hot rush of blood.

"I tell you this. There were several of us, a long time ago, and one of them was Farret. This was a long time ago. Then Farret comes back, with a vengeance. For some notion of vengeance. He is cruel, one of us learned that. He is unscrupulous, another one learned that. He is going from one to the other in a circle of bigger and bigger destruction, to feed something inside him. To guard something inside him from what I don't know. And maybe he doesn't know himself because he makes up reasons to act like an executioner. He does everything coldly, with insane logic, with some damn persistence which never stops. That's Farret. And then there's the last thing that happened, something different perhaps from the rest I told you. When I caught—when I ran into him, just last night, he was running from something as though the furies were after him. Caught by a master plan, the whole place wired to trap him—that's how he talked—and help me, help me, that kind of thing. More crazy talk I don't even remember. That's Farret!"

I stopped. It felt more like I had run out. It felt to me like the sum of the man and for the moment I didn't care whether Barnett had understood me.

"Where did you, uh, run into him?"

"Lamotte. Some town further north."

"Yes." Barnett looked up from his folder. "Did you know that this Farret had been in Lamotte before?"

"He was?"

"The police checked his name, of course, after you brought him in. Sixteen and a half years ago, if it's the same man. He crippled a local policeman there. Terrible beating."

I hadn't known it had been in Lamotte.

"And then last night, the thing with that old man in the station. You remember that, you mentioned it."

"Yes."

Barnett said nothing for a while, just looked across the room. Then he said, "Ah well," and looked at his watch. He picked up the phone on his desk and pressed a button.

"Is Mister Farret here yet?"

The answer was longish while Barnett said nothing. Then he hung up and said, "They're a little late."

I waited a moment but Barnett didn't say anything. He was looking down at his folder but I don't think he was reading.

"Did I make sense?"

He acted as if I had waked him up, and then he said:

"Oh yes. Of course," and looked down again. He looked at his hands. "Do you know, Mister Miner, why Farret likes you?"

"*What?*"

"Curious, isn't it?"

It was. But I remembered how Farret had come with me, how he hadn't acted the way I'd expected him to, with that snide, ill-tempered air of his. And in the station, the bastard had even defended me!

"I'll have to see him first, of course, but maybe I can explain it to you later."

"I don't think I want to wait," I said.

"Let me ask you one more thing, Mister Miner. The episode you described, alluded to, last night, in Lamotte. During the time you have known him, did anything like that ever happen before?"

"No," I said. "Never when I was around."

Barnett nodded. He stuck his fingers under the glasses, making them move up on his forehead, and rubbed his eyes. Then he let the glasses slide down again and looked at me.

"Well, I'd say that's likely. I have a report on his behavior for the few hours he was in jail. He was fine. Rational, calm, or rather, quiet. That sort of thing. Not pretty," he added.

"This means nothing to me."

"Yes." Barnett got up and walked to the window. "They are not easy to spot, necessarily. They act so sane, logical, most of the time."

"Who?"

"Paranoiacs."

"You mean Farret?"

"I haven't seen him, but it sounds like paranoia, of some degree. And Lamotte," Barnett turned around to explain, "was an episode. An episode where the whole structure, his whole ironclad structure, just started to give. And in that context, Mister Miner, you appeared on the scene, as a saving feature, so to speak. You were safe for him. That, I would guess, is the extent of his liking for you. Not that it will last," he said to his folder. And then, "Of course I don't know what went on in Lamotte, before you came, and maybe we never will know."

"Never will?"

"I'm no magician," said Barnett. "As a matter of fact, with the time given me, there's a chance I can't determine a thing about this man." He turned back to the window. "As I told you, paranoia can look very sane."

I was hoping this was a joke, maybe some professional joke among court psychiatrists. Ridiculous. Not Barnett. Barnett *meant* it!

I got up and the chair scraping made him turn around.

"You're not leaving, Mister Miner?"

"I'm leaving," I said.

If Farret managed to talk himself out of this corner he would more likely than not talk me into it. If they got him dead to rights, they wouldn't need me, but if he got off, then I needed elbow room.

"But Mister Miner—"

I stopped at the door and said, "I'm not under arrest, am I?"

"Of course not. I mean, not as far as I know."

"And that's why I'm leaving."

I turned to open the door but the door opened by itself.

"You leaving, Miner?"

It was hardly a question, the way Barnett had put it a while ago, but more like a taunt. That's how Lieutenant Harmond had meant it and he pushed me back to get into the door. His face was still like a country boy's but he needed sleep now, or maybe a scapegoat. He kept staring at me while he came into the office and the two cops with him, in uniform, stayed at the door.

That's all there was, Harmond and the two cops by the door. I was enough on edge now, I didn't care how I sounded.

"Where's Farret?"

Harmond paid no attention to me. He walked up to the desk and talked to Doctor Barnett.

"We don't mean to make a scene in your office, Doctor, but our problem is a little different from yours. You've got your patient...."

"Where?" I said.

"Wait your turn, Miner," and he stared at me.

Barnett saw the tension between Harmond and me of course, and he tried his best. He said, "Mister Miner, if you will appreciate his position, lieutenant, is under considerable tension when it comes to this matter. Please don't take

him up on it, but just try understanding it. The unusual responsibility of re-
questing psychiatric observation for someone else is not easy."

"Exactly why we're here, Doctor," and then Harmond looked at me. "He's
tried to dump Farret on us and run out last night in my office, he tried skipping out again this morning, and all that taken together doesn't look too responsible to me."

Barnett still tried to be soothing and said, "Well, lieutenant, Mister Miner
is still here."

"And we're here, so he stays," which was said to me. Then Harmond
turned back to Barnett. "Like I started to say, our problem is different from
yours. You got your patient, but we got to make sure we have Miner."

I looked down at the floor, hoping it would make me look calm. Actually,
I was flying apart. The best and neatest way to dispose of Farret was turning into a nightmare of threats. The police were suspicious of me, the psychiatrist wasn't sure he could gauge Farret and Farret, given half a chance,
would drag me into legal tangles. More than tangles, knowing Farret.

"We got the job, Doctor, of protecting a citizen. We can't have irresponsi-
bility in a guy who comes in and makes serious accusations like he did," and
Harmond jerked his head at me. "If Farret turns out all right, we got to have
Miner on tap to find out why he did the committing. We got to have him on
tap in case Farret wants to prefer charges. That's only plain sense. What if
every guy with a grudge comes around and has all his enemies put through
the indignity of a forced trial by lunatic doctors?"

"Well, as to indignity," Barnett started, but then Harmond apologized for
the use of the word, the same as a trial lawyer will do, after he has made his
point.

The point about Harmond was that he didn't like me. He had a legitimate
job to do, which he had explained well, but with a bastard like Harmond
against me I could only get hurt.

"All right," I said. "You've made it clear that I'm doing a serious thing. I'm
taking the responsibility. When I tried to leave, I was doing wrong."

Harmond didn't like my being so agreeable but there was nothing else for
him to say. But I had to say more. I had misjudged the step I had taken, and
I was now trying to judge things right.

"Doctor Barnett," I said. "If it's so difficult judging a case like Farret's, if
it's difficult in this particular case, what would make your judgment easier?"

"Well, first of all, observation will take more than a day. There are tests, interviews, colleague opinions, all of which can be facilitated by your being available to us. What would help also, Mister Miner, would be corroborative information. If there are other people whom you could call in, others who have
had a chance to see Mister Farret, all that would help."

Then the phone rang. Barnett picked it up and said yes, fine, yes. He hung
up and picked up his folder.

"He's here," and he went to the door. "We'll know more by evening."

After he had gone I left. I had to tell Harmond where I was going and then he sent one of his men along. I went to the hotel and stayed in my room.

I slept some and I smoked too much. I waited till four which was the time when Barnett had told me I could reach him by phone.

Worthwhile material, he said, but nothing conclusive yet.

I spent a bad night. Then I sweated out the next day. I had one more interview with Barnett and told him more or less the same things I had told him before.

"Were you able to enlist anyone else in this matter, Mister Miner? Anyone else who might give information?"

I hadn't. There was Metz, who was too sick. There was Lena, but I didn't know where she was. There was Getterman, who didn't know anything but his own fears. There was Jane, but I did not want to bring her back into this.

At four I made my call to Barnett again.

Nothing conclusive.

They would spend one more day with him, unless there was promise of new material.

That night I called Jane. To bring her back into it could mean Farret would remain safe. To leave her out of it could mean Farret would find us.

Jane left the ranch that night and flew to Baton Rouge.

Jane and I went to the state institution to see Barnett at ten. He seemed pleased to see Jane, even before she had said anything. When we sat down he explained.

"We've got some conclusive material at this point, and in my opinion at least, the man's syndrome is clear."

"Yours won't be the only opinion?" I asked him.

"There are two other psychiatrists and we're still waiting for the psychologist's report. Rorschach, some picture completion tests, that kind of thing."

"What did you find?"

Barnett smiled at his glasses because he was wiping them. Then he said:

"Among other things he's told me all the various matters which you didn't want to talk about. You needn't worry. This is psychiatric material, not a police matter. Anyway," and he became serious again, "there is always that grain of truth in a paranoid's delusional system. The little frictions with you, the escape from the island, made especially difficult because you had left with the boat, that sort of thing. But growing from that there is that wild flower of rampant suspicions and hates, all designed to externalize what he suffers on the inside. We'll let that go. Too much detail. But I at least, feel he needs to be institutionalized."

"And the others?"

"Yes. I'm particularly glad that this young woman has come, particularly glad that she's a woman."

That sounded highly peculiar to me but Barnett went right on.

"There has been one current demonstration in Farret's behavior which gives, *in vivo* so to speak, indications about the man's make-up. You were present at the time when he attacked the old policeman. The image of the old man seems highly disturbing to Farret. The psychiatric material would lead to that suspicion."

"Why suspicion? He attacked the old man."

"Yes. But he hasn't since. We introduced him to a situation involving an old man, but Farret did not take it up. His attention had switched. All he said was, 'You're dead,' and showed no further effect."

"You mean you got to see him beat up an old man before you can...."

"Of course not. But it helps as case material. Anyway, another precarious area of his make-up is the relationship he maintains towards women."

"He hates their guts."

"You've said it much shorter than I would have, and you're right."

"I don't want to see him again," said Jane. "I'd much rather not see him."

"You know him personally?" Barnett asked.

"We met."

"I'm not interested in details, but was it pleasant or unpleasant?"

"He was vile."

"I would just like him to see you," Barnett said to Jane. "I'm not interested in provoking a scene and for that matter he might not be inclined to make one. But seeing you would enrich his further speculations, the kind of thing we observe in interviews. Seeing a woman of his acquaintance might sharpen the material we gather from him."

We talked about it a little bit more and then we left Barnett's office. We sat in a waiting room since Farret had not been brought in yet.

"He won't come through here," said Barnett to Jane. He patted her hand when he said it and then talked about something else.

The reason I saw Farret was because I had gone out into the hall. There was a water fountain there and when I straightened up I saw Farret come down the long corridor, walking with hands in his pockets and talking to the man who was with him, who must have been one of the other psychiatrists.

Nothing happened when Farret passed me and I only think of the incident because of the way it made me feel.

Farret was not pleased to see me, I thought, but he made no display about it. He stopped talking to the man next to him and he kept looking at me. He looked stern but his face was mostly shut. We just looked at each other while he passed.

To me it felt somehow like a good-by. It felt empty between us, the same when I looked at his face and the same when I watched his back. Farret was done and past.

I went back to the waiting room and Barnett was getting up, taking Jane's arm.

I smiled at her and said, "It's over, Jane. Soon we'll be gone."

She nodded and went into the consultation room.

I couldn't hear all that was going on but, as Barnett had predicted, there was nothing violent. I could hear Farret's voice, fast and sharp, but he often talked that way. Several times I made out the phrase, "I wasn't finished with you. I wasn't finished with you," and then Barnett talking and a short moment later Jane came back out.

That was all. Barnett said good-by to us and asked me to call at nine in the evening. Possibly there would be a final word.

There was. Farret, one hour before my call, had escaped.

CHAPTER TWENTY

The police gave us a guard and advised us we could leave any time we wanted. We stayed one extra day with a guard. But the time made no difference. They didn't find Farret. And then the time was very short again, because Farret was loose, and only two steps left to the end. Getterman and me.

I talked to Harmond and said, "If I tell you where Farret is heading and what he has in mind...."

"Not interested. There's been no crime and the board never made their decision on him."

I called Barnett and told him the same thing.

"I'm powerless, unless the man is in my office. It's unfortunate that we did not reach a decision."

"He's sane? And he's safe from the law? Doctor Barnett, is there nothing that you can do?"

"Nothing personally, nothing professionally. It's a shame we did not reach a decision to constrain."

A shame. The Baton Rouge interlude could just as well not have happened, and he said it's a shame.

Farret was loose and had two to go.

"Doctor Barnett. How far can he go? Is he wearing some special institute garb? Would he have to steal clothes to get inconspicuous?"

"He wasn't an inmate, you know. He had his own clothes, all his own things which were in his pocket. No knives, of course."

I hung up. There were two to go, and with Farret's brain and with Metz's money still in his pocket he might go very far.

We took a taxi straight to the airport and got busy. We checked one airline desk after another. There had been no flight to San Francisco between the time Farret escaped and right now. The next flight to San Francisco was at twelve midnight and I bought two tickets. If Farret wasn't on that flight then I would get to Frisco first. I didn't expect him on the plane and he wasn't there.

"My father is next, John? Or is it you?"

"Farret doesn't know where I live. He knows where your father is."

I had called Getterman from Baton Rouge and I called him again on a two hour layover in Salt Lake City. There had been no answer. Then I checked flight schedules out of Salt Lake City and after that called the ranch. While I waited I talked to Jane.

"I'll feel safe looking for your father, only if I know you are safe, Jane. You understand that?"

"I do, darling."

"I don't want you to be in San Francisco."

"I'll wait for you, John. It's close to the end now, and it won't be long."

I squeezed her arm. I had made the call person to person to Edsel who was the oldest of my three men and most like a foreman. I wanted him because he would be best.

"This is John," I said, "John Miner."

"I can tell your voice, John. What is it?"

I asked him if Wilgant, the bush pilot in town, was out on a job or at home.

"He's free," said Edsel. "You need him?"

"I want you to fly down with him to Sacramento and pick up Jane who's coming in on a nine p.m. flight. Pick her up and take her back to the ranch."

"Fine. I'll be there." He didn't ask what this was all about but said only the necessary.

"And listen, Edsel. You got the keys to the gun case."

"Yes," he said.

"Edsel, till I'm back, you three men carry guns. Take rifles when you're out working, have a revolver near by when you're in the house."

"I'm listening."

"Two things. Don't you ever let Jane out of your sight, and till I'm back, you three men stay in the main house nights."

"Pauline will have a fit."

"She's to carry a revolver too. She's good at it."

He laughed.

"Any man coming by whom you don't know, Edsel, that man gets stopped. And tell this to the others."

"How about the sheriff?"

"Not yet."

"We'll handle it, John."

"At night, one of you has to be awake."

"We'll handle it, John."

"He's after me, Edsel, but look out for Jane."

"Right."

"He is thin, with black hair hanging down. Wears a pea jacket, maybe. Tall and thin with a dead serious face. Jane knows him."

"Don't worry."

"And take care of yourself."

We hung up and for a short time I felt better.

I put Jane on the Sacramento plane and watched it leave. It was the second time I had put her on a plane and the sight made me tense. Before my own flight time, I called Getterman's house again but got no answer. I had forgotten his office address and Jane wasn't here any more to give it to me. I let the phone ring a long time, but there was still no answer.

Chapter Twenty-one

Getterman's apartment faced the back where another building came close to the windows, close enough to show the details of bricks and mortar and cracks in the wall. The bricks were an old red which made the sight very dark, and on a day with no sun the gloom in the apartment became deep. There was a living room with furniture picked without care or love, there was a bedroom with just a bed and a bureau, a bathroom and the kitchen. The kitchen had no windows at all, just a vent. There was greasy fuzz on the grill of the vent.

Getterman's apartment was empty all day, looked empty now. Everything looked anonymous, like in a warehouse, and this did not change when Getterman came home in the evening.

He came home late. There was nothing for him at home and he never went there until after he had eaten his meal, seen a movie, perhaps, or had spent time in the library. He would spend his evening hours in the newspaper room in the library, reading this and that until closing time. The difference between himself and the drifters who sat in the reading room was a difference in looks. Even with his better clothes, with his better haircut, Getterman still looked the more pitiful. A lot of the men in the reading room sat there because they had nowhere to go, but it showed that they didn't care. Getterman still cared. He had nowhere to go and still cared.

He left the library at ten and walked for a while in the damp night air. He was hoping he would feel tired soon. Once he stopped to have a cup of hot chocolate and then he walked again. He wondered where Miner was and he wondered about his daughter, whether she could be as happy as she had looked the last time he had seen her, whether anybody could be that happy.

Then Getterman walked home, wanting to go to bed. He did not want to walk and think any more.

He let himself in and turned on one of the lights, a dim bulb in a wall bracket, not much good for any real light, but Getterman didn't care. He would turn it off as soon as he had taken off his coat and hat which he hung into a wall closet next to the entrance. Then he sat down on the couch in the living room because he was not yet tired enough.

If he were working at something which really occupied him, interested him, then there would not be a problem of having too much time to sleep. If he were still on his own, the way he had built it up on the island. So many years of work, legitimate work, and then the whole thing down the drain because of that gunrunning lunacy. Not that he had been a criminal, like some of the others in that terrible business. He had been a business man. The same kind of acumen, the same kind of contacts in fact, and the same work, in essence. And all down the drain.

The thought made him feel peevish, and then doubly so when he realized how his thinking had sucked him along. It was a good thing the whole business was down the drain and eight years gone.

It was time to go to bed. If he sat longer and thought in this way, the next thing would be the doubts; whether it was all down the drain. It wasn't, not till Miner came back.

Getterman coughed and stopped himself from thinking further. He went to the front door, latched it, chained it. The way Miner had told him to on the day he left San Francisco. Getterman locked the door and went to the bedroom. He did all this with an emphasis on the routine of it, to think less, to feel no fear.

Someone knocked on the front door.

Getterman just stood still because to do anything else would have felt like panic to him. The knock sounded again and this time there was a voice too.

A woman's voice. Maybe a woman's voice was all right. Maybe to breathe carefully now would be all right.

"Mister Getterman? It's just me. It's Mrs. Coons, Mister Getterman."

Getterman managed to say, "Yes?"

"Your landlady, Mister Getterman."

He had unwound by then and went to the front door. He unlatched it, unbolted it, and opened the door. His landlady stood there in a wide flannel robe and a sock was over her head, as if that would hide the curlers.

"Mister Getterman, I don't mean to bother you this time of night, but just in case you should want to know, I mean, not that I know anything about...."

"What is it? What happened?"

"Now you don't need to get excited, Mister Getterman, but it's just I heard you come in and me still up so I thought I'd just simply drop over and tell you. Not that it's anything."

This time Getterman waited. She would soon come to the point. She was patting her head and the curlers with the sock over them and she was smiling.

"Well, first of all there have been these phone calls. Of course I didn't come in to answer, you understand, but I know you don't often get phone calls during the day here. In fact, I don't ever recall...."

"Yes," said Getterman. "Yes—"

"So, anyways, there was the phone ringing for the longest time. Happened two or three times, maybe, I don't recall which."

"Oh," said Getterman. He could not think of anything else to say.

"Was it important, Mister Getterman?"

He had no idea. He hadn't answered the phone calls, not having been in the

apartment, and the only feeling he had about all of this was a growing and
sick uneasiness. Maybe Jane had called? Maybe something had happened. No,
not Jane. She knew his number at work, at the office, and that failing, she
would have called Mrs. Coons to deliver a message.

"Well, and then this young man came," said Mrs. Coons.

"What?"

"Oh, he was very nice. Very quiet and nice young man, and looking so tired.
What he wanted to know was, when are you coming home."

"What did he look like?"

"A nice young man. Well, not so young maybe, but young by me," and she
giggled. "Anyways, he said he'll get in touch. In the morning, maybe, or some-
time soon. I said, is it business? And he said, yes, it's business, private business, but he'd come back about it and not to worry."

"Not to worry?" It was all Getterman was able to fasten on.

"Yes. He get in touch with you?"

"Did he give his name?"

"No. He said you'd know. He said not to worry in the meantime, everything was all planned, and he'd get in touch."

Then Mrs. Coons left and Getterman closed the door. He bolted and
chained it by habit, not for any other reason. He felt much better now. It
would all be much better now because Miner was back.

Getterman went to the bathroom, then to the kitchen. He straightened a
towel on the rack, gave the tap a firm twist so it wouldn't drip in the night.
He went back into the living room where he looked at the couch which
showed the dent in the pillow where he had been sitting. He patted that back
into shape. He turned off the light, went to the bedroom door in the dark,
turned on the bedroom light before going into the room. He had forgotten to
straighten his bed in the morning, he noticed, because he could see the wrinkles. And the spread wasn't clean either. He went to wipe at the stain, which
seemed to be almost like dirt from a shoe. This was irritating, but Getterman,
now properly tired and ready for bed, did not get upset. He wiped, and then
it sparked.

A cigarette. How did a lit cigarette come, suddenly, out of nowhere?

"Pick it up, or there'll be a burnt hole."

Getterman whirled with the sheer force of his fright and it seemed an eter-
nity before he saw clearly. Before he saw more than the bulk of a black jacket,
black hair, black eyes, white face, black lines in the face because of the un-
shaven cheeks and the long chin.

"Don't make a noise," said Farret and came closer.

Getterman had not been about to make any noise, because his insides had
turned as stiff as ice, and then Farret hit him across the face, hard, breaking
everything or so it felt. Breaking Getterman all to pieces so that he fell on the
bed where he had meant to sleep.

When he opened his eyes he saw that Farret was there as before. Not a wild fear image in black and white, but worse, the real Farret.

He sat down on the edge of the bed and lit another cigarette.

"I'm glad you're scared," said Farret. "I'm glad to see this. It proves me right."

He smoked, as if he were ignoring the old man on the bed.

"I'm glad I'm at the end of the mission."

In a little while Getterman felt himself breathe again, though it was painful, but breathe again with a slow, cautious pain in his chest.

"Farret," he said. "What do you want?"

"Why you whispering?"

"Please, Farret. If you want money, look around. You'll see I don't have any."

"I don't want your money," said Farret. He pulled wads of bills out his pocket, made a noise with them, stuffed them away again.

"I got enough money to hire me a private plane all the way from Louisiana to here and you."

"Please—"

"Whisper! You sound better that way."

He got off the bed and stood there, looking down at Getterman. Farret's big collar was up, he put his arms on his hips, spreading the jacket like a wide cape, stood like that with his legs apart. There was a mirror on top of a bureau and Farret could see himself. He kept standing the way he was.

"You and me," he said. "And the end of the mission." He sounded like an old-fashioned preacher.

Getterman stared and started to raise himself up.

"Stay down," said Farret. "I can see you better."

Getterman fell back on the bed.

"Stay there and listen," said Farret. He dropped his cigarette on the floor and stepped on it without looking down. He kept looking at Getterman.

"I started out on this thing a long time ago, Getterman. The day you fingered me, the day you stabbed me in the back, all those years ago. I started to think and plan then. One of them did this thing to me, I kept saying. I lived through the kind of hell you and your kind never heard of only because I wasn't going to let you get away with cheating me. You were smart, Getterman. You threw me on all the wrong tracks. First Lena, I thought, but she was too dumb. Then Metz, I figured, but he was too sick. I had to find all that out, you covered yourself that good, Getterman. I admire that. I even got my suspicions about Miner, that slob, except he was in on something else. He was in on Lamotte. But I beat that too. That was lucky for Miner, or he'd have been on my list. And on my list, Getterman, nobody gets away with a thing! So then I saw it had to be you."

"What are you saying?"

It was a near screech. It was Getterman in his desperation trying to keep his bearings in the midst of all the insane accusations.

"I'm saying you knifed me!" said Farret, his face suddenly close to Getterman's.

Then Farret straightened.

"Like I said, Getterman, I admire that. You were good. I respect that and I'm going to show you how I respect that. Lie still!"

Getterman froze.

"I'm going to kill you slow, Getterman."

"God! Wait." He didn't get it all out because Farret slapped the word back into Getterman's mouth.

But the action helped. Getterman knew for sure now what he was afraid of, nothing vague now, no waiting for the right sign. Farret was going to kill.

Getterman jumped off the bed, he was trembling but he jumped off the bed and stood next to Farret. He could not stand anywhere else.

"Farret, listen to me. I don't know where you got all this or how you thought up all this."

"With this," said Farret and tapped his skull.

"All right, listen. Just listen for one minute."

"I'm listening," said Farret because he was so certain he was right.

"Just think why," said Getterman, the words racing each other, "why would I do this, ruin this business for you and all of us? When everything went, I lost everything. I lost the business on the island, I lost my money, they held me in jail. Duz put me in jail. I almost didn't get away in the end because of the mess, and now you stand there and...."

"You?" said Farret. He had never thought of Getterman as a man in jail. Getterman was the kind who put other people in jail, people like him, Farret. "Jail where?"

"Capitol. In the capitol. The day after they raided the transport. I swear, Farret. They came into my agency, the Duz men...."

"You never been in jail in your life," said Farret. "What jail?"

"On Domingue, the jail on Domingue. Heavens, Farret, I spent weeks there."

"I know that jail," said Farret. "I was in that jail."

"It was terrible, Farret. Why should I go through that, I ask you? The filthy cell with no window, the room they have in the basement, and that fat man who was there, Sperro. I'll never forget Sperro."

"Sperro?"

Farret knew Sperro. In the days before Miner had hired him, Farret had known fat Sperro in the capitol jail and some of the sadist's little tricks with thumb stringing and toe breaking.

"He give you a hard time, Getterman?"

The old man's jaw trembled so that he couldn't say what he had on his mind.

"He put you in the room he has with all the rats? All those hungry rats?"

"They weren't rats!" Getterman wiped spit from his mouth. "They were cats! Starving tom cats." Getterman tore open his shirt. He tore it till one arm was exposed, showing thin, long scars and the dents from punctures.

Farret looked down at his shoes. He took out a cigarette but did not light it. He held it in his hand, forgetting the cigarette because it was the third time now, and a bad time, to be almost wrong. Farret, no matter what else, went by the rules, and by the rules Getterman was the wrong man.

He had known about Sperro and his cats. Getterman had not fallen for the trick when Farret had called them rats, and the old man had those scars. How else would Getterman know about this? Why would Getterman go to jail, *and* suffer the brutality of Sperro if he were the mastermind of the doublecross.

"If that's so," said Farret. "How come you got out?"

"Money! All my money! Sperro and God knows who else got all my money?"

"How much?"

"All I had. I had fifteen thousand. I lost my franchise, too, and they shipped me off the island with nothing but the clothes on my back."

"Didn't you have a daughter?" said Farret.

"In the States."

The memory made Getterman weak, how he had landed back in the States with his suit still wrinkled from jail, how he had called Jane at her school and how he had to reverse the charges. She could finish her term, he had said, but that was all. Everything was over. When they had met she had not asked many questions. She had been eighteen at the time.

Getterman noticed after a moment that he and Farret were sitting next to each other on the bed, that Farret just sat there, thinking, and he himself too weak to think at all. He did not even move when Farret got up. Perhaps Farret would leave now.

"It's a good thing," said Farret, "that I believe you."

He would leave now.

"It's a good thing, because there is one more to go."

The old man looked up, not understanding.

"John Miner," said Farret.

Farret walked back and forth in the room, clicked the light switch a few times. He looked up along the wall and the ceiling and said something about the wires being built into the plaster.

"What did you say, Farret?"

Farret suddenly grinned. Then he said, "So."

Getterman thought it best to keep still.

"You paid out fifteen thousand in bribes?" asked Farret.

"All I had."

"All you had." Farret rubbed the side of his face. "Where was the fifty thousand we'd been collecting, huh? Fifty thousand bucks, unsplit, for shipments of over three months?"

"But that went to the States!" said Getterman, "You know that John always...."

"John Miner!"

"Huh?"

"He took it back to the States, didn't he?"

Getterman did not want to say anything, but he had to nod. If I don't nod, he thought, he'll kill me.

"Took it back when?"

"On the last run, Farret. The night everything went."

"Except John Miner. He didn't go to hell, did he, Getterman?"

"Please, listen to me, Farret. Miner hasn't got that kind of money."

"How do you know?"

"He works, Farret. He has a small ranch and works it like a dog."

"Ranch?"

Getterman shut his mouth, afraid he had said too much.

"How does a man buy a ranch, huh? Stock it, run it, keep it up, huh, Getterman?" Farret grinned without any humor. "I should have known this to start with. Lena is broke, you're broke, and Metz, with him fifty thousand wouldn't make a dent. But Miner! He sets himself up with a fancy ranch! He's the one got the fat out of this fire! Him! All the time him!" and then Farret walked up to the old man on the bed.

"Where is he?" said Farret, quite low.

The fear was no smaller in Getterman than it had been before, and Farret looked worse now.

But Getterman wouldn't tell.

Because if he told it would mean that Jane would be in this. So Getterman didn't tell.

First, he took the beating and then, when Farret stopped, the old man did not think of it as a relief. He did not care about now or later, except that he wouldn't tell, which absorbed all of him. He did everything Farret told him, except that one thing to tell. He got up when Farret said to get up, he went to the bathroom when Farret said that, and he stood by, dull now and far away, while Farret ran water into the tub.

"Get in," said Farret.

He had to lift the old man into the tub.

The water was cold, but only as a distant fact, not as something that mattered.

Then Farret talked more, but the old man didn't hear the words, just the sounds. Later he struggled, because it was nature, but he drowned in the tub of cold water without having told.

Farret found out about Miner's ranch in another way. He found a letter from Jane Getterman to her father, a letter which was in a coat in a closet, and it said there that she was staying at John's ranch a while longer, and there was the address.

Chapter Twenty-two

What's worse than a gray day in San Francisco is a gray morning in San Francisco. A gray and clammy morning when the day looks like it's never going to make it. At five o'clock the plane came down in the sog of it, and that's how I felt, too. Except for the sharp edge I'd had inside me ever since I'd left Louisiana.

It would wake Getterman to call him at the crack of dawn and scare him, but it would be best that way. I ran into the airport building to make the call and then realized it would be quicker all around to catch one of the empty taxis before the mob from the plane got them all. I took a taxi. Waiting another hour before reaching Getterman now wouldn't make much of a difference.

I told the cabby the address and sat back. He just nodded, which was fine because I didn't feel like talking to anyone. He handed a morning paper back to me and started to drive.

I sat with the paper in my lap for a long time. The cabby went fast and it felt good to watch him. I didn't look at the paper till we were in San Francisco proper and then I read it in jumpy pieces, again and again, because that was the only way I could get it down.

BATH TUB MURDER... police puzzled by unusual cruelty of the crime... corpse that of Alvin Getterman, discovered in the early hours of the morning by landlady who came to investigate banging front door of victim's apartment... banging in the wind... motive for heinous crime not immediately apparent... co-workers of Mister Getterman could not yet be reached for comment at this hour, though office building superintendent said, "he's been the same all the time, cheerful, friendly, always with a smile"... police following several active leads... early arrests... landlady held for questioning... she is the former Denise Dolarty, one time sweetheart of the notorious Biff Misher, executed in nineteen-thirty-one for his part in the fabled "silk wars" of the early twenties....

"Driver!"

"I can't go any faster if I tried, Mister."

"Turn around. Back to the airport!"

Farret was loose again. Farret was loose and only one left in the circle, myself!

How could he have made it? No flights between the time he got out of jail in Baton Rouge and the time I caught one. Private plane! The bastard was loaded with money! He must have hired a powerful two-engine plane, needing no more than one or two stops for refueling compared to the five stops the commercial line made, flying the shortest route to San Francisco instead of the big city route taken by the commercial line. Beat again, beat again. Per-

haps he didn't know about the ranch. But he must. The way he had made Getterman die—

"Driver!"

"What is it this...."

"The railroad station," I said. "Not the airport."

It would take me half a day to the ranch, going by rail. That's how the connections ran. By plane, I might have made it in about three hours.

I was broke, though. The trek all across the country and then back. I did-
n't even have enough left in the bank in Great Rock. And Farret? He had
started from Miami with ten thousand dollars. He had hired a plane for a three
thousand mile trek. Why not another for this hop, just over the Rockies.

I shut my eyes and took a deep breath. I took several, trying to let the cold
air go all through me.

When I opened my eyes the cabby was driving the way he had driven before, good and fast, good and skillful, and no more than five, ten minutes to
the station. That would have to be the way. Unless I called the police.

I got out at the station, I paid the cabby, and was in such a hurry now he
called me back for my suitcase. I got the suitcase and went into the station.

This would stop, I felt. It was over right now, forgetting small details. Not
anymore, from now on. I bought my ticket for the local that left thirty minutes later and then went to the phones.

I did not call the police. I was in this thing now, all the way, and right or
wrong, I could not call the police. Farret was mine. I could not call the police or hire somebody else, because Farret was mine.

I called the ranch and Pauline answered. I asked her only one thing, if everything was under control, and when she said yes, I said I'll be in by noontime.
Until then, I told her, the same holds like I explained to Edsel. She understood,
she said.

"Except this time," I said, "everybody stay in the house, in a room upstairs,
where you can see out. Just Edsel and George to stay outdoors, checking."

"We do that," said Pauline and then I had to hang up.

The half hour till traintime wasn't easy but I had gone through worse. It
would have been worse if Pauline weren't home, and the three hands: Edsel,
the old one who knew a gun and the sights of the land like his own hand;
Luke, who sang to the cows and could be a man next to you, like having another self; and George, with the build of a bull. And Jane. I had seen her react in this kind of thing so I didn't feel too bad about her. I loved her and it
meant that I did not have to know how she was every minute because—it's
hard to say properly—because I loved her.

I knew two more things: I knew about Farret, and I knew about myself. I
knew what I was after. I didn't know all the hows, but I knew *what*. Farret.

I got to Great Rock when the sun was high and clear and the cool air blowing across the green land from the woods had the purest feel of any season.

And maybe Farret was in all this somewhere, and that meant another kind
of a season.

I was the only one who got off at the depot, and the station master, a man
who owned three hundred pipes and spent most of his time in the small office
cleaning one after the other, didn't even come out for the train because it was-
n't mail time, freight time, or a time when a stranger got off the train. He
waved at me through the window where he sat with his telegraph key, his clip
boards and the long shelf of pipes. I went to the window and tapped on it.

"Anybody come in from out of town, the last twelve hours?"

"Norma did," he called back through the glass. "She's Powell's sister and
been living in Mormon Creek last twenty years. You don't know her, I don't
think."

"Anybody else? A man?"

He just shook his head and I left. I ran across the stone square in front of
the depot to the beer parlor, which is the first house you come to when you
go into town. There was a pickup parked there, and the shiny Buick which
was one of the cars the Terence brothers used for a taxi. Bob Terence was at
the long bar, eating pig's knuckles and drinking a beer. There were five or six
other people in the place who looked up and nodded at me or said hello, and
the bartender was at the cannon stove, shoveling ashes into a bucket. It was
cool enough, evenings, to make a fire.

I went over to Bob Terence who looked at me with his mouth filled with
food.

"I'm a fare," I said to him, and when he couldn't answer immediately, because of the pig's knuckles, "Your first fare today, Bob?"

He nodded and tried to grin. Mostly he nodded for me to sit down.

"Bob. I'm in a hell of a hurry."

He swallowed, just for my sake, because he wasn't done chewing.

"And I know why," he said.

He took my look to mean something innocent, something cagey but innocent, because then he said, "Because I seen her. So would I be in a hurry," and
laughed.

"Bob. I'll pay your bill if you leave off eating and drinking, Bob. I'm serious."

I must have looked it, because he got up with the beer not finished and more
pig's knuckles on his plate. He would not let me pay his bill and came out right
away.

"I can't take you into the ranch," he said. "Just your cutoff. I'm late picking up this woman Norma, Powell's sister, who's got to make the bus out of
Trilling. She's been living in Mormon Creek these last twenty years, but ever
so often...."

"Let Dick take her. He can drive her to Trilling."

"He ain't in town, John. Sorry."

I didn't argue. From where my cutoff started, it would take maybe five minutes walking to reach the ranch. I sat in the front with Bob and told him to rush it. Then I said, "Is your brother in Wapeko maybe? The airfield in Wapeko?"

Bob looked at me and said, "Yeah! How did you know?"

"Picking up a fare?"

"No. No plane coming in there but once a day, you know. Which was nine in the morning. He's taking a fare for the plane out."

"Whom did he pick up at nine in the morning?"

"You expecting somebody?"

I said, yes, I was expecting somebody.

"Nobody," said Bob. "There was nobody on that plane for Great Rock."

Maybe. It was twelve now and the plane had come in at nine.

"If he picks up a fare in Wapeko, on his way back, I'd want to know, Bob. Is there any way he can let me know?"

"Carrier pigeon," said Bob and laughed hard about it.

"When he comes back to Great Rock I've got to reach him. Does he stop at the Parlor?"

"You know Dick," said Bob. "Him and the pig's knuckles. You try the pig's knuckles yet they put up at the Parlor? I mean that new batch they put up a while back, the one I was eating from just now you walked in? No? Let me tell you something. You know who showed 'em how to put up that new batch? Your Pauline! Brother, you're living good if she makes the rest of your vittles the way she showed 'em how to put up them knuckles I been talking about."

He went on like that all the way to the cutoff and I didn't interrupt. I heard what he said but I was elsewhere. I was all over the big spread of land on both sides of the road, all along the woods coming down the side of the mountain, all through each corner of the ranch house, the outbuildings and the draw where the pasture land was cut in two.

"About that nine o'clock plane," said Bob. "You expecting somebody?"

"Yes. I said yes."

"I know." He laughed. "You bringing in a preacher?"

I let him laugh himself out and then I said, yes, again.

"I'm expecting a kind of a preacher," I said.

Then Bob stopped at the cutoff. I paid him, left a tip, took my suitcase. I wasn't forgetting a thing anymore. He drove off and I started running down the dirt road with the fir trees on one side and my fence on the other. The way the road wound I could not see the ranch yet, but I knew when I would see it, how it would look, what the next bend would show me. Everything felt and smelled close and familiar. This was mine and I never forgot that or the reason I was back now.

It was *zin-ng* first and then the report of the rifle.

There was a *No Hunting* sign on the nearest fir tree on my right and the sign had a hole in it now and the metal still seemed to be twanging.

By then I was flat in the ditch. My suitcase was in the road, showing just about where I was off to one side, and my heart under me seemed to be jumping around out there.

It wasn't fright. It was pure, open rage, held there, because so far I didn't see anyone.

"Jest yew stay put there or the next'n takes off yore left heel."

I exhaled very slowly. I stayed down where I was and only turned my head up when I saw his shoes at the side of the ditch.

"Mister— Gee, Mister Miner!" said Luke and lowered the gun very slowly.

I got out of the ditch and started brushing myself without looking at him.

"Mister Miner," he started again, "I'm sorry."

"Don't be. I'm glad you're this good."

"All I seen was what turned out to be you coming fast through the bend."

"Believe me, Luke," I said. "I don't want you to act any different. Till it's over," and I went back on the road to pick up my suitcase.

"You want me to go back with you, to the house?"

"Whatever you were doing, Luke, keep it up."

"You go on back to the house and never fear," he told me. "It's clear from here on till you get to the yard."

"I'll walk slowly when I get to the yard."

"Yes," he said. "You walk slowly there. I myself wouldn't trust that Pauline."

Then I left him and went the rest of the way to the ranch, moving slowly when I got to the yard.

But it wasn't Pauline who had me in her sights when I came into view. I heard the yell from the upstairs window, the curtain flew to one side, and then, behind the Winchester, Jane waving at me.

It was a wonderful thing, seeing her, the way she was happy, the way I felt seeing her there, even waving the gun the way no gun should be waved. But the sight of her, even had she been waving a two-headed snake, would have made me happy.

Inside the house I held Jane for a moment, but neither she nor I felt that there was much time for a kiss and for warmth, the kind of warmth that always needs time to come and to stay.

Then Pauline came down from upstairs and George came through the back door, from the place in back of the house where he had been guarding. He said, "Hello, Mister Miner. You're looking bad."

I smiled at him because I was sure he was right. "I'll make you some coffee," said Jane. "Then you can tell us."

"To me," said Pauline, "it looks like a bath would be good."

I nodded again and said:

"All right. First, I make a call."

George went to the back door, carrying his gun. Pauline went to the front door, and she carried a revolver. Jane stayed with me. I called the beer parlor in town and asked if Dick Terence was there. He had just come in. I asked him if he had brought a fare back from the airport, or a fare from anywhere coming back to town, and he said no. There had been nobody on the plane for Great Rock, there had only been four men who lived in Wapeko. And there had been no fare from anywhere along the road back to Great Rock, and no other plane due till next morning.

I hung up and felt a little bit better. There was time enough for a breathing spell.

"Good news?" asked Jane.

She smiled at me and looked so hopeful I suddenly felt like dirt. I felt terrible.

"There's some time now," I said. "Time to wait for it to happen."

She must have gone more by the tone of my voice, or by the tone I was trying to hide, because she said nothing after that, just put her hand on my face and stroked.

"Whatever it is," she said. "We'll wait. You're back now."

Jane has very large eyes. She has a well-defined mouth which is full and her wavy hair makes a beautiful frame for her face. She has a live look all about her, the way she stands or the way she walks, and to me that is the best about her. Then all I can feel is wanting her with me, no matter what else might exist between us or against us. I closed my eyes because her father was dead, which she did not know, and Farret was coming. I was sure Farret was coming.

"Go upstairs," she said. "Come on," and she took my arm. "Take a shower and then we'll talk about it. Come, darling."

But she hadn't been blind. I saw how still she was now and when we went into the bedroom she sat down on a chair and did not try to smile at me. I started to take off my jacket and then my tie and kept moving around without knowing where to put the things.

"Drop them on the floor," she said. "I'll pick up while you're in the shower."

I said all right, but the exchange hadn't helped.

"John," she said. "Don't let it eat up both of us, John."

I sat down on the bed and nodded. Then I looked at her and said, "Sit next to me. I'll tell you everything while you're sitting next to me."

She came over and sat down.

"Hold both my hands," she said, "and then tell me. If it's bad for you, or if it's bad for me, darling, if you hold both my hands it's better."

I took both her hands in mine and we sat next to each other and looked at each other.

Then I told her of the track Farret had made. Denver, Miami, Baton Rouge, San Francisco. I told her of Lena, of Metz, and about her father.

Her hands were very hard inside mine now, clamped with a real pain which I did not feel half as much as she must have felt it. And then she dropped back her head and started to cry.

She poured out. For a long time she did not let go of my hands, because that was our contact, and then when she did, leaning against me, she was really through crying and mostly the spasms were left, and her mourning.

"I'll leave you alone now," I said.

"Yes."

"Stay here, Jane."

"Yes."

I got up and left her on the bed where she bent over. I had the terrible image of Jane not wanting anyone, not needing anyone, or me.

I took off the rest of my clothes and went into the bathroom.

I took the shower very hot. I made it so for the simple dimensions; hot, cold, pain, pleasure, hard, soft—

Then the curtain rasped with a quick, sudden sound. The movement slapped cold air at me and a bright light from the window across the small room.

Jane was there. She has large eyes which look blacker sometimes than they really are, and a full mouth which was now part-open. Her skin looked already damp from the steam, with a sheen on her shoulders, with a firm sheen and a deep-shadowed curve rounding her breasts, and her belly sucked in with excitement, and her thighs full and strong.

"I want you," she said. "I want you, I want you!" Then the water was all over us.

Chapter Twenty-three

Pauline had the coffee made and some sandwiches on the kitchen table and we all sat down there after Jane and I came down from upstairs. George had whistled for Luke to come back from the road and Edsel rode in at about the same time from the rounds he had been making over the land. We kept the back door open and the front door, for the view, and except for the guns standing around in the kitchen and the long knife Pauline kept wearing inside her belt, it looked friendly enough in the kitchen with all of us there. The coffee smelled good and the three men ate like they always did and so did Jane. Or rather, I didn't remember ever having seen her eat with as much of an appetite.

"I see you took a shower, too," Pauline said, because Jane's hair was still wet, combed back straight from her head now and shiny like plumage.

"Yes, I did," said Jane and kept eating.

"And you're looking better," Pauline said to me, "with those city clothes off and no tie choking you up. Where'd you find those clean suntans?"

"Jane found them," I said. "And they got too much starch in them, Pauline."

"Tell her," said Pauline and nodded at Jane. "All I ever do here anymore is boil coffee."

"And put up pig's feet," said Luke. "You put up the damndest pig's feet, you know that, Pauline?"

"You can't have any," said Pauline. "Open-up day won't be for another week."

I lit a cigarette and the talk ran out. We drank coffee and they waited for me to tell them.

"The man's name is Farret," I said, "and for a reason he made up in his mind, for a reason that started before I ever came here, he wants me. He has killed. Now he wants me."

I smoked and looked at all of them. They were waiting to hear what their part was to be.

"He's on his way, though I don't know when he'll get here or how. I'm now telling any of you, all of you, that it's my fight. And if you have it in mind to go now, go. When it's over I'll be grateful if you'd come back."

"Don't insult us," said Edsel, and they all nodded.

I said thank you to them and got up. They kept watching me. I looked out of the house, to the yard, to the back where the land rolled with the bright sun over everything and in the quiet we heard a cow lowing gently.

"He wants me," I said. "And I want him."

They understood that and said nothing. Only Jane looked nervous now. She tried not to show it and looked away.

"He'll have to come to the house for me," I went on, "so we don't have to spread anymore. Jane and Pauline stay here, and George goes upstairs, the frontway window. Pauline upstairs to the back." I looked at Jane and said, "I'd like Jane to be with me. I'm staying downstairs." She nodded at me. Then I said, "Edsel, you sit in the barn, and you, Luke, in the stables. Those two buildings and this one make a triangle for us." Then I told them they were to stay put until dark. I wasn't sure yet what we would do during the night.

We got up because there was nothing else to say. We heard the cattle low again somewhere behind the dip.

"They're trying to come down to the low pasture," said Luke, as if the cattle had been telling him that.

"He's right," said Edsel. "The west fence needs work. I saw the place where they're trying to break through, when I was riding by before."

"Lazy like humans," said Pauline. "Too lazy to walk those hills for their feed," and that was the last light thing said by any of us for a long time.

The rest of the afternoon was mostly silence, and above all it was waiting. Perhaps this would take a long time, days perhaps, and we would get used to waiting or learn to live with it better. But not yet. Maybe Edsel in the barn and Luke in the stables had an easier time, being alone, but the three of us in the house kept a tight silence, not wishing to infect one another with the anxiousness and the edge of irritation which kept growing inside.

What we heard from outside were all the ordinary, small noises, the firs moving themselves in the faint wind, the weather vane on the barn making the swinging sound like a small sigh. No new sounds, but new now because everything was thick with suspicion.

At four we heard a car. Sound carries far at that hour. It was a slow sound, it even got slower, but stayed far away. Any other time it would just have meant the mail car slowing down for the box at the far end of the road, but now it meant almost anything. I went to the stairs and called up to Pauline.

"Yes," she answered, "I see the dust now."

She was at the front window with the field glasses up.

"It's the mailman," she said. "I see he's pulling away."

But it was no relief. I smoked too much and felt like in a cage.

At five George called me. But there was nothing. He hadn't seen anything, but wanted to tell me that the feed company had called in the morning, that the salt and the sacks of mash powder had come and they might have time to deliver today.

"You mean to tell me they're going to drive in here any minute or anytime during the day?"

"I'm sorry, John. I'm sorry I didn't remember."

It was after five and the feed company didn't answer when I called them in town. It was after five and they wouldn't be likely to deliver any more this day.

At six the sun hit the peak of the mountains and made long blue shadows which started to grow fast.

"You're not doing it right," said Jane. She took the cigarette out of my mouth and took both my arms. "You're building up and building up. Everyone is feeling it with you. Then comes the night. Then maybe another day. You see that, darling?"

I saw that. I looked at her and buttoned and unbuttoned the collar on her shirt, just to be doing something that took concentration. She held still while I did this and when I looked up I saw she was smiling at me.

"You're getting me all choked up," she said.

I grinned at her and relaxed. I looked at her hair, which was dry now, and rumpled it up so that it fell loose, the way it usually did. It had a good shine.

"You need lots of showers," I said.

"I know. Soon."

Then I called up to Pauline.

"Time to eat, Big Pond!" I yelled.

Her Indian name wasn't Big Pond, but Slow Water, and this was a way to get a rise out of her. She came clambering down the stairs, rattling dialect. When she passed me she said, "Mercifully, you don't understand my language," and went on to the kitchen.

Jane went with her, I went upstairs to the window where Pauline had been sitting, and George yawned in the other room, at the other side of the house.

It was like a coffee break. We would eat, we would talk a while, and then when it got dark in another hour or so, we would change plans.

"You hear something?" said George from the other room.

"No. Just the kitchen."

"A car. Sounds like a pickup."

I heard the pickup then but I couldn't see it because it was somewhere far on the highway.

"That damn feed truck, most likely," he said.

I told George to come to my window and sit there with the glass while I went downstairs. I left the gun by the window but had the revolver in my pants pocket. In a way, at that moment at any rate, it felt almost ridiculous to walk with that gun hanging out of my pocket to go down to see about a feed truck. I went to the kitchen to tell Pauline I was going out for a minute and that a pickup might come down the drive. I only said half of it, because Pauline was alone in the kitchen, ladling food into plates, and Jane wasn't there.

"Where is she?"

"Now, she ain't going far," said Pauline. "She's gone to bring food to that starving Luke and that starving Edsel."

George would be covering the yard. There was no need to tense up.

I ran out to the front, out to the porch, and the yard was empty. Jane was in the barn, next to the road, or in the stables, off towards the pastures.

"Jane? Where are you?"

"In the barn, John. I'm coming," she called.

"The pickup's in the road now," George told me from the window above.

"Stay there where you are."

I ran into the wide yard just as the pickup came through the last bend. The sacks were bouncing in back and the man was going hell bent for leather, because it was after five and he hadn't finished deliveries. He came to a fast stop, between me and the barn, and got out. I could just see Jane coming through the gate.

"You call me, John?" she was running.

"Stay! For God's sake, *Stay!*" I screamed.

Farret whirled.

Farret was clever. He paid no attention to me but leaped for Jane.

There were now four guns on him. Edsel, in the door of the barn, Luke in the Dutch door of the stable, George behind me on the second floor. And me, down on one knee for a better angle and the gun out straight, for the surest shot.

But it didn't matter. Farret and Jane were one target.

For a dead moment of time, nothing. Then Jane kicked. She kicked hard, hurting Farret so he had to slump, but his grip got tighter. But that wasn't enough for him. He slammed the heel of his hand into her face so that I saw how the pain made her shudder.

I almost broke, except what Farrett was saying held me.

"See this?" He was calling to me. He was showing me where his knee was in her back, his arm linked over her throat, and the other one back of the neck, for a lever.

"I can break her back in one half second. You know that, Miner?"

I knew that.

"You want me," I called to him. "Leave her."

"I'll get you," he said. "I'll get you, Miner."

He started to walk to the barn with her, dragging her. He stopped before getting there and said, "Call your man out."

I called Edsel to come out of the barn, to stay clear. Edsel circled around to the house.

"Anybody else?" Farret asked.

I didn't get to answer. There was a shot from the stables, a five hundred foot shot from Luke by the stable door, making Farret spin like a top, screaming, and a big splotch of blood on the side of his head.

But it was no good. The bullet had ripped off Farret's ear, I could see the frazzles. Farret, with the strength of his madness, crouched low, still holding Jane like a praying mantis, showed a gun. He cut the butt of it over Jane's head and then ran for the barn gate and through.

My shot missed him completely.

Just a thin slice of sun, blue-red, still showed over the peaks, and the dark-ness was creeping in from the east. The cattle always got noisy at that time, but it was far, far from me now. The closest thing to me was a lust for Far-ret. Or a lust for his corpse, or anything that would mean Farret was dead and Farret was over.

"George?"

"Yes, sir."

"You stay up there. Have Pauline put on the yard lights once I'm in the barn."

"Yes."

"Edsel?"

"I can hear everything you are saying," Farret called from the barn.

"Edsel?"

"Cover the back of the barn."

"Will do."

"Luke? Take the yard, but from closer than you are now."

"You ain't going in there, John," he called. "You ain't...."

"Shut up."

I walked to the gate which was a black hole with nothing to see inside. Maybe he could have shot me, or maybe the angle was wrong. I wasn't think-ing that way. I was thinking of the ugliest lunatic that was ever going to die through my doing. I stopped by the side of the gate, so that I could listen be-cause there was a sound in there which meant a lot to me.

Hard thunks of shoes, the rattle of hay, and then the way it always whis-pers when the fine dust from the loft sifted down to the floor.

Farret was up there. It was dark in the loft but I knew where he was and that he couldn't go anywhere. And that he couldn't reach me with a shot, if I walked the right way.

I slipped in and stood under the loft.

"I know you got a gun," he said, "but you know what I got."

"Jane?"

"She can't talk," said Farret. "I hit her too hard."

No. She wasn't dead. I had seen him hit her and she couldn't be dead.

"She isn't dead," said Farret. "I'm keeping her alive here."

"Farret," I said. "You want me. Come on down."

He laughed.

"Farret—"

He stopped laughing and then he said, "Hey. You know what I'm doing to her?"

I felt like I might explode with one terrible scream. I could hear my breath make a hoarse sound.

"Don't tell me, Farret. Don't tell me or you'll die harder."

I heard a sound above, a body dropping limp on the boards, and then foot-steps. Farret was walking. He had left Jane and was going up to the rim.

"Miner?"

"I'm waiting for you."

Hay dust sifted down. I couldn't see it because of the gloom, but there was the sound by the edge of the loft.

"You've been waiting," he said. "So, you've been waiting." He sounded stern, with a voice from high above. "And now I've found you."

"You come down from there, Farret."

"Quiet."

The voice was cold and mad. The high loft and the darkness in the barn took on cathedral proportions.

"I've searched and searched," he said, "and now I've found you. I've suf-fered through years of searching, and I've made my mistakes, because of your ruses."

"Listen here, Farret. You've got any kicks coming about losing out...."

"I can get you two ways now, Miner, two ways. I'm going to punish you through the girl and I'm going to punish you with my own hands."

I had to get him down. I had to get him away from Jane.

"For myself? No," he said. His whole language was changing. He was like a new person, or different. What he did was nothing new. It was old as vengeance and ugly as lunacy.

"You broke the code. You are a son of a bitch, Miner," he said, sounding as if he were using a biblical word.

"I can't hear you, Farret. Come closer."

"You're making fun of this even now? Listen, Miner. It's planned that you have to die, because of what you did. And I'm the one chosen. I'm the one knows the whole truth."

"Tell it," I said. Keep talking, keep talking yourself into a righteous cloud. Let the lunacy get into your eyes and blind you.

"There were only the five of us. I checked out all five of us. Lena didn't do it to me, Metz didn't, Getterman didn't and I'm the one who got it in the neck. That, Miner, leaves *you!*"

"I lost out," I said, but it sounded lame.

"You are the only one knew the delivery dates because you delivered. You and your short wave delivered, you son of a bitch. The transmitter on your boat was as good as an ocean liner's. You set up the ambush from out at sea, and you were the only one that made something good out of it."

"You got away yourself," I said. "Alive and kicking."

"I got away?" He started to scream. "I got away stripped down to nothing, nothing but the brains to see it was you all the time doing this to me! I stowed away on a shrimper that hung off the coast of Mexico for three boiling weeks! I got beaten and kicked when they found me, for messing into their lousy shrimp! I had to swim for it with the sharks and cudas when they wouldn't let me off when they found me! Me! Stinking like fish and crud. Me!"

It had been a lousy getaway for him, but it didn't balance his grudge. Only lunacy balanced his grudge.

I remembered almost the first thing he had said to me, before I had ever hired him. Balance the balance sheet, something like that. And all by the code.

I held the gun down now, letting it hang by my side, because it came to me that I might not have to use it. Just get him down from up there. Just make him come down alone.

"I didn't finger you, Farret. Are you listening?"

"Sure. I'm listening." He was almost bored.

"You switched routes for that last convoy, remember?"

"I always play the safe side of...."

"When did you switch routes, Farret?"

"That same afternoon."

"You remember when you told me about it? How you blew your stack telling me?"

Farret said nothing, apparently thinking.

"You didn't tell me in the afternoon that you would switch routes because you didn't see me that afternoon. You didn't see me because I was late, late by five hours coming into the island because of that cruiser that came into the bay. You remember that cruiser?"

Farret remembered it. He remembered the lights of the large ship in the black bay when he and his crew unloaded the arms.

"So I didn't know which way you were going to deliver till the time you unloaded. That's when you told me, mad like a shrew, because I had come in late delaying you for the long trek up the mountains, the longer trek you had picked all by yourself. That's why I couldn't tip anybody. You see that, Farret?"

Farret stood at the end of the loft staring hard into the darkness. Maybe he smelled sea smells from the bay in the island and leaf rot from the jungle road. All that was real. The arms pickup, the trek, the ambush. Where was the flaw? Where was the flaw to show him his victim?

"You're the only one made any money on this," was what he said.

"Money?" I laughed. "Why? Because I picked up the fifty thousand from Getterman's office?"

"And that's how you bought the ranch, living big, with private servants and gun men. I seen them. One of them hit me in the ear. My ear...."

"Shut up, Farret. Just listen. I left the bay with that fifty thousand the same night, the way we arranged it. But I was late. I was too late to pass the gale that was coming down the Gulf coast the next day. It was daylight when the coast guard gave me the signal because our timing was late and I ran into their patrol. Or maybe that was part of the ambush too, Farret, but they gave me chase."

"There wasn't a coast guard cutter could touch you and that one thousand horse power engine you had. I remember you said that."

"Just listen." I kept telling it to him because I was going through it again. Perhaps I told him with some hope of distracting him, hoping to make this seem more like a talk, but I mostly told it because I went through it again.

"No. They couldn't touch me. Not by eight knots, because their cutters aren't powered like a PT-boat." I took a deep breath. "Except in a gale, Farret. Not in a gale. I had the strength in the hull but not the right shape of a hull, not for twenty-eight knots in a gale! I started to plow. They dropped back and back but I started to plow, and more of it when I got into the shallows. I had to make the shallows and beach. I swamped the first time two miles before the reef. I wasn't worried about hitting the reef, Farret, I knew it, the whole length of it. I couldn't slow down because they were sure to radio for support, planes even, and I had to make it. The gale made eight foot waves in the shallows and then it went up to ten or twelve. You know what that means with one thousand horse power inside a fat hull built for a safe fifteen knots? I plowed! I dug the prow into the white water and then the green water. I drove the whole boat into the green at an angle that makes me sick when I think of it. You listening, Farret?"

"Yes."

"I sunk. I sunk half a mile off the reef, the boat, the whole fifty grand, me. Like you said, Farret, I swam for it with the sharks and the cudas. The worst was the reef. The reef is one foot below in calm waters. You know what it is in a gale? It's sharp white teeth all along the horizon."

I wiped my head and shut up. It had been the first time I had talked about all of it and I was glad it was done. That's how I had made it to the mainland. Wet, bloody, and beat. The finish, I had thought then, of that kind of life for me.

"You had the dough to buy a ranch," Farret said.

I almost laughed. It was true what he said. Half true. The money I had saved in the bank went in a month. A month of running, of hiding, of bribing myself back to another life.

The ranch? I still owned a shrimp boat my father had left me. An old boat, which had cost thirty five thousand when new. I sold it to the man who had been renting it and got eight thousand. I took the eight thousand, my only legitimate money, and found a place far away, mountains instead of water, and had taken this ranch.

I was back now. I was in the black barn with Farret's breathing above me, and the pale light from the yard outlining the door. Jane moaned.

"Don't touch her, Farret."

I don't think he heard. He said:

"You're smart, Miner. You're a twister. But look at it," and I heard him laugh, "it's got to be you, Miner. There's nobody else!"

His logic. Nothing had changed. Nothing gained but time to confuse my-self with those memories and time for Jane to start moaning.

His logic, his balance sheet, his code. That's how it must work.

"Don't you know who tipped this?" I said. "Don't you know how you lost?"

"Huh?"

"It wasn't Lena, or Metz, or Getterman. And it wasn't me. Do you know how they knew you would change your route, how they knew how to switch their ambush?"

"How, you son of a bitch? *How?*"

He was dying to know. He might even be willing to die to know.

"The route you picked at the last minute was longer and steeper, wasn't it, Farret?"

"I know that better than you."

"Listen to me. It's harder going. When you took that route, Farret, you al-ways added five extra bearers, right, Farret?"

"Yes."

"You hired five extra bearers that day. Where? In the village of Palmo?"

"I always got bearers there."

"Yes. I know. They all knew that, those who kept still because of the bribes and those who didn't, because they were Duz men. You see now, Farret? You see who tipped it off and broke the code?"

I could hear him breathe very heavily.

"*You,* Farret! *You* made the doublecross!"

Maybe I could have moved then, quietly. Maybe I could have shot and hit him. But I wasn't sure. I wasn't sure enough to risk Jane. Nothing was sure when there was no sound from above, not even breathing. He must break! He goes by this rule and he must break! It's his insanity.

Nothing. Nothing. Just the black barn, like a dead vault to me now, and the thin light in the yard. But it had been a good story, a plausible way to place the guilt! He *had* to believe it. We got ambushed and broken up for one hun-dred reasons, gathering for months. But for Farret it had to be one simple rea-son. One traitor, one man's guilt. I couldn't guess wrong.

"God!" he groaned. "My God. My God!"

I had him!

I let him groan for a moment and then I called up. "Come down, Farret. Now."

"Now? My God, Miner, don't you know—"

"*Now!*"

My sharp voice had been wrong. I should have played it the same way I did in Lamotte. Gentle, helping him, holding him up when his system broke. But the sharp voice must have been like the enemy to him.

"You filth," he said to me, and a shot tore through the boards over me and the slug smacked into the floor. "You filth! You and this bitch up here, you and your *plans!*"

"Stay away from her!" I yelled up, and out in the middle of the barn now I shot up towards him, once, twice.

I didn't see him. I missed him. I could hear him scramble and he was cursing.

"Here," he yelled, "first her, then you! Here!" and saw him stagger up to the rim.

He had Jane again, who was awake enough to moan in his arms and then he yelled, "First this bitch!" and he tossed her over the rim of the loft.

I dropped my gun running for her. An eight foot drop and I caught her. The impact buckled my legs and tore hard into my shoulders but I held. There was a gasp out of Jane, a sound which I couldn't gauge but which meant she was breathing. I ran towards the barn gate with her, yelling, "Hold fire, hold fire—" and ran out into the yard.

No one shot. Pauline came running and Edsel came from the back of the barn. I put Jane down on the ground and pushed back her hair.

The sight of her made me cramp up so that I thought for a moment I could never move. A bloody gash on her scalp, a swelling across her face, a pallor like sickness itself, and her clothes open—

"She's looking at you," said Pauline. "Smile at her."

She was looking at me. She took a breath and said, "Fine. Not so bad." And I gently put my hand on the side of her face. I did not manage to smile.

"Gimme your gun, Edsel."

He did. He stepped back and pointed between the two buildings where the corral was, and the grazing land behind that.

I ran, but with ease now, without panting. Once in the corral the moonlight seemed to turn on because now I was out of the orbit of the yard light. A misty light was over everything, with the shadows like pitch.

I looked back once and saw Edsel climb over the fence and Luke was coming, holding his gun. They did not try to catch up. They were following.

It was easier for me than for Farret because he didn't know the land. I knew that a man in the half-dark, running, would follow what he could see and would run where the running was easiest. That meant between the two knolls, down the fence, then to the draw. He would run that way for a while until something else happened inside his brain and he changed his mind. Before that, I would have him.

I was cutting him off, knowing the land. I could see him running, the pea jacket like a black hump on him and his legs going like pistons. I should hear him. I should even hear how the breath croaked in his throat. But there was another noise.

"The west fence is down," I heard Luke say.

Farret heard it and shot.

"You're next," he yelled. "So help me, you're next!" And the cattle had heard the shot because they were snorting now, grunting to get off their bellies.

"They've come through the break in the fence," said Edsel.

Farret was closer to them and saw more. They were part of my plot to him, or something insane like that, because he started shooting again. He hit one steer.

From what I could hear a lot of the cattle had come through the broken fence. They milled and snorted to get away, but panic hadn't taken hold yet and they wheeled.

"Watch them!" Luke yelled.

"They'll get him, John," said Edsel. He was winded. "What do you want us to do?"

I saw it too, the mass of the cattle with the wounded one somewhere in the middle. Then Farret fired again. I don't know if he hit, but he fired again and was making a sound in his throat like sharp metal.

"Luke!" I yelled. "Call them. Luke do your calling! You on the other side, Edsel, over left. Head them off! Save him, damn it, save him!"

Whatever they did it worked, while I kept running straight toward where I saw Farret, where the cattle were parting now like a heaving mass in the dark, with anguished noises.

"*Save him!*" I yelled once again and then Farret turned on me, shot once more, crouched.

They had saved him for me.

I could see his teeth and his hate and his gun and the smell of him then, which seemed like a strong stink all around me. I dropped the rifle and Farret roared at me with his arms out like the image he had made once before, like a praying mantis.

They had saved him for me and I killed him fast.

It is difficult to see clearly what is really over or what is something you want to be over.

Farret was dead and there were the police who didn't stay long. They had him for Getterman and they had him for something he had done in Lamotte. The feed company even came in on the thing, for the stolen truck. The police didn't stay long and I didn't care.

And the others were not much more real. Getterman had been killed. Metz, perhaps worse than Getterman, stayed alive a long time and without money. Lena had not gone back to Denver when she could have done so most easily. She waited until much later. By that time Hubert had left. Lena, I heard, then left to find him. I know nothing else. It is difficult to look back all the time.

Jane and I were the luckiest. There was even a note in the wedding mail which said, "For my part, may you live happily ever after," signed Luis Gambello. He had known where I was for some time.

Farret had made a long, ugly track. It was behind us, but it was always there.

THE END